A COIN FOR CHARON

MARLOWE GENTRY BOOK 1

DALLAS MULLICAN

CHARON
PRESS

A MARLOWE GENTRY·THRILLER

A COIN FOR CHARON

DALLAS MULLICAN

CHARON
PRESS

CONTENTS

A Coin for Charon

A Marlowe Gentry Thriller

Published by Charon Press

Cover design and interior graphics by Jeffrey Kosh - www.jeffreykoshgraphics.com

Interior design by Matthew Cox

ISBN - 9781078049481

CHAPTER ONE

G abriel knelt low, watching her struggle to breathe. The air, elusive, rattled in her throat, interspersed with pitiful moans. Her heart raced, pounding against his outstretched palm. Eyes filled with terror pleaded for the pain to end. A familiar feeling came over him—fingers tingled, stomach tightened, his head thumped with a dull ache.

He drew the Buck knife from his pocket and flicked it open. Boasting a five-inch blade, walnut handle with brass bolsters, and sharpened to a razor's edge, the metal glinted with the slightest turn. Gabriel admired the knife, relishing its weight in his hand and remembering the day his father had offered the gift, his tenth birthday —a relic from a discarded life.

Tracing his hand along her side, he located the spot between two ribs and positioned the tip. A quick thrust slid the blade into her heart. She died without another sound, only a shudder, and lay still. His hands numbed as *the feeling* released, and the tightness in his stomach relaxed, a pleasant light-headedness replacing the throb in his head.

His fingers raked the dog's thick, matted fur as a tear streamed down his cheek. No one would mourn a dead mutt in a city teeming with strays; only Gabriel grieved for her. Her distended belly and swollen teats marked recent births. He wondered if the pups would meet her same fate without a mother to provide sustenance and protection. Did they search for her now in vain?

He took her gently into his arms, eased her body into a bag, and sealed it. Hefting the bag onto his shoulder, he trudged to the alley's trash bin and lowered her inside. Gabriel gazed down on the black plastic and the lifeless form within. His thoughts wandered, indistinct and frayed, memories stalking the edge of remembrance, memories better forgotten.

He craned his head back, staring into a late afternoon sky darkened to deep purple and streaked through with crimson slashes. A crow, perched atop a telephone line, cawed out an eerie greeting to the approaching night. The haunting ambiance suited Gabriel's mood and offered an appropriate eulogy.

Rundown buildings stretched high toward the ominous heavens, blocking out the final rays of a waning sun. The gangly structures held a rank and heavy air that squeezed the life from these back streets. Windows set into the crumbling facades peered down like apathetic eyes on the people cowering below, watching over a domain in ruins.

Gabriel rolled his head on his shoulders, hearing his neck creak and pop. He wiped a tear from his face with a sleeve and entered the store. Henry leaned over the counter, a plump cheek balanced in one palm, elbows resting on the wooden surface. Years of hard work caused the big man to hunch a little and his ample belly to peek from beneath his t-shirt. Henry owned the grocery store, selling food while giving away the area's juicier tidbits of gossip.

"Go okay?" asked Henry.

"She is at peace." Gabriel spoke with reverence, as if losing a dear friend rather than a sick dog that had wandered into the alley to die.

Henry arched one bushy, gray eyebrow at the severity in his voice. "Yeah … well, I'm glad you were here and knew what to do. The thing's groaning gave me the heebie jeebies. Planned to call Animal Control, but who knows if they would've showed. I pay my taxes, should buy a little dependability, but no, can't count on anything in this damned city."

Gabriel kept silent. It was never a good idea to interrupt one of Henry's rants. Most things perturbed Henry in one way or another. He had opinions and loved to express them with a touch of victimization and vitriol. On his best days, he could out hyperbole any politician's filibuster.

Henry slammed a hand down on the counter. "My store's been broken into four times in a year. *Four times.* Think they catch anybody or recover any of my merchandise? Hell no. But let me go a single mile per hour over the speed limit, and a whole mess of cops are there to give me a ticket. Dirty bastards." He huffed with disgust. "Anyway, I wouldn't have any idea how to put down an animal, not without hurting the poor thing worse."

"A mercy. No creature should suffer needlessly."

"True, too true. So how *did* you know what to do? Not something you pick up on the fly."

Gabriel stiffened and looked away. "I … I spent some time working with animals."

"Can't say I envy you the chore, don't think I could handle the job. Not if I had to kill 'em. I'm probably the only hick in the South don't even like to hunt. Hell fire, I feel guilty 'nuff cuttin' into a rare rib-eye. Still eat it, mind you, but feel a little bad about it. I couldn't ever work in one of those slaughterhouses. Don't see how anyone could get used to it."

"Everything can become acceptable with repetition," said Gabriel, unable to mask a bitter tone.

"You got a stronger constitution than me. Where'd you pick up such knowhow?"

Gabriel reddened further. "I-I t-traveled, saved my money, looked for a place to settle, and took work where I could. Farms always needed extra help."

Henry's eyebrows rose. "Must say, I didn't figure you for a farmhand. Can't see you busting broncos or milking cows. I mean with the way you talk, and the way you carry yourself. I thought...."

Hell, I don't know what I thought. Saw you as some sort of college boy, I reckon. Anyways, I wondered how someone like you ended up here. We got former bankers and lawyers living right out there on these streets though, so nothing should surprise me."

Gabriel's gaze turned downcast. He absently tapped one shoe against the floor and rubbed sweaty palms along the sleeves of a blue, checkered button-down.

"I'm sorry, Gabriel. I didn't mean to embarrass you. It's just you talk all proper, and the way you act.... Well, you don't seem like the normal drifter."

"No, it is all right. I discovered early on how different my speech and mannerisms appear to others. I am striving to speak and act normally, but doing a thing a certain way for so long is difficult to change."

"You know, when you first came to the neighborhood … what was it, a year ago now? You were a fish outta water. Honestly, we didn't know quite what to make of you. I'll tell you though, wasn't you changing none made us think so highly of you, getting to know you's what did the trick." Henry stepped around the counter and placed a hand on Gabriel's arm. "You never got a bad word to say about anyone, and help everyone around here whether they ask or not."

"It is the least I can do. All of you have been good to me," said Gabriel, uncomfortable with the compliments.

"Maybe so, but you've gone above and beyond the call. Hell, you've fixed everything in this store, run errands, and now put down a sick dog for me. You're a godsend."

"Thank you, Henry. It is good to hear." Gabriel's shoulders lifted.

"As for changing, don't you change one little bit. Normal's overrated if you ask me. What's normal anyhow? Anything makes you different from the scum around here's a good thing in my book. Stay exactly the way you are, I say."

Gabriel appreciated the sentiment. He still felt out of place in the city. A year was too short to alter a lifetime of isolation. Fortune had led him to Henry and a handful of others like him, but the city could be cruel and unwelcoming.

To some, Gabriel remained invisible. In the streets or stores, they might stroll right through him like a ghostly image if he did not step aside. To others, his strange speech and behavior gained a contemptuous glare or a snicker. To all but these few, he was insignificant.

"Must say, you chose a hell of a place to park it. Satan's bunghole, this place," said Henry.

"It is not so bad."

Henry exhaled through fluttering lips. "Good Lord. I don't wanna know where you've been if this place ain't so bad. Anyway, glad you're here now. I'm pretty fit for sixty-five, if I do say so myself, but managing this place ain't as easy as it used to be. Sure's nice havin' a strong lad around to lend a hand."

"I am happy to assist in any way I can."

"I do wish you'd let me pay you something for all you do around here. It'd cost me minimum wage at least to hire someone. Feel like I'm taking advantage of you." Henry knocked the dust from a rag and wiped down the counter for the third time in as many minutes.

Gabriel browsed through the magazines on a display rack. "You helped me to gain employment. More than enough repayment for anything I have done for you."

"Not much of a job though. Think I got the better end of the bargain. You gotta be up at the ass crack of dawn to work outside in this cold all day, Christ on a stick. When summer comes you won't be thanking me none."

"I do not mind the work or the hours. My past jobs often required I wake at daybreak and work until after dusk. When there are fields to tend, animals to feed, stalls and pens to clean, it matters little if the weather is inclement or pleasant."

Henry grunted in agreement. "A bit of luck my cousin owed me a favor. Act of God, he actually delivered on it. How's he treating you out at the hospital anyway?"

"Well. I have grown quite fond of Paul and the crew."

"Really? You're the only one. Never saw eye to eye on much, Paul and me. Always thought him a bit of a prick to tell you the truth. We once duked it out at a family reunion, no clue what about, both drunk most like. Paul's got one of them mugs just makes you wanna punch it." Henry laughed and mimed a jab in the air. "So anyways, now you mentioned it, I'm more than a little curious how you went from growing up in the sticks to becoming all educated and classy like. Always did wanna ask."

The chime above the front entrance rang out its unmistakable note, a sound like a bird's chirp, albeit a sick one. Gabriel slouched with relief. The answer to Henry's question would require a lengthy story, and not one he cared to share. He had walked away from the past and hoped to leave it far behind him.

Wanda Felton waddled down one of the aisles. Her dress, a delicate lavender, swished back and forth, and a cloth handbag thumped against her thigh. She paused between canned goods and soft drinks to tsk at some item's price. Still spry for eighty years old, her eyes gleamed with intelligence and wit.

Once she came within earshot, Henry said, "Don't be coming in here busting my chops today. I'm in no mood for your sass."

"It wouldn't matter if you were in the mood. I'm way outta your league," she said.

"And what league you in? The League of Extraordinary Pain in the Asses?"

Wanda shook her handbag at Henry. "I'll have you know this is loaded, and I know how to use it. You got my groceries ready, or you going to stand there ogling me all day?"

"Might already be blind from catching sight of you as it is. I got your groceries—just hold your taters. All but the cold stuff, anyway. Started to wonder if you'd show, feared they'd go bad, so put 'em back in the fridge."

"My appointment at the beauty salon ran a bit long." Wanda preened and puffed up a freshly sculpted blue-gray beehive with one hand.

"Beauty salon? Ha! More like construction site."

Wanda swung her purse toward him. Henry flinched as the projectile narrowly missed making contact.

"Hey," he said in mock disbelief.

"You look beautiful as always, m'lady," said Gabriel with a slight bow.

"Now see, there's a real gentleman. You're such a sweetie, Gabriel. Why if I were twenty years younger…"

"You'd still be forty years too old." Henry raised his hands in a defensive posture.

This time Wanda's purse struck against the anchor entwined in rope tattoo, a souvenir from Henry's merchant marine days inked on his forearm.

"Christ, you crazy old bat, that hurt." Henry rubbed his arm, feigning injury.

"You deserved it. I know you're jealous Gabriel's getting all my attention." Wanda turned up her nose.

"Jealous hell, thankful more like."

Gabriel smiled at their playful bickering. When he had first met the pair, their antics had left him confused and disturbed. They both had a good laugh at his expense when he objected to some playful insult Henry had hurled at her. He soon learned they shared a deep affection and this repartee was their way of expressing it.

The three meeting at Henry's store had become a Thursday ritual. Gabriel arrived and assisted with any needed tasks, such as stowing supplies in the back or stocking the coolers. Around five p.m., Wanda came in for her weekly groceries, and after she and Henry finished badgering each other, Gabriel carried the supplies home for her.

"Are you waiting on me, Gabriel?" Wanda asked each week.

"But of course. I would not miss an opportunity to assist a lovely lady with her burden." His customary reply, to which she blushed and giggled like a schoolgirl.

They said their good-byes to Henry and left. On the two-block stroll to Wanda's apartment, she said, "You know, I saw you this morning at the bus stop. That bum pestered everyone in line for money and not a one would give him a cent. He gave up before reaching you, but you chased him down and handed him a few dollars."

"I could spare a small amount."

"You have a big heart, Gabriel, but you need to be careful. These people are pests, like insects, nothing but nuisances. Don't go thinking they have any gratitude for what you give them. They've forgotten you the moment they walk away. At least until they see you again and remember you're an easy mark."

Gabriel frowned, looking thoughtful. "Everyone has a story. Perhaps some made mistakes, leaving them in a hole from which they cannot find their way out. Maybe some terrible event in their lives brought them so low. Should they suffer forever for past mistakes?"

Wanda seemed to toss the thought back and forth in her head. "I guess not, but most are plain lazy or no good."

"I admit my intent is not altogether altruistic. To see them hungry and destitute, knowing I can do some small thing to alleviate a modicum of their suffering yet doing nothing, distresses me greatly. I do it to avoid my own ill feelings as much as to help them."

"A big heart, yes sir. Well, you go on doing what you're doing if it makes you feel good. Don't listen to me. I'm old and cranky. I remember what this neighborhood used to be like, and I resent what it's become."

Wanda and Henry were among a few dozen holdovers—those unable or unwilling to move on once the area began to devolve into a haven for crime and poverty. Block by block, they watched their neighborhood become unrecognizable. Like a portentous black cloud, degenerates and homeless flowed into the area. Property values fell as crime rose.

Most of Westside's previous residents pulled up stakes and sought greener pastures. A few, however, thought they could ride it out, hoping the influx of destitute creatures merely a temporary situation. Not until ten blocks in every direction had fallen to drug dealers, prostitutes, and criminals did they realize the undeniable truth. For many, the drop in their property's value precluded selling without losing everything. Others refused to budge and stood their ground, ignoring the sad fact no victory would come from their defiance.

"You should have seen it. This neighborhood was so nice—full of families and quaint little stores, flowers grew in the medians, and dogwoods bloomed every spring. Kids would ride their bikes on the sidewalks and play in the hydrants in the summer. Now look at it. Nothing but obscene bookstores and strip clubs. Makes me sick." Wanda turned a little green at the mere thought. She glanced across the street at two men shouting obscenities at one another and shook her head. "You should get out of here while you can. Believe me, it sneaks up on you. Wake up one day, it's twenty years later and you're still stuck in this sewer. You need to get to college, a better area, find a nice girl."

"I possessed so little money when I came here and remained very naïve about how the world worked. I suppose I thought I would arrive in the city, become someone important, and live in luxury. A child's dream," said Gabriel. One of the men shoved the other and stormed off.

"Can happen, too, but it doesn't come from simple hard work anymore. You've got to know the right things, meet the right people. You won't get those things here."

Gabriel rubbed the day-old stubble dotting his chin. "I will most certainly think on your wise counsel, milady. As for a wooing a pretty girl, no need, I have you."

Again, she giggled and playfully rapped him on the arm. "You flirt, you."

He assisted Wanda with putting away her groceries, each item in its proper place. Gabriel considered himself neat and orderly, but Wanda kept an immaculate home. Not a speck of dust or hint of clutter existed throughout the entire apartment. Heirlooms and knick-knacks from a bygone age sat lined in prim rows along shelves and tabletops, arranged like a pristine antique shop.

Once they completed the chore, Wanda said, "I know you won't let me pay you, so on Sunday you're coming over for pot roast. The carrots and potatoes cooked right in the pot, just the way you like 'em. No arguments."

"No arguments forthcoming. You are well aware I cannot refuse your delightful company. With the additional allure of your delicious cooking, I am powerless to resist."

"A flirt *and* a flatterer, you'll charm the world if you set your mind to it."

Gabriel stepped outside to the dark. He hated the city at night. Days were bad enough, the sun spotlighting horrid conditions of squalor and filth. At night, every creeping crawling thing felt the rule of shadows granted reign over darkened alleys and dim streets.

Rats scurried underfoot, indifferent to the steps of humans. They feared nothing but the legion of feral cats that roamed the backstreets. The scrawny felines perched along window ledges and trash bin lids, yellow eyes scanning the dark, tails swishing against cracked brick walls the color of dried blood.

Every city housed its vermin, this one no different. Men, women, boys, and girls sold their bodies and their dignity beneath flashing neon signs. Junkies bought death by the vial next to boarded-up storefronts. Homeless vagrants huddled underneath tattered awnings, clutching tight the last drops of whatever liquor they were able to hoard—their only shelter against the bitter cold.

They might have been happy and safe in a better world, in a different world. Now they measured success by surviving another day. Lost and degraded, they devolved into vicious or lame animals.

His heart broke as he watched their daily struggle with a crippling empathy. What little he might do for them was never enough—never enough to satiate their hunger, never enough to quench his need to help them.

Each time he walked down the street, it brought more reminders of how far this city remained from his childhood dreams. Oh, there were those sections where mansions rose, limousines traveled, and the residents knew no want, but for the forgotten masses of Westside, such places seemed mythical.

Gabriel had envisioned living in one of those affluent areas. Places full of lights illuminating cheerful faces, glamorous fashions, and sleek cars. He came here hoping his past might fade into dim memory and a new adventurous life might begin. Instead, he witnessed only decadence and despair. Hands tugged at his clothes, begging for a morsel or a dollar. Despondent voices propositioned a myriad of pleasures to mitigate the pervasive misery.

As he sauntered toward home, Gabriel tried to banish such thoughts. He tried to ignore the rotten smells of trash heaped along the sidewalk, the foul odors emanating from fetid waters pooled in the gutters. His mind drifted, giving little notice to his surroundings.

His attention struck on a girl up ahead, sitting back on her heels with a half-eaten Big Mac clutched to her face. She reminded him of the squirrels back on the farm, the way they would guard a found nut with twitching, bushy tails and furtive glances, nibbling away, yet ready to bolt at the first sign of danger.

The girl appeared young, but her eyes were old. He could tell experience had taught her to be wary. Skinny, with stringy, dirty-blonde hair, more dirty than blonde, the last few crumbs slipping through her fingers as she finished off her meal. When she sensed his stare, she stiffened. Gabriel moved to skirt her position, trying not to frighten her, but she stood and approached him.

Obviously deciding he did not present a threat, she came close, tossed back unkempt hair, and slid open the top of a faded, red blouse. In a sad effort at sexual enticement, she exposed part of one small breast tattooed with a yellow butterfly.

"Hey mister, wanna have a good time?" she asked in a voice devoid of seduction.

Gabriel harbored every intention of refusing the offer, giving her a couple of dollars—which was all she really wanted—and being on his way. As he reached for his wallet, a shock lanced down his spine. His hands felt as if they'd been thrust into a bed of angry ants, his head pounded with the thunder of discordant timpani drums, and his stomach clamped tight, doubling him over.

"Jesus, mister, you okay?" the girl asked, one delicate hand reaching out to steady him.

When he raised his face, she stepped back in alarm. His visage had changed. Gone now the placid demeanor of a benevolent stranger, replaced with cold scrutiny. A thin smile, lacking any humor or warmth, lined his mouth.

"Yes, I would very much like to have a good time," he said in a dead voice.

She seemed unsettled and relapsed into timidity. After gathering herself, her need overwhelming apprehension, she said, "Oh yeah ... just down here."

The girl took his hand and led him into the adjacent alley. "My ol' man keeps a place down here. You got a cigarette?" She peered up at him expectantly.

"I do not smoke."

"Hmm, I could use a smoke. Think I've seen you around. You live near here?" She constantly rubbed her arms as they walked while casting anxious glances into the alley's shadows.

Gabriel nodded and remained silent, allowing the girl to rattle on, her voice sinking to background noise in his head. Her nervous conversation confirmed a lack of experience with this particular occupation. Yellowed bruises dotted her inner arms and discolored teeth peeked out of fleeting, false smiles. Perhaps eighteen, she appeared no stranger to desperation. A junkie turning tricks when necessity demanded it.

A few hundred feet into the alley, she hopped onto a fire escape leading up the back of an apartment building, a slum teetering on the verge of collapse. Rusting metal squeaked and wobbled as they climbed to a fourth-floor window and ducked through. The smell of mildew, dust, and a variety of filth pervaded the confines. A thick layer of grime covered the walls, paper wrappers lay strewn upon a floor discolored by stains, and drug paraphernalia littered a small wooden table: used syringes, a bent spoon, and a cigarette lighter.

The girl sat on the bed. A long crack showed in the headboard, running diagonally from one end to the other. The sheets, which may have been white once upon a time, had become a sullied yellow. One leg, the front right, was broken, causing the bed to tilt to one side. Gabriel gazed at the girl as she reclined on an elbow and thought it a fitting metaphor.

He looked into her eyes, dead like the button eyes on a doll, but beneath swam a torrent of emotions—fear, pain, disappointment—all piling layer upon layer over so few years. What tragedy or misjudgment brought her here? Gabriel felt a wave of compassion wash over him. He would not accept what she offered, but offer her a gift instead ... mercy.

"It's twent—uh, fifty bucks. You don't get the goodies 'til I get paid. House rules." She tried to sound playful and portray herself as a savvy veteran of the streets.

Gabriel stood at the kitchen counter. Noticing a long meat fork, he picked it up and rubbed it clean on his jeans. Polished now to a meticulous shine, he stared at his disfigured reflection in the gleaming metal. The *feeling* remained, but had left him numb. It would not dissipate, he knew, until released.

A single bedside lamp cast a feeble light over a third of the room. Shadows crept along walls hued by a flashing vacancy sign outside the window. One side of the girl's face hid in darkness, the other glowed in scarlet neon.

"I don't have all night, you know. We gonna do business or not?"

With bright, white knuckles, he gripped the fork and turned to the girl. His eyes shone with deep sympathy. Her longing ... her resignation was clear. He walked toward her, the sharp implement raised beside his face.

"Yes ... to business."

CHAPTER TWO

T hat goddamned noise. A swarm of hornets buzzed through
his skull—chitinous legs scratched to get out. Marlowe
Gentry slung one arm across the nightstand, knocking the
alarm clock to the floor. The noise continued unabated.

The phone ... shit.

He felt blindly along the table's surface until his fingers touched
his cell. Taking it in hand, he placed it to his ear.

"Yeah, Gentry. Where? Got it ... be there in thirty," he said in a
sleepy, haggard voice.

Kicking a leg outward, he sent an empty bottle of Jim Beam
rocketing into space. Ol' Jim. His best friend ... and his worst enemy.
They must have tied on one hell of a drunk last night—like most
nights. The little drummer boy beat out a dum-dum-dum rhythm in
his head.

Marlowe lay on his back, one arm rested against his forehead. He
felt Katy's warmth, the soft outline of her body pressed to him. Sitting
up slowly, he waited for the vertigo to subside and prayed for the
pounding in his head to take a break. He glanced back at Katy's side of
the bed—empty ... for a long time now.

It seemed like yesterday they were all together and happy. Marlowe and Katy made truth of the old cliché, love at first sight. After a whirlwind romance, they married in short order. Abandoning previous dreams and ambitions, they decided to settle somewhere scenic and safe. They would raise a dozen children and live in domestic bliss.

But that's the thing with dreams, they usually only come true in fairy tales.

Marlowe's legs wobbled unsteadily as he stumbled to the bathroom. He felt like shit, and judging by the guy in the mirror, looked even worse. He sorely needed a shave, but lacked the motivation. Splashing handfuls of cold water onto his face opened his eyes a smidgeon wider. He ran wet fingers through thick, wavy brown hair suffering from a bad case of bedhead.

After a quick shower, piping hot, Marlowe bemoaned the realization he might actually be alive after all. He picked his suit off the floor, dark navy wool, half of a two-for-one special at Men's Warehouse. The thing showed more wear than he did, which said a lot. He hand-pressed it, knocking out a few wrinkles, and dressed, draping a solid burgundy tie around his neck.

He peeked into Paige's room. Sound asleep, although sometimes it could be hard to tell. She had not spoken in almost two years, and moved zombie-like, arms and legs stiff, eyes glassy. The last time he'd heard her voice—a terrified scream—replayed in his dreams every night. Two dozen shrinks and a medicine cabinet full of pills had failed to snap her out of it. He missed the days when her rumbling footfalls would storm down the hall before she burst through the bedroom door, flew onto the bed, and demanded he make her pancakes.

Mable, their live-in nanny, apparently slept in as well, or simply avoided him. He did regret cussing her out last night in a drunken stupor. In Marlowe's defense, he had warned her not to mess around in Katy's closet. She insisted the clothes were turning musty. Marlowe informed her, not so gently, if she washed or cleaned away a hint of Katy's scent he would skin her alive.

After a moment of watching his daughter lie still, he hung his head and trudged to the kitchen.

Instant coffee. He hated the shit, tasted like an oil slick, but no time to brew the good stuff. Too bad, he could go for some Dunkin' Donuts Dark. Marlowe shrugged on his black, wool topcoat, took his mug in hand, and grabbed a stale bagel on his way out the door.

Shutting the door of his Ford Explorer hit him like the sound of a gunshot. The radio he'd neglected to turn off blared as he turned the key in the ignition. The evil bastard in his head heard it all and started to bang on those infernal drums again. This was not shaping up to be the best of days.

When did I last have a good one?

He drove down Highway 79 and hit I-59 at Tarrant, driving toward Mountain Brook, passing the Birmingham Zoo on his left. He, Katy, and Paige had often visited the zoo. Paige could stare at the monkeys for hours. Katy had mixed emotions; she loved to watch the animals, but hated the fact they were caged. Marlowe took a sip of coffee, burning his lip and swerving into the emergency lane.

Damn it. Stay in the here and now, Marlowe.

1099 Meadowview Lane sat in a pricey suburb filled with mammoth houses and ritzy cars. The Haves certainly enjoyed their opulence. Three families could live comfortably in any one of these homes. These people believed their wealth provided security from crimes of this nature, or any crime for that matter. They were wrong.

When he arrived at the scene, his day went from shit to a big, heaping pile of shit. Dozens of EMTs and uniformed cops scurried about the grounds like ants seeking the asshole who'd kicked their mound. Neighbors meandered in their yards, trying to get a glimpse of whatever horror had occurred next door. Every print, TV, and radio media outlet appeared to have half a dozen reporters on scene.

What a cluster fuck. How'd they get here so soon?

He hoped the uniforms had sealed the area before the vultures arrived. Every scrap of information that got out made his job more difficult. He had no idea what had happened here; a murder obviously, the only reason to call him in. Still, with the pandemonium, it did not appear a normal break-in/homicide or domestic violence matter. He could have checked the news on the drive, but his head still recoiled from the possibility of sound.

Getting to the house proved a chore, which irritated him further. Uniforms had set up a perimeter, and he saw no way to the house without fighting through the crowd. As he forced his way through the throng, belted by shouted questions from reporters and angry concern from neighbors, Marlowe fought the urge to throw up a middle finger.

A young uniformed officer stood guard at the house's front door. "Detective Gentry … victim's on the second floor."

Marlowe nodded and proceeded inside. He noticed a woman seated on the living room sofa—head in hands, body racked by sobs, inconsolable. Next of kin, he guessed. Maybe she found the victim. Officer Maria Marquez sat close to the woman, speaking softly, trying to conduct a preliminary interview and having little success by the looks of it.

He met his partner, Spencer Murray, at the top of the stairs. Spence suffered under the delusion he was the spitting image of Denzel Washington at thirty-five. Marlowe might concede he was marginally handsome, but Spence's estimation broke with reality. Dressed in a fashionable tan slim-fit suit, Spence leaned casually against the bannister wearing a smile out of place for the occasion.

"You look like shit, bro. Should really give the firewater a rest," said Spence. Never a simple good morning or hello from Spence; if he opened his mouth, good chance a wisecrack followed.

"Thanks, Mom. I'll let you know when your opinion matters."

"Grumpy, too. Well, that's nothing new. It's why we love you … your charm."

"Can we get to work? Please?"

Despite hassling one another, and though he could chafe Marlowe like no one else, Spence served as a surrogate brother and best friend. He'd stood by Marlowe through a world of hurt and put up with his moodiness and ill temperament. Marlowe trusted no one more than

Spence. Even so, he was not about to tell him that; no need to swell his head any bigger.

"Had a late night myself. You know the secretary down at Morgan & Starling? The one with the huge …" Spence cupped his hands in front of his chest. "Man, the chick's like a gymnast. She did this thing with her legs…."

"You're incorrigible." Marlowe shook his head.

"I don't know that word, but if it means hung like a horse, then yes. Yes I am."

"Spence. Murder. Crime to solve." Marlowe pushed his way up the hall.

"Fine, party pooper. You're no fun at all."

As they advanced into the bedroom, Marlowe froze at the sight of a body lying on the bed—bluish-colored skin, lips impossibly red. His world went bright white.

Katy quaked with fear. Naked except for blue panties and socks, nickel-sized burn marks dotted her torso and abdomen. The knife's edge against her throat bit into the skin. A thick stream of blood trailed down to pool at her collarbone. From a dark shape behind her arose maniacal laughter.

A crimson wash flooded in behind Marlowe's eyes. Screams and whispers rose and fell like a tide crashing against a rocky shore. The room spun. He thought of the merry-go-round that had caused him to throw up as a kid. Bracing himself, he fought to keep from passing out.

After a long moment, his knees stopped wobbling, and the red storm receded. Marlowe remained propped against the wall, pale, hands trembling.

"Hey man, you all right?" Spence stepped to Marlowe's side, helping steady him.

"Yeah, fine," Marlowe said as his equilibrium stabilized and the color returned to his face.

"My office, Gentry." Lieutenant McCann walked up and grabbed Marlowe's arm. "The second you're done here." His stern tone left no room for argument.

Marlowe nodded weakly. That would not be a fun conversation.

McCann stayed wound tight, and right now, he appeared ready to pop a spring.

"What the hell was that? The lieutenant did not look pleased," said Spence.

"Never mind. What we got?" Marlowe placed a hand to his forehead and forced the residual image from his mind.

"A house of horrors. Vic is Melissa Turner, twenty-eight. Koop puts the time of death between eleven p.m. and one a.m. Found the body at seven a.m. The bastard had all night to do his thing. Must have known she would be alone."

"Forced entry?"

"Back door. Nothing fancy, pried it open. Alarm system wasn't armed. There's no sign of a struggle, so we're guessing he came in while she slept. Christ, I haven't seen anything like this since...." Spence stiffened. "Oh shit, sorry man. I didn't think."

"Forget it. Let's just get to work, okay?" Marlowe had no desire to visit those old, still-oozing wounds. There appeared to be more than enough wounds in this room already.

"Gentry, a little green around the gills, my friend. I would have thought you used to this sort of thing by now," said a gray-haired man of about sixty, standing near one window. His eyeglasses dipped onto the tip of a hawkish nose as he surveyed Marlowe over their rims. "You also look like a bum. Although I am not certain the two bear a causal relationship. Did you sleep in that suit?"

"Screw you too, Doc." Chief Medical Examiner Dr. Fredrick Koopman, affectionately known as Koop, smiled at the jab. "What are we looking at?" asked Marlowe.

"See for yourself." Koop pointed to the floor beside the bed.

"What the hell ..." Marlowe rounded the bed and stared down at what he assumed were the victim's internal organs laid out neatly on a white sheet. They stretched outward from the wall beneath an open window toward the bed. If he did not recognize them as organs, he might have thought the display a work of abstract art.

"A real artist, this killer. I detect a Grünewald inspiration." Koop tried to maintain his serious demeanor.

"If you want to be a comedian, Koop, try to leave the obscure references to Dennis Miller. He gets paid for it, and even his aren't funny," said Spence.

"Not obscure. You are simply uncouth and uncultured."

"Knock it off you two. Koop, continue please," said Marlowe.

"Fine. Nearest the bed, we have the lungs side by side. Below those, various organs—kidneys, liver, stomach. Lastly, the heart bisected, split open like a melon at lunchtime. You'll notice the markings beside each stage of the totem, painted in the victim's blood."

Three groups of symbols were scrawled alongside the horrific pattern of pulpy tissue: 'ζωή' beside the lungs, 'σκοπός' next to the liver, kidneys, and stomach, and at the heart, 'θάνατος.'

"What do the symbols mean?" asked Spence.

"I think they're Greek." Marlowe stared at the bloody writing while unconsciously fingering the grip of the Glock 21 in his shoulder holster.

"It's certainly Greek to me," said Koop with a subtle grin.

"But what do they say?" asked Spence.

"I know what Greek writing looks like, doesn't mean I can read it," said Marlowe. "Everything removed from inside the body? What happened to the rest? Intestines and all?"

Spence gestured at the window. "We found a bag full o' bloody mess thrown in the trash out back. Made a couple of uniforms toss their cookies."

"I'm guessing the other viscera did not meet the aesthetic design the killer desired," said Koop.

"Doc, what's with the arms?" asked Spence.

"No idea of their meaning. The killer severed both arms at the shoulders, the skin flayed to a point where only a thin strand remains attached to the muscle. As you can see, the skin is drawn downward. The image that comes to mind is ... wings." The arms stretched parallel to either side of the lungs, and the *wings* of skin fanned toward the wall.

"What else? Give me the full rundown," said Marlowe.

"There is a contusion on the forehead above the hairline. I believe a blow to the head rendered the victim unconscious. Death delivered from cuts to the carotid arteries and the jugulars. I found a hole in the ceiling over the bathtub that looked as if a large screw had been forced into the beam. My theory is the killer suspended the victim inverted over the bathtub and exsanguinated her."

"Treated her like a goddamned deer." Marlowe scowled.

"Not much room in the tub," said Spence. "No more than a couple of feet from head to ceiling. Vic was what? About five-five?"

"A hoist wouldn't require much space if choked up all the way," said Marlowe.

"Perhaps," said Koop. "Though the killer attempted to tidy up after himself, we found traces of blood in the tub, on the floor, and on the bathroom walls. Once the body was drained of blood, he removed the organs, washed them clean, and brought them here for this totem. Impossible to remove all the blood in such a way, so you see the halos outlining each. Still, all in all, quite impressive."

Marlowe and Spence moved in for a closer inspection while Koop continued. "After laying the body on the bed, he filled the abdomen and sewed it closed. For a final touch, he placed a coin over each eye and set a small cross fashioned from two small, cylindrical metal pieces and bound with copper wire on the victim's neck below the chin."

"He filled the body? With what?" asked Marlowe.

"Flowers. I'm not certain of the types. I'll know more after I get the body back to the lab."

"Hey, didn't the Greeks do the coins on the eyes thing? I saw it in a Brad Pitt movie. *Troy*," said Spence.

"You and your pop culture knowledge. You might have read it in a book years ago. If you read, that is. But actually, you're right for once. Make a note of it. We'll see if we can track down a connection between the coins and the writing … or whatever it is. A lot of symbolism all over this thing to sift through," said Marlowe. He looked at Koop. "Murder weapon's a knife? Scalpel, maybe?"

"Doubtful a scalpel, more likely a very sharp knife, six-inch blade, approximately. I'll know more after a full autopsy."

Marlowe fidgeted. "And when will that be?"

"A few hours. I should have my preliminary findings by late afternoon. Thorough tests and a full report will obviously take longer."

"Fine, we'll check in with you then." Marlowe waved at the door. "Let's get the photographer in here. Pictures of everything, lots of pictures. Koop, you can have the body once she's done."

"Very well. Until we meet again, gentlemen," he said with a nod.

"Spence, I want everything bagged and tagged. Check the bathroom, I'll search out here." Marlowe began with the nightstand and dresser drawers while Spence examined the bathroom cabinets.

Spence's voice echoed from the bathroom. "Got a shitload of pills in the medicine cabinet—Ambien, Xanax, Ativan, a couple of different prescribers."

"Bottle of Oxycodone out here. Mixing this stuff would've killed her sooner or later without our guy's butcher job." Marlowe replaced the bottle in the drawer and took down a framed picture from the wall; the victim and a small boy, her arms wrapped around him, both smiling. In the background, swing sets and a seesaw.

"Who's the woman downstairs?" asked Marlowe.

"Sister, Carrie Mellick. She found the vic. Messed her up pretty good." Spence circled one finger in the air around his ear.

"Let's head down and see if she can point us in a direction."

The sister had not moved since they'd arrived. She rocked on the sofa, wiping her nose with a Kleenex. The box looked nearly empty, the wastebasket beside her full. Trails of mascara ran down her face, lipstick was smudged, eyes outlined in chalky black—a sad clown.

When she saw the two detectives approach, tears welled in her eyes anew.

"Ms. Mellick, I'm Detective Marlowe Gentry, this is my partner Detective Spencer Murray. I know you've answered some questions already, but would you mind answering a few for us?"

"Of course, anything I can do," she said.

Marlowe flipped open a pad to take notes. "You found your sister at seven this morning?"

"Yes." Carrie blew her nose on a pathetic scrap of overused tissue.

"Did you see anyone near the house? Anyone? Whether you knew them or not?"

"No, I come over most days near the same time. There's hardly ever anyone around. Sometimes a neighbor passes on their way to work, or maybe out walking the dog."

"Anyone pass this morning? Any dog walkers?"

Carrie shook her head. "No, I didn't see anyone."

Spence glanced at the windows, scoping the front yard. "Anything about the house seem different? Anything out of place or missing?"

"No, not that I noticed." She dabbed the tissue on her reddened nose and peered bleary-eyed about the room, before shaking her head again. "No. No one."

"What can you tell me about your sister?" Marlowe tried to sound sympathetic. "Where did she work?"

"She did work at an accounting firm, but she hasn't been there in over a year."

"Why is that?"

Carrie pointed to a picture of the same boy Marlowe had seen upstairs, this one a school photo. Good-looking kid, bright eyes, a mop of white-gold hair; he appeared to be nine or ten years old.

"Dalton, her son. He died of leukemia in July. Melissa stopped working when he got really sick, didn't go back afterwards."

"We found a lot of medications upstairs," said Spence.

"All Melissa's. I worried so much about her. After Dalton was gone, she became so depressed. She stayed in bed most of the day. I don't know how she got all those pills. I've thrown away more than I can count, but somehow she always had more. I really thought she might kill herself."

Carrie took the picture of Dalton from Marlowe and stared down, tears falling from her cheeks onto the glass. "She was so destroyed by Dalton's death. That's why I came every day to check on her. She wouldn't answer the phone, so I had to come. Every day I feared finding her dead, but I never imagined ..." She leaned forward, clutching her knees, unable to process the tragedy.

Marlowe placed a gentle hand on her forearm. "Do you know of anyone who might have a reason to harm your sister? Arguments, grudges? She was divorced, I take it. What about the ex-husband?"

"No, she stayed a total recluse for the past year. No one would have anything against her. She wasn't married. Dalton's father never entered the picture. He bolted before Dalton was born."

Marlowe glanced around the room—crystal vases, big screen television, a pool outside the glass double-doors to the rear of the house. "Impressive house for a single mother/accountant."

"Melissa worked because she wanted something to do more than needing the money. Our family owned Mellick Aeronautics, so we've always been wealthy. The company merged with Lockheed Martin several years ago. When Mom and Dad passed, we both inherited some money … well, a lot of money."

Spence jotted something down. "Both parents are deceased?"

"Yes. A car accident in '98."

"I'm sorry to hear that. Who's the beneficiary for your sister's estate?"

Carrie blanched. "Well, I am, but you don't think …" She started bawling again. "I would never …"

"No, no of course not. We just have to ask," said Marlowe. "That's all for now. Thank you, Mrs. Mellick. The officer has your statement. We'll contact you if we need anything further."

Carrie reached out and grabbed Marlowe's wrist. "Please catch the person who did this to my sister."

Marlowe nodded and squeezed her hand. Turning to Spence, he motioned toward the door.

Once outside, Spence said, "You sure you're all right? I thought you were going to take a header back there."

"Spence, drop it. I'm fine."

"Okay, okay. What do you make of the sister?"

"I think she's going to need some serious therapy after seeing what she did. We'll check her story. Money's always a good motive, but she's genuinely upset. I seriously doubt she possesses the strength to do what our killer did to the victim. Possible, I guess, but highly unlikely. I don't make her as the perp."

Spence crossed his arms over his chest. "Yeah, and with no husband in the picture—obvious suspects ... zero."

"This isn't an argument gone too far or a personal vendetta. Nope, you were close before when you started to say you hadn't seen anything like this since the Churchill Murders. This is only the beginning. Things are about to go from bad to really fucking bad."

"Shit. There goes my Bahamas vacation. Thought I'd take Miss Huge Boobs along, play naked Twister."

Marlowe could not stifle a chuckle. "I'll meet you back at the station."

"What do you think the lieutenant wants?" asked Spence.

"I have an idea. Fill you in after, okay?"

More than an idea. Marlowe knew exactly what ate at the lieutenant. He tried to think of some way to avoid their little conference, but McCann would not let it go, no chance. Marlowe was certain he would not take him off the case. They needed him on this one, and although the lieutenant would rather swallow his tongue than admit it, Marlowe stood several cuts above the rest of Metro Homicide's class of detectives. One of the reasons the higher-ups had looked the other way since ... well, since the shit went down and he lost it for a while.

Okay, maybe shooting a couple of guys and seeing his wife in a pool of her own blood might screw with some people's heads. Not to mention dealing with an eight-year-old daughter who had watched her mother brutally murdered right in front of her eyes. Even so, Marlowe had handled it pretty well. One tiny, nervous breakdown and everyone got all concerned. He had remained on the job, hadn't he? He retained the highest solve rate in Homicide. So why all the fuss?

Who in this job had not seen their share of horrific shit? Everyone lived with some kind of nightmare the past refused to swallow. The lieutenant, more than most, should understand. Vietnam vet like him, probably hiding a little post-traumatic stress disorder in his closet somewhere.

McCann put up with Marlowe's moodiness and reclusiveness, but he probably figured this case would get too big to cut corners with a head case. Marlowe's best guess was he needed reassurance there would be no going off the deep end again. The lieutenant had picked the perfect time to walk by, catching that spell back there, which likely strained his confidence in Marlowe's mental stability.

Marlowe's immediate concern, however, lay in discerning any possible pattern in this crime scene. He possessed an uncanny knack for seeing links and connections others missed—the minute details and discrepancies that at a glance seemed inconsequential. For all his training and natural acumen, so far nothing jumped out.

The ritual appeared finely detailed, meticulous in its planning and execution. He noted a few signs of inexperience, but overall, a clever and determined mind lay behind the murder. Marlowe held a begrudging admiration for this type of killer. They displayed a certain sick artistry. He also knew a sad story usually lurked in the background of such psychopaths, minds fractured by terrible abuse. Even so, nothing mitigated his hatred for what they became—or his desire to put a bullet in them.

Marlowe could not avoid the lieutenant forever; putting it off only delayed the inevitable. After another twenty minutes of staring at a bloody room, he knew he could do nothing more with the case until Koop completed the autopsy and lab tests. Plus, he needed more information on the victim, which would take time. He despised waiting—patience not among his paltry supply of virtues.

Out of excuses, Marlowe climbed into his SUV and headed toward what promised to be an epic ass chewing.

CHAPTER THREE

The image on the screen resembled a cross-section of cauliflower, stained with various colored dyes. The doctor droned on, directing attention to areas on the display with a laser pointer. Max Bannon's eyes followed the pointer, but his mind registered little. The little red dot darting across the screen made him think of cats.

"All four lobes are compromised. The nexus of the malignant cluster is here at the cerebrum midline, encroaching on both the temporal and frontal lobes. Additional lesions appear on the occipital and parietal lobes. Glioblastoma multiforme—which has metastasized throughout the brain topography." The doctor sounded as if he were reading a bicycle assembly manual.

Blah blah malignant *blah blah* lesions *blah blah* metastasized—he heard the words floating around him, echoing off tin walls. Two weeks from his thirty-fourth birthday, and Max was dying. Not how he'd planned for his life to turn out. Obviously, someone forgot to give God the memo.

The doctor continued spouting terms Max had never heard, could not pronounce, and would not remember. He thought of all the plans he had for the future—restoring his '70 Mustang, coaching the boys in Little League, taking Maggie on that cruise she wanted so badly.

Maggie. How can I tell Maggie with things so hard already? This will shatter the kids.

"How long?" he asked the doctor. "How long do I have?"

"Let's cross that bridge when we come to it. The invasiveness of the malignancy rules out surgery, but I want to get you on chemo and radiation immediately. We need to attack this with an aggressive treatment plan."

"How will it affect me?" Anxiety caused Max's hands to tremble.

"The cancer itself may produce some debilitating effects, such as progressively worsening headaches, seizures, anemia, personality changes, vision impairment, possibly even hallucinations, among others. We'll need to keep a close eye on your symptoms. The chemo and medications can have some noticeable side-effects as well."

"How bad?"

In many ways, the idea of chemotherapy and radiation frightened him more than the actual cancer. No one enjoyed vomiting constantly, but Max had a particularly severe aversion to it. A sympathetic vomiter, just hearing about someone throwing up made him gag.

He didn't consider himself a Calvin Klein model to begin with— too thin, with thick, uncontrollable brown hair that always seemed to have a cowlick somewhere, narrow, dull brown eyes, an unsightly mole on his left cheek—the prospect of hair loss did not strike him as appealing. Some guys could pull off the bald look, Max had a strong suspicion he would not be one of them. His head seemed shaped like an egg now that he thought about it.

"Effects can range from non-existent, to mild, to pretty nasty. It depends on the patient. Most commonly, we see fatigue and nausea. Kidney infections and other related problems can occur. I'll send you home with some information outlining what to expect and complications to watch out for."

The doctor reviewed the file before him. "I see you're married.

Good. You'll need to have someone with you around the clock. If you don't have someone at certain times of the day, I can recommend a few agencies with very good attendants to supplement your supervision."

"I need constant babysitters?" asked Max, dismayed.

"I wouldn't look at it that way, but yes, you need someone with you. As we discussed, the effects of the cancer and the medications can cause a number of reactions. We don't want you to harm yourself by falling or suffering any other accidents."

"This is all ... a bit overwhelming," said Max. He possessed a gift for understatement.

"I know it is, but you're not alone, Mr. Bannon. Engage your support system—doctors, family and friends, clergy. Which brings me to one final recommendation, and I can't stress enough how valuable this is. Your emotional state is going to be as important during your treatment as the physical. We have a wonderful program here run by an excellent psychologist. Please consider utilizing their services. Here is a card with their information."

Max took the card and stuffed it into his jeans pocket. Some doctor guiding him through self-affirming bullshit, not a chance. What good could it really do? He might as well take up yoga or tai chi.

"Maintaining a positive attitude is essential, Mr. Bannon. I'll have the nurse get you some literature on the way out. The more you understand the process, the less fear you may have."

Yeah, right.

Max left the hospital feeling numb. He sped through the denial stage headed toward the *why me* phase. He did not understand. No smoking since his early twenties, and then only for a couple of years. Not a great diet, too much junk food, but he exercised. Maybe not running or aerobics, but he was not a couch potato. He worked in the yard and took hikes through the woods. No beer gut or love handles yet.

All because of a little headache, a migraine or something. Not goddamned cancer.

Granted, the headaches had increased to the point he felt his skull would crack open. His regular doctor recommended seeing a specialist, who sent him to the oncologist. No easy chore keeping all the doctors' visits secret from Maggie. She suspected he stayed out drinking, and normally he did just that after an appointment. Without insurance, he could not afford the prescribed painkillers, so Max substituted copious amounts of alcohol to dull the pain.

Maggie. Their marriage held on by a slender thread at present. He asked himself again, how could he tell her? He came up with the same answer … he couldn't. Even so, he did not see how he could hide frequent trips to the hospital for chemo, blood tests, and check-ups. And when the effects started showing?

Max could not go home, not yet. His head hurt, and his apprehension of facing Maggie tied his stomach in knots. A couple of beers might dampen the ache and lend a little liquid courage. He thought of Maggie again and decided a couple of shots might be better.

He stopped at his usual haunt. A place where everyone knew his name, or at least the bartender did. They would probably dedicate a stool in his honor—a memorial to his devoted patronage. Convenient the bar was so close to home.

Wouldn't want to die in a car wreck while driving under the influence, now would I?

Max's humor grew darker right along with his life expectancy. His face must have conveyed his mood, as the bartender sat a drink on the counter before Max took his seat.

"Tough day?" asked Bob. Bob the bartender, imagine that.

"Tough life." Max dragged a stool to the counter.

"In that case, first one's on the house. Second costs double though. Then they go back to regular pricing."

"You're a freaking riot, Bob."

"Don't I know it. So, what's got you so down in the dumps?"

"Ever have one of those days when God looks down and decides to take a piss right where you're standing?"

"Been there. Except it wasn't God—three ex-wives," said Bob, wiping the counter in slow circles.

"I hear ya." Max flicked at a peanut on the counter and watched it spin.

"Look at the bright side."

Max looked up, curious to hear about this supposed bright side.

"You don't have cancer."

"You're a real pick-me-up, Bob."

"What I'm here for."

Bob went about his business and left Max to nurse his drink in peace. As he stared at his disjointed reflection in the shot glass, thoughts whirled by at light speed. A thousand fears fought for dominance, each more terrifying than the last.

The alcohol helped the headache, but did nothing to alleviate the dread of dealing with Maggie. Even driving under the speed limit, the trip home passed far too quickly. Part of him wanted nothing more than to keep going right on past. Just drive until he ran out of road and then keep on driving.

If he had not lost his job, or if he could find another one, maybe things would be different. If a frog possessed wings, it wouldn't bump its ass every time it hopped. Ifs and buts, the sad story of his life.

He pulled into The Bannon Stead, as Max liked to think of it, a one-level home sitting on two acres. Nothing fancy, but he loved it. A creek ran along the edge of the property and disappeared into a forest behind the house. The large backyard provided plenty of room for the boys to play and Maggie to keep a small flower garden. Max enjoyed sitting out on the deck with a cold beer, watching the sunset. His castle, all he'd ever wanted within its boundaries.

Cody and Austin played outside and came running at the sound of his truck pulling into the driveway. At least they appeared happy to see him. The two best things he had ever done, or would ever do. Cody, ten, looked like his mother: the same deep, brown eyes—eyes that melted Max's heart whenever in pain or begging for some desired toy. Austin, six, was more like his pop. Unfortunate, that; God willing he would grow out of it.

"Hey champs," said Max.

"Dad, Cody won't let me on the tire swing," said a petulant Austin.

"He won't get off if I let him. Austin doesn't take turns right," said Cody.

"You guys have to share. The swing isn't going anywhere. You have all the time in the world." The last statement meant more to Max than to his sons. His face dropped. Catching himself, he forced a smile. "Maybe we can put up a second swing later in the week."

"What did you bring us?" asked Austin with excitement and attempted to rummage through Max's jacket pockets.

"A big hug," said Max, arms held wide.

"Aww, I wanted a candy bar. Come on Austin, race you to the treehouse," said Cody as the two boys turned and dashed toward the backyard. No hugs given.

Max watched them go. His mind saw them as infants, so tiny in his arms. He imagined the grown men they would become—grown men with wives and kids of their own. He hoped they were better fathers and husbands and did not make his same mistakes.

Max stepped through the front door to a cyclone.

"Where the hell have you been?" asked Maggie, her voice several decibels above normal.

"Needed some hoses for the truck." He tried to move past and avoid the inevitable confrontation.

"They sell hoses at the bar? I smell the liquor on you." Maggie picked up a handful of papers and waved them in his direction. Betty Boop on her sweatshirt jumped up and down.

"You know what I've been doing? Fighting with the power company, trying to keep our electricity on. We have two dozen bill collectors leaving message after message on the phone. I've stopped answering it because I don't know what to tell them. They're calling me at work now." Her face turned red as a beet; steam might come gushing from her ears at any moment.

"Try to understand. I need you to support me right now." Max pinched his face into a well-practiced expression of discouragement, which never worked.

"Support you? You need some support, do you?" Max realized too late he had said the wrong thing. Maggie stormed forward, one pointed finger wagging inches from his nose. "I'm working my ass off to keep crumbs on our table. I'm raising two boys practically alone while you're out doing God knows what. I bathe in cold water and live in a cold house. I'm so stressed all the time I feel like I'm losing my mind. And you … you need support? I need support, Max. I need some goddamned help."

"I'm trying. I put applications in every day. I go door to door to every business. The job postings on the internet never reply, or send me form rejections. I search all day long."

"Do you? You say you do, but how do I know?" Maggie stood glaring at him, hands on hips.

"You calling me a liar? You think this is easy for me? I've never been out of work this long in my life, and now I can't even get a job at McDonald's. I'm a journeyman electrician with over ten years of experience, and I can't get a job flipping burgers."

"It's been more than a year. The news says the unemployment rate is falling and businesses are hiring. Maybe you can't get another electrician job right now, but there must be something."

"No one in construction is hiring, you know that. The housing market is still way down. I'm not qualified for office jobs—no college. Low paying jobs won't hire me because they see my resume and think I'll only be there until I find something in my field … and they're right. So they hire the kid who will work there for a while, can't blame them."

"I don't blame *them*. I blame you. Be a man. Take care of your family. You think I can pay our bills with what I make at Denny's? Two bucks an hour and tips, give me a break."

"I guess I'm not a man. Maybe you should find one."

"Self-pity now? Jesus, Max, this is all so predictable. It's not about you. It's about your family, those two boys out there. Do you know Austin didn't eat lunch at school because he thought we couldn't afford it? He's been saving his money so he could help us pay the bills."

Max felt like someone kicked him in the gut; an ant could piss on his head he sank so low. His sons going without, his wife stressed to her breaking point. Some father and husband he'd turned out to be. And now ... not even enough life insurance for a funeral. They should just toss him into the river.

"I'll talk to him, both of them. I'm sorry, Maggie. I'm so sorry."

"I know you are, but sorry isn't enough anymore."

"Believe what you want, but I am doing the best I can. You don't understand what it's like for me. I'm the man of the house. Everyone is looking at me. They all see me as a loser."

"No one matters except us. You and your goddamned male ego. That's why you don't take a job at McDonald's, too damned proud. Well, pride doesn't pay the bills. "

"That's not true. I'll do whatever I have to, dig ditches, anything." Max tried to ignore her glare. Her disappointment in him killed something inside.

"What about you? You're on me all the time. Think your hounding me helps?"

For a long moment, she glared at him, fists shaking. Max thought she might hit him for that one.

"God, we've done this so many times it sounds like a recording. I can't do it anymore."

Most times Maggie would be in tears by now. The anger bled from her face. She had moved past being upset toward not caring at all. He needed to defuse this fight before it got out of hand, if it had not already. "Me either. Let's give it a rest until we've cooled off. We'll work it out, we always do."

"No, you still don't get it. I'm *not* doing it anymore. I'm taking the kids to stay with my sister. At least I'll know they're fed and have electricity."

"Maggie, no." He said it on reflex, but truthfully, he thought her leaving for the best. If he told her about the cancer now, she would stay out of pity and obligation. He couldn't take that. It would be better for them to leave. He did not want his sons to see him waste away. He did not want Maggie taking care of him when he started shitting his pants and vomiting all over himself. She could barely stand to look at him now. Max couldn't stomach the thought of pity and disgust in her eyes.

"My mind is made up, Max. If you get a job, we can talk and see where things stand, but I can't make any promises. We've done a lot of damage. I don't know if we can fix it."

That night, Max slept in Cody's room while Cody slept with Austin. Cody protested, but little Austin seemed thrilled. He planned to build a fort from boxes and bed sheets for them to *camp out*. Maggie intended to leave the following day. She instructed Max to move into their bedroom in the morning and stay there until she and the boys were gone.

His concern should center on Maggie and the kids, on the possibility of losing them, but he could not shake the terrors his imagination threw up behind his eyelids. Besides, it appeared a near certainty he would lose his family, one way or the other. Sparing them his descent seemed the only mercy he could provide.

As Max tossed and turned in a bed too small and unfamiliar, Cody's soldiers and cowboys seemed to stare at him with contempt from the shelves. Shadows moved through the room, ghastly shapes creeping along the walls. When sleep came, it did not come alone.

A LONG HALLWAY, GRAY AND STERILE, STRETCHED OUT BEFORE HIM. Seconds of silence gave way to a soft hum vibrating in the back of his skull. The sound rose and fell in sync with the flicker of overhead lights.

He stumbled ahead, each step a labor, as if trudging over a floor coated with tar. Max passed a room on his left. Within, a pulsating mass grew from the far wall—fleshy, yet black with rot and pierced through with a myriad of tubes and wires. The mass undulated, convulsed, and burst, spewing a torrent of vile fluids on the floor. An overwhelming stench of decay engulfed him. Heart monitors blared; straight lines ran across their screens. He staggered back. The warning buzz and hum joined, exploding into a thunderous cacophony of metallic ringing—like a million brass cymbals all clanging at once, struggling for a unison they could not find.

Max raised an arm to his face, hiding his mouth and nose in the crook of his elbow. He stumbled away from the ghastly sight. The second room held a sea of corpses, each in various stages of decay, laid out on cold steel gurneys. The nearest stood and faced him, beckoning him closer with spindly arms, pale and venous. His emaciated body appeared too thin and fragile to remain erect.

"Brother," rasped the corpse, reaching, pleading.

Max screamed, but the sound existed only in his mind. He recoiled, managing an uncoordinated sprint for a few places before falling to a hopeless stride along the hallway's endless journey. Three figures came out of the murk in the distance, standing abreast, two smaller than the other. He longed to stand with them. A deep yearning threatened to sap his strength. All his will bent toward reaching them, yet each step forward pushed them further away.

He walked the hall for a thousand lifetimes, never drawing nearer to those distant shapes. Those he loved and needed, he had lost forever. The cold gray embraced him. The hall elongated and constricted. On hands and knees rubbed raw, he crawled on, praying for an end.

Max snapped awake. Sweat soaked his shirt and the bed sheets. He glanced at the clock.

Fifteen minutes? I only slept fifteen minutes?

He felt as though he'd spent hours trapped in that hallway. He understood most of it, deciphering the dream's images did not require one to be Sigmund Freud. Max had to get a grip on his fear, or it might drive him crazy before the cancer could kill him.

After waking from the nightmare, he abandoned further attempts at sleep as futile. Max rose and went to the computer. He usually stayed away from self-diagnosis by internet, or looking up any illnesses online.

A bit of a hypochondriac by his own admission, surfing the web for possible ailments was like pouring gas on a fire. He was unable to watch a television program about a disease without feeling every symptom. Ironically, he loathed doctors and refused to see one unless deathly ill.

Max read over the papers the doctor sent home with him and typed in the term for his cancer. Clicking on the first link, The Mayo Clinic, his fears were confirmed.

Glioblastoma multiforme—a grade four cancer, the most common malignant primary brain tumor. Standard prognosis with treatment is six months to a year. Survival rate after one year 42%, after eighteen months 17%, after two years 4%.

Great. Just freaking great.

Max wondered when the countdown started. How long were the tumors infesting his brain before discovered? He might be a month or more into his six-month expiration date already. Those estimates said *with treatment.* What if the treatment proved ineffective? Did that shorten the prognosis?

As he read, each described symptom needled at some part of his body. His vision seemed to blur. Max's hands trembled, which might mean the onset of a seizure. He scrutinized his reflection in the mirror above the computer. Yes, his gums looked a little white, could be anemia.

The room rotated. The walls waved back and forth. Sweat beaded on his forehead.

I'm going to throw up.

He dashed to the bathroom, his pulse thundering in his temples and chest.

I'm having a heart attack. Is that something that can happen with this?

Everything around him closed in, squeezing, he could not breathe. He huddled in a corner, knees pressed to his stomach.

It's a panic attack. Settle down. Let it pass. Oh my God, I'm really going to die.

He needed to talk to someone. He felt so alone, terrified. Maggie was out of the question. He could not tell any of his friends. They were all Maggie's friends as well. Out of concern they would talk, and it would get back to her.

Max dug through his jeans pockets and found the crumpled card —*Patient Counseling Services.* He carried the card across the room in two hands and set it by the phone. First thing in the morning, he would make the call.

CHAPTER FOUR

Becca's hands shook. Hot coffee splashed near the cup's rim with each step. The porcelain-against-porcelain rattle of cup on saucer set her nerves further on edge. Michael had woken in a foul mood this morning. Out late drinking with his friends, he now nursed a nasty hangover. His discomfort usually found a way of becoming *her* discomfort.

Her movements slow and deliberate, Becca eased forward to where he sat on the sofa. His scowl did little to encourage confidence. One step away, her hand slipped and the cup tumbled into the air. It crashed down to the carpet, spilling onto Michael's shoe and pants leg.

"Goddammit, you stupid bitch. Can't you do the simplest thing without fucking it up?" Quick as a cat, his fist flew out, punching Becca in the stomach. She doubled over with a whoosh of expelled air, tears stinging her eyes. "That's a taste of what you're going to get if that shit stains my carpet. Now I have to change. You stupid bitch. I swear you don't have the sense God gave a rock."

He started to walk away, but turned and backhanded her across the chest, sending her onto her rear. Becca gasped for breath, her breasts throbbing madly. He grunted with disgust and continued toward the stairs. His cussing dwindled to indistinct grumbling as he moved out of earshot.

Becca angrily wiped the tears from her cheeks. Not angry with Michael, she expected his actions; the abuse had stopped shocking her years ago. No, she was angry at her own weakness—the timid mouse, so afraid. Each time, and the episodes became more frequent with each passing month, she hated herself for allowing it. Thinking back, she could not remember how it started. Why hadn't she walked out the first time?

The story sounded so clichéd as to be sickening. Michael hit her, she threatened to leave, he cried and begged, promised never to do it again … and she believed him. How stupid.

He didn't bother to cry or beg anymore. Well-conditioned as she'd become, his threats were now enough to keep her cowered and afraid to leave. Ironically, the more vicious the situation became, the less she considered fleeing. Fear could be a powerful motivator, but also an equally powerful restraint.

Maybe she suffered from a version of Stockholm Syndrome. In those cases, the victim developed a strong attachment to their captor and often viewed them with positive feelings. Becca felt nothing for Michael—not love, not even hatred.

Even in the beginning, she had not believed in him as much as in the dream. The dream of how things were meant to be. Love at first sight, leading to a beautiful, white gown in a picture-perfect wedding. A house with a picket fence, complete with two happy kids. They would grow old together, still in love after all those years, reclining in rocking chairs, basking in the warmth of the sun.

Giving up on the dream meant killing a part of herself, the part that believed in things such as love and happily-ever-after. Too late, she recognized the dream for a lie. When she woke, the walls rose up around her. The cage door slammed shut, a captive unable and unwilling to break free.

Becca went to the bathroom, pulled her long, dark hair into a ponytail, and rubbed ointment onto her sore abdomen. She swallowed a couple of Advil and appraised the newest token of

Michael's affection. A large purple bruise ached and overlapped his last gift, marring a shapely figure. It hurt to lift her arms as she readied for work. She brushed her teeth and dabbed makeup onto dark circles under eyes, normally brilliant blue, but today, bloodshot and dull.

She waited for the front door to bang closed and proceeded to the bedroom to dress. Numbness set in after a while. The bruises rarely faded before new ones took their place. It surprised her what a person could accept over time. The horrible became commonplace, its horror lost in the repetition.

This did not mean she no longer feared the next punch or the next kick. Nor did it mean she did not yearn to escape the abuse. No, it simply meant she accepted there was no way out. Michael had effectively clipped her wings. She could sit at the open window, staring out onto a world full of promise, yet remain unable to fly free.

Rebecca Drenning, this is your life ... for bad and worse.

Once in her Volvo, she felt a little better. Becca's car remained her one sanctuary from Michael ... from everything. Her mother had bought it for her to take to college more than a decade ago, and she still loved it. Memories of happier times felt infused into the upholstery. Old songs playing from the stereo filled the interior with the pleasant past.

Becca popped Tori Amos into the CD player, took a deep breath, and drove away. The music and the vibration of the road always soothed her, like an irritable infant lulled to sleep by gentle motion. She wanted to keep driving. Drive until the wheels fell off, or until she found a place hidden from the world, whichever came first.

She arrived at work already dreading the return home. Becca wanted the day to last forever. She wanted to lose herself in the daily routine, lose herself in others' problems and ignore her own, at least for a little while. The simple act of sliding on her long white coat caused her chin to lift a little higher, the slouch in her shoulders to rise a fraction.

"Good morning, Rachel," said Becca as she arrived at the nurses' station and took her clipboard in hand.

"Good morning, Doc." Rachel, Becca's head nurse and general do-everything sidekick, looked up from typing notes into the computer. Fifty-five, with the body of a linebacker and the face of a cherub, Rachel could intimidate or enliven with the subtlest change in posture. Rust-red hair in a bob cut framed kind eyes and a mischievous mouth.

Rachel had been with her since they started the practice, her knowledge and skill managing to keep Becca sane in those early days. She'd needed someone experienced and smart to see her through the learning process of starting a new business. Despite being brilliant in her field, she had been a complete novice in matters pertaining to operating an office.

Rachel stood, stepped close, and placed the back of her hand to Becca's forehead. "You feeling okay? No fever, but you look a bit peaked."

"I'm fine, rushed to get ready this morning." Becca looked away and attempted to avoid Rachel's scrutinizing stare.

"Michael again, right?" Rachel also served as Becca's confidant and best friend. She knew about Becca's marriage and about what she endured.

"Let's not talk about it now. What's on the schedule?" Becca perused her clipboard.

"Full day. We're booked up. Your first appointment is a referral from Dr. Curtis."

Dr. Curtis, a neurologist, often sent patients to Becca for counseling. Many of those under his care displayed great difficulty accepting or even understanding the nature of their afflictions. He referred patients with Alzheimer's disease and dementia, as well as head trauma cases.

"Okay, let's get to it," said Becca. "Show him in."

Becca took a seat in her leather chair and waited for Rachel to escort in the patient. She read over his file as she waited—early onset dementia. Only sixty years old, yet suffering substantial memory loss with episodes of erratic behavior.

"Mr. Clemons, please have a seat." Mr. Clemons was currently undergoing inpatient treatment for a fall, a fractured left ulna. Dr. Curtis hoped this visit might assist with his emotional stability.

"I think I'm lost. I must have taken a wrong turn. Can you direct me to the foreman's office? I'm here about the job opening." He shambled into the room holding his injured arm as if the covering cast might prove adequate protection, while aiming a distracted smile nowhere in particular. Blankness swam in his eyes.

"Mr. Clemons, I'm Dr. Drenning. You're in the hospital. Dr. Curtis asked me to meet with you." She kept her voice calm and even. Perhaps a key word would bring him around.

"Did Clare come with you?" Clare, his oldest daughter, brought him in and visited every day. Hopefully, the mention of her name would trigger recognition.

"Clare? Clare's away at college. I miss her, but she'll be home for Christmas." He brightened at the sound of her name, but the look of confusion returned.

"Clare brought you to the hospital. Remember, Clare visited yesterday?"

"I ... uh ... yes, Clare ..." He searched the photos on the walls, trying to find anything familiar. He turned toward Becca, staring.

"Who are you? What am I doing here? My arm hurts. I want to see my doctor."

"If you'll sit down, I'd like to talk to you. I understand you've been having some trouble remembering things?"

"I don't want to talk to you. I want to go back to my room." Mr. Clemons, obviously agitated, tugged at the neck of his shirt as if it choked him.

"We'll take you back to your room right after you and I have a little talk, okay?"

"No, I want to go now. You can't keep me here. I want to go." He screamed at Becca and advanced in her direction, shaking a fist. He was addled and panicked; the situation escalated toward dangerous.

"Mr. Clemons," said Becca sharply, "sit down this instant."

The tone and volume of her voice froze Mr. Clemons in his tracks. Lucidity filtered back into to his eyes.

"What? Where … oh. I'm … sorry doctor." He slouched into the seat. "I'm so scared. I know what I'm hearing and seeing, but my mind won't accept it. It's like I'm not me anymore."

"I understand. We're going to help you, I promise." Becca sat across from him, her voice soft and soothing now.

Over the next half hour, she guided Mr. Clemons through some mental exercises and key words that would help anchor his mind and encourage memory recall. As the session concluded, he thanked her profusely and seemed more confident in himself. Becca felt the same sense of satisfaction she always felt after a successful session. Most often, results were not so obvious, but each small step for a patient was a victory for her as well.

The remainder of the day passed without incident. Most of the sessions were follow-ups, which always went smoother, Becca having previously developed a report with the patient. Finally came her last appointment of the day, a new patient recently diagnosed with a malignant brain tumor.

Rachel came to the door and ushered in a defeated-looking man. "Doctor, this is Max Bannon."

"Hello, Mr. Bannon, I'm Dr. Drenning. Please, have a seat. How are you feeling today?"

The man moved as if he were already dead. Shuffled steps, head down, he sat in the chair, keeping his eyes on the floor. Becca could tell at a glance, this would be a challenge. Max Bannon considered his end a done deal.

She rose from behind her desk, took the seat opposite her patient, and waited, uncertain if he had heard the question. Only recently diagnosed, she assumed the knowledge still overwhelmed him. He could not accept his situation, or worse, accepted it too readily—the certain finality of it.

"May I call you Max?" Becca asked. He nodded almost imperceptibly. "Max, I know this feels insurmountable, but it isn't. I've seen many with your condition live for years."

"What kind of life?" he asked without looking up.

"Okay, straight talk. Yes, the percentages are against you. Denying

44

the severity of your condition can mean giving up as much as making it unbeatable. You have to find a middle ground. Come to grips with the possibility you may indeed die. Come to peace with it. Yet, don't give up. If ten percent of people with your type of cancer live, why can't you be among the ten percent?"

"I can't find the middle ground. I can't find any ground. Wherever I try to stand, I just keep falling down."

"I see you're married with two sons. Surrounding yourself with those who love you is a powerful medicine. You'll fight for them and for yourself.

"My wife left me and took my boys."

"I'm sorry to hear that, Max." Becca needed to pivot the discussion. "You still see your sons though, right? The old adage, *out of sight out of mind*, is true. Without them around, you feel more alone. The need to fight lessens. If no one cares, if no one is there ... why bother? You need to stay in close contact with your sons. Maybe you can even reconcile with your wife."

Max shook his head while tapping his fingers distractedly against his blue jeans. "No, I don't think so. But what you said, that's how I feel. Why bother? No one will miss me. My death will only improve their lives."

"That's the fear and depression talking, Max. You obviously love your family very much in spite of any problems in your marriage."

His knuckles whitened as he clutched the edge of the seat. "I do, more than anything."

"Do this for me. Think of a memory, your fondest memory involving your family."

Max sat stone still. Becca waited for a time. "Is there—"

"I remember baseball," he said.

"Baseball? Okay, what about baseball?"

"Cody played. He wasn't very good, couldn't hit the ball. He always swung before the ball got close enough. One of the other fathers lived vicariously through their sons—you know the type—took it all so seriously. He screamed at the boys from the bleachers—harsh things, too harsh for little kids." Max scratched at the back of his neck. "Well, Cody struck out for the third time, and this father went off on him."

Becca nodded, taking notes.

"'Park him on the bench. God he sucks. He's killing us,' the guy yells. Cody was devastated, everyone in the ballpark heard. I walked up to the man and said, 'Hey, they're only kids.' So he gets in my face, yelling. 'Kids? What the hell are we teaching them? What the hell is going on these days? Everyone gets to play; everyone gets a trophy. It doesn't matter if they did nothing to help win. We got to teach them early, winning matters, being the best matters.'"

Becca shook her head, but kept quiet.

"'I see your point, I do,' I said, trying to take the heat down. I tried to tell him they're too young for that, they're just kids trying to have fun. He kept on screaming. 'Fun? You call losing fun? Figures you'd say that, cause your kid sucks. He's the worst player I've ever seen. Look at him crying like a little pussy.'" Max wiped a hand over his mouth.

"I reared back and hit him as hard as I could, right in the breadbasket. He folded like a busted straight and fell sideways off the bleachers. The whole place went quiet, and I looked over at Maggie where she sat holding baby Austin. The look on her face ... I thought it would embarrass her, what I did, but she didn't look ashamed or humiliated. She was ... proud of me."

"You stood up for your son," said Becca.

"We fight constantly now. Every time she looks at me, her face filled with disappointment, anger, disgust, I always think about that day at the park. I want it back."

Once Max remained silent, she said, "That's the kind of fight you need now, Max. Fight for your family. Focus on what you can control. Keep a positive attitude and maintain your treatment regimen. Fight."

"Easy for you to say. You sit here all day telling others how to cope, how to live, but you don't understand, not really. I bet you're around suffering and pain all the time, but you can't really understand it, not until it's you." Max appeared near tears, fists in tight balls thumped against his thighs.

"You know what? You're right. I don't know exactly what you're going through, but I have worked with hundreds of people in your situation. Some give up, some fight. You want to know the difference between the two?"

Max looked up, waiting for the answer, an answer he desperately needed.

Becca reached out and squeezed his forearm. "Purpose, Max. There's some reason inside them pushing them on. Maybe it's something they want to accomplish and can't give up on the desire to live—they need to meet that goal. Perhaps they simply refuse to be beaten, a stubborn will refusing to allow anything to defeat them. Others are not ready to leave the ones they love. All find a purpose, a reason to fight."

"I don't have a reason. When my wife left and took my sons, every reason I had for wanting to live left with them. The only reason I'm even trying the treatments is that I'm terrified of dying. I'm not afraid of being dead. It's the pain, the slow wasting, and all the tests. I don't want what's to come." He seemed unaware of the tears coating his eyes or the thin line of snot running toward his lips, his gaze a million miles away.

"You can't let fear paralyze you. Fear, if you let it, will keep you fixed in place. You won't be able to look toward any possible future except the one you most dread. You've got to fight it." Becca had said these same words to countless patients. She hoped they did not sound as empty as they felt. More so, she prayed the words contained truth and were not just little white lies meant to soothe fears, a pointless salve on a gaping wound. "You've heard the saying *'you can't always control your circumstances, but you can always control how you react to those circumstances'*? Decide how you want to face this ordeal. Do you want to face it with fear and give up? Or do you want to face it with strength and dignity? It's completely up to you, Max. No one can tell you how to live or how to die. Make your choice and fight with every ounce of will. If not, you'll find yourself trapped in a nightmare...." Becca froze. A thought slammed into her mind, followed by a wave of anger.

Max stared at her, puzzled. "Doctor?"

She tried to gather herself. "I'm sorry, what did you say?"

"Nothing. You stopped speaking mid-sentence and looked a little odd for a second."

"Did I?" asked Becca. She blinked a few times and shook her head. "Well, at any rate, think on what we've talked about. Don't give up, Max. If you're going to beat this, you have to fight it. Medicine and treatment won't be enough. But more than that … live. Cherish every day, make the most of what time you have left, whether that's one year or a hundred. What would you regret if you died tomorrow?"

"So many things I could never count them all. I regret that I couldn't keep my marriage together. I regret I can't take care of my wife, my kids. It would be easier to name the things I don't regret. A much shorter list."

"Work toward removing those regrets. Always wanted to do something? Do it. Don't want to leave on bad terms with your wife, kids, friends? Talk to them. Fix it. Let the future come on your terms. Taking control of an issue will dilute feelings of powerlessness and give you some peace." Again, Becca felt the thought strike at her consciousness. This time, however, she could not pretend to overlook its relevance to her own life. Anger welled inside her.

Keep it together. Focus on your patient.

Max turned his head downward. She could tell he was not ready, maybe he never would be, and he did not have a great deal of time to flip the switch. Most in his predicament went through this stage, belief in the inevitability of their deaths—the no hope stage. Many never moved beyond it. Working with hundreds of patients had given her a good compass for which direction one would go. She feared Max had already lain down and now waited for the fast approaching end.

"I'll try, Doc," he said without any conviction.

"That's all you can do. Just try. See you Thursday?"

"Yeah, I'll be here." His every word dragged, down-tuned and in slow motion. His walk out the door carried the same defeat, body rigid, steps lurching in despair.

Becca leaned back in her chair. Max Bannon was dying. He faced the hardest road anyone could ever travel. Everything she told him carried with it truth that must be seized upon to give him any power over his situation. She could not force him to believe it.

Yet, what disturbed her during their session was how every word applied to her, her situation, her refusal to believe and to fight.

Dr. Rebecca Drenning … hypocrite. She preached the sermon and ignored it in her own life. A scam, a hoax, a run on those who desperately needed the magic elixir. Becca sold snake oil to the sick, and saddest of all, she needed the cure as badly as they did.

CHAPTER FIVE

"Have a seat, Gentry," said the lieutenant.

Marlowe entered the office, pausing to glance at the dozen or so detectives and staff of Homicide Division busy with the day's assignments before closing the door behind him.

Lt. Claude McCann, a big, Irish stereotype—close cropped, red hair over steel gray eyes, a flame-colored mustache crowning thin lips that twitched whenever he was annoyed, which seemed most of the time. With the sleeves of a white cotton button-down rolled to his elbows, his jet-black tie hanging loose around his neck, he stormed around the room like J. Jonah Jameson. The residue of cigarette smoke permeated the office, a poorly kept secret behind a closed door and blinds. The acrid atmosphere made Marlowe's eyes sting.

McCann gestured at his computer screen, open to the news. "What a mess. The Seraphim Killer. The media is already calling this psycho the Seraphim."

Marlowe rubbed his eyes for second and asked, "Seraphim? Why Seraphim?"

"Why? Because some asshole coughed up info on those ghastly arms, wings, whatever. I don't know if a reporter got in before we sealed the scene, or if one of our people spilled it. If it's the latter, and I find out who, my size twelve boot is going up their ass."

"It's kind of catchy though. Better than something cliché like The Angel of Death. I mean if you're going with an angel motif." A mischievous grin played at the edges of Marlowe's mouth.

"Can the jokes, I'm in no mood." The lieutenant possessed no sense of humor on his best days. He had two settings—angry and pissed-the-fuck off. He thundered around his desk, pounding a fist into his palm to accent each syllable. "I hope I don't need to say this, but I'm going to anyway. It'll make me feel better … and I can say I told you. Nothing like plausible deniability in my position."

Marlowe fought the urge to roll his eyes.

McCann never smiled, so one always had to assume complete seriousness.

"This is going to get out of hand in a hurry if we aren't careful. This Seraphim shit is only the tip of the iceberg. We're on the Titanic headed right for a world of hurt. You're the best we have, so I need you on this, but your head better be in it. All the way in … got me?

Marlowe nodded.

"What a mess. A goddamned hack-and-slash serial killer. They're supposed to be in New York or Chicago."

"Oregon," offered Marlowe.

"It wasn't a question. Point is, they shouldn't be killing people in my city. Let 'em go to Atlanta or Miami if they want a warm climate. Now we've got a second in five years. Do I need to tell you how the first one turned out?"

"No, you don't," said Marlowe through clenched teeth.

McCannt actually seemed ashamed for a second … a short second. "Yeah, well…. Anyway, this one is a hundred times worse. Last time out, eight murders, but we managed to keep it local and without causing mass hysteria."

Marlowe felt the need to rub his eyes again. His mouth would taste like an ashtray when he finally got out of here. "I seem to recall twenty-four-seven coverage. My face on most of it."

"Sure, all local, not the national press. Birmingham Metro wasn't hung out there as an example of an inept police force. Okay, so maybe some middle-aged men shit their pants for a few months, but we didn't have a whole city on the verge of panic."

"The victims were confined to a singular age group and race," said Marlowe. "Most people figured they were safe and got off on the Hollywood-style media frenzy."

"Yeah, and with this one no one knows. Anyone could be next on the chopping block. This go round, just the one murder so far and I already have CNN, MSNBC, Fox, the major networks and local stations crawling up my ass. You can't throw a rock without hitting one, which sounds like a good idea now that I think of it. Everyone in the country is going to be glued to this like O.J. in a Bronco. The higher ups want it solved … yesterday."

"I can handle the press. I dealt with them before."

"The hell you will. Two years ago, you served them an educated pretty-boy face. Everyone loved it—media, viewers, even the brass, but that was before the shit it the fan. I don't intend to rehash the past with you other than reminding you of the fallout, and the mess it caused. _I_ will handle the press. You don't so much as sneeze in a camera's direction. And for Christ's sake, keep Murray away from them."

Marlowe suspected rehashing the Churchill Murders was the main reason for this meeting, but if the lieutenant wanted to play it subtle, Marlowe didn't mind—subtlety not being McCann's strong suit. Still, the less they discussed the specifics of the Churchill case, the more Marlowe would like it.

"We're on it, Lieutenant. We're doing everything possible. Koop will have the preliminary autopsy this afternoon, and Spence and I will comb through the victim's background. It's not microwave crime solving. We'll work it as fast as we can."

"Speed is secondary, let the brass sweat. Getting it right—that's top priority. By the book Marlowe, every step. When we catch this son of a bitch, it's got to be iron clad. Any defense attorney worth their salt is going to use your past against us. All that business with the Churchill case is going to come up. They'll say what happened to you affected your judgment. We need to be ready and have every contingency covered. You're a straight arrow, I know that, but this one has my panties in a bunch."

"I understand. I've got it under control." Marlowe tried to appear confident and sound reassuring.

"Do you? That episode back at the crime scene didn't look under control to me." Lieutenant McCann glared at him like a disappointed father.

"I'm fine, really. I didn't eat breakfast and got a little queasy for a second." Marlowe doubted the lieutenant bought the lame explanation, so he added, "What happened before is only greater motivation. I know better than most what happens when we get it wrong. I want this guy more than anyone."

"Up for debate, and I don't have time for it. You haven't been the same since. You're a surly, moody bastard these days—not that I can point fingers in that regard." McCann leaned against his desk, not quite sitting. "Some say I can be less than pleasant on occasion."

Marlowe's eyebrows went up. "You, Sir? Nonsense."

"Stow it. My point is, you get the job done, and that's all I want. But, I don't want you going all Charles Bronson on this thing. You're a cop, not a vigilante. Last time was close to home, I get that. This time, no shrink will pull your ass out of the frying pan. Understand what I'm saying?"

"Yes, sir. By the book." Marlowe snapped to attention, one hand at his brow in a salute.

"By the fucking book." McCann turned his back with a dismissive wave and ignored Marlowe's flippancy.

Marlowe exited the lieutenant's office, his mood soured. The mere mention of the Churchill Murders felt like a spike jammed into his eye. He worked hard at maintaining a case of selective amnesia, and the constant reminders did not help. In truth, he did not need it mentioned—most everything reminded him. He stopped in the hall thinking of Paige, the hollow long-gone look in her beautiful eyes. Marlowe closed his eyes, weathering another memory of her screaming. *It would've been kinder if—*

"Still in one piece?" asked Spence, coming up behind him.

Marlowe jumped. His barbed retort stalled as Spence offered him coffee. "Thanks."

He walked in silence to his desk and plopped down. Spence rounded to his chair on the other side.

"Yeah, a real teddy bear, our boss." Marlowe took a long sip, and sighed. "Read me the riot act about how he expects this case handled. Nothing we didn't know, but he loves the sound of his own voice."

"Sounding a bit resentful there, partner. I know Lieutenant's worried the press will try to stir up old shit into this mess. With you being lead on both cases, it's easy fodder for them to dig through to add a dash of scandal. Bunch of garbage divers, the lot of 'em." Spence put his pen down and rotated his seat to face Marlowe.

"Nothing to find," said Marlowe. "They broadcast everything but my shoe size the last time. One of those bloodsucking bastards even tried to sneak into Paige's room at the hospital."

Spence grumbled. "The Churchill Murders made horror movies look like Saturday morning cartoons. With this new nutjob, and the god-awful things he does, it all adds up to ratings. You know they'll run at this thing from every angle over and over again. The talking heads will eat it up and spew it out for a public that gets off on this shit. This is real life CSI, Law & Order, and Hannibal Lecter all rolled into one."

"What are you saying? The Churchill case is over and done, sealed and put to bed. I did what I had to do—in self-defense."

"I know. Righteous shots all the way. You wouldn't be here if they weren't. The department would have you behind a desk or out to pasture. I was there, remember? For most of it anyway. But you know the media, they're entertainment now, fighting each other for viewers. They haven't cared about *news* for years. All of 'em go for the lowest common denominator."

"Is this heading somewhere, Spence?" Marlowe felt his patience wearing as thin as his socks.

"The lieutenant has legit concerns, is all. I've seen what it did to you, how it's still inside you. The threat of a loose cannon running wild on this case is not an added worry we need. This thing is pulling up a lot of shit for all of us. You were the most affected before, so it has to be needling at you. "

"I'm fine. The shrinks cleared me. I dealt with it. But hey, if you and McCann think you can catch this guy without me, by all means be my guest."

"That's not what I'm saying and you know it. Cut the defensive crap for a minute and think. If you allow this case to pull you back down, you may not make it out this time. You barely recovered before. I don't want to see you sink into that pit again. Stay with me, okay?"

"I'm headed to the morgue to work on catching a killer. If you want to join me, and stop playing shrink and priest, the car's this way." Marlowe stood and pushed past Spence, not waiting for an answer.

For two years, he had tolerated the concerned glances, the whispers. Everyone seemed to think him a breath away from eating a bullet, and although he would never allow anyone to know it—he was. Not a day went by he did not think about it. If he didn't have Paige to take care of, Lord knows they'd have found him on the floor right next to Katy.

On the job, with something to focus on, he could manage. The quiet, he hated the quiet. Those moments alone, sitting in his dark, empty house, waiting for the alcohol to kick in, when the relentless images assaulted him, Marlowe would stare at a bullet for hours, twirling it between two fingers, thinking how easy it would be. One quick squeeze of the trigger, and bam, all over. One bullet to shatter the images once and for all.

Only Paige kept him going. The idea of giving up and leaving her an orphan repulsed him. Although sometimes, in the darkest moments, he questioned if she would be better off without him. Every mute glance, every dead-eyed stare accused him of not being strong enough to save Mommy. Nevertheless, Marlowe soldiered on, bottled it up, and tried to ignore it. Maybe not a stage in the grieving process, but the only way he knew to cope.

He could not discuss it with anyone, could not stomach the pity. One more hand on his shoulder mouthing some useless platitude and he might explode on the lot of them. They meant well, he knew that, and somewhere deep down he even appreciated the sentiment; even so, on the raw surface, he wanted them to take their condolences and sympathy and shove them up their asses. Just leave him the fuck alone.

Focus on the job. On what you can control. The here and now.

If he did not keep his head in the game, others were about to understand his pain in a whole new way. He would not wish the experience on his worst enemy. To spare them, and maybe even find a little peace for himself, he needed to catch this maniac. Marlowe hoped Koop turned up something to help. The clock continued to tick, and Seraphim was no doubt already hunting his next victim.

"Ah, detectives," said Koop as they entered the morgue's examination room.

Marlowe always found the chill and sterility of the morgue relaxing. Most likely, the least dangerous location on earth. The dead rarely presented a threat to anyone. They knew their place and kept their opinions to themselves. The dead never bothered Marlowe. The living, on the other hand, always made him wary.

"Find anything interesting?" asked Spence.

"Much and more, step over here," said the doctor, waving a hand toward the center of the room.

They followed to where the victim's body lay. The armless corpse resting on the cold, steel table made Marlowe's head swim again. So much for the dead not unnerving him. He managed to mask his unease and nodded to Koop. The doctor positioned the overhead light and pulled back the sheet, revealing the body.

"As you can see, the killer separated the sternum using bolt cutters, or something similar. Though I can think of nothing similar to bolt cutters that are not bolt cutters." Koop smirked. His humor went unappreciated, so he continued with his findings. "The jagged edges indicate a breaking of the bone rather than sawing through. A bone saw leaves smoother edges and a more even separation."

Koop removed the ribcage, placed the sections onto an adjacent table, and pointed to the interior cavity. "It appears I guessed correctly. A hunting style knife sliced the organs free."

"Our killer has medical expertise?" asked Marlowe.

"Doubtful. A knife rather than a scalpel suggests not, and the cuts themselves confirm it. The killer sliced and cut whatever held the organ in place, like someone working on a Thanksgiving turkey. I do not detect any surgical precision in the method. Also, and more telling, look here...." He indicated a round contusion high on the victim's forehead. "My assistant pursued a degree in veterinary medicine before switching to forensics, fortunately for us. He recognized the mark. Jonas, care to enlighten our guests?"

A freckle-faced kid of about nineteen approached and stood to one side of Koop. A college kid interning with the department, he could not seem to make eye contact with the older men, addressing his comments to his shoes.

"Well ... I-I ..." Jonas stammered.

"Speak up lad, they won't bite you," said the doctor.

"A captive bolt gun, uh ... made the mark."

"A what?" asked Spence.

"It's a device used to subdue livestock before bleeding them out. It knocks the animal unconscious, so they don't feel anything. On large animal rotation, I saw the procedure performed several times. It's considered the most humane way."

"Humane slaughter. Now there's an oxymoron for you," said Spence.

"Like our vic, though." Marlowe glanced at Koop. "So, you're thinking the killer works or worked in a slaughterhouse?"

"Or on a farm processing their own meat." Jonas returned his stare to the floor.

"Great, only a few gazillion farms and slaughterhouses in Alabama." Spence tossed his hands into the air.

"It's a start," said Marlowe. "What about the flowers in the body cavity, any luck there?"

"Yes, Google. Wonderful invention," said Koop. "The flowers are species found in abundance across the southeast—wildflowers blooming almost year round. The yellow are a type of daisy, the purple are known by the common name Carolina Wild Petunias."

"Short answer ... no help. Anyone can get them from virtually anywhere," said Spence.

"Also, the coins placed on the eyes are British half pennies. Britannia embossed on the back holding a trident, George V on the front. This version was the most abundantly minted, running from 1911 to 1936." Koop repositioned his glasses with an index finger.

"Those must be rare," A glimmer of hope sparked Marlowe's eyes.

"Ah, but there's the catch. These are replicas. Cheap brass and aluminum," said Koop.

"Meaning we can't trace them?" Spence huffed a disgusted breath and rubbed tension from his neck.

Koop shook his head. "You can try, but I'm guessing you won't get anywhere. Cheap coins like these are used as children's toys and fake currency in theater plays, among others. A slew of uses in England for costume antiques."

"Maybe he's from England." Marlowe paced about, tapping his index finger to his thumb. "We can try checking immigration and passenger manifests for incoming flights and see how many Brits have recently arrived in the city. Though even if that's the case, he could have landed in Atlanta and driven over, or simply have been here for years. Another needle in a haystack."

"There's one other thing," said the doctor. "We found adhesive residue, most likely from duct tape, on the victim's skin inside each breast. The same residue was found on the lapel area of her top, along the buttons and button-eye holes."

"Why?" asked Spence.

"Modesty? He kept the victim's breasts covered during his operation. No blood on any of the clothing suggests the body was wrapped before exsanguination."

"Ok, that's weird. Not like this whole thing isn't weird as hell, but why would someone who planned to hack her up worry about seeing her saucy bits?" asked Spence.

Koop shrugged. Finished with his examination, he pulled the cover over the victim's head and cut off the overhead light before snapping off his latex gloves. "Toxicology results will take a week. We know she took several prescriptions, and with the use of the bolt gun, I doubt the killer used additional drugs."

"Good to know about the tape residue, but not much help at the moment. We'll mark it for a profile workup," said Marlowe. "Spence, let's get some people looking into slaughterhouse workers going back ten years. Farms with livestock processing, current and former hands, owners, the works."

"What are we looking for? Have to narrow it down a little more than that." Spence jotted the instructions into his notepad to pass along to the staff.

"Anyone who might have walked off with one of those captive bolt gun things—anyone with access to one. Run every name through the databases. Anyone with priors, tag them for an interview. Plus, put in a call to every county sheriff's department in the state. Have them send people to question farmers and slaughterhouse supervisors about anything odd or suspicious, like stolen or missing bolt guns. Interview everyone with access to the guns. Also, check manufacturers for sales. I doubt this guy bought the gun on the up and up, but maybe if he stole it, we'll find an order for a replacement."

"That's a lot of work. They ain't going to like it," said Spence, his eyes wide, head tilted to one side."

"I don't care what they like. Ask nice, but if they offer you lip, tell them the governor will be giving them a call. Next, run this killer's MO through VICAP, NCIC, and the rest."

Spence closed his notebook. "You'd think this fucked up totem would have made it onto our radar."

"Maybe, maybe not. You saw those Greek symbols. Did you notice how they looked like a child writing their name for the first time— thick and rigid, concentrated? This wasn't a practiced hand. The sutures are haphazard and cautious as well. This looks like a first run through with the complete ritual." Marlowe paced the floor, his thinking cap pulled down tight. "I think he's killed before. However, it would be less refined, perhaps only a few signatures similar to this one. He's evolving, finding a ritual that best expresses his message."

"Message?" asked Spence.

"No one goes to this much effort and detail without having something they wish to convey."

"So what's he telling us?"

Marlowe stared at the door. "I have no idea, but I know someone who might."

CHAPTER SIX

Gabriel positioned the rake against a pile of leaves, hefted the heap waist-high, and deposited it into the wheelbarrow. Almost done with this section of the hospital grounds, he took a deep breath and gazed over the yellowed area. Beneath layers of dried, brown leaves lay a dead earth. Dead but for a time; soon it would live again, green and vibrant.

He knew his purpose now. More than a purpose … a calling. The cool air felt invigorating. The sun on his face seemed the kiss of divinity. And why not? Chosen to be a mortal instrument in the hands of the gods, he stood above the triviality of menial tasks.

Gabriel leaned against the rake, his dark green jumpsuit over-warm in the sunlight, but chilly on his back. He watched the doctors, nurses, and patients scurry from across the hospital complex. All of them appeared so busy, lost in the need to be somewhere. None of them could appreciate the quiet moment and revel in the simple value of living.

A sharp whistle brought his head around. Paul waved Gabriel over to where he leaned against the riding lawnmower, inspecting its engine.

Paul stood back and kicked the tire. "Goddamned piece of junk.

I've told them a hundred times we need a new one. Can't see why the hell we cut the grass in winter anyway. Ain't no fucking grass to cut. I'm moving leaves around the lot is all. Hand me those pliers, will ya?"

Gabriel reached into the toolbox. As soon as his fingertips touched the cold steel, his mind leapt to a different time and place.

HE FOLLOWED HIS FATHER OUT INTO THE FIELD. AT TEN YEARS OLD, HE had taken on more responsibility around the farm. His father owned a small spread, but it contained everything the family needed. In a garden, they grew tomatoes, okra, several kinds of beans, lettuce, cabbage, and corn. An orchard sprouted apple and peach trees, and wild grapes and blackberries grew near the wood line.

They passed a pen full of pigs, chickens in their coop, and a half-dozen milk cows milling about the grounds and pasture. Athena, a recent addition courtesy of a large cantankerous sow, seemed to think she was a puppy. Each time Gabriel entered the pigpen, she ignored the slop in favor of rutting at his feet and following him around the enclosure. He developed an attachment to the little pink nuisance. She soon became a pet and then his best friend. If he ventured outdoors, Athena shadowed him.

Mason, Gabriel's father, propped himself against the tractor's front tire. A long white scar, where hair would not grow, ran from his temple to well behind his right ear. He did not know how his father received the scar, but assumed one of the horses kicked him, back when they owned horses, before Gabriel's birth. Mason could not hear or speak, presumably due to the injury.

His father motioned with one hand, twisting it left then right. Gabriel understood and reached into the toolbox for a pair of pliers In addition to being unable to hear or speak, Mason was illiterate, which caused communication between them to develop slowly over time. They had evolved their own language of gestures and expressions.

Gabriel handed the pliers to Mason, who took them with a smile. His father had trouble with most things and became confused easily;

yet, when it came to the farm, he had mastered repairing the equipment, tending the fields, and caring for the animals. Gabriel followed at Mason's heels as Athena did at his own, absorbing everything his father did.

Mason nodded toward the tractor's seat. Gabriel bounded onto the footstep and up behind the steering wheel. Mason gave the bolt one last turn and shook the pliers at Gabriel, who hit the starter. The old John Deere fired right up. Mason smiled his lopsided grin and Gabriel clapped with delight.

He let Gabriel drive the tractor into the barn. Once the rumble of the engine stilled, the sound of Mother's voice called out.

"Time for nourishment, my angels."

Gabriel dashed for the back door with Mason limping along in his wake. Elisabeth smiled at their approach.

"Did you slay the dragon, my prince?" she asked.

He bounded up to her. "Yes milady, all is quiet in the realm."

"How marvelous. Following our meal, I thought we might continue our reading from *King Lear*," said Elisabeth.

Gabriel shifted a stone near the step with a toe before offering a slight nod.

"You have your heart set on Henry V again I take it?" said Elisabeth.

Gabriel looked up with a smile. "I love that one best."

"I know you do. All boys love stories of battles and heroes." She tousled his hair. "Very well, Henry V it shall be."

The family did not own a TV or a radio. An old record player sat in the den, where many nights they listened to Mozart, Beethoven, Aaron Copeland, and Glen Miller. Other than tromping through the woods, Gabriel's primary entertainment came from playing with his coins and reading.

His mother had given him a large vase filled with coins. Each depicted a woman with a sort of pitchfork on one side and a man's head on the opposite. He liked to arrange them into shapes and designs and watch the sun shine down on them, bursting into stars of light.

He possessed five books—Homer's *The Iliad* and *The Odyssey* in one volume, John Milton's *Paradise Lost*, Virgil's *Aeneid*, Edith Hamilton's *Mythology: Timeless Tales of Gods and Heroes*, and a Bible. He read each more than a dozen times through, and knew all of his books cover to cover. Gabriel could recite long passages from all of Shakespeare's plays, having heard his mother on a thousand readings.

Following their meal, the three sat around the den as Elisabeth recited Henry V's Saint Crispin's Day soliloquy.

"...From this day to the ending of the world,
But we in it shall be remember'd;
We few, we happy few, we band of brothers;
For he to-day that sheds his blood with me
Shall be my brother; be he ne'er so vile,
This day shall gentle his condition:
And gentlemen in England now a-bed
Shall think themselves accursed they were not here,
And hold their manhoods cheap whiles any speaks
That fought with us upon Saint Crispin's day."

Elisabeth lacked the male tone for Henry V, but Gabriel could still hear the king rallying his men for battle. The passage always sent chills up his spine. He pictured the rows of mail-clad knights, their steel swords glinting in the sunlight. Such bravery they displayed, facing death without fear. Gabriel felt certain he would become a knight someday. He envisioned himself in steel armor, seated upon a rearing stallion, a brightly colored banner waving in one hand, a sharpened sword in the other.

Mason slept in his recliner, chin firmly fixed to his chest, a thin line of drool tracing down his jaw. Occasionally, his legs might kick out, or a hand slapped at something unseen floating in the air.

"I believe our king is ready for bed." Elisabeth gently nudged her husband and nodded to Gabriel.

Gabriel helped his father to the bedroom and assisted him in removing his boots. Once in the bed, he fell asleep in seconds, snoring loudly. A child in his mind, Mason feared the darkness, so Gabriel clicked on the nightlight plugged into the wall by the door in case his father woke.

As Gabriel reentered the den, his mother spun about the room, dancing to some inaudible music. Her elegant lines showed practice and experience. Dress streaming about her, she twirled on a toe like a ballerina.

"Isn't this concerto simply divine? I recall this dance from the first time I performed Miranda in *The Tempest*. The Globe was spectacular then, filled with adoring fans." She whirled across the floor, eyes on distant sights only she could see. "There's nothing ill can dwell in such a temple: if the ill spirit have so fair a house, good things will strive to dwell with't."

Gabriel did not reply. He realized long ago many of the people his mother spoke of no longer lived, and those she spoke *to* were not present. She existed in times and places far removed, decades or centuries long past.

Some days, she was an actress performing Shakespeare at the Globe Theater, other days, a poet in Victorian England trading verses with Alfred Lord Tennyson, Robert and Elizabeth Barrett Browning, and Matthew Arnold. Every so often, she claimed to be an Oxford professor at the turn of the 20th century.

On her more cogent days, she taught him to read and write. She instilled in him an understanding of the Bible and Greek mythology, and instructed him on the nuances of all his beloved books. Everything he read and learned merged into a worldview teeming with gods and heroes, strife and triumph. As a child, Gabriel looked out beyond the boundaries of his little farm at a land ripe for conquest and adventure.

By the time he turned fourteen, however, Gabriel's childish dreams had receded behind the demands of his days. Constantly in his father's shadow, he now knew every facet of the farm. He could repair any tool or piece of equipment, knew how to manage the garden, and how to tend to the animals. A simple smile from Mason after he mastered some new task always made him swell with pride.

He loved his mother, but worshiped his father. Their silent

communication spoke deeper than Elisabeth's highbrow words—her stanzas and verses. He understood his father's every gesture. The childish dreams of Odysseus and Hercules, Samson and David, faded. Now, to be like his father seemed enough. He yearned to see things grow from the earth, and to become a man of the land—an inheritance bequeathed from one who loved it and had shown him how to love it as well.

Mason limped down a row of beans, a pouch filled with insecticide in one hand. Each time he shook the batch over a stalk, his face tightened in a grimace. Gabriel touched his father's arm, studying him with concern. Mason waved it away and continued his chore.

Later that afternoon, his father tried to move a piglet from one pen to another. As he lifted, he made a pained sound and dropped the animal. Gabriel rushed to his side. His father smiled weakly and indicated for Gabriel to complete the task for him, stumbled to a nearby bucket, and sat, discomfort evident in his posture.

Over the next few weeks, his father's condition worsened. He appeared pale, a yellow tint to his eyes and gums, his skin, paper-thin. Mason's every movement seemed strained with effort, distress pinching his face. Although mentally slow, his father had always been a strong man. Gabriel knew something was very wrong.

As Mason's health continued to decline, greater responsibility fell upon Gabriel's young shoulders. His mother's lucid days came fewer and further between. He made his own meals and performed most of the work around the farm.

In addition to his regular duties, Gabriel now handled all their dealings with Mr. Hayes, who bought their surplus produce and meat to sell at market. In the past, he had assisted Mason with conducting business, making sure buyers did not take advantage of him.

Gabriel began to accompany Mr. Hayes to market in his father's place. Mr. Hayes felt it important he learn how transactions worked and how to negotiate the best prices. On one trip, his abnormal upbringing came into stark view.

"Okay, let's set up over there. Yep, a good spot. We'll catch folks coming both ways—headed to the animal pens and back out toward the parking lots," said Mr. Hayes, pointing this way and that. "Be sure to put the best-looking goods on the counter."

"Yes sir," said Gabriel, eager to please.

"Don't let anyone talk you down. Our prices are more than fair. If anyone gives you a hard time while I'm out of the stall, just tell 'em to take it or leave it." Mr. Hayes patted him on the back and walked down the path between vendors.

Gabriel stood behind a makeshift counter, selling bushels of vegetables and baskets of fruit. The crowd buzzed with shoppers. People came from several counties away to seek out the freshest foods for dinner, while farmers appraised livestock divided into neat rows of pens.

He enjoyed going to market. The sights and sounds of the crowds moving about overwhelmed him at first, but soon, curiosity replaced trepidation. It had not taken long, however, to discover none present quoted Shakespeare or recited Tennyson.

A boy, about his age, stepped up to Gabriel's stall with a sneer. "Hey, how's that crazy family of yours?"

Gabriel tried to pretend he had not heard. These trips, simply listening and watching, confirmed Gabriel's life lessons were quite different from those of others. He could not recall his mother ever speaking in a manner similar to those he encountered here. Her words leapt from the pages of his books, a vernacular which had not progressed beyond the eighteenth century.

Outside the farm, he felt as if he watched a future world from a portal far removed. In order to avoid embarrassment, he allowed Mr. Hayes to do most of the talking, keeping his own interactions limited to handing over purchases.

"You deaf like you're ol' man?" asked the boy. "Y'all are strange, you know that? Your dad's dumb as a brick. But hey, we always get good deals off him. At least when the other guy ain't around. Cause your dad can't add for shit."

"Do not speak of my father in that way," said Gabriel, his face drawn in anger.

"Do not speak of my father in that way," mimicked the boy. "What the hell are you? Probably bat shit wacko like your mom."

Apparently, his family's oddities were common knowledge. Gabriel could not guess how the boy knew about his mother, but rumor and gossip found a way of spreading. His eyes tearing, Gabriel hung his head, fists balled tight.

"Oh, gonna cry, little baby? Man, you're a real weirdo," the boy said, walking away.

A quiet fury burned in Gabriel's belly, not with the boy as much as with himself. He should not have allowed him to speak of his family so disrespectfully. However uncomfortable he felt with his odd speech and mannerisms, it did not mean he feared danger or confrontation. His books taught him chivalry and courage. So, why had he not defended their honor?

Shame.

Gabriel longed to fit in, to be a part of the world and not only a spectator. Yet he could not carry on a simple conversation without his strangeness thrown into his face. He feared his mere appearance gave away his naiveté. Could others see an eccentric mother, a slow-minded father, simply by looking at him?

On the return trip with Mr. Hayes, Gabriel wanted nothing more than to be home. Surrounded by his animals and his peculiar family, he would ignore the world beyond the fences. No more would he allow foolish dreams or the disparagement of others to taint his love for his life.

When he arrived home in late afternoon, he did not see his father in the garden or the pens. He needed to find him, spend time with him, and remember. Remember their bond and the devotion they shared. With age, a new perspective crept in, threatening to undermine the life he knew and turn his eyes toward distant horizons. He needed to crush it, banish it from his thoughts. His father was the anchor keeping him steady, a solid foundation on which he could stand. To be like his father must remain enough.

He did not find Mason in the house, and Elisabeth had not seen him for some time. Gabriel scanned the garden and pasture, finding no sign of his father. As he walked toward the barn, he startled when a thunderous boom echoed across the field. Gabriel dashed toward the barn and flung open the doors.

Mason lay against one wall, a spray of crimson misting the air. Pieces of skull and brain painted the area above his body. His shotgun rested near a limp hand, the serenity of death frozen on his face, anguish replaced with peace.

"Hey, space cadet, where you at?" said Paul.

"I am sorry," said Gabriel, snapping back to the present.

"You look a little off. Maybe you should take your break."

"Thank you, I believe I will."

Gabriel sat on a bench beneath one of the oak trees. The image of his father's face still lingered in his mind.

Serenity in death, anguish replaced with peace.

The thought brought with it comfort like a sweet melody.

Gabriel recalled the young prostitute and the grieving mother; both wore the same expression as his father. Their eyes seemed to see another world, a better world, in those final moments before he placed the gifts for Charon upon them. Gabriel flipped a coin into the air … and smiled.

CHAPTER SEVEN

Marlowe leaned against a wall at the back of the room, watching Professor Kaplan deliver his lecture. His hand struck down in an abbreviated karate chop, driving a point home. A hall full of students sat transfixed by the charismatic presentation. Not an easy thing to do, keeping fifty college students engaged in a lecture on the history of world religions, but the professor seemed to be doing just that.

Marlowe could not hide his smile. Peter Kaplan, his old college roommate, had majored in theology and world religious history while banging every co-ed at the university and drinking every frat boy under the table. In Peter's defense, he was not a believer, but simply possessed a keen interest in religions and mythologies. Still, everyone called him Father Kap, whether an insult or a playful moniker depended on who addressed him.

Dashing would be the best word to describe Kap, that, and a cad. Movie star good looks blemished only by a white scar above his left eye, an old basketball injury suffered when he stepped into an elbow on a box out. Whenever he flashed his devilish grin and batted those bright blue eyes, skirts went up and hearts melted.

The class concluded and Kap caught sight of Marlowe. He rushed forward and took him in a great bear hug. "Why didn't you tell me you were coming?"

"Why? So you could hide all your good liquor?" Marlowe returned his friend's embrace.

"From you? Never. Come on, my office is just down here."

The two strolled the hall like the bright-eyed students they once were. Marlowe felt a wave of nostalgia. While working toward his degree in psychology, and then law school, he spent the better part of six years on this campus. So many good memories.

He met Katy here. They spent more hours than he could count on the university's quad or in the local pubs. Marlowe recalled long nights in the library and longer ones in each other's dorm rooms. Fond memories.

Yet everything, every memory, seemed tainted now. All the sights and sounds of campus life conjured competing emotions. One was warm and cherished, but a different feeling, equally strong, drowned the other in grief. Marlowe shook the thoughts from his mind and forced a smile.

"You've lost weight," said Kap as they took seats in his office.

Marlowe scanned the books, icons, and pictures, always impressed with Kap's ability to find new places to store his ever-increasing hoard.

"Yeah, getting into fighting shape." Marlowe flexed a bicep. Still muscular and fit, he had to admit his pants and jacket were considerably looser than in the past.

"If you plan on fighting a scarecrow. You need to put some meat on those bones. Why don't you come over to the house this weekend? Teagan will make you a good home-cooked meal."

Teagan, Kap's latest TA girlfriend. He seemed to find a new one every few semesters.

"Can she make anything besides Fruit Loops? Is she even old enough to use the stove?"

Kap laughed. "Screw you. I'll have you know she makes a mean linguini in a red wine sauce."

"Maybe. Right now I'm up to my ass in alligators."

"All work and no play, you know? You haven't always been so serious. Where's the wild man I roomed with? This new reclusive Marlowe is a real downer. I need the Sundance Kid to my Butch Cassidy." Kap had an irritating habit of smirking after most sentences, as if some joke hid inside everything he said.

"I have no idea what you referring to. I've always been a standup guy, no clowns in my closet."

"No? Shall I refresh your memory?" Kap's infernal smirk widened. "I seem to recall the matter of a certain video camera placed strategically in the girls' showers."

"Nope, wasn't me," said Marlowe with a smirk of his own.

"You invited me and half a dozen other guys over for beers and viewing entertainment. We hoped to catch a peek at Stacy Phillips in the buff; instead, we got more than we wanted of the only person who used the showers that night ... Ms. Potters. Three hundred pounds of rolling wet flesh, boobs sagging to her waist. She found the camera."

"Yeah ... she couldn't just take it down." Marlowe shuddered.

"No shit." Kap cackled. "That woman did the nastiest things marginally resembling a dance I've ever seen."

Marlowe had not laughed so hard in ages. After a moment, he wiped the tears from his eyes. "Jesus, I did forget about it. I couldn't eat for a week."

"You forgot that? I still have nightmares." Kap struggled to get his own laughter under control. It took him a while to compose himself. "Good to see you laugh. I know you haven't done much of it in a while."

Kap moved his chair closer to Marlowe's, his voice growing serious. "I hope you know I'm always here for you. I figured you had enough well-wishers around, and I didn't want to pressure you about talking. Not a day goes by I don't think about you and Paige."

"I appreciate it, Kap. But you were right. Too many people were hounding me. Talking was really the last thing I wanted to do."

"I get that. Just know I'm here if you need me. So, I assume you didn't come all this way to relive Ms. Potters?"

"Ha, you got me. No, I'm afraid this isn't entirely a social call. I need your expertise."

Kap arched an eyebrow. "Was that a compliment?"

"Despite being an egotistical dick, you still know stuff."

"Touché."

"I need you to take a look at some photos, tell me what you see from a religious point of view." Marlowe laid out a dozen pictures across Kap's desk.

"Shit, Marlowe." Kap averted his eyes, a hand pressed to his belly. "You can't show me something like that while I'm still thinking about linguini in wine sauce."

"Sorry, I should have mentioned they're a bit graphic."

"A bit?" Kap collected himself and moved one photo free of the others. "Well, right off, placing coins on the eyes of the dead is Greek in origin."

"I thought the same."

"The original Greek myth asserts the coins were payment to the river boatman Charon in order to grant the dead passage across the river Styx and into the underworld. Doesn't necessarily peg it though, placing coins or other objects on the eyes of the dead was subsequently employed by many cultures."

"But the writing is Greek too, correct? There must be a connection," said Marlowe, pointing to the symbols.

Kap examined the three symbols. "Perhaps. The first word positioned by ... are those lungs? Christ. Anyway, the first is the Greek word for life. Next is purpose, and finally, death."

"The killer obviously knows Greek. Greek ethnicity or ancestry? A scholar wannabe?"

"Doubtful, these translations are very literal. Anyone could plug the English word into an online translator and get the corresponding Greek word. No real knowledge of language or myths required."

"You're not helping me here, Kap. Show me what your high-priced education bought you."

"Hold your taters, amigo. Life. Purpose. Death. It's ambiguous. It could suggest the progression of life—we're born, we live, we die." Kap scratched his head and stared at the photos.

"Hmm. In Judeo-Christian mythology, God made Adam from the dust of the ground, and breathed life into him. In the Greek, Prometheus shaped man out of mud, and Athena breathed life into his clay figure. So, the word Life next to the lungs could mean birth, Purpose next to the pile of organs could be *lived life*—the act of living, and of course the heart cut in half ... death. Life, Purpose, Death.

"However, in many Christian belief systems, our purpose *is* to die. This world, this life, is simply the pathway to true life—the afterlife. Therefore, life's purpose is death."

"Interesting. What else do you see?" asked Marlowe.

"Well, the wings are likely Christian—angelic. So is the cross, of course. Look here." Kap pointed to a photo displaying the full totem. "See how it's positioned facing the window? The arrangement doesn't appear meant for an interior viewer. It wasn't placed for you, the police, or anyone in the room to see, but directed for someone observing from outside."

Marlowe leaned in and looked over the photo. "But it was on the third floor of the house. There were no homes or buildings nearby tall enough to see into that room. Unless he planned on viewing it from a helicopter, I don't see it."

"God," said Kap, matter-of-factly.

"What?"

"The display is for God, or the gods, to see. The totem is an act of worship. This murder wasn't committed out of malice or sadism. It was an act of love," said Kap, lines creased his forehead.

"You've got to be kidding me."

"No, the coins and the cross are both symbols of blessing. The window is open. Before coroners and mortuaries, the departed lay in state in the home for family and friends to say their goodbyes, pay their respects. They would leave a window open so the soul could leave this world and fly to the heavens. I assume it's the reason for the wings."

"The killer must have known the victim to care so much about them. You don't love a stranger to this degree." Marlowe bent over the desk, arms taut against the surface.

"Love thy neighbor as thyself, ring a bell? But no, I don't think that's it. The symbolism suggests universal themes. The love that god or the gods have for their children, their creation."

"He sees himself as a god?" asked Marlowe, trying to get a grasp on this new information.

"No—an instrument carrying out God's will." Kap retrieved a book from a shelf, and flipped through the pages. "The mish-mash of Greek and Christian mythologies is perplexing—one polytheistic, one monotheistic. They have many themes in common, but no believer of either would confuse one for the other."

Kap pointed to a passage in the book. "See here, widespread practice of worshiping the Greek gods gave way to Christianity around the fourth century with the Emperors Constantine and Theodosius. Of course, Paganism continued even under the threat of execution for a long time. You can still find small pockets of worshipers. There's currently a group petitioning the Greek government for permission to worship the gods at the ancient sites. With the country now primarily Christian, they're fighting an uphill battle."

Kap shook his head. "Sorry, more information than you probably needed. Short answer, I'm not sure why your suspect has married the two mythologies."

"No, it's useful to know. More than likely, we aren't looking for someone trying to usher in an age of Greek Paganism. Killer prophets … no thanks."

"I agree. This murder is strictly personal for the killer. There will be something important about the victims, some reason why there are chosen, but the grand scheme is not for the masses." Kap closed the book and returned it to the shelf.

"Flowers were placed inside the body, any idea what that means?"

"Flowers? I'll do some research, but nothing comes to mind in Greek or Christian burial rites involving flowers per se. Flowers are common with funerals and have been employed since ancient times. Traditionally, they conveyed hope and sympathy. Also, they served the practical purpose of disguising odors before embalming came into use. Judging by this ritual, the flowers probably have a personal meaning to the killer."

"Thanks Kap, most illuminating." Marlowe slapped his friend on the back.

"Always happy to help. I'll bill you."

Christ, how Marlowe hated that smirk. "Now how about some of the good stuff I know you have hidden in the bottom drawer."

Past midnight, Marlowe sat alone in the basement of the police station. A single lamp lit a small area around the wooden table. Its green shade caused an eerie glow to touch the surrounding darkness.

Hours ago at Paige's bedtime, he'd called home and asked Mable to put her on the phone. His daughter had said nothing; only her soft breathing came over the phone as he told her how much he loved her and apologized for working late. She stayed on the line until he had wished her a good night's sleep, and hung up without giving the phone back to the nanny.

He stared down at the manila folder before him, reluctant to open it. Across the cover in bold type print read, 'Case HOM-09-127.'

The Churchill Murders.

Seven victims in all, each seared repeatedly with a cigar—head, chest, abdomen, legs, even genitalia bore deep, red circular wounds— the zodiac symbol for the Gemini carved into the stomach. Death came by strangulation with a leather belt.

Teddy Brumbeloe.

The psycho managed to stay off the radar. His history remained sketchy, but led Marlowe back to Hilltop Orphanage. The length of his stay there, as well as how he ended up at the orphanage in the first place, went up in smoke, quite literally. The facility burned down in the early eighties. The destruction of the records prior to the age of computer backups made ascertaining details on Brumbeloe's background difficult. More information later came to light, but by then it was too late.

Teddy encountered his victims, white men in their fifties, in the course of working in a tobacco shop. Not terribly clever given the burns on the bodies and the butts left behind. Still, the tactic proved smart enough to claim multiple victims before the police caught on. The men were apparently stand-ins for his father, whom he'd killed and wanted to keep on killing.

He was not stupid enough to target recent buyers. Teddy knew how to bide his time and wait for the right moment. In some cases, he waited several weeks between spotting his target and acting. He never selected regular customers. Most of the victims placed orders over the phone and had them delivered, so the murders did not remain confined to an area near the shop.

In time, Marlowe connected the dots and the investigation turned in Teddy's direction. Marlowe sent uniforms out to question every owner and employee of stores selling Churchill brand cigars, the brand used in the murders. There were more such establishments than anyone would have guessed, dragging the investigation out still further.

It turned out all six men bought cigars from one particular store, a discount tobacco shop at the corner of 5th Avenue and 38th Street. Tucked out of the city proper, it took a while to come up on the list of sellers. Once investigators visited the place, Teddy got wind of interest coming his way and disappeared. The owner had no idea where he went, only that he did not show up one day and never came back.

Marlowe tracked Teddy through a score of reluctant informants by bribe and bully to a small, rundown house on a deserted backstreet in one of Birmingham's worst outlying areas. No judge would grant a warrant. What Marlowe possessed and could describe loosely as evidence remained circumstantial at best.

"No harm in taking a look," Marlowe had said to the lieutenant. "It's the best lead we have. Maybe we'll get lucky."

"Some luck would be nice right about now. Okay, check it out, but nothing else. If you turn up anything concrete, call it in. You got me?"

"Got it."

"Take Kirkpatrick and Bateman with you. Better safe than sorry."

A shack more than a house, roughly a hundred yards separated the crumbling structure from the road. With the nearest neighbor a quarter of a mile away, Teddy picked a good place to stay out of sight. Thick pine trees made it doubtful anyone would notice activity from a distance, and dense, high shrubs made peeking through the windows risky.

A beat up Olds Cutlass sat parked in the driveway. Little more than a hunk of metal with rust dotting the frame like tender scabs. Inspecting the car's interior revealed nothing more than empty beer cans and cigarette boxes. One witness had mentioned seeing a similar vehicle shortly after one of the Churchill Murders. Still circumstantial —not enough.

"How do we play this?" asked Spence.

"Direct approach, we don't want to spook him. Take Kirkpatrick around the back. I'll take Bateman with me to the front. If you see Brumbeloe, radio."

"Got it," said Spence.

"If he's here, we only want to talk. We don't have anything to hold him on, so go easy. We're looking for anything to give us probable cause for a search. Hopefully, we can get inside and have a look around. Maybe he'll slip and say something we can use."

Marlowe waited for Spence and Kirkpatrick to disappear behind the house, and motioned Bateman to follow. He did not hear any sounds emanating from inside, or see any motion beyond the curtained windows.

More beer cans littered the yard near the shack. Bateman stepped on one, causing an audible crunch and earning a 'you dumbass' glare from Marlowe. When he got within ten yards of the door, edging up on the line of shrubs, a gunshot rang out.

"Get down," yelled Spence.

Marlowe pointed to the front door, then to his eyes. Bateman understood and aimed his gun at the entrance. Marlowe crept around the corner of the house. If Brumbeloe engaged Spence and Kirkpatrick, Marlowe might take him by surprise. No such luck. As he rounded the wall, Marlowe came face to face with a fleeing Teddy Brumbeloe. A flash of silver announced a gun.

"Drop it, Brumbeloe," shouted Marlowe.

Teddy seemed less surprised than Marlowe. Obviously, he expected more police in the front of the house and had prepared for it. His gun drawn, no fear in those hateful eyes, Teddy bore down on him like a wounded bear.

"Fuck you, cop," shouted Teddy at full charge.

There had been no time to think, only react. Teddy's gun came up; he fired twice. Marlowe dove to the ground, the shots whizzing past overhead. He hit hard on his shoulder, rolled, and returned fire. Teddy stumbled backwards from the force of the blasts and collapsed; blank eyes stared into the sky. One bullet had entered his stomach, the other hit center mass—heart shot. He died before he hit the ground.

Marlowe stood over the body, his breathing ragged, heart racing. Not how he planned it, but Teddy's fingerprints and DNA should tie him to the murders. Marlowe hoped they would find more evidence inside to make this a slam-dunk.

"Call it in, Bateman," said Marlowe. "Forensics and a meat wagon."

With probable cause obtained, the hard way, Marlowe and the team entered the house.

"No neat freak, Teddy, this place smells like piss," said Spence, riffling through the litter. Dirty dishes sat on the counters and in the sink. Stains on a ratty mattress did not warrant a guess.

"Got something under the mattress," called out Bateman. "Loose floorboards. And lookie lookie, a cigar box half full … Churchill brand."

"News clippings over here." Kirkpatrick retrieved a book from behind a plank inside the closet. "Articles on all the kills. Didn't figure Teddy for a scrap-booker."

"And the motherfucking mother lode." Spence stepped out of the adjacent room holding six leather belts. "I've got a Benjamin says I know where these came from."

Analysis confirmed the belts did indeed belong to the victims. Teddy's fingerprints matched those found at the crime scenes, and his DNA dusted the cigar butts. It should have ended there, The Churchill Murders solved, Marlowe a city hero ... but it didn't. Marlowe missed the clues. He failed.

Marlowe drifted back to the present. It took a moment to remember the basement. The eerie, green glow added to the disorientation. He stared down on the list of victims:

Herman Brown- age 51

Adam Henry- age 55

Arnold Partridge- age 56

Richard Castings- age 54

Christopher Marlin- age 56

William Farrid- age 52

Katherine Gentry- age 31

That last name branded itself into his mind's eye. The despair and self-loathing he had felt for so long roiled in his gut. It was changing— a metamorphosis turned relentless depression into something else. Something hot and raw ignited within him.

Rage.

His fury needed an outlet, somewhere to aim itself before it burned away every remnant of his humanity. Most frightening of all, Marlowe possessed no desire to quell the black hatred growing inside him. The pain seemed diluted, the grief a faint whisper crying from a distance. His humanity could take its leave if it meant a cessation of his suffering. To hate felt ... better.

All the love he lost, his stolen future, needed an enemy—a surrogate for his revenge. '*An act of love*,' he heard Kap say. One word seeped into his mind. One word set the flame of rage ablaze. A seething bonfire. One word ...

Seraphim.

CHAPTER EIGHT

With her last appointment of the day completed, Becca returned to her desk. She needed to dictate the day's notes, but her thoughts scattered, drifting from one worry to another. Unable to focus, she sat back, sighed, and gazed around her office—a spacious room overlooking the hospital grounds. Framed degrees and licenses hung on the walls, photos with her mother and college friends sat on her desk.

Becca had come so far from nights spent waitressing to pay college tuition. Her mother would happily have paid her way, but Becca wanted to make it on her own. Academic scholarships helped; still, they did not cover everything. Between a job, school, and a hundred other responsibilities, she slogged through twenty-hour days on minimal sleep to avoid student loans and arrive at this position. Now, respected by her peers and appreciated by her patients, she should be enjoying the fruit of all her hard work.

Just the opposite, she felt no sense of accomplishment or satisfaction in her career. For so long, this place had existed as an oasis from her other life—the life she feared and wanted only to escape. Now it encroached here as well. No place seemed removed from the specter of home ... and Michael.

Becca lifted the snow globe from her desk—a pretty little thing, a pink castle inside. She turned it over and watched the tiny flakes cascade down onto plastic towers, bright yellow banners flying over miniature battlements. Michael had given it to her long ago, back when something passing for love and passion still existed between them. Before the distance grew, before she became the object at which he aimed all his resentment and frustration, before the screaming and belittling … before the beatings.

She found it impossible now to remember how it started; no one event sparked the cycle of abuse, apology, abuse. Instead, little things had built over time. She let him get away with it, like a child going undisciplined, and the infractions continued and worsened. One memory stuck in her mind that crystalized the disintegration of their relationship.

It was barely into their third year of marriage. Michael knelt outside beside a poor excuse of a motorcycle, turning one bolt and then another. Becca watched him for a time and shouted, "Michael, dinner's about ready."

"I think it's a lost cause." Michael entered the house, grease and grime covering him from neck to elbows.

"Ah, I hate that for you," Becca said with a grin.

"I know you do." His tone carried frustration and anger. She could not be certain precisely how he intended his reply, but prayed the bike received the lion's share of his displeasure.

Michael's temper flared more often lately. A minor annoyance could escalate in seconds to a full-blown rage. Now, whenever she sensed his mood turning, she tried to placate him or ease his mind away from the source of his ire.

"I'm sure you'll fix it. You're so good with repairing things." Her smile shifted to an uncomfortable pressing of her lips. "If not, you can sell it and get a new one."

"A new one? That's your answer? If something's not just the way you want, toss it out, right? Maybe *I* won't be what you want one of these days." His voice rose, his stance like a coiled serpent.

"I didn't mean anything. I only meant you could get a new bike, one you really like. One you wouldn't need to spend all your time working on, but could actually enjoy."

Michael huffed. He retrieved a beer from the fridge and stood staring out the window at his motorcycle. He bought it at a garage sale for four hundred bucks. Becca wasn't sure what he had expected for that price.

"I could place an ad in the trading magazine for you," Becca said.

Michael spun so fast beer flew from the bottle, splashing across the wall and floor. He glared at her from a mere stride away. She retreated a step, maintaining distance to stay out of striking range.

"You gonna sell my shit? *My* shit?"

"No … I only offered…."

"You don't touch my shit. You hear me?" he screamed, his face bright red, and moved toward her, a fist clenched. He froze. His mouth turned downward, and his cheeks drooped. His body seemed to go limp, and his eyes went dull. He set the bottle on the counter and left the room without another word.

Becca felt relief to see him go. She couldn't remember when his temper had begun to show. Certainly, he never acted this way before they moved in together. Handsome and charming, Michael had treated her like a queen.

No, it started after. At first, simply a raised voice, and then came the verbal abuse. Next, threatening postures—shaking his fist at her or getting in her face. Finally, a shove turned into a slap. The latter had only occurred once, and he swore it would never happen again. He did seem so upset afterwards, and she believed he really regretted his actions.

An hour after Michael left the kitchen, he still had not returned. No sounds came from upstairs.

Did he go to bed? At two o'clock in the afternoon on his off day?

She crept up the stairs and peeked into the bedroom. Michael sat on the edge of the bed, head in hands.

Is he crying?

Becca had never seen him cry. Even when his mother died, his brash demeanor remained locked in place. He mumbled.

"I don't want to be like him." Racking sobs shook his body.

"Like who, baby? What's wrong?" Becca sat close and wrapped her arms around him.

"I won't…. I can't…." He ran his hands roughly through his hair, plowing at his scalp.

"What is it? Talk to me." He frightened her more now than in his worst temper tantrums.

"I don't want to be like him. I can't be like him…."

How long she sat there holding him, she could not guess. She held him until he fell asleep. Michael slept the night through, tossing and turning, muttering and fighting at the air. Becca did not sleep a wink; his outbursts chased her from the bed. She sat in the rocking chair next to the window and watched over him.

The next morning, he acted as if nothing had happened. He avoided her questions and refused to discuss the matter. It was the last time such an occurrence took place. Becca never learned the identity of the *him* Michael had referred to or the person's role in his depression. His father, she assumed. Michael never spoke about his father.

Perhaps the episode explained why she stayed for so long. The psychologist in her saw Michael's pain, one brief glimpse of a frightened boy cowering in the dark. She knew something terrible ate at him deep inside. Maybe she believed she could save him and help him deal with the demons he battled. Becca felt sorry for him.

She did not want to recognize when the demon within him seized full control. Trained to help the helpless and offer hope to the hopeless, she couldn't accept he had fallen beyond saving. An unrealistic faith in her own abilities, her ego as much as his brutality, kept her caged.

Becca flung the snow globe across the office. It struck the wall, dead center of her framed Doctorate of Philosophy in Clinical Psychology degree. The glass exploded outward, sending shards raining into the air.

Damn it. What's happening to me?

84

"You okay, Becca?" asked Rachel, rushing through the door. "It sounded like a gunshot went off in here."

Becca leaned over the shattered frame, picking the glass off the floor. "The frame fell off the wall. I'm fine."

Rachel raised an eyebrow. "Hmm, the snow globe fell off the wall too?"

Becca reddened with embarrassment. Rachel did not miss much. She possessed a keen eye when it came to looking out for Becca, watching over her like a lioness protecting her cub. In regard to Michael, Rachel's claws were always sharpened and ready.

"Michael again?" asked Rachel.

"What else? But you know, I've had it this time. Speaking with Mr. Bannon, it hit me: Everything I say to my patients is advice I should be heeding myself. In many ways, I'm as terminal as he is. I've got to get control of my life. Right now … it's not a life at all."

Rachel set her hands on her hips. "Do you know how many times you've said the exact same thing?"

"I mean it this time. I've taken all I can stand. I'm done."

"Do you know how many times you've said *that*?" asked Rachel, her lips pursed in that pedantic manner Becca loathed so much.

"I'm already down, no need to keep kicking." Becca tossed the globe, along with the glass shards, into the wastebasket.

"I'm not, Honey. I'm on your side, you know that, but talking isn't going to get you out of the situation." Rachel spoke while pouring a cup of coffee and offering it to Becca. She seemed to have a sixth sense for what Becca needed.

"I know, but it's harder than you think. So many what ifs. I'm scared, Rach." Becca sipped the hot coffee and stared at her distorted reflection in its inky, black surface.

Rachel nodded and placed a hand on Becca's shoulder. "I know, Sweetie, I really do. And I know how hard it is, but is it harder than staying with him?"

"I don't know. I don't know anything except I'm at the end of my rope." Becca twirled her hair over one finger, a habit she exercised when frustrated or upset. "How can I be so strong and self-assured here and so fearful around him?"

"I bet it didn't happen overnight. Assholes like him have a way of creeping into your head. I doubt you even realized the level of control he had over you until it was too late."

"True. I wish I could go back to the moment I first started giving in and change it somehow."

"You can't undo the past, but you can break the cycle. You get upset and reach a breaking point. When the shit hits the fan, you're determined to make a change, but soon the moment passes and the urgency fades, allowing time for the fear to worm back in. Don't let that happen this time," said Rachel with maternal concern.

"I tell myself this is it. I don't deserve this treatment. I deserve something better. But the fear *does* worm back in. It's so powerful." Becca's gaze locked on to Rachel. She needed an anchor, someone to compel a hidden reservoir of will and strength inside her.

Rachel smiled and gave a playful wink. "You, more than anyone, know the first step is making a decision. The back and forth, fighting with yourself, is what drives you mad. Once you decide—really decide—much of the pressure disappears."

"You're telling me the same things I have thought a thousand times. It helps to hear them from someone else. Confirmation, you know? I want to go through with it this time, but I don't even know where I would go. He'll find me and things will be worse," Becca said, her voice broken, disheartened.

"You can stay with me and Bill. Bill will love it. He enjoys debating psychobabble with you. And let Michael try bringing his sorry ass to my house. I'd like to see him try."

"How is it I have all these degrees, and you are a better therapist? Rach, you have no idea how much I value you. I'd be lost here without you. You're like a second mother."

"Well, listen to Mom and leave the jerk."

"Thanks Rach. I love you." Becca embraced Rachel.

"I love you too, Doll. Now get home, pack a bag, and get over to my house. We'll worry about the bulk of your things later."

"Okay."

On the drive home, her resolve waxed and waned. Envisioning Michael's reaction sucked her confidence dry. Trapped. No less than Max Bannon with his cancer. A thousand meaningless banalities she espoused on a daily basis rang in her mind, *make your life what you desire today, for tomorrow may be too late*, nothing but drivel doled out to dull the fear, lessen the angst.

She spent a lifetime in study, learning the workings of human psychology, and in the end it all boiled town to the luck of the draw. She taught people how to deceive themselves, nothing more. Max did not ask for his lot, and neither did she. They both found themselves confined by chance.

Less than a one percent chance, a one in two-hundred shot, Max Bannon would develop his cancer. There was a better likelihood of being struck by lightning on a clear day. Yet, the odds no longer mattered for Max.

Becca had married a monster. What were the odds of that? How many monsters existed, mingling in amongst normal people? Perhaps Max bore some fault for his condition—poor diet, tobacco, drug or alcohol abuse, bad genes. What about her? Did she overlook the signs, ignore the warnings, and allow Michael to deceive her? Maybe, but ignorance did not equate to fault, not for Max, and not for Becca. They were ... victims. That remained the hardest part to stomach.

Becca snapped back to reality as her house came into view. She pulled her Volvo into the driveway. Unease twisted in her gut as she looked for Michael's car.

Shit, he's here. Time to pull up the big girl pants.

She heard Michael's voice raised in anger before entering the front door.

"Listen asshole, you're making a shitload of cash. Do you think you can move that shit without me? I want my cut or next time you're on your own. I can make life very difficult for you.... No, not a threat. A promise. Fuck with me and see what happens," he yelled into the phone, slamming his fist against the wall.

He made Becca's decision for her. If she stayed, tonight would get ugly. She could not stand another beating ... would not stand another.

She snuck past the den where Michael continued screaming into the telephone. Once in the bedroom, she grabbed her suitcase and threw in as much as it would hold. Taking one last look around the room, she couldn't help but notice that virtually every item—every piece of furniture, every decoration—she had chosen and purchased with her money, same with the entire house. Michael's paycheck always went toward some new *toy* he wanted, or seemed to evaporate into the ether.

For a second, anger became more dominant than fear. This was her house, how dare he force her to leave. He should be the one leaving.

The unfairness of the situation made her want to scream. Nonetheless, Becca, more than most, knew life was rarely just or fair, and if she must lose so much to rid herself of Michael, then so be it.

Steeling herself with a deep breath, she tiptoed down the stairs. Each step seemed to scream out under her feet. Every breath exhaled sounded like a gale wind roaring through a canyon. She thought Michael would surely hear the thundering *boom boom* of her heart beating against her chest, or the rumble of the suitcase banging against her leg.

At the bottom of the stairs, she paused. Standing only a few feet from the foyer, Becca went statue still and listened. Silence.

She waited, pressed to the wall, and prayed he was still on the phone. Michael might turn the corner at any second. If he caught her now, in his present mood.... A sound from behind made her jump, her pulse breaking the sound barrier. Nothing, it was nothing.

"That's more like it," Michael said. "We're doing good business. People love their drugs, no need to screw it up with infighting. Have I ever let you down? Hell no. You keep your end and I'll keep mine. So, when's the next drop?"

Christ, her heart could not take much more of this. Becca crept to the front door and cracked it open; the joints groaned. She held her breath, hands trembling.

Steps? Is he coming this way? No, thank God above.

Michael had not heard her drive up, too busy yelling. Now however, he might hear her leaving. Desperate, she remembered a similar getaway from one of those cop dramas. She put the key into the ignition, placed the gear into neutral, and let the car roll. It inched backward as she guided the steering wheel, walking along just inside the driver's side door. As the grade of the driveway increased, the car picked up speed.

No longer able to keep pace, the car's momentum jerked her hand from the wheel and knocked her to the pavement. Becca watched in horror from her backside as the Volvo raced into the street. If it collided with the street lamp, the commotion would give her away. Michael would be furious.

Luck, for once, was with her. The Volvo came to a halt as it bumped into the far curb. No harm done ... whew. Becca picked herself up and jogged to the car, slipping in and pulling the door closed without a sound. She drew a hand down her face, waiting for the panic to fade. Seconds later, she rolled the tension from her shoulders, and drove away.

Rachel lived on the other side of town, a twenty-minute drive at best. Becca allowed herself, for the first time, to consider that this would work after all. Michael would not hound her at work: too risky for him with so many people around. He might cause a scene at Rachel's, but Rachel and Bill would not tolerate it.

Almost there, almost free.

The red and blue lights flashing in her review mirror brought her back to reality.

Oh, shit.

Becca fixated on them like a deer at an oncoming truck. Dare she run? Her brief spark of independence died. She had no choice but to pull over. Terror clutched her heart, bile rose into her throat as she gripped the steering wheel so tightly a stinging sensation ran through her palms and fingers. She stared into the night, floating in a haze.

A *tap tap* on the window made her jump. The butt of a flashlight rapped the glass a third time, and then turned its glare into her eyes.

Pressing the lever, she lowered the window to keep him from bashing it in.

"Going somewhere, my love," said Michael, still dressed in his blue police uniform.

"I didn't want to disturb you. Your conversation sounded heated, thought I'd take a little drive and give you some privacy." Becca prayed he could not hear the fear in her voice.

"Very thoughtful of you." His sneer radiated pure venom.

He shined the light into the back seat—on her suitcase. His eyes narrowed, hard and mean.

"Packing heavy for a little drive."

"Michael ... I ..."

"Shut up. Here's what's going to happen. You're going to turn this car around and drive right back home. Then you'll call that nosy bitch friend of yours—you were headed to Rachel's right? You'll tell her you changed your mind, everything's fine. Then ... then my sweet loving wife, you and I are going to have a long talk about loyalty and commitment. Remember? Until death do us part."

CHAPTER NINE

Max leaned back in the chair and tried not to look at the IV tubes piercing his arms. A bag hung above his head, containing a substance that looked like piss, and might be, for all he knew. The yellow liquid dripped from the bag in large teardrops, a slow journey taking it through the plastic tubes and into his waiting veins.

The bleeps and clicks of monitors made his skin crawl. Or was the chemo already affecting him?

Max felt another panic attack coming on. He might vomit on himself, or maybe pass out. He needed to get out of the chair, out of the hospital, and into the open air. Only once before could he remember feeling so frightened ... so trapped.

A few weeks after Max turned ten, he and his friend Tony took a hike into the woods behind his house. A frequent venture, it remained one of the few escapes for the boys to escape parents' prying eyes. Strange they had never come upon the cave before—more a giant hole dug out beneath the stump of a fallen tree. It looked deep, diving down and turning in before snaking beneath a rock overhang. The temptation to explore proved too much to resist for the adventurous boys.

Max climbed down first, discovering the burrow deeper than it appeared from above. He gazed up from a good ten feet below. By the squeamish expression on Tony's face, Max knew he was having second thoughts.

"Chicken-shit coward," Max yelled. "Fine, baby, I'll go by myself."

Max crawled fifty feet or so through the muck before reaching another opening—a cave proper. He stood surrounded by stone walls covered in droplets of moisture that trailed down, wetting the ground under his feet to thick mud.

"Max," called Tony. "You okay? You need to come back up now."

Let him sweat, thought Max, refusing to reply. He felt along the rock, finding sturdy roots thrust downward from the trees above, their jagged edges hanging like stalactites from the roof. Max basked in the discovery of a new world, a subterranean domain just for him. Tony yelled incessantly now, he would alarm Max's parents if he kept it up at that volume.

Fine. Max got onto his hands and knees, set to reenter the tunnel, when he heard a crash echo from the distant end. The earth around him shook, spraying debris into his hair.

"Max," called Tony. "The stump fell into the hole. I don't think you can get out. Max, can you hear me?"

The cave, which seemed a fantasyland moments ago, now drew in around him like a coffin. Max had seen his great uncle in a coffin once. He had imagined how it must feel in that little bed with the lid closed tight, six feet of dirt dumped on top.

The fear started in his legs, knees wobbling, feet sliding in the mud. His chest tightened, he couldn't breathe. The stump might have cut off the air—he might suffocate. Fear escalated into terror, and in seconds, Max went from courageous explorer to sobbing child.

Tony must have heard his cries. "I'm going to get your dad, hang on."

Max's father arrived in minutes and tried to remove the stump, but it stuck fast, too heavy. He tried digging around it, but needed to return to the house and retrieve a shovel and an axe. Two hours buried beneath the earth. For ten-year-old Max, it seemed an eternity.

He felt the same suffocating feeling now, lost in a deep, dark cave with no way out. The chemicals burned as they slithered through his veins. Max dug his fingernails into the armrests. A frightened child crouching in the dark surrounded by rock and mud

... who could free him this time? He wanted to pray, but no one ever listened.

Following his first round of chemotherapy, Max desired nothing so much as simply being home alone where he could throw up or pass out without embarrassment. The doctor instructed him not to drive, but he did not have the money to waste on a taxi, and no buses ran so far out of the city. He took it slow, already feeling weak and a little lightheaded.

Max had barely stepped through the door before the nausea hit like a tornado. His world spun round and round. Max wanted to die. They said that sometimes the cure was worse than the sickness. They were right. Sadly, this might not even be a cure, but just another layer of shit on a shitty life.

His head pounded again, his skin clammy and cold. Sitting with his forehead resting against the coolness of the toilet bowl, Max knew he could not do this, not alone. He fumbled through his pocket and retrieved his phone.

"Hello," said a woman's voice.

"Laura, is Maggie there?"

Laura, Maggie's older sister, huffed and said, "Oh, it's you. Maggie can't come to the phone right now, Max. I'll tell her you called...."

"It's ok, I'll take it," said Maggie in the background. After a bit of rustling noise, she spoke into the phone with a mechanical voice. "Hello, Max. What do you need?"

Not a good start, he already regretted making the call. "I wanted to check on the boys," he said, his voice carrying fatigue and depression.

If Maggie noticed, she made no comment. "Oh, they're doing great. Playing with their cousins, running around like wild Indians."

"Good ... that's good. Uh, how are you?"

An exasperated intake of breath came from the other end. "I'm fine, Max."

"I ... I miss you. I didn't realize all I was losing until you were no longer here."

"Don't do this, please."

"What? I just wanted you to know...."

"It's only the moment, the right now of it, Max. We haven't gotten along in years—even before this. You know that. The kids are happy now. All the fighting really affected them, it drove me crazy, and it couldn't have been a picnic for you either."

"No, but things got so hard. Anyone would get frustrated. Families work things out. It can't always be easy."

"It was never easy for us. We married too young and too stupid to know what it all meant, or what it would take. Maybe we wanted independence from our folks, or really did think we were in love, even if we didn't have a clue what love required. I don't know ... but it wasn't enough."

Max sighed and stared at the muted television. The insects on the screen crawled along the underside of a tree limb, clinging to the bark. It amazed him they didn't fall. A program about the mating habits of the praying mantis. Max clicked the set off.

"I've done nothing but think about how I can fix things. Maybe there's still time." His voice came off haggard, lacking any conviction.

"You can't fix it. There's nothing left to fix. I've thought about nothing else as well." Maggie paused, and Max knew what came next. "I won't be coming back. We made the kids miserable, and each other. They deserve better. We deserve better."

"They deserve better than me, you mean."

"Oh no, Max. I would never come between you and your sons. They need their father."

Max went silent, his voice flying with hope. For the best really, that this moment of weakness had not brought them back. A moment of weakness, nothing more. Max still did not want them around to see what he knew fast approached him. He simply needed to hear a voice. A little human contact to let him know he was not already dead. A moment of weakness.

"Hey, why don't you come and take the boys to the park. There's a nice one a few blocks up the street from here."

His throat tightened. "You wouldn't mind?"

"No, of course not."

"Thank you. I'd like that."

Max cleaned himself up and tried to look presentable. The fatigue still weighed on his body, but the worst of the effects had calmed. With his head clearer, he felt better about driving. When he arrived at Laura's house, Maggie answered the door. He had forgotten her beauty, how her smile made his knees weak.

Don't know what you've got until it's gone.

Hardships and frustrations had clouded his view of her. So self-obsessed with how things affected him, he lost sight of her. Now he viewed her clearly through the eyes of regret.

"You feeling okay?" she asked. "You look pale."

"I'm okay, touch of a cold. I won't get too close to the boys."

"If they didn't catch it from their cousins, I doubt they'll get anything from you. None of them ever wash their hands." Maggie turned and called into the house. "Cody, Austin. Your dad's here." She waited a few seconds. "They're coming … I think."

The two boys came shuffling down the hall, appearing displeased. "Do we have to?" asked Cody. "I want to stay and play with the puppies." Ten years old and already bigger than Max had been at fourteen. A diet seemed in order, cut out the fast food, but Max no longer possessed the right to mandate one.

"Cody, it's your dad." Maggie admonished her son, aware of the effect his words might have on Max. At least she granted him that modicum of concern.

"It's okay if they don't want to go." Max could not completely mask his hurt.

"No, they want to. Really. You know how hard it is to compete with puppies. They don't even know I exist with puppies, a trampoline, and two cousins to play with.

"I did a flip on the trampoline," said Austin, proudly. Since turning six, he had become a brazen daredevil.

"You did? That's great," said Max.

"I can show you. You wanna see?"

Already Max felt like an intruder in someone else's life. "Maybe later. Let's go to the park for a bit first."

As they walked down the sidewalk toward the park, Max began to feel dizzy. The world changed hues. For a second, he thought the sun had dipped behind the clouds, but a gray overcast sky hid the sun today. The world did not tint darker; the clouds shifted from red, to bluish, and then orange. Max braced, hands on his knees.

The boys ran ahead, pushing each other, and squealing away at a full sprint. Max worried he might not be up to the task of watching them. It hit him what a liability he was becoming. What if he fainted and one of them got hurt? He could never forgive himself, and neither would Maggie. So many concerns raced through his mind.

Once at the park, the boys played on the monkey bars while Max fought to retain equilibrium. Mercifully, after a time, the feeling passed and the world settled. He felt so tired. His legs, like wet noodles, dared him to stand.

"Cody, Austin, come over here a second." Max patted his knee.

They took their time, but made their way to him. "Boys, I want you to know how much I love you. What's going on with your mom and me has nothing to do with you."

"It's okay," said Cody. "We like it at Aunt Laura's. We get to play with Marcy and Jimmy."

"They have a swimming pool. We can swim … well, when it gets warm," said Austin.

"Can we live at Aunt Laura's forever?" asked Cody. "The puppies need me to take care of them."

"I like it 'cause I don't get cold at night like at home," said Austin, smiling.

"Yeah, and they get more channels—the movie ones." Cody looked down and tapped his sneaker in the dirt. "Theirs never gets cut off either."

Max's heart swelled within his chest. Anger, hurt, self-pity, self-loathing all whirled within him. "Let's head back, okay."

He did not need to say it twice. The boys dashed off, laughing as they went. Max watched them go. They did not need him. Maggie did not need him. It hurt to admit, but he felt some relief in the realization as well. They would be fine without him.

He followed them back and said his good-byes, receiving a

superficial hug from each boy. Austin lingered for a second, as if somehow sensing more finality in his words.

Max waited for the boys to disappear into the house. "Thanks for letting me see them."

Maggie looked at him with complete sincerity. "I promise you, I will never keep your sons from you. And I promise not to make this any harder than it has to be. Us, I mean."

"Promise?"

"Promise," she replied.

So many promises broken. He promised to take care of her and to provide for her. They vowed to stay together for richer or poorer, in sickness and in health. The only vow they would keep in the end ... *until death do us part.*

MAX DROVE TOWARD HOME ALONG COUNTY ROAD 15. HE LOVED THIS country. He grew up here, would die here—sooner than hoped, but still. Never any desire to travel or live elsewhere tempted him. His ambitions had always revolved around a home and family right here.

He loved the smell of fresh pine needles in the spring and dry, brittle oak leaves in the fall. Max even liked the unpredictable weather. Warm and raining one day, cold with snow flurries the next, no two days ever the same. He celebrated hunting and Crimson Tide football in the autumn and winter, and fishing, camping and Braves baseball in the spring and summer. What could be better?

He thought becoming an electrician like his father would ensure a good job, providing enough money to keep his family comfortable. He possessed no desire for great wealth, no dreams of becoming someone important. A decent house and a loving family. Enough for any man.

When the housing bubble burst, the dream went the way of so many fortunes and retirement plans. No one built and no one bought. No new houses going up meant electricians, carpenters, and plumbers circled the ailing job market in a holding pattern, waiting for the day buyers and investors regained confidence.

Eighteen months and still waiting. Living off unemployment checks did not cut it. Not enough money to keep the power on even if they ate Ramen noodles every day. Worse, the checks ran out months ago, and the noodles were running low as well.

Worst of all, however, was the wound to his pride. Max was an excellent electrician and a hard worker. In ten years with the company, he used three total sick days. First in the door, last out, he loved his job.

Now no one wanted him—not employers, not his wife, not his kids. Everything he had believed about himself, he now questioned. Maybe he *was* selfish and lazy. Perhaps it took losing his job to reveal the real Max.

He drove on, lost in torturous thought. The voice on the radio droned on about the Seraphim Killer, which seemed to be all they talked about anymore. The media sure could milk a story. Max stopped listening, his attention fixed on the scenes passing by the window, until up ahead, Unity Baptist Church came into view. A sad smile inched across his face. He and Maggie had married in that church. They took the boys there on Easter and at Christmas. Without realizing it, he pulled into the parking lot.

Comfort. He needed something, anything to relieve the tension, anxiety, and sense of loss. Max did not consider himself very devout, but in the South, religious indoctrination came by osmosis. He believed in God and Jesus, he guessed, but never saw the need to overdo it. He prayed sometimes, but never got any answers, or maybe he asked the wrong questions. Perhaps God had gone deaf, or simply grown too uninterested to listen.

He stepped into the church, a small building that could seat a hundred on a Sunday—a rare occurrence these days. Max lurched down the aisle, remembering that walk over ten years ago. A day filled with terror and exhilaration, feeling stiff in his tuxedo, watching Maggie approach, his heart pounding.

He sat in a pew near the middle of the hall and stared at the picturesque scene painted beyond the choir loft. A waterfall cascaded down into a pool surrounded by a lush meadow. He tried to put himself into the mural. He wanted to feel the cool water on his dangling feet, the sun warm on his face, God looking down.

"Max?" said a voice from behind. "Max Bannon, well I'll be. I haven't seen you in here since Easter." The man stood with one hand resting on the pew, a welcoming smile on his face. Max could not recall ever seeing Reverend Mayer so casual. It somewhat spoiled the effect. Not dressed in his customary suit and tie, the t-shirt and jeans he wore made him look more Wal-Mart shopper than church pastor.

"Hi Reverend, I was in the area and felt a need to stop in."

The pastor's brow furled. "Everything all right?"

No sense in playing coy; he needed counseling, comforting. Maggie wouldn't, maybe a pastor could. "I have cancer."

Concern rose in Reverend Mayer's eyes. He tugged at the collar of his shirt and sighed. "You know, Max, cancer isn't the death sentence it used to be. Treatment has come so far. Four months ago, doctors diagnosed Mary Chilton with breast cancer, and now there's no sign of it."

"I've got stage four brain cancer. Prognosis is pretty bad."

"Oh, I'm so sorry Max. How are Maggie and the kids holding up?"

Max's head fell, his stare locked onto the dark, gray carpet. "Maggie took the kids. They're staying with her sister." Defeat laced his every word.

Reverend Mayer moved in, taking a seat beside Max. "Max, look at me. I want you to listen to me now. I know things seem desperate. Life hasn't turned out like you hoped or planned, but God can't be surprised. You are exactly where he wants you to be."

"Is God so cruel?" said Max with a sardonic laugh.

"Cruel? No, not at all. I know saying we don't understand God's plan and we just have to trust may ring hollow right now, but it's true." He eyed Max and shook his head, as if mentally waving away a line of thought. "I'm not going to sit here and preach inspiring verses to you. You are headed to a better place when you die, but that isn't what you need to know right now." He leaned back, gazing up at the vaulted ceiling. "You have a great opportunity before you, Max."

Max shot the pastor a confused glance.

"No, really. Throughout the Bible, God sent his angels with messages for those he called for his purposes. He still does. They come to do his work on Earth. They guide us. There's a spiritual realm existing all around us. As you move closer to the veil separating life from death, your ability to feel and see that realm increases. I've sat at too many bedsides, heard too many things the dying hear and see, to discount it. Open your eyes, Max. Open your heart. You can be a great instrument for God's purpose if you let his will guide you. Your life's purpose is revealed as you approach death. Isn't it a wonderful thought?"

Max listened, trying to commit the words to belief. A hope his life, or his death, might mean something. He wanted it to be true. Perhaps something he said or did in these last days would change things. If he could be remembered well by Maggie, by his boys. If they held a fond memory of him, if they could be proud of him, death would not be so bad.

"Will you pray with me? I want you to talk to God in your own heart and ask for his hand to touch you. Beg for his angels to come to you and offer you purpose, and with that purpose … peace."

Max closed his eyes and prayed as he had never prayed before. In that moment, he thought he understood a tiny fraction of what Jesus felt praying in the Garden of Gethsemane, begging for the cup to pass from him. Max felt the weight of his own cross. When he lifted his head, Reverend Mayer no longer sat beside him.

Max peered around the hall, but the pastor was nowhere in sight. He stood and noticed Emily, the church's custodian, vacuuming the carpet at the rear of the building. Funny, he did not hear her before.

"Hi, Emily, good to see you again," he said, approaching her.

"Oh, hi ya Max. Good to see you, too." A thin brunette, Emily maintained the church's interior while her husband Vernon tended the grounds. A poor couple with three children, the church had given them jobs and provided a single-wide mobile home to live in.

"Did you see where Reverend Mayer went? I wanted to say goodbye."

Emily looked at him, puzzled. "Sorry Max, the Reverend ain't here. He's down near Montgomery preaching a revival."

"But … I just …" She must be mistaken. He started to object, but Emily's baffled expression made him hold his tongue.

Max stepped from the building. Outside, the sun burned through gray clouds, its rays shining almost singularly on one of the stained glass windows. Max gazed on the multitude of shimmering colors. It depicted an angel with wings stretched wide, surrounded in a glow and hovering in the air, a trumpet held to pursed lips.

CHAPTER TEN

"Good news, bad news," said Spence, plopping a stack of papers onto Marlowe's desk. "Bad news—no luck on the bolt gun, it appears to be an older non-penetrating model. After the mad cow scare, most farms and slaughterhouses switched to non-penetrating guns to avoid brain matter contaminating the meat. Thousands sold, no way to track it down."

With hundreds of man-hours spent chasing the bolt gun lead, Marlowe had lost count of how many agencies statewide were looking into it. Since they had nothing to show for it, the lieutenant would verge on blowing a gasket. Even so, tracking all potential evidence remained essential. They never knew when the slightest clue might strike pay dirt.

"And the good?" asked Marlowe.

"We got a hit on the MO search. Two, actually. A girl—junkie/prostitute on Westside, and a man—financial investor, both with those weird coins left on the eyes. We found a small cross on the man's body."

"Sounds like our guy. The girl?"

"No good info on her. Name's Nikki Baker, no known address. She has a rap sheet— possession and solicitation. A vagrant found the body in an alley and alerted a passing uniform. Vagrant didn't see anything. Well, he did, but JFK coming out of a UFO shaped like a fire-hydrant probably isn't helpful."

"Not so much. Have some uniforms canvass the area door to door. We'll come in behind them to check it out. What about the man?"

"Matthew Young, twenty-nine, some kind of bigwig investor with one of the firms downtown. A road crew found his body near the abandoned warehouse out at the Furnaces. His car was parked at the site with the key still in the ignition."

"I assume we have *his* home and work addresses?"

Spence nodded.

"Good. We'll start with him."

MATTHEW YOUNG WORKED AT SPECTRUM FINANCIAL SERVICES ON THE 22nd floor of the Wells Fargo Building. Spence, not a fan of elevators, airplanes, or anything more than two feet off the ground, normally took the stairs. Yet not even he wanted to walk up twenty-two floors.

Wells Fargo boasted a glass elevator. Riders could gaze down on the entire building as they rode. No gazing for Spence, he kept his eyes locked onto the chrome doors, humming nervously to himself. Marlowe occasionally kicked his foot against the glass, making Spence jump every time. He spooked him whenever they used an elevator, and it never grew old.

They exited the elevator and approached the receptionist desk where a pretty, young woman sat talking on the phone. Her hands acted out the dialogue, gesturing and waving.

"No way, he didn't," she said, obviously not a business call. "What did she do?"

Marlowe reached across the counter and pressed the lever on the cradle, ending the call.

"Hey, what the …" she said.

Spence held up his badge.

"Oh, sorry." She tried to mask her embarrassment. "Welcome to—"

"Save it, Sweetie, we know where we are. Point us to the person in charge," said Marlowe.

"Uh … sure. One second." She punched numbers on the keypad. "Mr. Bolton? Two police officers are here to see you. Yes sir." She hung up. "Mr. Bolton will be right out, if you would follow me."

She led them to a conference room situated in a corner of the building, three walls enclosed in glass windows and overlooking downtown. Spacious, even elegant. For a second, Marlowe considered that he chose the wrong line of work. Only for a second; he hated being cooped up inside all day. No amount of money seemed worth it.

Portraits of the three senior partners adorned the conference room wall, wearing smug expressions only the ridiculously wealthy could muster. A 52-inch flat screen inset into the opposite wall played an infomercial advertising services the firm provided. Spence stayed as far from the windows as possible.

"Can I get you officers anything?" asked the receptionist.

"Detectives. No thanks, we're good," said Marlowe.

Spence watched the girl's backside as she sashayed from the room, a short plaid skirt, pink and green, swishing back and forth.

"You're a real cretin, you know? She can't be more than twenty." Marlowe shook his head in disbelief.

"How old they have to be?"

Marlowe huffed. "Nice place. I wonder how Mr. Young went from penthouse to coins on the eyes.

"Yeah, we still have no idea how Seraphim is choosing his victims. A low-rent prostitute, an out of work accountant, and this guy. I don't see an obvious connection."

"We have squat on the killer, so the victims are the best bet. Seraphim is too precise to grab people at random. No, he has a plan, a grand mission. We have to determine what it is."

Spence leaned to the side, keeping the receptionist in view two seconds longer. "And how do we do that?"

"The more victims, the more clues, a pattern will form. We just have to spot it."

"Connect the dots, huh? With dead bodies? Let me know when

you're going to tell McCann your method. I don't want to be anywhere around."

"Yep. Unfortunate, but to figure out what Seraphim is all about, we need to know who he is and what he wants. He isn't going to invite us over for polite conversation, so the only way to get to know him is through his work."

"Detectives," said a man entering the room. Tall, handsome, sixtyish, sporting a well-tailored Italian suit, charcoal-gray, he struck a commanding presence. "I'm Clyde Bolton, Managing Partner here at Spectrum. I assume you're here about Matthew."

"Yes, what can you tell us about him?" asked Marlowe.

"Terrible tragedy. Matthew was one of our best investors ... or so we thought."

Marlowe cocked an eyebrow. "Meaning?"

"Let's say some of his dealings proved not to be completely kosher. We only discovered the problems after he ... well, left the firm. Matthew owed a large sum of money for gambling debts and attempted to cover them with some risky, quick-turnaround investments using his clients' funds."

"Uh oh, not good," said Spence.

"To put it mildly. When those investments fell through, he lost a great deal of his clients' money, as well as all of his own. His situation became dire, as you can imagine. He still owed on the gambling debts, and now he would be let go from the firm, without any money of his own, and most probably facing jail time." Mr. Bolton gazed out the window and smoothed the lapels on his coat."

"I'm guessing he bolted before you could confront him," said Marlowe.

"He did. His secretary, Sandra, said he seemed near to tears. She heard him slam about in his office before lumbering out and rushing past her. He didn't say a word, just left. That was the last we saw of him. We informed the investors, the SEC, and the ASC. A few days later, we learned of his murder. Very sad, he once had a promising career."

"We'd like to look around his office," said Marlowe.

Mr. Bolton gestured to the door. "I'll have Sandra show you the way. Technicians performed a thorough search of his computer and discovered his shady practices. They also found multiple transfers to an offshore account, suggesting sizeable payments to his bookies."

"We can trace those if need be, but it will take some time. Not an immediate necessity."

Spence and Marlowe went through Young's office, rifling through drawers and cabinets, but turned up nothing useful. Maybe they would have better luck at his home.

As they drove I-65 South toward Young's home address, repaving crews slowed their progress.

"No wonder it takes years to complete these projects. Look at 'em, standing around smoking cigarettes and drinking coffee." Spence pointed with righteous indignation. "This is how my hard-earned money is spent? I'm tempted to write my congressman."

"Spoken like a true disenchanted tax payer."

"I'm just saying. How many breaks does a person need?"

"Work a lot of hard, manual labor in the freezing cold, do you?"

"Ruins my manicures." Spence held up one hand and admired his nails. "Anyway, I'm thinking ..."

"Does it hurt?" asked Marlowe with an evil grin.

"Screw you. As I was saying before being so rudely interrupted, we have a prostitute and a gambler. I'm thinking this could be a mob thing. Granted, substantial gambling debt and a ghetto hooker don't seem to go together, but the mob is known to be involved in gambling and prostitution, along with drugs."

"I very much doubt it. Still, worth looking into all the same. Melissa Turner liked her prescription drugs. The sister said she threw a lot out, but Turner always kept a bountiful supply. Might fit the mob angle."

Spence shook his head. "Only thing is, the mob isn't a big player in Birmingham."

"Not directly, but some of the gangs may work with them. We'll check with the Feds, and Vice might have some information. From what I know, the mob doesn't do this level of ritualized killing. This is very personal. Kap called it an act of love. I wouldn't get my hopes up."

"Act of love? Jesus, I've had some crazy exes. I've heard of jealous wives lopping off the husband's fun rod, but this degree of *love* is something else all together." Spence unconsciously covered his crotch.

"Anything can be twisted by a deranged mind—love, religion—you name it. The thing is, the suicide bomber killing for religion, or the serial killer murdering out of some twisted version of love, they all believe in what they are doing. For them, the faith is real; the love is real. Thinking of them as simply crazy is a mistake. And Seraphim isn't going to stop unless we catch him."

"How do you know? Maybe once he accomplishes whatever wacked out mission he's on, he'll just disappear."

"If God came down, in person, and told you to do something, would you do it?" asked Marlowe, an eyebrow raised.

"Yikes, good point. What else did your friend Kap have to say?"

"I filled you in on most of it. The one question he couldn't answer was the mixing of Greek and Christian mythologies. After Christians moved into the Mediterranean area, a lot of crossover occurred, with Christian beliefs becoming dominant. Our killer seems unable to separate one from the other. The mythologies are blended into one system."

"All this religion stuff spins my noggin. Give me a simple passion murder or gang shootout any day," said Spence.

"I'm not certain the religion/mythology angle isn't chasing our tails anyway. The victims are the key. Hopefully, something in Young's home will give us a clue as to why Seraphim picked him."

"I know you want there to be a link, but what if he is choosing them randomly? Could be simple opportunity."

"The hooker may be, but Turner, a shut-in living in a nice neighborhood? And now Young, a high-end investor? No, my gut says Seraphim killed them for a particular reason."

"You're the expert. I'm just here for moral support."

At last, the freeway congestion broke up, and they rounded the off-ramp into the suburb of Hoover. Young's home, a nice single-level modern, sat sandwiched between dozens of near identical houses on a tree-lined street, all screaming yuppie.

Marlowe and Spence crossed the yellow crime scene tape and entered the front door. The interior was decorated in a nauseating mix of Boca do Lobo, probably knock-offs, and Ikea. Clearly, Matthew Young defined himself by his place in a social pecking order. Keeping up with the Joneses and scaling the corporate ladder may well have led him to cutting corners in order to feed his ambition.

"Wife and kid are staying with family. I'll start at the back of the house," said Spence, and moved down the hall.

Marlowe perused the living room area. He walked to a rack of glass shelving near the TV that held various knickknacks—a crystal oval inscribed with Top Investor 2nd Quarter, two blue ribbons affixed to a 4H badge, and several photos. One photo depicted Young, his wife, and his daughter posed on a beach, framed by the ocean and sun.

Katy sat beside him, digging her bare feet beneath the heated sand. Paige tiptoed into the water, squealing and running whenever the waves lapped over her feet.

"We have the perfect life," said Katy, her dark glasses reflecting the sun and surf from under a wide-brimmed hat.

"Perfect," said Marlowe, watching Paige like a hawk. The little daredevil was bound to try deep sea diving if not kept under close watch.

"It's only beginning. Before long, Paige will be in school. She'll get all A's and graduate valedictorian. She'll excel in college, where she'll meet a great guy, get married, and have beautiful children. You'll be Grandpa."

"Slow down there," said Marlowe. "Let's get her through preschool first."

"You just don't like the idea of grandpa."

"Actually, I do," he said with a smile.

"Once Paige is off on her own, we'll retire and buy a big RV. One with a kitchen, shower, big bed—the works. We'll travel around the country staying at all those cute bed and breakfast places. Then one day we'll come right back here, sit on this beach, and remember how we saw it all, all those years ago."

"Sounds like a plan to me." He leaned over and kissed her neck.

Darkness. A hallway formed in his memory.

Marlowe heard Paige crying from somewhere up ahead. He entered the kitchen to find Katy clutching a man's hairy forearm pressed against her neck. Her stomach convulsed with heavy panicked breaths. Paige's sobs grew louder, overshadowed by laughter.

Marlowe swiped his hand hard across the shelves, sending the photos and trophies flying and the display case crashing to the floor. Picking up a lamp, he slung it against the television set, shattering the screen. He tore around the room, upending furniture, breaking vases, and throwing a clock through the glass of a coffee table.

Images, crimson and wet, assaulted his mind. He could not make them stop. They bled together into scenes filled with torturous emotions, overwhelming in their intensity. Marlowe's mouth opened in a silent scream.

Spent, breath coming in gasps, he collapsed onto the sofa, his palms pressed tightly against his eye sockets.

Hold it together, goddammit.

Spence came rushing in and halted at the doorway as his eyes tried to make sense of the devastation strewn across the room.

"What the hell? Marlowe, you okay?" he asked, worried, and more than a little stunned. "Jesus man, what did you do? This isn't a narco raid."

Marlowe did not answer. Raising his head, he stared at Spence as if he might attack him. Spence took a step back, surprised by the violence in his stare.

"Marlowe, it's me, snap out of it. You're worrying me, bro." Spence inched forward and squatted down to eye level with Marlowe.

Marlowe shook the torrent from his mind. He gazed at the broken glass and fractured objects. Kneeling, he started absently picking up the debris, then stopped and plopped back into the seat.

"I know what you're going through. Well, I don't, but I understand it. You're my partner. I've been with you since all that shit went down, and watched you caught in this spiral. You live in a dark pit. It breaks my heart that I don't know how to help you, but you've got to hold it together. We need you on this one. Whatever I can do for you, you know I will, but you've got to stay in the game. Stay in the present, nothing you can do about the past."

Marlowe nodded. "Reading fortune cookies again?" He smiled weakly. "I'll handle it. This thing is pulling up memories I've tried damned hard to bury. I'll be strong, don't worry."

Spence did not appear placated. He stared at Marlowe, concern etched across his face. "You really are scaring me."

"Listen, if I'm going to cash it in, you'll be the first to know. After all, you're singing at my funeral, right?"

"Not funny. And I'm dancing, not singing," said Spence, obviously feeling some relief.

Marlowe gently shoved his partner toward the front door. "Let's get outta here."

THAT EVENING, AN ANXIOUS FEELING FOLLOWED MARLOWE HOME. RAGE and pain had ambushed him at Young's home and now clung to him like a resistant infection. An insidious disease wormed through his flesh and bones, sapping his strength and will.

He paused on the porch, one hand raised in the robotic motion of inserting the key in the door. Painful memories stiffened his body as he plodded into the house. They exhausted him. So tired—tired of the haunted past, the thorny present, the hopeless future.

Marlowe thought of Paige. He knew he would not be up for any Father of the Year awards, but getting through to her on any level seemed beyond anyone's expertise. An army of doctors had failed; how could he do anything? How could a damaged man fix a damaged little girl?

A strangled sob leaked from his lips. He needed to spend time with her and feel something other than anger and hate. She represented the last remnant of anything good still hiding within him. So unfair, he knew, to expect a despondent child to serve as the instrument keeping his humanity alive. Marlowe stumbled along a treacherous path toward a precipice, each step led closer to the void.

He stepped into Paige's room. She sat on the floor, placing jumbo jigsaw pieces into a puzzle—an image of a white horse pranced on the box. Paige peered up as he knelt down, and then averted her gaze back to the puzzle.

"Honey? How ya doing, Babes?" said Marlowe in a soft voice.

Paige did not respond, oblivious to him as she attempted to set a piece into puzzle. The piece was ill-shaped to fit where she wanted to it go. Marlowe gently took the cardboard cutout from her tiny fingers and inserted it into the proper spot.

Paige paused, stone still. She leaned forward and retrieved the piece. She stared at it for a moment before repeating her attempt to place it where it did not belong.

"Honey, Daddy really needs you to talk." Tears coated Marlowe eyes as he raked his fingers through her long, blonde hair. She looked so much like her mother. "Please … tell me how to help you."

Paige withdrew her hands and rested them in her lap. Marlowe choked back tears that would not fall. After minutes of silence, he took Paige into his arms and carried her to the bed.

"Okay, Pumpkin, time for bed." He tugged the covers up to her chin. "I love you so much, Baby Girl." He leaned in to kiss her atop the head. Paige stared at him, no recognition in her eyes.

Marlowe sat at her bedside long into the night, long after she fell asleep.

CHAPTER ELEVEN

G abriel walked down 21st street headed toward his lunch date with Wanda. A pleasant day, cold, but with blue skies and the sun shining, the brisk stroll felt good. In a cheerful mood, he looked forward to his friend's company; not to mention, he had not eaten since yesterday.

Approaching Wanda's building, Gabriel noticed a rather rotund man standing at the entrance. He wore a red cap turned sideways on his Neanderthal-shaped brow, and a thick, gold chain around his neck.

As Gabriel came near, the man offered a crooked tooth grin. "Hey dude, need a pick me up?"

He pulled a small, clear bag from his jacket containing what looked like tiny crystals. Gabriel tried to sidestep him, but the man moved into his path.

"No thank you. I am visiting a friend. If you would kindly step aside and allow me to proceed."

"If you would kindly step aside and allow me to proceed." Red Cap laughed and mocked Gabriel's speech. "What the hell are you supposed to be? Some kind of robot?"

Gabriel's face darkened. The man's words conjured another

memory from long ago, and triggered the feelings that encounter had stirred—anger, guilt, shame. He squeezed his fists tight, something cold swirling inside him.

Red Cap seemed to sense the change, and after a moment of indecision, hardened. Lumbering forward, he taunted Gabriel, pounding one meaty hand against his chest.

"Go ahead shithead ... jump," said Red Cap.

"You leave him alone," called Wanda from the doorway. "I've told you to stay away. You don't belong here. I don't want you peddling your drugs outside my home."

"I do what I want, bitch. Ain't a fucking thing you can do about it."

"I can call the police," replied Wanda, refusing to be bullied.

"Police don't do shit. Call 'em. See if I care."

"I will." Wanda shot a belligerent glare at the big man and took out her phone.

"I wouldn't do that if I were you, old lady. You don't wanna mess with me." Red Cap retained his intimidating posture, but unease flitted across his eyes.

"Yes, this is Wanda Felton, I live at ..."

"Fine, I'm going, but you done fucked up, bitch. This ain't over." He lumbered away, casting the occasional menacing glare over his shoulder, implying he did not fear Wanda or the police. His leaving indicated otherwise.

"Gabriel? Gabriel." Wanda shook his arm. "Are you alright?"

He remained fixed in place, his scowl burning a hole in Red Cap's back. The man disappeared around the corner with Gabriel still glowering after him. Finally, feeling Wanda jostle him, he blinked a few times as if waking.

"Sorry milady, what?"

"Are you okay?"

"Yes ... yes, fine." Gabriel tried to cast off the raw emotions.

"Don't worry about that scum."

"I ... I should have defended you. Defended your honor, but ..."

"No, don't you worry about it. You're a gentle soul, Gabriel, not a mean bone in your body. You stay the way you are. There's too much hate and hostility in the world already," she said with a sweet smile. "Well, come on in, lunch is getting cold."

After their meal, they sat in her small living room sipping iced tea. Throughout lunch, Wanda continually cast furtive glances toward Gabriel, as if trying to discern some hidden secret. Her scrutiny made him uncomfortable, so finally he asked, "Is there something wrong, milady?"

"See that box on the shelf there? Get it for me will you?" She seemed to have been waiting for the question.

Gabriel retrieved the box and handed it to Wanda. She opened it and removed a ring—silver with an opal stone. She held it up between two spindly fingers; pretty, albeit cheap, he liked the glint of the gem.

"I gave this ring to my husband when he came home from Korea." Her head turned downward, a sadness creeping into her voice. "I made a big mistake once, Gabriel. While my husband was away at war, I got so lonely. I thought he would never come home. Another man showed me attention, and I needed someone...."

Gabriel remained quiet. He could tell this confession was not easy for her, but, for some reason he did not understand, important for her to share.

"It only happened the one time, but it ate at me all the many months my husband was away. When he returned, I gave him this ring and begged his forgiveness. I guess I wanted him to scream at me, threaten to leave me. I thought I deserved punishment. He didn't, though. Just smiled ... actually smiled and said he understood. Said he still loved me, nothing had changed."

"A good man, your husband."

"Yes ... yes he was," said Wanda, unconsciously smoothing her dress. "It took a long time for me to forgive myself. Before he died, he placed that ring in my hand and told me it could absorb all my regret. He told me to hold it tight, remember he loved me, and let my guilt seep into the ring. Let it take away my shame and pain."

"A pleasant thought, if only such things were possible."

"But they are. Maybe not really, but it's a symbol, a symbol of giving up the darkness inside you. The ring reminds you—reminds you that the darkness is gone."

Gabriel stared at the ring. Puzzled, he did not understand what Wanda needed him to comprehend. "There's goodness in you Gabriel, but also a lot of hurt. I saw it the first day I met you. Pain like yours is from either loss or regret, and I think you have plenty of both."

She reached over, placed the ring into his palm, and closed his fingers around it. "I want you to have it. Let it take your pain. I don't know what you're dealing with, I don't want to know, but that kind of guilt will eat you up. Believe me, I know too well. Let it go, Gabriel. Forgive yourself."

"Thank you, milady. I will treasure it always."

"No, it isn't meant to be an always thing. Give it your regret, forgive yourself, and when the time comes, give it to someone who needs it more than you."

GABRIEL LEFT WANDA'S DISTURBED BY THEIR CONVERSATION. He worked so hard at shutting out the past, but now her guidance stirred thoughts he did not want to contemplate. A life left behind, yet one refusing to remain locked away, constantly pounded at the door, demanding release. The cage he built within his mind could no longer contain it. The memories flooded in.

"Mother?" said Gabriel.

"This ignorant present, and I feel now the future in the instant," said Elisabeth. "O, never shall sun that morrow see."

Since Mason's death, Elisabeth steadily slid into insanity, her days of rationality almost nonexistent. Strange that a deaf, dumb, and dim-witted man could provide the slender thread tying her to reality. She slept more hours than spent awake. The world she resided in seemed filled with ghosts, none of which Gabriel could see or understand.

The full responsibility of running the farm now fell to him. He worked morning and night, trying his best to keep the garden tended, the animals fed, and everything in good repair. Only sixteen, he found himself thrust into manhood and faced with decisions he lacked the experience to make. Bills fell behind, crops rotted unsold, and several animals succumbed to illnesses.

The outdoor chores were only a portion of his daily tasks. Elisabeth no longer cooked or cleaned. Gabriel prepared her meals and often fed her—many days she would not eat on her own. He felt guilty, but in truth, his duties outside the house were a blessing. They removed him from her constant need and her ravings.

"Come on," he said to Athena, opening her pen. She grunted a happy greeting and followed Gabriel to the barn. Entering the building still filled him with an odd sensation. Each time he ventured inside, he half expected to see his father lying against the wall, the remains of his fragile mind upon the hay and dirt. Gabriel never recoiled from the feeling. Though he missed his father, this place harbored an attachment to his memory. He found it comforting, an oasis from the burden his life had become.

He sat between two hay bales and opened his copy of the *Aeneid*, Athena sprawled at his feet, content in his company.

Surely as the divine powers take note of the dutiful, surely as there is any justice anywhere and a mind recognizing in itself what is right, may the gods bring you your earned rewards.

Gabriel prayed the passage contained more than ancient tenets belonging only to a long gone age. He lived in a hope always somewhere a day, a week, a year removed. Dreams of other places, cities filled with beautiful sights and sounds, teased his desire.

His mother's voice, screaming, broke the silence. He rushed out of the barn, Athena at his heels, to find Elisabeth kneeling in the dirt wearing only her nightgown. She tore at the thin weeds growing there, pressing reed and root into her hair.

"The mind is its own place, and in itself can make a heav'n of hell, a hell of heav'n," she screamed at someone no one but she could see.

"Mother." Gabriel ran to her side.

"Ease would recant vows made in pain, as violent and void. For never can true reconcilement grow where wounds of deadly hate have pierced so deep."

"I don't understand. Tell me what I can do." Tears streamed down his cheeks. Fear mingled with disgust, concern with shame. He shook her, attempting to raise Elisabeth from whatever depths now drowned her.

She lifted her eyes to the sky and, in a voice torn from the deepest pits of her despair, yelled, "Only in destroying I find ease to my relentless thoughts."

"Mother, it's me. It's Gabriel, please look at me."

She sat quiet and still for a long moment as if paralyzed. Then her gaze slowly turned toward him. "Gabriel? Oh, Gabriel, my angel."

"Yes, mother, I'm here." He took her into a tight embrace. His arms sought to reassure her, to make her believe everything would be all right.

"Nor love thy life, nor hate; but while thou livest live well—how long, or short, permit to Heaven." Her shoulders slumped, her spirit broken, the words seemed a prayer lifted up by the dying.

"I will. I promise. Now let me get you inside. You must lie down." He helped her to her feet and guided her into the house. Once in her bed, she lay curled on her side, staring into nothingness.

Gabriel's hands trembled. The worst episode yet. He feared the time quickly approached when he could no longer care for her. What would he do then? There was no choice but to do his best to keep her safe. Safe from the demons that sought to claim her mind, safe from the calamity that was herself.

The next morning, a night removed from his mother's outburst, found his fear and frustration diminished. A warm day for a change, the sun rode a clear, cloudless sky.

"Athena," he called out. She seemed more dog than pig and might believe herself human if her haughty attitude were any indication. At Gabriel's call, she always came and waited, snout pressed to the pen's gate. Today, however, when he reached the gate she was not there. He scanned the pen, but she did not appear amongst the other hogs. Perhaps she had rooted out again, and he would find her eating herself sick on the chickens' feed.

He walked around to the coop, but found no Athena. A shriek

carried on the breeze coming from the forest. The silly girl went and got herself caught in a briar patch. He smiled, and began the long stroll across the pasture. Naomi and Ruth, the two remaining milk cows, eyed him for a moment, and then continued grazing on a hay bale.

Now several yards into the forest, Athena's squeal repeated. Her cry sounded muffled and faint. He could not tell if the distance or perhaps the trees and foliage gave the sound its subdued quality, but feared Athena's condition muted her call. Gabriel ran toward the sound as fast as his feet would carry him. Tearing through the brush, low branches slapping against him, he listened, trying to pinpoint her location.

Closer now, she must be over the next hill. Frantic with worry, Gabriel did not see the steep embankment. He stumbled and fell, tumbling head over heels. His downhill slide dumped him into a gully where Athena lay on her side a few paces away—one leg caught in a metal trap, her free legs feebly kicking at the air. The area around her was stained black, browned leaves and dirt saturated in her blood.

Although the land belonged to his family, they rarely came this far from their cleared farmland. Hunters often encroached into the forest to shoot deer, squirrels, and rabbits. Gabriel occasionally heard the echo of a gunshot, but he had not known about the traps.

Predators had come in the night, gouging large chunks of flesh from Athena's flanks. The horror dawned on him; he forgot to put her in the pen after attending to his mother. This was his fault. Gabriel fell to his knees, tears flowing.

Athena suffered in so much pain. Her squeals gathered new strength seeing Gabriel close. He thought to carry her home where he might do something, anything, to help her. Leaning over the trap, Gabriel attempted to separate the closed teeth. Athena thrashed furiously, summoned what strength remained in her, and let out a piercing, agonizing screech.

Gabriel could open the trap no more than an inch or two, not enough to free her captured leg. He could not save her; the damage inflicted was too severe. Kneeling beside her, he stroked her coarse hide. The heartache of her impending loss crashed down on him. Gabriel stared into her eyes, pleading with her to get up, to be well again.

His fingers felt on fire, his head squeezed by an invisible vice, a crushing force blinded him. Cold pressure clenched his stomach as he clawed the ground, fighting the feeling. Urgency built within him, bubbling and boiling, seeking release.

He heard whispers drift through his mind. Voices rose like a Gregorian chant in some beautiful language he did not know. *The feeling* seemed to merge with the chorus, coalescing into a tangible symphony. Louder now, insistent, filling him.

Gabriel dove onto Athena, the knife Mason had given him as a birthday gift clutched in his hand. He drove the blade into her over and over. Rising and falling, it plunged into her body until his strength failed. Finally, he collapsed in exhaustion.

Athena appeared so peaceful. Her cries silenced, her eyes shut as if in a deep sleep. Reaching out, he touched her bristly skin, already growing cool. Gabriel thought he felt her spirit soar. He had released her—set her soul free from its pain-riddled flesh. A smile came to his lips.

Gabriel trembled with the power of the memory. He had not thought of that day for a very long time. It was the first time he felt the feeling. No ... *the blessing.*

After that day with Athena, the blessing came many times. A deer, wounded by a gunshot to its hind leg, wandered out of the forest. A dog hit by a car on the road staggered into his mercy.

The young prostitute was the first time he experienced the blessing with a person. It frightened him, but soon an exhilaration filled him. He understood his purpose. His calling.

The gods called him to be their mortal instrument. They showered the blessing on him, demanding it pass through him and onto the chosen—those crying out for release from the pain of suffering an unwanted life.

The man in the nice suit and fancy car offered him a ride. A man who should have avoided him, ignored him, but instead gave him a ride and allowed Gabriel to guide him to the abandoned area out near the Furnaces. What more proof was required to prove the hand of Providence directed him?

Even so, those two were sloppy and crude, so much blood. Most unbecoming of the gods' work, a matter he soon rectified with the grieving mother. A grand display to Their glory, for Their worship, and for the salvation of the chosen.

THE MEMORIES LINGERED OVER THE NEXT DAYS, HOVERING HIM LIKE halo. Elation filled Gabriel when at last he again felt the divine touch. *A new* chosen one. He sat on the edge of the bed stroking the woman's hair, nudging a lock from her face. She appeared angelic in the moonlight streaming through an open window. Peaceful, serene, free.

"Do not fear, your pain is gone now. Soon you will walk the fields of Elysium. The gods heard your pleas, took notice of your suffering, and deemed you righteous. You go now to a better place to live a blessed and happy life free from the woes of this world."

Her skin, the color of porcelain, seemed to glow—a new life born in the cold rigidity of death. He cut the last suture, admiring how neat the crisscrossed threads appeared. His art, his worship, showed practice, each stage of the design now steady and elegant in its construction. A beautiful arrayal.

"O death, where is thy victory? O death, where is thy sting?" Gabriel placed the cross on her neck.

"Precious in the sight of the Lord is the death of his saints." He set the coins upon her eyes.

Gabriel stood, gathered his tools, and started for the door. Reaching for the knob, he stopped, and walked back into the room. He leaned down and pressed his forefinger into the bisected heart, coating it in blood, and stepped to the wall behind the bed where he wrote one word.

CHAPTER TWELVE

More than two dozen detectives and subordinates sat in the briefing room. The lieutenant had ordered the whole department to drop whatever they were doing. Commotion filled the air as the group offered their varied opinions as to the meeting's purpose. All present were well aware of the latest Seraphim murder, but how that changed the investigation's parameters remained anyone's guess.

Marlowe entered, followed by Lieutenant McCann and Spence. As everyone took their seats, Marlowe moved to the lectern. He nodded to Dr. Koopman, who attended the briefing with his assistant in tow. Jonas seemed more out of place here than in the morgue, eyes flitting from one person to the next as if encountering aliens on some strange planet.

"Okay, we have our first good lead. It appears Seraphim's targeting people who are depressed—very depressed, suicidal," said Marlowe.

"You're kidding, right? That's half the city. Everyone's on Prozac and in therapy. The economy's in the shitter, unemployment rates at all-time highs. We'd have a tougher time finding people who *aren't* depressed," said Detective Marty Vines, a slight man with a snub nose and sunken eyes.

"And anyway, how would the killer know?" asked Officer Kirkpatrick.

"Patience, young Skywalker," said Spence.

"We're not talking stressed out or a case of the blues here. These people are at the cliff's edge ready to take the dive. They've reached the point where they believe death is preferable to living."

"Still," said Kirkpatrick, "I don't see how anyone could know that."

"I'm about to tell you," said Marlow. He pointed to the first photo on the board behind him. "The first victim, Nikki Baker—street kid, prostitute, junkie. Multiple counts of solicitation and a couple of busts for possession. The ER treated her for an overdose ... twice. We can safely assume her life wasn't peachy."

"Quite a leap from overdose to suicidal. Hell, what junkie hasn't overdosed at least once?" said Bateman.

"By itself, maybe. In total with the other victims, not so much," said Spence.

Marlowe moved to the next photo. "Matthew Young lost a ton of his clients' money and all of his own when he fell in deep with some nasty characters. He was looking at a career in ruins, bookies coming to take their pound of flesh, and probable jail time. His coworkers said he seemed ready to jump out his 22nd floor window.

"Melissa Turner's son died of leukemia. Her bedroom contained a pharmacy of sedatives and antidepressants. Her sister believed she was suicidal. We contacted the prescribing doctors, and they indicated she suffered from severe depression."

Finally, Marlowe pointed to the last picture tacked onto the far end of the board. "Now, Seraphim himself has given us the knot tying it all together. The latest crime scene included a new signature. The word *Anticlea*—written in the victim's blood on the wall above the bed."

"What the hell is that? Sounds like a venereal disease," said Vines, to snickers from the group.

Marlowe ignored it and continued. "Anticlea, Odysseus' mother in Greek Mythology. She committed suicide while grieving for her son away at war."

"Okay, and …" said Kirkpatrick.

"Patricia Wilton is the latest victim. Her son was killed serving in Afghanistan," Marlowe waited for this information to sink in. "Based on the religious symbolism Seraphim leaves in his rituals, it's my guess he believes he's saving the souls of his victims—keeping them from committing suicide. In Christian theology, to some at least, suicide means a straight trip to Hell. Or, it could mean he believes he is ending their pain and sending them to a better place. Either way, there's obviously a religious/suicide link."

"Okay, maybe there's a link, but I still don't see how he could know," said Vines.

"I'm getting to it. All these victims have something in common, unless Seraphim truly does have God on his shoulder pointing them out. In which case Vines is right, he can't possibly know their emotional state. I don't think God or anything supernatural is guiding the killer, do you?" Marlowe asked the group. Some shook their heads, most averted their eyes from Marlowe's stare.

"So, there's a doctor, shrink, pastor, someone somewhere who counseled all our victims. A staff member, custodian, member of a congregation, someone who overheard them and is targeting them with this knowledge."

"How the hell do we find them? Might as well toss a rock in the ocean and hope it doesn't get wet," said Bateman.

"Glad you asked. We're going through each victim's background with a fine-toothed comb to find where each went for treatment, counseling, or comfort. Might be they have a common friend they talked to, or maybe they all called the same help line," said Marlowe.

"You've got to be shitting me." Kirkpatrick threw up his hands.

"Leave no stone unturned. Think outside the box on this one. Consider anything along these lines that they might have in common. It's there, people, and we're going to find it."

"Jesus, Gentry, there could be hundreds of people for each victim." Bateman echoed Kirkpatrick's concern and looked none too happy with the prospect of this particular task.

"Yep, and we will look at every one of them. Seraphim is hitting his stride. He's confident, and worst of all, he believes in what he's doing. Find the link, folks," said Marlowe, scanning the room, making eye contact with each person. Satisfied there were no more questions or complaints, he waved at the door. "Okay, get to it."

As the room emptied and a grumbling police force began work on the intensive undertaking assigned them, Spence, Koop, and the lieutenant stepped up to Marlowe.

"Nice speech," said Spence.

"That's a ton of man-hours, not that I'm complaining. We've got a blank check on overtime. You really think this will lead us to Seraphim?" asked McCann.

"I do. I don't believe he's psychic or divinely guided. He's finding his victims in a more mundane way."

"Some people believe in that shit. I hear there are psychics who work with the police sometimes," said Spence. "Locating missing persons, bodies …"

"Urban myth," said McCann.

"I saw it on …" began Spence, but pulled up short at a scowl from the lieutenant. "Fine, they don't."

"Suicidal persons," said Koop, rubbing his chin. "Interesting. I once considered suicide, but lacked the patience for the seven day waiting period."

"No one would let you have a gun with a hundred year waiting period," said Spence.

"We should listen to the resident expert on suicides. Our friend Spencer has caused many of them," shot back Koop.

"Would you two shut up? For Christ's sake, you're like little kids," said McCann.

"Am not," said Spence.

"Are too," said Koop.

The lieutenant's face went red. He grunted and turned to Marlowe. "What's your next step?"

"While the team checks backgrounds, Spence and I will head to Westside and try to run down info on Nikki Baker. We struck out with Young; no one saw anyone with him when he left work. No luck locating any stops he made. The Furnaces are out in the boondocks, so no witnesses on that end either. I'm hoping for better results with the girl. Signs point to her being the first victim. There was no trace of ritual involved. My theory is he took her on impulse. He didn't plan it, at least not like these last two, so maybe someone saw something."

"Uniforms have been all over the area," said McCann.

"Yeah. Still, we need to give it another pass. I have a tough time believing no one knows anything. The girl lived in the area, someone saw her that day. We need to jog some memories." Marlowe tapped his temple with an index finger.

"Folks in that area aren't keen on talking to cops. Uniforms aren't always brimming with tact. Maybe, they'll be more talkative with us," said Spence.

"Sure, those of us in suits are the picture of sensitivity. Okay, keep me in the loop," said McCann, walking away.

"The lieutenant should really see someone about his condition," said Spence.

"Condition?" asked Koop.

"The stick up his ass. Seems chronic."

"He does suffer from a pain in his posterior region, but it is not a stick." Koop gave Spence an impish look.

"Koop, don't you have some bodies to carve up or something?" asked Marlowe.

"I do have someone on ice at the moment, now that you mention it. Adieu, gentlemen."

Once the doctor left, Spence said, "This is pissing in the wind, you know."

"It's what we have. May take some time, but all these victims have someone in common, and that someone is Seraphim," said Marlowe.

"These vics did have some fucked up lives. Not saying it's right, but I can see how they wanted to check out. Like you said, they didn't have a bad day and get down in the dumps. They were dealing with some major league heartache. What I don't understand is why they didn't do the deed themselves if they were so depressed. What were they waiting for?"

Marlowe paused, his mind filled with the image of Paige's emotionless face. "Hope."

They took the stairs and exited the back of the building into the car lot. Winter refused to give up the ghost and blasted the city with another round of sub-freezing temperatures. Spence, wearing a navy pea coat over a sweater and jeans, pulled the collar tight around his neck and blew out a stream of breath visible in the cold air. Marlowe, in his topcoat, button-down, and dark slacks, was comfortable with the chill, showing no sign he registered the sudden forty-degree drop since stepping outdoors.

"Say again?" said Spence, puzzled by Marlowe's answer.

"People in their emotional state are standing right on the line between swallowing the pills or pulling the trigger, and trying again to find a reason to live, to keep going. The line is hope. If they can find something in the future more powerful and promising than the pain of the past and present, they'll step back from the line. If they can't, they jump across."

"Sounds like you understand them a little too well, brother."

"You've never been there? Never hit a spot where the present felt unbearable, and you had trouble seeing the future improving matters?" Marlowe took his seat behind the wheel of the Explorer and cranked the engine.

"No. I mean, of course I've had bad shit happen. I was all set to play football for the Tide and broke a femur. It didn't heal right, so no more scholarship. For a while, it felt like life was over. Football had always been my dream, all I wanted to do. But down deep, I always believed it would pass, sooner or later."

"You're lucky then. We can sit back and tell someone all day long how things will get better, but for some, they just can't see it. And for some, it won't ever get better. Maybe Nikki would have found a way off the streets eventually, but we both know the odds were against her. Likely she would have overdosed, gotten some disease, or a john would have killed her. Melissa Turner, you think she would have ever learned to live with the loss of her son? Perhaps, but it's the moment that matters. These people can't see the future. Same with Matthew Young."

"I get what you're saying, but others have gone through the same or worse and pulled out of it," said Spence, reaching down to crank the heat up another notch.

"Pain is relative, I guess. My pain is the worst in the world, because its mine. I can't feel your suffering or you mine. We can sympathize with each other's pain, but not experience it."

"Yeah, I had a friend whose mom died around the same time I broke my leg. Losing a mother is way worse than losing a football scholarship, but I focused on my own misery, what I lost. I wasn't there for him."

"Exactly. In the moment, the future doesn't exist and hope is elusive. Hope is only part of it, though. There's a big difference between wanting to die and actually killing yourself."

"True, everyone fears pain. Plus, what if they botch it? That would scare the shit out of me," said Spence. "Keep me from doing it—the possibility of ending up a vegetable or something. I guess I can see how a killer who will do for you what you can't do for yourself might be appealing to people in their situation."

They traveled over the cobbled street of Morris Avenue and turned left toward Westside. The inner defrost had yet to completely clear the windshield, forcing Marlowe to scrunch forward and peer through the lower half. He rubbed his sleeves against the glass and grunted irritation when it did little good.

"That's what worries me," Marlowe said, sitting back at a red light. "We don't have a Ted Bundy or John Wayne Gacy here. We have a Dr. Kevorkian. If we don't paint this picture right, he could turn into a sympathetic actor. People hear about what he's doing to the victims, but they don't see it. They can't wrap their minds around it. A man saving people from hell or assisting them to commit suicide, some crackpots will actually think it's okay, even admirable."

"We live in one screwed up world, my friend. There's always people who idolize these monsters. Even the ones with no sympathetic intentions. Hell, Charles Manson got married in prison I think. Bundy had scores of admirers. Regardless, there are these psycho groupies out there," said Spence. He poured out two cups of coffee from his thermos and handed one to Marlowe.

"True, and Seraphim is just the kind of killer they love to emulate. I'm surprised we haven't seen a copycat or two yet. Or someone thinking they are in league with him. The tag Seraphim, all the religious symbolism, begs for some kind of sick disciple."

"Jesus, that's all we need."

"You mentioned Manson. He talked his *family* into killing for him. Four devotees butchered a pregnant Sharon Tate, then Leno and Rosemary LaBianca. Manson wasn't even there to encourage them. They worshiped the guy, did whatever he said." Marlowe shook his head. "Then you have people like those who drank the Flavor Aid on the command of Jim Jones. Happened again with the Hale Bopp Comet group—the Heaven's Gate cult. The list goes on and on."

"Why do you know this shit? It'll rot your mind." Spence cut his eyes at Marlowe from the passenger seat while sipping gingerly from his coffee mug.

"I took several classes on abnormal psychology, and I've read pretty much every book on serial killers written."

"Not the smartest idea with what you've gone through, is it?"

Marlowe nodded and tightened his grip on the steering wheel. "I needed to understand ... or try to. Anyway, imagine you're one of these suicidal types. Maybe you believe committing suicide lands you in hell, or you just can't do the deed yourself for some reason. Now, you learn there's an angel out there granting salvation or release ... whatever. What would you do to gain said angel's attention?"

"Great, like I wasn't already having nightmares over this thing. You know, I really hate you and your big brain sometimes."

CHAPTER THIRTEEN

"I'm sorry, Mr. Bannon." The doctor closed the file and peered across his desk. "The malignancy isn't responding to treatment, and with the metastasis into the liver and lungs, I believe at this point, continuing will only cause discomfort without benefit."

Max felt a cold hand grip his heart and squeeze. Why so surprised? He had expected it. Still, during the treatment and his sessions with Dr. Drenning, Max had held tight to a sliver of hope. Now, he felt that sliver evaporate.

What now? Sit back and wait to die, he supposed. Or worse, sit back and wait for the pain to become excruciating. Wait for his mind to turn to mush.

"Aren't there some experimental treatments you can try? Clinical trials, maybe?" Funny, he had been so afraid of the chemo and radiation, and now Max would give anything for another round if it would help.

"No, I'm sorry. We've exhausted our treatment options."

"What about alternative treatments? I've seen those on the internet."

"I could not recommend any non-medical treatments. I'm unaware of any that have proven more successful than traditional methods.

Chances are good they would only be a waste of your time and money. However, if attempting some other form of treatment will give you comfort and the strength to cope, then by all means."

"What do I do now?" Max asked in a hollow voice.

"You'll be more comfortable at home. Surround yourself with loved ones and try to value the time you have left with them. I've notified hospice. Someone will contact you to come by and show you how to use the morphine, as well as the proper regimen to control any pain."

"There's nothing else I can do? Just wait to die?" asked Max, hoping against hope the doctor might suddenly change his mind.

"I encourage you to continue your sessions with Dr. Drenning. She may have techniques to help with managing your fears."

Max left the doctor's office feeling more defeated than ever. Silly to hold out hope, he had read the percentages and knew there was little chance of remission. Still, he did not want to die. More so, he did not want to live in pain and dementia.

In the hospital parking lot, a crisp coolness accompanied the afternoon breeze. Winter began its slow march toward spring. Birds perched on low limbs sang, hastening its approach. Max yearned for winter to linger a while longer. It seemed more fitting. A time when things died, and the world fell silent in sleep, waiting for rebirth.

His legs felt weak, all strength sapped dry. He sat on a bench and watched the groundskeepers work. Max would miss the simple joy of working with his hands, feeling the dirt between his fingers. Connecting all those wires and circuits, watching the lights come on and knowing he had a part in illuminating this home or that building, one little corner of the world.

He told himself again that he should not drive, should not have driven for weeks now, but spending money on a cab seemed such a waste. His money needed to stretch a little longer—not much longer. He drove toward home, keeping it under the speed limit. Safety first.

Home safe and mostly sound, Max went to the fridge, grabbed a soda, and sat on the sofa. The house felt strange, too quiet. It was never quiet with the boys around. The little demons tore through constantly, voices raised, accusations flying of something or other. Max actually missed it. He even missed Maggie's nagging.

He set the drink on the arm table and closed his eyes. He might nap for a minute or two—just a short one to get his strength back.

THE SMELL OF FRESH PINE FILLED HIS NOSTRILS. ENCASED IN WOOD, THE tight fit pressed against his prone body on all sides, the hard surface raking his hair and his toes, the lid an inch from touching his nose. Max panicked.

Barely able to lift his hands, he placed his palms to the lid and pushed with all his strength. Dirt dribbled in around the pried cover, falling into his eyes and mouth. He gagged and shoved, a scream of desperation escaping with the exertion. The lid gave, bursting upward.

He sat up, gasping for air. No more than a foot of earth had covered the coffin. Two shovels lay beside a mound, the diggers having decided filling the hole not worth the effort.

He climbed from the grave and stood staring in disbelief. This could not be real. A dream … a nightmare, surely. No preacher presided over this funeral; no tombstone marked the place of rest; no flowers or footprints evidenced where mourners came to pay last respects.

"Pretty shabby turnout," said a raspy voice.

He looked up toward the sound and saw a large crow gazing down, a amused aspect in its black, probing eyes.

"What?" said Max, questioning his senses. "Did you speak?"

"Wasn't the wind, bright boy."

"What is this? Why am I here?"

"You're dead. Well dead and not dead. Mostly dead."

"I don't understand."

"Humans, you are a slow bunch aren't you? Your heart stopped beating, they put you in the hole, but your spirit ain't quite flown the coop yet," the crow said with as much of a sneer as a crow could sneer.

"What happens now? What do you have to do with this?"

"I'm a guide of sorts. I'm here to take you to the next plane. You're moving on up."

"But I can't. I'm not ready."

"No? What's left? Nothing. You had nothing, you got nothing."

"That's not true. I have to fix things with Maggie. I have to raise my boys. They need me."

"Hmm, let me enlighten you. Maggie marries a dentist, pretty well off—definite upgrade, no offense. Cody becomes a successful contractor, more or less a chip off the ol' block, should make you happy. Austin becomes a decent professional golfer—dentist dad's a member of a country club. So, no worries. Everything turns out peachy, see?"

Max clenched his hands. "No. I don't believe you. They need me. I know they do."

"This is already starting to bore me. You going or staying?"

"I have to stay."

"Your call, but don't say I didn't warn you."

The crow took flight, disappearing after a time beyond the distant horizon. Max sat on the loose dirt, unsure of what to do. He did not know this place, did not know where he could go. The crow's words stung deep. Part of him wanted to crawl back into the grave.

"I'm pleased you decided to stay," said a different voice, gurgled, as if spoken under water.

Max turned to see a monstrosity. It appeared vaguely human, but moved like liquid. Black and oily, it flowed across the ground.

He grabbed a rock, and flung it hard at the thing. The stone passed through the figure, concentric ripples spanning out from where it struck.

"Now, now, no need for hostilities."

"Who are you?" Max backpedaled. "I thought I would return to my life."

"You will live what life remained to you. The final months of an insidious disease await you. As for me, I have many names. You will call me Pain."

Wires, barbed with razors, shot up from the ground, entwining Max's arms and legs, pulling tight and anchoring him in place. He struggled to break the binds, but the sharpened tips only dug in deeper. Max screamed in torment. Pain drifted forward, a shadowy hand reaching out to touch Max's forehead ... and all went black.

When he opened his eyes, Max found himself strapped to wooden beams in the shape of an X—legs spread, arms upraised. Pain stood near the far wall, placing instruments on a table. Terror filled Max, he tried to cry out, but no sound would come. Agony hit him. The stump of his tongue lolled about the back of his throat; He gagged on the vile, coppery slime sliding down his throat. Thick, dried blood caked his chin and his chest.

Pain approached, holding a bucket sloshing with water, droplets splashing over the edge. He placed light fingers along Max's abdomen. Seeming pleased with the spot, he reached into the bucket and pulled out a slender eel-like creature more than six feet long. The thing thrashed viciously as it swung inverted from Pain's hand.

Pain held it up for Max to admire. It possessed no eyes, only two rows of needle-like teeth set in a large, oval mouth. One row of teeth turned one hundred and eighty degrees clockwise, the other, the same degree of rotation counter-clockwise. Max's imagination could not help but picture the wounds such a bite would inflict—penetrating, tearing.

Pain unsheathed a curved blade, set the tip against Max's skin, and drew it downward. At the scent of fresh blood, the eel-thing gyrated madly. Pain shoved the ferocious creature into the open wound and grunted with satisfaction. Trapped in silence, Max's inaudible scream ripped through the ether, sending monsters and gods hiding their heads in fear of such terrible agony.

For a thousand years, Pain entertained Max with his tricks and delights. Each time Max felt certain there could be no worse torture, nothing more heinous to imagine, Pain proved him wrong.

One day Max found Pain gone and his restraints loosened. Leaning forward slightly dumped him onto his face. The open door seemed a million miles away, and the silver light beyond an appalling lie. He dragged himself toward the door, fingernails raking the floor for purchase. Outside, he erupted into maniacal laughter. Under the full moon, surrounded by a forest he knew well, bloody and broken … Max wept.

HE WOKE WITH TEARS DRIED UPON HIS FACE, HIS SHIRT STILL DAMP, lying naked in the backyard of his home. Tall pines stretched into the night sky, a full moon hovering above. Wide slashes covered his body; his fingernails were stained with blood. The memory of the nightmare slammed into his consciousness. Every sight, smell, sound, and feeling seemed the remnants of an actual occurrence.

He stood, staggered into the house, and made it to his bedroom. Max picked up the bottle of pills from the bedside table. After pouring the capsules into his palm, he counted twenty pills. He hoped it was enough as he slapped them into his mouth. Max did not recall what the pills were intended to treat, or what they were called. He washed them down with the glass of lukewarm water that remained on the table from the previous night.

He knew now, he could not face what was to come. He did not fear dying so much, but the dying process … *this* dying process. Max sat on the edge of the bed. Nothing to do now but wait … it was over.

What if it doesn't work? What if it makes things worse?

How can things possibly get any worse?

What if I go into a coma? They'll call Maggie and the kids. They'd be forced to care for a vegetable. They don't even want to be around me. My kids will see me wither away—shitting on myself, my brain nothing but soup.

Max stood on wobbling legs.

Not too late, please don't let it be too late.

He lurched into the bathroom, fell to his knees, placed two fingers down his throat, and threw up into the toilet. Nothing. Again, he gagged and vomited.

There they were. Small plastic orbs floated on the surface of the water. Frantically, he counted. One … two … did he miss one? No … twenty, there were twenty.

Thank God, oh thank sweet Jesus.

Max collapsed against the bathtub. He had never felt so exhausted —physically, emotionally, spiritually. So tired. Max Bannon, the most pathetic person to have ever lived. Dying, wanting to end it, and not having the balls.

In that moment of perfect silence, a voice came from the bedroom television: *Sources within the department say the Seraphim is targeting people who are deeply depressed or suicidal. Police have not yet determined how the killer becomes aware of his victims' mental and emotional conditions, but many healthcare officials are concerned those in need may forego care out of fear. More on this story as it develops. Now let's get a first check on weather with meteorologist....*

The television voices melted into a clutter of meaningless sound.

Maybe Max would luck out and win the lottery. Maybe the Seraphim would find him and do for him what he could not do for himself. He had an ample supply of luck … all of it bad. He'd never been in the habit of wishing. He didn't even toss pennies into the fountain. Max had always believed hard work got a person what they wanted. So much for that theory. Maybe he had saved up all his wishes, and this one would count for all of them. One wish....

Let Seraphim find me.

CHAPTER FOURTEEN

T hey drove down 21ˢᵗ Street at a pedestrian pace. "Want to get there today?" asked Spence.

"Patience, my son, it's a virtue," replied Marlowe. He sped up to beat a yellow traffic light.

"I try not to have those, cramps my style."

Traveling into Westside seemed like passing through a time warp. Southside contained the city's nightlife—dance clubs, restaurants, boutique shops. Banks, law firms, and corporate headquarters lined Northside in skyscrapers. Westside had little more than rundown buildings, slum apartments, and raunchy strip joints with the accompanying vices aplenty.

"Stop here," said Spence.

"I thought you were in a hurry."

"In a hurry to get somewhere. Your NPR listening habits give me a headache."

Marlowe pulled into a no parking zone in front of a store sporting a faded sign reading HENRY'S. The chime overhead as they entered sounded like a sick canary. Spence appeared to know the place, navigating the rows to the coolers, where he plucked out a bottle of some pink liquid.

"Granny's Old Time Cherry Lemonade." Spence held up the bottle with a pleased grin. "Only place in the city where I can find this sweet elixir of the gods."

"Looks like pixie piss," said Marlowe with a scowl.

"You have no taste, bro."

They made their way to the front of the store. An older man stood behind the counter, looking perpetually displeased about something. He narrowed his eyes and what might have been a growl rumbled in his throat.

"Detective Murray, long time, no see. And each day I thank God for his small mercies. What brings you to our hairy armpit of the city? Oh wait, did you recover my stuff? At least tell me you caught the crooks."

Spence looked at him with faux surprise. "What? Did you get robbed again?"

"Did I ... why you worthless ... you cops are no good for anything. Useful as a warm bucket of piss, as LBJ used to say."

"LB who?" said Spence.

"Lyndon Johnson, our former president," said Henry with a reproachful glare.

"Sorry, I only go as far back as Carter. He was the peanut guy, right?"

"Shame on you. You're probably serious too. You young'uns forget how important history is. You think you know everything, when you can't even pull your pants up."

"Henry," called a voice from behind the coolers, "where would you like these boxes unpacked?"

"Just leave 'em, Gabriel. I need to clear some shelf space first."

"Finally get some help around here?" Spence asked.

"Yes, and out of the goodness of his heart. He's a godsend, and a polite young man. Actually respects his elders. You could learn a thing or two."

"I learn stuff all the time. Watch Jeopardy at least once a week." Spence picked a speck of lint from his coat and flicked it nonchalantly into the air.

"If you two are about through with this verbal lovemaking, we have work to do," said Marlowe.

"Ah, the brains of the operation," said Henry. "What does that make you? The brawn?"

"The looks," said Spence.

Henry gazed at the ceiling. "Christ on crutches, get him outta here."

"First, do you know this girl?" Marlowe displayed a photo of Nikki Baker. "Sorry about the … well."

The picture showed Nikki from the neck up, quite dead. No photos of her living seemed to exist—none with the DMV, online social sites, nothing.

Henry blanched at the sight of her stone-colored image. "Ah, no, I don't know her." He turned his head away.

"Sorry about that," said Marlowe. "Okay Spence, work, this way."

"See ya around, Henry," said Spence.

"Not too soon." Henry bared a sorry excuse of a grin and offered them a dismissive wave.

Marlowe and Spence stood on the sidewalk, studying both directions.

"Any brilliant ideas?" asked Marlowe.

"Nikki's body was found in an alley a few blocks up, behind an old apartment building. Uniforms searched the place room to room, but couldn't determine where she stayed. Most of those apartments get junkie squatters holed up in them. All kinds of clothes and shit left behind, so it's impossible to tell who stayed where. They cased the place for a few days, but nothing turned up."

"Somebody knew her." Marlowe stared into an alley. "She didn't live here, turning tricks and buying drugs, without someone knowing her."

"I've got an idea. We need to talk to Trixie."

"Trixie?" asked Marlowe.

"Kind of an unofficial mayor of the area, nothing happens here she doesn't know about. Dealt with her a lot when I worked Vice."

"We've got to start somewhere. Lead the way."

Patricia "Trixie" Wilcox owned three of the four strip clubs on Westside. All low-rent dives featuring dancers only the inebriated would pay to see naked. Still, they offered something appealing to the undiscerning tastes of Westside—a warm or cool spot to park it (depending on the weather), cheap drinks, nude girls, and a host of illegal substances and activities.

A real American success story, Trixie. She started out turning tricks on the streets before replacing her pimp under mysterious circumstances—they found him dead with his severed penis shoved into his mouth. Rumor had it he tried to short her on her cut and knocked her around for arguing. Trixie referred to him in anger as Dickbreath on many occasions.

After a short investigation, Trixie walked, and soon ran most of the working girls. She saved her pennies and bought a club, then two, then three. Now the prostitutes had a sympathetic runner and safe places to work—all the dancers dually employed.

Marlowe followed Spence through Git Nasty, the pounding rap music and gyrating lights making his head hurt. Only three customers were in the club at this time of day. One sat at the bar nursing a beer. Another reclined in a booth with a well-endowed dancer/waitress. Marlowe didn't want to guess at what was going on under the table. A sad-looking fellow stared bleary-eyed at the pencil-thin stripper spinning around the onstage pole.

They proceeded to the back of the club and came to a red door guarded by the largest man Marlowe had ever seen.

"Tiny," said Spence.

"Don't call me that," said the bouncer.

"Sorry, Reg-i-nald," he said, accenting each syllable. "We need to see Trixie."

"You got an appointment?" Reginald smirked, his massive biceps bouncing in time with the music. Dark skin hid his expression in the dim lighting, but when he smiled, there was nothing subtle about it.

"I've got a badge, and I've got a phone here with Vice on speed dial. Now every girl in here might, and I stress *might*, be twenty-one; but we would need to shut this place down while we check. Could take quite some time."

The smirk disappeared from Reginald's face. "Wait here," he said before disappearing into the office.

After a moment, he returned. "Go on in."

"Thanks big guy, been a pleasure," said Spence.

"That mouth of yours is going to get you killed one day," said Marlowe.

"Maybe, but not today."

Trixie's office looked like one of those tasteless Valentine's Day inspired rooms at a bad whorehouse. A heart-shaped bed sat against the back wall, red carpet and red velvet curtains framing this disaster of space. An attractive woman stood behind a large, cherry wood desk.

Not what Marlowe expected. Trixie appeared no more than five-feet tall, maybe a hundred pounds soaking wet. Golden brown skin and black hair hanging to her waist accentuated a dancer's figure. A keen intelligence shone in her almond-shaped eyes. She wore a dark purple top, sequined in gold, thin straps at the shoulders, and tight, black cloth pants. How such a diminutive woman ousted one mean pimp, kept a few dozen girls in line, and inspired fear in the criminals of the area defied comprehension.

"Hey there tall, dark, and yummy," she said in a soft accent. Trixie rounded the desk, yanked Spence downward, and planted a kiss on both cheeks. "And you," she said, looking Marlowe up and down. "Mmm mmm. Though a shave and a suit with a few less wrinkles would pretty up this picture. What brings you two hotties into my fine establishment?"

"Trixie ... as beautiful as ever," said Spence.

"You dog, looking for a freebie? You know I don't work the sheets anymore, but you want to take me out, treat me all nice like a real lady, maybe you'll get lucky."

"Do you know this girl?" asked Marlowe, already nauseated by the repartee.

"All business this one, huh?" Trixie took the photo. "Sure I know her … or knew her, poor thing. Not one of my girls. I tried to get her off the street a couple of times, but she shacked up with a real loser."

"A pimp?" asked Marlowe.

"He wishes. A playa-wanna-be that calls himself Raze, trying for cred. We call him Li'l Marv. Don't call him that though, not if you want him to talk to you, hates it. Real name's Marvin Lister."

"Know where we can find Mr. Lister?" asked Spence.

"Sure. Brightbrook Apartments. Fourth floor, I think."

"Brightbrook?" Spence raised an eyebrow. "Nikki was found in an alley right behind there."

"If you knew this, why didn't you tell the authorities?" asked Marlowe.

Trixie gave a sarcastic laugh. "You kidding, right? Well, they didn't ask. They don't care about no Westside junkie hooker. They figured some crazy john offed her. Probably right, too. Shee-it, can see her damn window from the alley where they found her. Shouldn't a' taken much investigatin' ta find it."

"You deal with a lot of mean-natured johns?" asked Spence.

"Not with my girls. Once in a while, some dickbreath kicks it a bit too frisky. A talk with Reginald shows 'em what's what real quick. Now the girls working independent, can't say. Plenty of bad boys on the streets."

"All right, thanks for your help," said Marlowe.

"Thanks, Trix," said Spence.

"You boys come back. I'm sure I can find something you'd like." Trixie struck a suggestive pose devoid of subtlety and accompanied by a devilish grin.

They drove the six blocks down 38th Street and pulled into the alley behind Brightbrook Apartments. Shreds of yellow crime scene tape still littered the area.

"What do we know about Marvin Lister?" asked Marlowe.

Spence punched the name into the onboard computer terminal. "Small time dealer, nothing big. Most of his rap sheet is possession. Looks like he wants to swim in the deep end, but so far the sharks aren't letting him play."

The detectives entered the building, stepping over a drunken vagrant. Spence flashed his badge to the man in the enclosed booth, who informed them Lister was in Room 412, barely glancing up from his porno magazine. An out of order sign affixed to the elevator sent them to the stairs. Spence didn't complain.

Apartment 412 sat at one end of the corridor on the right. Spence stepped up and gave the door a hard rap. "Police," he called out.

Shuffling and bumping emanated from inside. After a couple of minutes, footsteps came to the door and it opened two inches, stalled by a chain. A rodent-faced man peeked out.

"I ain't done nothin'." Dark circles shadowed his bloodshot eyes.

"Mr. Lister, we need to speak with you," said Marlowe.

"Name's Raze, asshole. You got a warrant?"

"You aren't under arrest, and we don't want to search your apartment. We want to ask you some questions about your girlfriend, Nikki Baker," said Spence.

"Ain't my fucking girlfriend, nasty skank. Besides, she's dead." Raze attempted to shut the door in their faces.

Marlowe slid his shoe between door and jamb. He clenched his jaw tight; he was losing patience with this guy … and fast. "That's what we want to talk to you about, if you'd open the door."

"Fuck you. I ain't got nothing to say."

Marlowe thrust his shoulder into the door, snapping the chain, and sending Raze stumbling backward. Marlowe pounced on him, grabbing him by one arm and the long rattail dangling down his back. He hustled Raze toward the far window and pressed him to the wall, one hand moving to clutch his throat, the other opening the latch. Once opened, Marlowe shoved Raze up to his waist out of the apartment. Raze hung four stories above the pavement below.

"Jesus Christ, I said I don't know anything, honest." Raze's streetwise accent disappeared with his bravado.

"Listen, you slimy little fuck," said Marlowe, his voice dripping venom. "I will drop you in a heartbeat. Think anyone will ask questions about a two-bit junkie splattered on the asphalt? That's exactly what you deserve, but she didn't deserve this...." Marlowe shoved the photo of dead Nikki into Raze's face. "Look at it. Look!"

"Oh, God. I ... I didn't do it, man. I just mo—" Raze shrank in on himself. "Fuck."

Spence ran over, presumably to stop Marlowe, but hesitated at the almost-confession.

"What's that?" Marlowe pushed him an inch farther out. "You just what?"

"M-moved the b-bitch!" Raze trembled, his voice stuttering with terror, his eyes darting downward to the pavement every other second. "I found the bitch all Freddy Kreugerized. Figured you fuckers would do me for it. Alls I did was move the little skank, swear."

Marlowe pulled him in by his legs and held him eye-to-eye by a fistful of shirt. "You know moving a body is a felony."

Raze shivered. "S-so's shovin' my ass out the goddamn window."

Marlowe grumbled and let him drop to the floor. Raze curled up like a frightened child cowering before an angry father. "Did you see anyone with her before you found her?"

"N-no man. I got mah own shit ta' deal with." Raze scrunched up his face. "Shit was a real horror show. You gotta know how it looks ta have her dead in here."

"Yeah, real damn inconvenient," said Spence. "Looks like you're all kinds of broken up over it."

"Man ..." Raze shook his head. "Shit was so messed up. Big-ass coins on her eyes, blood all over. Nikki's gone, man. I didn't wanna go down for it, 'cause I ain't got nothin' ta do with it."

Marlowe stared at him for a long moment. "He's not Seraphim. He may be a moron, but he's not our killer."

Raze slouched, whispering something about Jesus.

Spence looked around. "We need to get a team in here. 'Course, probably a waste of time at this point. Too much contamination."

"Sorry for your loss." Marlowe flicked the photo onto Raze's chest.

Spence pointed at Raze. "Don't think of going anywhere. I'm sendin' a patrol car by soon to take you to the station."

"Aww, shit." said Raze, pouting.

"Maybe, and maybe a few hours with the mug books will jar your memory. We need you to tell us every person Nikki knew—her regular johns, friends, etc."

"Shit," repeated Raze.

Marlowe stared at him. "You help us out, maybe we don't care too much about you moving her. Was there anything else around you tossed?"

"Naw, man." Raze wiped his finger back and forth under his nose. "Just them coins, an' the cross. Stuffed it in her pocket, wrapped her in the sheet an' went down the fire 'scape." He let his head hit the wall behind him with a *thud.*

Marlowe wandered the apartment, not seeing much of interest until he spotted a knife block in the kitchen, missing the large fork. "Seraphim wasn't planning this. He chose the murder weapon for convenience. Nikki was first."

"What's that?" asked Spence.

"Unplanned." Marlowe turned to face the bed from the kitchen, stalking toward it. "He probably came up here acting like a john. The ritual hadn't evolved yet. This was by the seat of the pants."

Spence followed Marlowe to the door and turned back to Raze with a grin. "Oh yeah, you might want to change those pants. See ya round ... Li'l Marv."

In the alley, Marlowe tramped the pavement like a caged animal, clenching and unclenching his fists. "We need to get forensics down here."

"What the hell, Marlowe? Next time we're going to play good cop/bad cop, you might let me in on it. Christ, what's gotten into you?"

"I've seen you do worse with a suspect."

"Yeah, *a suspect*, and one I knew was guilty. First, you ransack a victim's home, now you threaten a witness. This isn't you."

"He's more than a witness. We could bring him in for tampering with a crime scene, but his contacts might help us out. No idea where

Seraphim's trail's going to go. Might be an ace we can play when the time is right."

"Stop ignoring me." Spence glared. "You're better than this. If you let yourself start down this path, you aren't going to like where it takes you. You're a good cop, a good man. Remember who you are, what you're about."

Marlowe tightened his jaw. "Back off, Spence."

"Fine. But you better get a grip on what's eating at you. I'll cover your ass best I can, but you're on a short leash with the lieutenant. You wanna keep Raze on the hook and not file him for movin' the body, that's gonna come back to bite you."

"I'll handle McCann. I'm getting tired of the babysitting, Spence. Do us both a favor and mind your own fucking business."

Spence stepped back as if physically slapped. He fixed Marlowe with a wide-eyed glare before shock faded to concern. He started to say something more, but thought better of it, shook his head and got into the car.

They drove back to the station in silence. Marlowe could tell Spence itched to rehash their argument. Spence never could keep his opinions to himself—one of the things Marlowe liked about him. He never had to wonder what Spence thought, or where he stood with him. Right now, however, as for this subject, enough already.

They arrived at the station and walked right into a shitstorm.

"What's going on?" asked Spence.

"Media got wind of the symbols, the Greek ones. The suicide angle, too. McCann is going nuts in there," said Detective Vines, keeping one eye on the lieutenant's office in case he made a sudden appearance.

When the lieutenant's door flew open, Vines became engrossed in paperwork.

"Gentry, Murray. Get your asses in here," yelled McCann from his office doorway.

Vines appeared ready to crawl under his desk.

They entered and took their seats while the lieutenant slammed around the room. "Goddammit. Have you heard? The media is broadcasting the translations of those Greek words. And worse, they're reporting on the suicide angle. This is a goddamned disaster."

"Someone is feeding the media scraps, a few morsels at a time. Upping the price with each serving, I'm betting," said Spence. "They got onto the coins and cross last week."

"We still have the flowers. And we withheld information on Nikki Baker and Matthew Young. There's plenty still unknown to the public for use with suspects," said Marlowe.

"Plus weed out the crackpots claiming they're Seraphim," said Spence.

"You don't get it, either of you. Every shrink, hospital, and clinic in the state is crawling up my ass. Can you imagine the PR nightmare for us if a crazy kills someone because they quit getting treatment, or stopped their meds because they feared someone there might be the Seraphim?" said the lieutenant.

"Shit," said Spence.

"Exactly. I swear, whoever leaked this will wish they were dead when I get a hold of them." McCann mimicked snapping something in two over his knee and sat down hard behind his desk, the chair groaning under his weight.

"Still no idea who?" asked Marlowe.

"Not a fucking clue," said Lieutenant.

"I've got a friend at WRZK. I'll drive over and see if she knows anything," said Marlowe.

"Like she will offer up a source giving them these kind of ratings," said Spence. "Damn reporters'll sit in the tank for months before they rat."

"Do it. It's worth a try. This has got to stop. The mayor and the captain are on me like ticks wanting this thing solved. I can't take a piss without a reporter waiting to hold my cock. Now this shit. Nothing worse than an overeducated, egomaniac doctor with a valid point."

"Anything turn up connecting the victims yet?" asked Marlowe.

"Not yet. I've got the whole station working on it. If it's there, we'll find it," said the lieutenant.

"It's there. It's got to be." Marlowe wondered if crossing his fingers would help.

MARLOWE PULLED INTO THE PARKING LOT AT WRZK. A TRICKY BIT OF business indeed, getting Natasha Peirce to give up a source … actually, no chance. He needed to think of a different ploy. Time for a little carrot and stick.

Natasha was a looker, much of the reason for her quick rise to on-air reporter. However, to think her a nothing more than a mouthpiece in a skirt would be a huge mistake. Natasha possessed a sharp intellect fueling her curiosity and unmatched ambition.

Marlowe found her hawking over the shoulder of some poor lad in the film room, dictating edits.

"No, pan to the fire. Move it there. Now close up on me. No, no." She grumbled. "Good Lord, what do they pay you for? Do I have to do it myself?"

Natasha struck an impressive presence. She stood a shade shorter than Marlowe, with long strawberry-blond hair and a supermodel's figure, none of which seemed to impress edit boy at the moment.

He threw up his hands, calling surrender. "Fine, you wanna do it? You do it."

"Natasha," said Marlowe.

"Detective Gentry, I wondered when I'd get a visit from you. Care to make a statement?" she said with a sarcastic grin

"Not today, and if you ever want another statement from me or the department, you might want to clue me in on this source of yours."

"I'll be right back. Edit the third take while I'm gone," she said to edit boy, then faced Marlowe. "Source? Why Detective, I have no idea what you're referring to."

"Can it Natasha. Your station has been first with reports since this Seraphim mess began."

"We're good, what can I say," said Natasha, flicking her hair over one shoulder.

"You can tell me who is feeding you the information, for a start."

"Come on, you know I'm not going to do that. It's a solid source. You wouldn't be here if it wasn't."

"Listen Natasha, we have our asses in a sling here. This guy is going to keep on killing, and the details you release make it difficult to weed out all the wackos trying to take credit. Plus, when we catch him, we have that much less to use. Help us out a little."

"I'll tell you what. Promise me an exclusive when you catch him. With both with you *and* the killer. Deal?"

"You know I can't make that kind of promise. Yeah, I'm lead on this, but the higher ups make those calls."

"Well, in that case … sorry, I can't help you." She turned back toward the film room.

"I can promise to do everything in my power to get you the exclusives, and I'll personally feed you bits that won't hurt the investigation," Marlowe said to her back, eliciting a quick about-face.

There's the carrot. Now for the stick.

"However, you know I can make your job as tough as you can make mine. Anger the department, and you can forget any help on future cases. Next time, you might not have a source in your pocket." Marlowe watched the wheels turn and lock into place behind Natasha's baby blues.

"Fine," she said, after a split-second hesitation. "I never met the source. Phone calls only. I sent his payment to a P.O. box. Voice sounded like a young guy. Sorry, I don't have much more."

"It's a start. More than I had two minutes ago. Thanks Natasha."

"Sure thing." Marlowe watched her walk away, and shook his head. He was hanging around Spence way too much.

Natasha had not given him much to go on, but he had a sneaking suspicion he might know the culprit. Nothing solid, he could only keep his eyes and ears peeled in that direction and hope for a slip up. Something told him a young man recently into a wad of cash might want to buy himself something nice.

CHAPTER FIFTEEN

In the weeks since her failed escape attempt, Becca felt like a bird trapped in a cage while the cat prowled hungry below. Michael called repeatedly at work until she assured him she was on her way home. Once home, he watched her every move. His anger flared with the slightest perceived provocation. Fresh bruises marked her with his reprimands.

So, little surprise she anticipated arriving home this evening with apprehension. She claimed to work as late as she thought believable. Michael knew her schedule well enough to sniff out a lie if she pushed it too far.

Becca stepped through the door praying he might be asleep or something, anything to avoid interaction. No such luck; Michael greeted her wearing something that shocked her … a smile.

"Glad you're home," he said. "Big news. I'm up for sergeant."

"That's … that's great. I'm happy for you." Becca tried with all her might to summon a convincing smile.

"For us. The bump in pay will be nice. You'll still make more than me, but …" The last sentence bore a noticeable drop in enthusiasm. "Anyway, I thought we'd celebrate. I put a couple of T-bones on the grill. We can watch the game together."

"What about Ed?" she asked. Eduardo was Michael's partner on patrol, and his usual sidekick.

"Humph, he's got his kids or some shit." Obviously, Ed was his first choice, and he seemed none too pleased with the snub.

Becca rarely ate meat and did not consider herself even a cursory sports fan. Not that Michael cared. This evening centered on him, with her a mere prop for his celebration.

"Well, let me change." Becca went upstairs to the bedroom and changed into sweatpants and long-sleeved t-shirt. This, in its own way, made her more nervous than his outbursts. She harbored no affection for Michael, not for a long time. Any need to fake it had passed years ago.

She knew he met secretly with more than one woman to satisfy his desires. It did not matter; Becca would thank the hussies if she could. Why he seemed so intent on keeping her and maintaining their hollow marriage puzzled her. The psychologist in her supposed it boiled down to control, a need for power.

He lacked such control in his job; it being no secret his commanders viewed him as average at best. She doubted he had any real chance of making sergeant. Michael did not possess leadership skills. He made a good foot soldier, but anything more should remain above his pay grade.

As Becca entered the kitchen, Michael finished off another beer and placed the bottle next to empties on the counter. She blanched at the sight.

"Here ya go." He handed her a plate. The meat looked rare—just how Michael liked it. The runny meat's mere appearance made Becca queasy.

"Thank you," she said, trying to mask her revulsion.

"Come on, I've got a hundred bucks riding on the Raiders."

Becca nibbled on the steak and jumped each time Michael screamed at the television. He went through four more beers during his meal. His speech began to slur, his tirades at a dropped pass grew more vehement.

Another six-pack later, Michael appeared well lit. The Raiders did not cover the spread, driving him into a fury.

"Fuck the Raiders. They never cover. I must be fucking crazy, betting on that bunch of losers." Michael clicked off the set and slammed the remote down on the coffee table.

Becca's fear steadily increased with every passing minute. She knew this play well. It wouldn't be long now before she became the focus of his irritation. Yet, surprisingly, he calmed and moved to sit close to her. Her body stiffened; she pushed herself into the cushion.

"You know … it's been a long time," he said in a slurred, soft voice. "I know I'm not always easy to get along with, but I still love you." He nudged his head against her neck, making her skin crawl.

"Michael." She wiggled free of his embrace. "This was nice, and I am so proud of you. You're great at your job, and I'm sure you'll get the promotion, but I'm really tired. I just want to go to bed."

"Exactly what I had in mind." Michael clumsily pulled her shirt above her mid-section.

"Michael. No." She shocked herself with the rebuke. Becca pushed around him, but he caught her arm and slung her back onto the sofa, the force whipping her head back.

"No? You tell me no?" His face went crimson, his grip digging into her skin. He tore her sweats with a loud ripping, spread her legs, and struggled to push his pants to his knees. Pressing himself to her groin, he tried to nudge her underwear to one side.

Becca's terror blinded her to any possible repercussions. She shoved Michael hard and kicked out with all her strength. Her foot connected squarely with his testicles, a soft *pop* rewarding her effort.

Michael fell to the floor moaning, hands holding his crotch, his face bright red. He flopped about and tried to get to his feet, but collapsed during the attempt. Becca dashed for the stairs.

"You fucking bitch. I'll kill you," Michael screamed.

Becca grabbed her cell phone from the nightstand, flew into the bathroom, locked the door, and dialed 911.

"Becca," Michael yelled. He entered the bedroom and stood outside the bathroom door breathing pure hatred. "I'll bust this fucking door down. Open it, now."

"My husband is trying to kill me. Please help me." She jumped back and dropped the phone as the door thudded from an impact. Her only salvation was that Michael could barely stand, much less ram through the door. He tried several more times, each collision causing the ships on the walls to rock on their seas, only paintings, but the tidal wave was all too real.

Finally, the room beyond went quiet. Becca huddled on the toilet seat, clutching her shattered phone. She prayed the call went through. Soon, Michael would try again, and, drunk or not, the door would not hold forever.

An hour passed, and Becca began to lose hope. They did not get the call. No one was coming to save her. If Michael came through the door, she would fight. She would have to … and fight for her life.

Becca heard him moving outside. She picked up the plunger and frowned. Not much of a weapon, but the bathroom did not exactly house an armory. Hairspray. Good substitute for mace, she thought. Too bad she no longer smoked; a lighter could make it a mini-flamethrower.

The door handle jiggled. Becca braced and prepared herself.

A knock on the door, and a voice, "Miss, you alright in there? It's Officer Cotts, open up. It's okay now."

Becca cracked the door and peeked outside. A police officer stood looking at her with either concern or impatience, difficult to discern which, from his naturally pinched nose and narrow eyes. "It's okay, I promise. We have Michael downstairs."

"He tried to kill me," she said, finally allowing the tears to stream.

"Now, I'm sure that's not true. I've known Mike for ages. He's a hothead, but that's all."

They walked down the stairs. Michael stood with two other officers in the living room. They were laughing.

I'm going to throw up.

"He tried to rape me," she said in a despondent voice.

"What? You're his wife, he can't rape you," said Cotts, an incredulous expression on his face.

She stared at him, mouth agape, eyes wide. Then understanding slid down her face. They would do nothing. They would protect their own and rationalize her accusations away. Calling them only delayed the inevitable. Maybe she survived tonight, but what about tomorrow, or next week? Becca realized now more than ever, she lived on borrowed time.

"You have to understand how much pressure our job puts on us. Michael's out there every day risking his life to protect you and everyone in this county. You've got to cut him some slack. Stay out of his way when he's in one of these moods. You'll be fine, okay?" Cotts patted her on the back, his condescending tone pushing her lower.

Becca could not speak. She simply stared past Cotts, watching the patrol cars' lights spin round and round. The alternating red and blue flashes lulled her into a trance. Her expression shifted from distressed to vacuous, all feeling drained away. She felt like one of those plodding zombies in a late night horror flick. Dead, without emotion, hungry for something she would never find.

After the police left, Becca tried and failed to compose herself. Michael would stay away for a few days, of that much she was able to insist on. She called Rachel, not wanting to be alone right now. Possibly a mistake. Rachel cared deeply for her, but played the overprotective mother's role a little too well. Becca just needed her presence, not her endless advice and admonishments.

Rachel rushed right over. She took Becca into her arms, cooing everything would be all right. Like a child waking from a nightmare, Becca desperately needed to hear those words, and for now, would even pretend to believe they were true.

After sitting Becca down, Rachel's motherly instincts kicked into full gear. "You most certainly will not be going to work tomorrow. You're a mess. Look at you. That man tried to rape you, might very well have killed you. Monica can call your patients. We can close down for one day. Jesus, you deserve that much."

"No, I need to go. I need something normal, something I can control. I feel so helpless, so goddamn weak. I need to work."

Rachel softened. "I guess I can understand that. At least cancel a few, make it a half day."

"Alright, have Monica reschedule my after lunch appointments." She knew she spoke, but the words seemed to emanate from somewhere far away.

"That's my girl. Come here." Rachel enveloped Becca in a crushing hug. "I love you, and I'm always here for you."

"I know you are. Thank you, Rach."

The next morning, Becca tried to keep everything normal. She needed to stick to her daily routine, nose to the grindstone. Rachel proved a godsend. She cooked breakfast and had piping hot coffee waiting.

They took separate cars to the hospital after Becca assured her she would be fine alone tonight. She whipped the Volvo into her designated spot, took a deep breath, and headed for the building. As much as she tried, however, she could not get last night out of her head. The feel of his hands on her, like a stranger's.

You're his wife.

She still heard that phase in her mind, whirling around like a tormented ghost haunting the bell tower. Becca did not want to be his wife, not anymore. She hadn't for a long time. Trapped with no way out, if she ran, he would find her. He really could kill her and get away with it. He would make up some story, and his cop friends would sweep it under the rug.

She knew now, without any doubt ... Michael would kill her. Intentionally or by accident, it was only a matter of time. One beating would get out of hand and go a little too far. Only a matter of time.

Becca wanted nothing more in that moment than to turn around and run. Give up her home, her career, and run. Flee to some place where Michael could never find her. With his contacts and access to databases, did any such place exist?

She could change her name and take on a whole new identity. Silly, she would have no idea how to accomplish such a thing—new Social

Security card, driver's license, and so many other matters. This was not some movie where she could track down the shady guy in a back alley to draft her a new life. No way around it, Becca remained a captive to her fear.

A thought seeped into her mind, one she never believed she would ever consider. One way out that Michael possessed no power to stop. Even death must be preferable to the hell she lived in. Every day, she coached patients through this same despair, but Max Bannon had it right, everything seemed so much different when you were the one in the shitstorm, and not some hypothetical exercise, or observing someone else's life.

As she walked, the idea frightened her less and less. Like opening a door and feeling sunshine when all she had ever known was the cold, the fear disappeared in that instant. A power to control her own fate gained a foothold. No longer to be at the mercy of another, but take matters into her own hands.

With her mind focused on such dire thoughts, she stumbled off the paved path and right into one of the hospital's groundskeepers.

"Sorry," she mumbled, barely glancing at the man.

GABRIEL'S HANDS STUNG, HIS TEMPLES THROBBED, HIS STOMACH TENSED. He steadied himself and watched the woman walk away. He looked upward and smiled, another chosen led to him.

After signaling Paul that he was taking his break, he followed the woman into the hospital, staying well back. A needless ploy, she paid no attention as she hurried down the hall and took the elevator to the fifth floor. Gabriel noted it and proceeded to the stairs. Once on the fifth floor, he strolled along the corridor, glancing nonchalantly into each office.

In the third office on the right, he saw her put on a white coat and take up a clipboard. He read the plaque beside the entrance—Patient Counseling Services - Dr. Rebecca Drenning.

The blessing eased, but would remain, quiet and waiting. Gabriel returned to his duties, letting his mind meditate on the tenets of his worship. The sculpted marble faces and majestic physiques of the gods stood before him, expectant of his offering.

The doctor's pain beckoned him, crying out to him for release. Only a little longer must she suffer. Soon, the good doctor would receive his blessing and find all her cares relieved.

CHAPTER SIXTEEN

Unable to reschedule that day's appointments, Becca slogged through her sessions. She counseled her patients on autopilot and registered little of what they said. Her mind, lost in a fog of dark thoughts, could not focus. That evening, she struggled to sleep, but found herself staring into the black above her, the same bleak shade swirling within her.

The next day, Rachel worked her magic and cleared Becca's afternoon. She had to admit, in her present state of mind, she couldn't give her patients the attention they deserved, and worse, felt in no mood to listen to their problems. Not that her sense of sympathy lessened with her own concerns, but all the misery and hopelessness —so many looking to her for answers—all compounded her powerlessness, her growing despair.

Becca did not want to return yet again to an empty, silent house filled with the echoes of anger and pain, so instead, she decided to visit her mother. She hadn't seen her mother since her birthday, and they had not spoken in over a month.

They were not estranged, just busy. Mary Tolbert, attorney extraordinaire, kept a more hectic agenda than even Becca's. Plus, with her court schedule, even sneaking in a brief phone conversation proved challenging. Becca hoped, with a little luck, she might snatch a few minutes with dear ol' mom.

Why this sudden need to see her? Perhaps not so peculiar, she thought. After all, children always ran to mother when hurt or frightened. Becca felt both. A thought of Michael pressed ice into her heart. Maybe she needed to say goodbye before ...

She stepped up to the reception desk at Morry, Tolbert & Stalk. "Hi Sarah, is my mother in the office today?"

"Dr. Drenning," said the woman with a bright smile. Sarah had sat at that desk for twenty years, greeting clients and answering phones. She predated most of the attorneys at the firm.

"Thought I'd surprise her. If she's here."

"She'll love that. You're in luck, Mary's in today. I think a hearing got canceled last minute. Let me ring her." Sarah punched in the number. "Mary, you have a guest. You're daughter's here."

Sarah yanked the phone away from her ear. Becca heard an exclamation from the other end. "I think she's a wee bit excited to see you. You can go on back, same office as always." Sarah grinned.

Becca headed down the hall, nodding to secretaries and attorneys. She knew most of them and stopped here and there to inquire after families. The attorneys, in expensive suits and dresses, all appeared so confident. She envied them. Still, she more than most knew the outward masks hid dark places and secret fears. Becca wondered what worries and horrors she might uncover with any one of them on her sofa, under her scrutiny.

She entered her mother's office, which never failed to impress. A large oak desk sat before a wall-length floor-to-ceiling window, a myriad of skyscrapers glinting beyond in the afternoon sun. Numerous awards and plaques of appreciation adorned the walls. Photos of her mother with Ronald Reagan, Jimmy Carter, Bill Clinton, Bush one and two, were proudly displayed. Not one to hide her accomplishments, Becca's mother.

Mary rotated in her plush leather chair and practically leapt over her desk when she noticed Becca standing in the doorway. She hugged her tightly and stepped back, appraising her, a hand on each shoulder.

"You look tired, angel. Aren't you sleeping? Can't one of those doctors prescribe something?"

"It's been a tough week mom."

"Well, lie down on my couch and tell Dr. Mom all about it."

"Hey, I thought I was the psychologist."

"Tsk, not today you're not."

Becca sighed, no use beating around the bush. This was why she had come after all. Still, she was unsure of how much to tell her mother. If she told her about the beatings and the rape attempt, Mary would be on the phone to the Chief of Police, hell, maybe the Mayor, before Becca could stop her.

"You know things haven't been good between me and Michael for a while now, but recently they have gotten worse. I can't take much more."

Becca shook her head and began to cry.

Mary moved close, putting an arm around her daughter. "Listen to me right now. You stop crying, not another tear." Mary took Becca by the hand and guided her to the sofa. "I know a thing or two about bad marriages. The trick is to get out while the getting's good. Don't stay until things are so bad one of you do or say something you can't take back."

Becca averted her face, hoping Mary did not see her guilty expression. "I know. I'm just scared. I don't think I'm strong enough."

"Nonsense," Mary said, "I doubt you remember this, but when you were about six you decided you deserved a puppy. Your father adamantly opposed the idea, but you persisted. He thought himself clever, your father. He knew someone with a German Shepard that had recently had a litter of puppies. The momma dog acted mean on her good days, but with puppies to protect, she became Satan incarnate."

"I remember. The momma dog's name ... Precious." Becca smiled at the memory.

"Oh, the irony." Mary shook her head. "Anyway, your father's devious plan was to show you how dangerous dogs could be, and how hard they were to deal with. He felt certain you would run screaming and that would be the end of any talk of puppies. Oh boy, he couldn't have been more wrong.

"You walked into the pen, your father and the dog's owner standing close enough to snatch you out of harm's way, and approached dear old momma. She lunged, the chain restraining her snapped like a cracked whip. You didn't flinch. With one eye on a chubby, white furball—a female pup you had already set your heart on —you turned to momma dog, one hand on your hip, pointed right at her and said, 'You stop that right now Precious. I'm taking that puppy home. I promise to take good care of her and love her with all my heart. I know you don't want to lose your baby, but you can visit anytime you want, and we'll come to visit you. Now you settle down.' You sounded like a little adult. Your father said he could barely keep from busting out laughing.

"The owner's jaw hit the ground when Precious stopped barking and sat back on her haunches. You reached out before he could get to you, and by the time he placed a hand on your shoulder to jerk you away, you were scratching Precious behind the ears. She licked your hand and then promptly laid down in the shade."

"She could have taken my hand off." Becca laughed while looking at her hand, surprised it was still there.

"Could have, but your desire proved stronger than your fear. That stubborn, willful child is now a beautiful young woman. The same streak still runs through you, I see it. That fearless little girl will jump out if you look for her. She isn't hiding, and she isn't gone. She wants you to find her. Remember who you are, who you want to be."

A crushing weight lifted. Becca stared at her hand a moment more, and made a fist, unable to help but smile. "Okay, maybe you are the psychologist here after all. I actually do feel better. Thank you Mom, I knew I came here for a good reason."

"Mom will always have a Band-Aid ready for your boo boos." Mary stood, her arms crossed, and looking rather pleased with herself. "I'm always here for you, whatever you decide. If you want to leave him, and I think you should, you have a place with me."

"It's complicated, Mom, but thank you. I know now I can handle it and find a way out of this mess."

"That's my girl," said Mary, hugging Becca tightly. "We've been missing each other like ships in the night for far too long. Next week, Thursday, we're going for dinner. I won't take no for an answer."

Becca headed home feeling more at ease. She guessed all mothers possessed an uncanny ability to calm their children, and children never grew too old to need their mother's soothing voice and wise counsel. A soft lullaby after a nightmare, Mary had sung just the song Becca needed to hear. Surely, Michael was no more dangerous than an ill-tempered German Shepherd to a little girl. She'd stood up to the monster once; she'd do it again.

Once home, she took a beer from the fridge, sat on the sofa, and propped her feet up. It relieved her to know she would not need to work at avoiding Michael tonight.

Becca knew neither her mother nor Rachel fully understood why she could not just up and leave Michael. They had not been there the night he chased her down. Nor were they with her daily to appreciate the level of control he wielded over her. It shamed her, but it was true.

She had no idea how she planned to deal with him. The head-on approach would be suicide, possibly literally, and after her visit with Mary, Becca now firmly rejected suicide as an option.

Now, the thought of killing herself seemed like a mental exercise. She didn't think she'd have gone through with it, but in that moment, it had seemed ... reasonable. A healthy mind snapped back from the precipice. She flicked her fingernail at the bottle, staring at the suds, thinking of patients who couldn't.

It frightened her to think on how far she had fallen. She needed to find a way of escaping Michael and gaining her freedom.

The first step, she knew: maintain resolve. Michael would return home and things would revert to their version of normal. She needed to remember last night, not the horror and fear, but the fact it happened. Like hanging her little black dress up when she worked out, the size four she was determined to remain able to wear, she needed motivation to stay focused, stay the course. Becca could not allow herself to fall back into acceptance.

Recent events had left her exhausted, she did not realize how much until she stood. Turning in early seemed like a great idea. Her mother guessed correctly, Becca slept only in fits and turns lately, and not a wink the last few nights.

Becca went to the bathroom and washed her makeup off. After placing a Fiona Apple CD into the stereo, she set it on repeat and slipped into her PJs. The bed greeted her with sweet, soft comfort. She fell asleep before her head sank fully into the pillow.

GABRIEL PLACED HIS TOOLS INTO THE TOTE BAG—BOLT GUN AND cutters, hoist and gambrel, knife, plastic ties, wrap, duct tape, white sheet. He took his Bible from the shelf and sat on the bed. Jeremiah 29:11: For I know the thoughts that I think toward you, sayeth the LORD, thoughts of peace, and not of evil, to give you an expected end.

Take me as your instrument. Use my hand to deliver your peace to the sufferer and spare her the true death, so she may find rebirth in your glory.... Amen.

He grabbed his bag, walked out the door, and made his way to the store. In the alley sat Henry's pick-up, which he rarely drove, an ancient Mazda B2000 older than Gabriel.

Every time he used it, he heard Henry's voice in the back of his mind. "Use it whenever you want, but I warn ya, don't go too far. Damned thing's as likely to break down as get you home."

Gabriel did not like borrowing the truck due to its condition, and because he had previously only driven the tractor around the farm, and Mr. Hayes's truck once or twice. On his previous *missions,* the bus had sufficed, but in this case, necessity demanded his own transportation. He took it slow and drove to the hospital.

He remembered where Dr. Drenning parked her car, and after punch out, he sat in the truck and waited, an eye on her Volvo. Once she left the parking lot, he followed. The doctor possessed a lead foot, and keeping pace in the sluggish Mazda proved a chore. He was certain he had lost her more than once, but soon sighted her again, darting in and out of the rush hour traffic.

Dr. Drenning's home was in one of the more affluent subdivisions of the city where the rust bucket he drove would certainly be noticed, so he circled the neighborhood at a distance, getting a feel for the area's layout. After pinpointing the doctor's house, he pulled to a stop and examined the street map he had taken from Henry's.

The house abutted a wooded area, which according to the map stretched some distance to the east and ran parallel to Hillcrest Road. Gabriel proceeded down Hillcrest to an abandoned lot, formerly serving the now defunct Sam's Salvage, and left the truck. A trek through the woods brought him right to Emerald Lane.

He walked along the woodline, staying out of sight. Dressed in jeans and button-down shirt, he did not stick out as a criminal type, but the community was small. Very likely all the neighbors knew each other and might take note of a stranger.

Gabriel felt confident the gods would shield him from any seeking to disrupt their plan, but even so, no harm in being cautious. He made certain of his position behind Dr. Drenning's house and reentered the woods. Now, he needed only to await the cover of darkness.

When night fell, it brought with it a multitude of stars, all shining bright like candles lit especially for Gabriel's ritual. Standing at the edge of the forest, he watched the lights go out one by one. He waited another hour and crept to the back door.

Using his small crowbar, he pried the door open with minimal noise. He paused and listened. No sound stirred to indicate movement within the house, or that anyone heard his entrance.

With the curtains drawn, he needed his flashlight to navigate the darkness. He moved up the stairs and into the bedroom. Gabriel hovered at the bedside, gazing down on her sleeping form. He removed two coins and the small silver cross he had fashioned from his bag and placed the items on the nightstand in preparation for later.

The blessing had been a faint itch at the back of his skull since encountering the doctor. Once he looked into her eyes and prepared to bestow it upon her, the blessing would come again with full intensity. He braced himself for the touch of the gods. With the bolt gun raised, he leaned forward, bringing the tip toward her forehead.

A cell phone vibrated atop the bedside table, pumping out rock music. Gabriel nearly dropped the gun and jumped out of his skin. The woman stirred. Groggy, she groaned and rubbed her eyes.

Gabriel stumbled backwards, alarm stuttering his steps. The blaring phone covered the noise of his clumsy retreat. He bumped against closet doors, reached behind his back, and opened them without taking his eyes off the doctor. He wedged himself inside an instant before she sat up and grabbed the phone.

"Hello," she said in a sluggish voice. "Mom? No, it's okay, I turned in early." The doctor raked fingers through her hair and listened to a warbled voice on the other end. "You were right; I was really worn out.... Yeah, I'm feeling much better. Everything is going to be fine. I really believe that now...." She paused for a moment, listening. "I know you are, I promise to call if need anything.... Thanks mom, I love you."

Listening to her, hearing the optimism in her voice, Gabriel felt the sting seep from his hands as if drawn from heated water. The tightness in his stomach and head faded.

The blessing had ... disappeared. He sensed nothing.

Shocked by the blessing's sudden absence, Gabriel fell to his knees. Panic engulfed him, tightening his throat. His body shuddered, his elbows knocked against the wall behind him. What was happening? How could he have been mistaken?

A small lamp atop the nightstand clicked on, sending light through the slatted door. Gabriel held his breath. The woman's head swung in his direction. Not fear, but puzzlement pinched her features. She crept toward his position, her shadow dancing through the glowing slats. The doors rattled and pulled ajar. A crease of light widened inches from his face. Gabriel crawled back into the closet and stood.

She flung the doors apart. Her mouth gaped. No question she saw his shadowy outline trembling in the darkness. Gabriel aimed the flashlight's beam into her eyes, disorienting her. He lunged forward, tackling her to the carpet and slamming the butt of the flashlight into the side of her head. She fell to the floor and lay still. Reacting on impulse, he lifted her into his arms and laid her unconscious body on the bed.

Gabriel fought to control his confusion. Hunched forward, hands on knees, he tried to catch his breath and calm the anxiety. The door seemed to have relocated; he could not find the exit. Frantic, his thoughts spun in a kaleidoscope of fractured images—wings flapped, stone eyes stared. Sights and sounds filled his mind in a maddening progression.

Finally, he regained some measure of control and hurriedly gathered his bag. He staggered from the bedroom, dimly aware of his surroundings, and made his way outside.

Once in the woods, Gabriel wandered for hours. Every tree looked the same. Every trail seemed to lead in circles. Unsure of his location, he roamed directionless until a pinprick of light caught his eye in the distance. Guided by the faint illumination, he exited the forest and found himself on Hillcrest Road more than a mile from the salvage lot. He staggered to Henry's truck in a fog.

Not until he arrived at his apartment and put away his tools did it occur to him that he had left the coins and cross on the table. He sat at his small desk, wringing his hands, and tried to understand what happened, what went wrong.

Had the gods abandoned him? Did he anger them somehow? How would they show their displeasure with this failure?

Gabriel felt alone. The gods withheld their favor and their guidance. He prayed for hours, but no answers came.

CHAPTER SEVENTEEN

Becca woke the next morning with a vicious headache. She rubbed her fingers across a large knot on the side of her head. The slightest touch sent sharp pain radiating outward from the lump. She blinked at the open closet and clothes littering the floor.

She staggered to the bathroom and pulled on her robe. The knot looked like a goose laid an egg on her head. A thin line of blood trailed from beneath her hair to below her chin. After wetting a washcloth in the sink, she rubbed the streak away.

What the hell happened to me last night?

Becca faintly remembered a dream involving a bright light shining in her eyes, but the dream, along with most of last night, remained fuzzy. Maybe she sleepwalked and mistook the closet for a doorway.

Returning to the bedroom, she scanned the area, looking for anything else she might've broken. The standing lamp in the corner leaned to one side, but she did not see how it could have inflicted such an injury. A small bloodstain on the rug near the closet caught her eye, coming with a flash of a silhouette. She turned toward the bed and saw the items lying on the nightstand. Definitely not hers, and not Michael's as far as she knew.

Strange coins. A woman holding a what? Pitchfork? She did not recognize the man's face on the opposite side either. Confused, she turned a coin between her fingers. How did they get here? It seemed somehow familiar. *I've seen these coins somewhere—*

Realization hit her like a bucket of ice water. The coin slipped from her fingers seconds before she covered her mouth with both hands and trembled. Her gut did a backflip as she sank to sit on the edge of the bed.

A serial killer was in my house.

Lately, every TV and radio station was inundated with it. People at the hospital chatted on their breaks about it. Hell, Rachel made a remark about him two days ago when the suicide angle went by on the news, something about the police interviewing mental health professionals. Unless someone did not own a television, or never watched or read the news, they knew every detail of the case. A few of the dedicated cable news channels covered the story twenty-four hours a day with every type of analyst opining their theories. She remembered the reports instructing anyone with information concerning the Seraphim to phone Birmingham Metro Homicide.

For ten minutes she stared at her phone before remembering what it was.

"Homicide," said a gruff male voice.

"Yes, my name is Dr. Rebecca Drenning. I live at 2211 Emerald Lane. I think … I think the Seraphim Killer attacked me last night."

"Gentry," called Officer Kirkpatrick, holding the phone between neck and shoulder. "Got a woman on the horn, a Dr. Rebecca Drenning. Says Seraphim attacked her last night. You want to take it? Sounds like a crackpot wanting attention to me. Address is 2211 Emerald Lane."

"Nice neighborhood." Marlowe took his feet off his desk and sat up. "You say she's a doctor? Could be a crank, but worth checking out. Tell her we're on the way."

"Doctor? Detectives are en route to your home. No problem, just sit tight."

"Have a team on standby. If it's for real, I want forensics ready to work the scene. Send a couple of patrols to do a ride through of the area, and get me everything you can on Drenning."

"On it," said Kirkpatrick.

"Spence, you catch that?" asked Marlowe.

"Yep, right behind you," said Spence, grabbing his coat.

Normally, Marlowe wouldn't personally investigate a tip unless the patrols turned up something concrete, but at present, they were batting zero and needed a hit. His gamble with Raze was a close call. He'd run with the story of the killer moving the body for the time being. Panic. A first time impulse. Spence had been right, forensics got nothing from the place but sick at all the luminol glowing everywhere. Body fluids from a hundred johns all mixed into a useless Jackson Pollack on the walls, floor, and ceiling. Marlowe shuddered at the thought.

They hovered as Kirkpatrick ran a background on Dr. Drenning. When it came back clean, they headed out.

Spence sipped his coffee as Marlowe navigated the snaking suburban roads. Some theologian on the radio espoused his opinion on the symbolism in the Seraphim's ritual—wrong on all counts. Marlowe reached down and switched it off.

"Think there's anything to this?" asked Spence. "No one's gotten away from this guy yet. If the attack happened last night, why is she calling this morning?"

"No idea," replied Marlowe, his stare fixed on the road ahead.

"You're Mr. Talkative."

"Just hoping for a break. I felt certain the suicide angle would have turned something up by now. There's a link there, pissing me off we can't find it."

"We have everyone on it, and so far we haven't found a single doctor, therapist, preacher, friend—hell, not even a mailman in common." Spence popped the last bite of his bacon, egg, and cheese biscuit into his mouth.

"Makes no sense. How is he finding them? What's his connection to them? He works or frequents places where he is privy to people divulging their problems. We've listed every possible source. We're missing something. Some avenue for counseling or comfort we haven't thought of yet." Marlowe reached up and adjusted the rearview mirror for the umpteenth time.

"Does anything concerning this case make sense? The guy hacks people up and seems ashamed or shy about it, covering up their privates. He blends Greek and Christian symbolism in no discernable method, and stuffs wild flowers in for good measure. It's pot luck, throwing in the kitchen sink."

"No. There's a purpose behind it." Marlowe drummed his fingers on the wheel. "Every symbol and detail means something to Seraphim. I can't seem to get my mind around it."

"Well, bud, if you can't, don't look at me. This puzzle work, that's your area."

"And right now I'm getting my ass kicked."

Spence clicked the radio on, switching it to a music station. "Ya know what they say, man. Misery loves company. You've got plenty of it on that account."

Spence's comment made the gun under his arm heavier. He thought of Paige and clenched his jaw. For an instant, he resented her. Because of her, he suffered. He let it go with a hard breath.…

No. I can't do that to her. This bastard is getting to me.

They pulled into the driveway at 2211 Emerald Lane. Not quite as grand as the Meadowview house, but impressive nonetheless. Spence whistled through his teeth.

"Whew, nice house. What does this gal do?"

"Shrink, psychologist. Works at the hospital. Husband's a cop," said Marlowe.

"You know him?"

"Not personally. Kirkpatrick said he's volatile, bunch of excessive force complaints lodged against him. Nothing stuck. Good for a hammer, but no finesse. Name's Michael Drenning, drives patrol for county, and been with them a while. Up for sergeant, according to Kirkpatrick."

"Why didn't he make the call? Seems he would want to be in the loop, especially if he's bucking for a promotion."

"I wondered the same thing," said Marlowe. "Let's see what we can learn."

Dr. Drenning met them on the front porch. Pretty woman … more than pretty. Long, dark hair purposely arranged over a nasty knot that still showed through. Maybe five-five, with a nice figure obvious even beneath her t-shirt reading *Property of UAB Medical School* and dark green scrub pants. Something in her eyes and posture reminded Marlowe of Katy.

She led them into the living room. The doctor seemed unsure of what to do with her hands, fidgeting, picking at her shirt, and constantly pushing her hair behind one ear.

"Can I get you anything? A soft drink, tea or something? The tea is sweet." Her voice sounded layered with fatigue more than fear.

"Tea would be nice, thank you," said Marlowe.

"Nothing for me thanks." Spence peered sideways at Marlowe as Becca walked to the kitchen and wiggled his eyebrows.

Marlowe returned the look with a glare of his own. Still, he watched her move into the kitchen. She extended an arm to a high cabinet and retrieved two glasses. Her shirt lifted a few inches above her waistline, revealing bruises shaded from purple to fading yellow.

Becca returned and handed Marlowe the tea before taking a seat on the sofa. "I'm not sure what I can tell you. I didn't see anything. I remember hearing a noise in the closet. I went over and opened it. A bright light flashed in my eyes, and then nothing until I woke this morning. I don't even remember staggering to the bed. I thought it was a dream until I felt the bump on my head and found the weird cross and coins on the table. I still don't quite believe the Seraphim from the news attacked me, but it unnerved me enough to call you."

"You're very lucky, Dr. Drenning. We can't confirm it was Seraphim until the lab does some tests. Let's assume it is until we know different. Any idea why he might set his sights on you?" Marlowe narrowed his eyes and watched her reaction closely.

"No, none. I know the news said he goes after depressed people— people close to suicide. I'm certainly not suicidal."

"You haven't seen anyone, or talked to anyone, about problems? No consultation with fellow doctors about personal concerns?"

"No. I guess you know I'm a psychologist. I help others with emotional and mental problems all day." Dr. Drenning tapped her foot and thrummed her fingers against her thigh.

"Doesn't mean you don't have some of your own. You're human after all," said Spence.

"True, but I don't. Nothing serious anyway, and I haven't spoken with anyone about depression."

"Maybe you had a tough day recently and spoke to a friend about it. Someone who might have off-handedly mentioned it to someone else," said Marlowe.

"No, nothing like that," Becca said, twirling her hair around an index finger.

"You don't remember fighting the assailant off? A struggle?" asked Marlowe.

"No, I really don't remember anything. It's all just a few flashes in my memory, nothing clear. Probably a man, that's all I can say for sure."

"And you didn't get a look at him? Maybe some small detail— tattoo on a hand, a scar on his arm, anything."

"The light in my eyes made it impossible to see. It was so bright. I'm sorry, I'm not being very helpful," she said, frustration clear in her voice.

"Probably hit her with a Maglite." Spence winced at the mark on her head. "Cops carry those."

Becca's face paled.

"You're doing fine," said Marlowe, lightly touching her knee. He quickly withdrew his hand after catching a sly wink from Spence.

"Thanks. I'm trying. Do you think he might come back?"

"I don't think so. But just in case, we'll station an officer outside the house for the next couple of days. Do you want someone to shadow you at the hospital?"

"No, there's security. I'll be fine at work. But I would appreciate you stationing someone outside the house. I'll sleep better knowing they're there." She smiled weakly and returned Marlowe's gesture, softly squeezing his forearm. "Thank you for helping me."

"Just doing our job, ma'am," he said, stiff, with discomfort only Spence seemed to notice.

And notice he did. Spence was getting far too much enjoyment out of this for Marlowe's liking.

"Your husband's with County isn't he? Where was he when this happened?"

"Huh, h-he's out of town for few days." Becca glanced away, a slight blush on her cheeks.

Marlowe's eyes narrowed with suspicion, but he let the line of inquiry drop. "We'll keep you updated on what we find, but don't worry. I think you'll be perfectly safe." Marlowe handed her his card. "Call if you need anything, Dr. Drenning—day or night. My cell number is on the back. If you see anyone you don't know around your house, or notice anything out of the ordinary, give us a buzz."

"Thank you … and call me Becca."

As they walked from the house, Marlowe could feel Spence's eyes on him. He tried to ignore him, but it quickly grew irritating.

"What?" he asked sharply.

"Getting a little cozy with the good doctor weren't you bud?"

"I don't know what you're talking about. I asked the relevant questions. You know, like cops do."

"Mmm hmm, right. Oh Detective Gentry, thank you for riding in on your white horse to save me from the bad man. You're welcome little lady, just doing my job." Spence leaned back, laughing himself silly.

"Screw you." Marlowe sped up in an attempt to put some distance between them.

"I'm telling you, sparks were flying. You two didn't even know I was in the room. All googly eyes locked on each other. How long since you had a date, anyway?" asked Spence, matching Marlowe's pace.

"She's married, for Christ's sake."

"Happily?"

"Screw you … twice."

Spence laughed until he had trouble catching his breath. Even Marlowe smiled and shook his head. He did hope Spence choked on his coffee.

With his hand on the door latch, Marlowe noticed Koop and Jonas unloading their gear from the Forensics van. He let go and walked over.

"Koop, what are you doing here? No dead bodies," said Marlowe. "I only needed a sweep for prints and fibers."

"His majesty the lieutenant decreed I oversee all evidence in this case, from inception through world's end."

"Glad you're on the job. You've been around since the world's beginning, so you of all people should know the end when you see it," said Spence.

Koop scoffed at the remark, but refused to dignify it with a response … for once.

"Good idea. Coins and cross are in the bedroom. Teams are working the entire house."

"I'll take them back to the lab and have them compared against the others. You're thinking definitely Seraphim?"

"Looks like," said Marlowe.

"Well, better get to it," said Koop, moving toward the house.

Marlowe watched Jonas pulling equipment from the van. As he stepped to the passenger side door, Jonas reached in and retrieved an expensive looking leather jacket. He slung it over his shoulders and thrust in his arms, running his hands over the supple fabric.

Appreciating a nice new coat?

"Jonas, sweet jacket." Marlowe casually stepped up behind him.

Jonas jumped. "Scared the shit out of me, man. I … I mean Detective." He hesitated a second "Huh, thanks."

"New isn't it? Still has that great new leather smell."

"Had it awhile, don't wear it much. Too heavy. Doesn't get cold enough most of the time. Alabama winters, ya know."

Jonas, obviously nervous, propped one foot on the van's side step, tied his shoes and tried to avoid eye contact with Marlowe. Marlowe was not certain if Jonas's unease rose from his shyness around superiors or something else. When he noticed the brand new Nike tennis shoes, he had a much better idea which.

"Run a marathon in those, and it'd feel like clouds under your feet."

"Yeah, I guess." He was giving it away—the subtle twitches, the thin line of perspiration in this cold.

"Natasha Peirce is paying you well, huh?"

Jonas could not hide his surprise. He stiffened and refused to glance Marlowe's way. "I don't know what you're talking about."

"No? Selling info on the Seraphim to reporters is something that slips your mind?"

"N-no w-way. I just …" His ashen face and shaking hands were all the confession Marlowe needed.

"Save it. I'm tempted to run you in for obstruction and interfering with an investigation."

"No … how did you … how did you know?"

"I didn't." Marlowe smiled. "Not for certain. Not until now."

"Shit," said Jonas, hanging his head.

"Since turning you in to the lieutenant would mean Koop's name got mud on it as well, here's what's going to happen. You'll go back to the morgue and tell Dr. Koopman you're quitting. Give him whatever reason you want. Then leave, no notice, just leave."

"I can't. I'm only an intern, and it goes toward my scholarship. I won't get another job if I quit without giving notice. Dr. Koopman will be pissed."

"I promise it will be far less than the lieutenant. If he gets wind of this, you might see jail time."

Jonas paled further. "I … I could say you're mistaken. You … you don't have any proof."

Marlowe had to admire the balls on the kid. "Yeah, you could do that. Who do you think they'll believe? A decorated senior homicide detective, or a lab geek intern?"

When Jonas offered no reply, Marlowe said, "Glad we have an understanding. Take care, Jonas."

CHAPTER EIGHTEEN

After the detectives left, Becca allowed her emotions free reign. She sat on the sofa, hugging her knees against her chest. It must be Michael trying to frighten her, to let her know how far he would go to keep her. It worked. Terror laced through her every thought. As a cop, Michael could find out everything about the Seraphim, even information the police withheld from the public and the press. He could kill her and get away with it, make it look like another Seraphim murder.

Michael was mean and controlling, but would he really go so far? Would he threaten her like this? He wasn't normally one for subtlety; if true, his ingenuity surprised her.

She turned on the television and tried to push the fears aside, to forget this entire mess, just for a little while. Her mind wandered to Detective Gentry. Something in the way he looked at her made her anxious, but also excited. Such depth in those dark, green eyes— passion, focus. Hard eyes, but underneath swam kindness and sympathy that seemed genuine. Not a man to put on affectations. No, what you saw was what you got with the detective.

Stop it. Like I need any more complications in my life.

She flipped through the channels, finding nothing but news about Seraphim, the last thing she wanted to see right now.

Why can't some campy comedy be on when I need it?

About to click to the next channel, she froze. The screen showed a two-story house in a scenic subdivision encircled by hordes of reporters ... her house.

WRZK has learned an intended victim of the Seraphim escaped an attack last evening. Dr. Rebecca Drenning is now the only known person to survive this killer....

She rushed to the window. Half a dozen reporters were set up outside her house, mounted lights and microphones everywhere. Vans with raised antenna arms lined the street. And storming up the drive ... Michael.

He shoved past, nearly knocking her to the floor. Anger radiated off him in waves, his eyes darting about the room as if looking for something to throw or break. This could get bad.

"What. The. Hell?" he said, unconcerned if the reporters outside, or the next state over, heard. "Have you lost your mind?"

"What? He attacked me. What was I supposed to do?" asked an incredulous Becca.

"Tell me. Let me handle it. I am a cop, you know. It's sort of what I do."

"You're not high on my list of people to trust." Her belligerence shocked even her. *There's my Becca,* said Mom in her mind.

Michael eyes squinted to hateful slits.

"I can't have fucking reporters and the goddamn police around here."

Ah, so that was it. He worried they would get wind of his little side enterprise. Of course, Michael did not try to frighten her. He'd never be able to come up with something so clever. He wanted to protect himself. Which meant ... the Seraphim *did* attack her.

"I don't understand how the reporters even found out."

"You really are stupid, aren't you? They're dialed into police scanners and have people camped out at Metro. Any call goes out from dispatch, they check into it. Anyway, when the detectives working that case leave the station, the reporters follow. They can't take a piss without a flock of those vultures swooping in. It ain't rocket science. For someone so smart, you sure are dumb as a bag of rocks." He glared out the window.

"Sorry dear, but you weren't exactly my top priority when I woke and discovered a serial killer had been in my house."

Michael spun toward her and took a step forward, but held up. Not even he would strike her with the world observing through a dozen camera lenses. Maybe that's what gave her the sudden nerve to defy him. Or maybe she just did not care anymore. Now two psychos seemed to want her dead. She felt stuck between huddling in a corner in fear, and laughing at the utter absurdity of it all.

Michael pointed his finger at her, teeth grinding so hard she heard his jaw pop. 'This is not over,' his eyes screamed with piercing rage. He stormed out the front door, got into his patrol car, and sped away with the whole city watching.

"They're the same?" asked Marlowe.

"The same," replied Koop. "The coins and cross found at Dr. Drenning's home match those Seraphim left at the other crime scenes. No mistake, it was him. By some small miracle, I even got a partial index off one of them the Doctor didn't smudge."

"So you know who this is?" Marlowe's heart raced with hope.

Koop held his hands up. "The Red Sea exhausted me. I only work *minor* miracles now."

Spence chuckled. "Damn, I knew your ass was old." He pivoted his head toward Marlowe. "Still, this makes no sense. She didn't appear depressed, certainly not suicidal. Think your theory is wrong? And how the hell did a little thing like her get away? I have trouble believing she overpowered him."

"She didn't. He let her go," said Marlowe.

"What?" said Koop and Spence in unison.

"Gut feeling, but she was out cold. Even if she fought, he subdued her in the end."

"Maybe she hurt him. He left to heal up and regroup," said Spence.

Marlowe paced the floor, one hand rubbing his chin, deep in thought. Could he be mistaken? No, suicidal ideation was the only possible connection. "We need to follow up with Dr. Drenning. Something's out of kilter."

Spence grinned. "Why don't you handle it by yourself? I've got some … well, things to do."

Marlowe offered a surly expression in reply. Spence and his attempts at matchmaking. He seemed to forget Dr. Drenning was married, and more, a key witness in the biggest case this city had seen since the 16th Street bombings. Even so, Marlowe felt in no mood to argue. Frustrated, he waved and walked toward the exit with Spence chuckling in the background.

A thousand thoughts whirled through his mind as he drove toward the hospital. Marlowe tried to grasp them one at time, but they coalesced into nonsensical images or danced out of focus. Something about Dr. Drenning, Becca, stirred emotions he had fought every day for five years to suppress.

Visions of his family never left him, always close, and the accompanying emotions were dangerous. Since the first Seraphim crime scene, controlling those feelings had grown more difficult. Already he had lost control on more than one occasion, and each brought him nearer to obsession. Most frightening of all, he found himself not wanting to resist them anymore. His thoughts turned in a direction he would have thought abhorrent five years ago.

Life, or more aptly death, had changed him. Now, he could imagine how good it would feel to let go and give in to the rage. How quickly could he get to Seraphim with the chains off?

Too many goddamned rules. Did the city want to be safe or not? There was a price to pay for safety. They clung to their civil liberties while expecting him to keep the wolf from the door with one hand tied behind his back.

If he could kill his idealism, smash the moral compass, things would be so much easier. Find the evidence by any means necessary and follow where it led. Any person with nothing to hide should not care if he looked around their house and possessions. Why should they need a lawyer just to talk to him?

He teetered at the top of a slippery slope from which turning back would prove impossible, he knew. Frustration had him so damned exasperated. He had to find something to break this case fast, before it drove him mad.

Arriving at the hospital, he pushed the thoughts away. He needed his mind sharp. Breaks did not fall out of the sky. A suspicious look, an off-hand comment, any tiny detail could make the difference. With his mind so clouded, the essential clue might slap him in the face and he would not recognize it.

Marlowe found Patient Counseling Services on the fifth floor. His timing proved fortuitous, as Dr. Drenning wrapped up early with her last appointment. He sat in the waiting room half-listening to a program on a "whole wellness" approach to cancer.

A nurse, stout in both stature and demeanor, escorted him to the doctor's office. Dr. Drenning sat at her desk and rose when he entered the room. Before, at her home, without make-up and her eyes showing a lack of sleep, he found her lovely. Now, however, she struck an impressive figure indeed.

Her black, silky hair fell over her shoulders, glistening in the afternoon sunlight streaming in from the window. When she smiled, an infectious smile, he felt certain his heart skipped a beat. Marlowe took her in fully, some inner mechanism behind his eyes controlling him. He marveled at her every feature, from the outline of her body beneath the lab coat, to the tiny heart-shaped birthmark on her neck.

As frightening as his own feelings, her eyes, the most brilliant blue, seemed to pierce through his veneer and see what no one else could see. He felt naked before her gaze. Shifting his stance nervously, he pulled his jacket tight, and buttoned it closed.

Focus. Christ, you aren't sixteen. Keep the hormones in check.

"Dr. Drenning, thank you for seeing me." Marlowe attempted to wipe the sweat from his palms inconspicuously, raking them along his sleeves.

"Not at all. And it's Becca, remember."

"Right, sorry. I wanted to let you know we've confirmed Seraphim did invade your home."

"I don't understand. The news said the killer only came after ..."

"That's what I needed to talk to you about. I noticed some bruising around your waistline."

She reddened and averted her eyes. "Yes ... well I ... he must have done it when I tried to fight him off."

"I don't think so. Seraphim never hurts his victims. No injuries are inflicted while they are conscious; in fact, he seems to take great measures to ensure it doesn't happen."

"Maybe it was different with me. Maybe the others didn't fight back." Becca tapped a shoe against the floor and twirled her hair around one finger, a tell Marlowe had noticed before.

"We don't know for certain you did fight. The positioning of those bruises suggests the person who caused them purposefully placed them in an inconspicuous location. The Seraphim would have no need to do such a thing. I think they were put there by someone trying to hide them, someone covering up their abuse. Someone like ... a husband."

Marlowe studied her reaction. The logic in his theory bore its share of holes, but he committed to the play. It was obvious his guess was spot on. Becca appeared on the verge of tears.

"How did you ...?" she said, her voice breaking.

"After I noticed the bruises, I suspected. Most husbands would be at their wife's side after such a traumatic event. I've seen many domestic abuse cases, and the signs were all there. Your office clinched it."

"My office?"

"No sign of your husband. No wedding photos, no pictures of a vacation, nothing." Marlowe waved one hand around the room.

"I like to keep it professional." She turned her face away from him, refusing to make eye contact.

"There's a photo of you and … your mother? Another there with a friend, colleague maybe?"

"Okay, okay. We have our problems, and perhaps Michael can get carried away sometimes. That doesn't mean I'm suicidal." Tears inched their way over fluttering eyelids, spilling down her cheeks. It did not please him to prove his hunch correct, but it did provide some answers.

"I know what it's like to feel trapped in a life you don't want. One where pain is the only constant you can count on. Every day you think you can't take it anymore. To just want peace." He was not certain why he said it. The words came from somewhere deep inside, and he knew the accompanying hurt must have shown on his face.

"Will you tell me? I need to hear." The urgency in her tone disarmed him. He held his secrets and emotions close, reluctant to share them. Quid pro quo was not his normal method of getting a witness to talk, yet, her vulnerability weakened his guard. The fact she reminded him so much of Katy did not help.

He considered her plea for a long moment. Marlowe had not discussed it with anyone. Even the department shrink the brass demanded he talk to could not get more than a few words out of him. He suspected they finally cleared him out of sheer annoyance. Marlowe took a deep breath. "Do you remember the Churchill Murders from a few years ago?"

"Of course, the news ran it day and night. You were on that case?"

"Lead detective, yes. I spent eight months chasing the sick bastard. Teddy Brumbeloe, a real piece of work. We tracked him to a rundown shack and took him out. Wasn't the plan, but he gave us no choice. Gave *me* no choice."

"I think I recall that. I thought you looked familiar."

"Yeah, they plastered my face on everything. City's hero. The brass loved it, and I didn't shy away. Only one problem. We only had it half right."

"What do you mean?" asked Becca.

"Remember the killer's MO? Cigar burns all over the victim's body, strangulation with a leather belt, and the sign of the Gemini carved into their stomachs? We decided early on, the Gemini, the zodiac symbol represented by the Twins, referred to the dual killings. Always two men in their fifties, killed a few hours apart. I suspected two killers, even voiced my theory, but always enough time existed for one person to make the trip between murders." Marlowe straightened in his seat, uncomfortable with the retelling.

Becca crossed her legs, hands in her lap, and listened intently.

"Plus, we found only one person's DNA at the scenes, other than the victims' of course. After Teddy went down, no one even considered another psycho remained out there. The higher-ups wanted to ride the wave of public support, and didn't want me bucking matters. I wasn't doing much bucking anyway, content with my temporary fame."

"You shouldn't be so hard on yourself. It doesn't sound like anyone could have known."

"Maybe not, but I feel like I should have. It seemed obvious in hindsight, when it turned out the killers were twin brothers. Teddy and Frank. Parents must have been Roosevelt fans. They seared their victims with the same type of cigar their father burned them with as children, and strangled them with a leather belt just as he had beaten them with.

"As identical twins, of course any DNA at the scenes would match. A one-killer theory seemed air-tight."

"But you didn't know any of this at the time, right?" Becca fiddled with a gold locket hanging at the hollow of her neck.

"No, we didn't learn any of their background until later. So, I'm at a bar with some fellow detectives celebrating our great victory when I get a call on my cell. My wife's number, but a man's voice."

Marlowe slipped back to that terrible day.

"Hello Detective Gentry. Enjoying your day in the sun?"

"Who is this? How did you get that phone? Where's my wife?"

"Oh she's here. Wanna talk to her?"

"Marlowe, he's got Paige. Oh my god, he's got our baby." Agonized desperation filled Katy's voice.

"You took my family from me, now I'm going to take your family from you."

"Hurt them and I will kill you. You hear me, you bastard!"

Despite Marlowe fighting to hide his feelings, pain and guilt pushed to the surface. "The phone went dead. I drove home, breaking every traffic law on the books. When I entered the kitchen, Frank held Katy with a knife poised against her neck, my little girl cowered, terrified in the corner. He killed my wife, Paige's goddamn mother, and the bastard made us watch."

"Oh my god, she saw …" Becca's hand went to her mouth for a moment. "I can't begin to imagine …"

"I tried to talk him down. I fucked up. I should've shot him. Maybe, if I had, Katy would …"

Becca leaned forward and touched his knee. "It's exhausting to tread water in a sea of doubt. You'll never know. You'll never come up with answers to make the questions stop. Don't do that to yourself."

"I know. I feel like I'm drowning sometimes." Marlowe averted his eyes, fingers digging into his thighs.

"How is your daughter coping now?"

"It's been tough. After the murder, she spent six months in a *facility*. They wouldn't let me see her for the first several weeks, which was hell. But I knew she needed help, and I wasn't in any shape to care for her. I had my own... well, issues. The doctors finally sent her home after telling me she might snap out of it in a day or year. The bastards didn't know a damn thing. It's been almost two years, and Paige still hasn't spoken a word. Two years... not a word. Sorry, I know they're your colleagues."

"I understand." Becca shook her head with a wistful smile. "No offense taken."

"I hired a nanny trained to work with special needs children, got my shit together, and went back to work. I had to. I would've gone crazy sitting home."

The overwhelming sympathy in Becca's eyes nearly broke him. He had believed every tear he would ever cry drained away long ago, but it took all his will now to hold the flood back. Every time he thought of Paige's impassive stare, he imagined her little voice asking him why he let Mommy die.

"I'm so sorry. I can't imagine what you must have felt, what you must still feel. I hear such heartbreaking stories every day, people battling for their lives, but to see your family that way ..." She stared down onto her lap. When her head rose, Marlowe knew she was ready. "You're right. Michael has beaten me for years. I took it. I guess I thought there wasn't anything I could do about it. You can't understand ... or maybe you can, with all you've seen and been through. His control over me, my weakness, didn't happen all at once. It crept in over ten long years."

Becca paused. Marlowe could tell she struggled with how much to tell him.

"He raped me ... or tried to. I called the police, but they defended him. It made me feel like I'd fallen deep into a hole I'd never be able to climb out of. Michael could do whatever he wanted to me and make up any story he liked. I did think about suicide. Anywhere I ran, he would find me. I saw no way out. Still, I could never kill myself. I wallowed in self-pity for a bit, but snapped out of it quickly and reconciled to finding another answer."

"Good," Marlowe said. "Good for you."

"So, you think that's why Seraphim came after me?"

"Yes, and I think it's why you're still alive."

"What do you mean? I don't understand."

"First, I need your professional expertise. Tell me about empathy. Could a person tell another felt suicidal without knowing them or even talking to them? Just by watching them?"

Becca considered the idea. "Hmm. Well, look at the way you figured out I am being abused. Your training and experience allowed you to see the signs."

"True, but I saw bruises and other tangible clues. I checked out your husband and found the complaints for excessive force. I didn't just look at you and know."

"Yes, but you picked up on traits and signs. You're a cop. You see a person acting suspicious, it piques your interest. You watch them and determine they're a threat of some kind. You've seen it enough times to know what constitutes suspicious."

"I think I see where you're going."

"Me, I deal with emotional issues. A person comes into my office, and in seconds, by their expressions and body language, I have a good idea of where they are emotionally. I know a therapist who deals with substance abuse, she can tell an addict almost immediately by their physical tics and traits."

"So, it's possible this guy could be attuned to some signs severely depressed people exhibit?" asked Marlowe.

"Possible, yes, I think so. Have you seen the dogs who can tell their owner is about to have a seizure and lie on top of them to protect them from hurting themselves? There are all kinds of similar stories. Some people also seem to have a naturally heightened sense of empathy. If he possesses this heightened sense, and his past placed him in constant contact with a depressed person, he very well might have honed an ability to decipher almost imperceptible signs."

"Shit," said Marlowe.

"What? It's a good theory."

"If it's simply empathy, if that's how he's finding his victims, there won't be a link between them for us to find. We're left with praying he slips up and gets arrested for something else. His fingerprints don't match any in our databases, so unless he's printed and we get a hit … we need to get lucky." Marlowe stood, his mood turning sour. "Thank you for your help. You've given me a lot more to consider."

"No, thank you. You know, for sharing your story. It meant a lot. I really needed to hear it."

Marlowe smiled and turned for the door.

"Detective … you'll catch him," said Becca.

"Thanks. And call me Marlowe."

CHAPTER NINETEEN

Confusion slid downward into angst. Gabriel could not understand what he had done wrong. He felt the blessing, sought out the chosen to bestow the gods' touch upon her, and then nothing. Her eyes held the fire of life, a desire to live. Nowhere within her did he find hopelessness, the crushing despair leading to final resignation.

He knew all the signs. Every gesture and expression spoke to him. He recognized the chosen—their downcast eyes, tears leaking behind their lids, their slow ponderous mien—unseen by all but him. In still others, he saw the quiet wringing of hands, a desperate spirit yearning for release. All were different, yet all the same.

Within his books, he searched for answers. The gods of the Greeks remained silent. Milton's deity offered no more than Zeus or Apollo. He took his Bible from the shelf, scanning verse after verse. Finally, the story of Abraham offered a revelation.

Commanded to kill his son, Abraham took Isaac to the altar and prepared to take his life. A test of his faith—would Abraham defy God? Would he elevate his own desire to keep his son above God's will that Isaac die? Abraham passed the test by surrendering to God's decree.

Gabriel understood now. He did not fail. Taking the woman's life would have been the failure. The gods teased him with the blessing, and then withdrew it to test his obedience. The message was clear. His actions must conform to their will, for in their will lay purpose. Acting in defiance of their will constituted no more than murder, a death devoid of higher meaning.

He lay on his bed, relief washing over him. In his mind, he felt Aphrodite's hands caress his body—the only carnal pleasure he allowed himself. He pictured her face, her form—the perfection of divinity.

She kissed him. A halo of light fanned out above hair the color of brass and gold. Her breath smelled of honey, her neck held the fragrance of heaven. A body sculpted from marble, yet soft. With a tender touch on his face, she straddled him. Her body undulated, rocking, rising in passion and urgency. He moaned as his seed spread out across his belly. Gabriel slept deeply, nestled in dreams of contentment.

The following morning, he rose early, feeling his spirit renewed. Thursday, his day to meet Henry and Wanda, but not until later in the afternoon. He had time to search, to seek out the chosen. There would be no test this time. This time the blessing would not fade until bestowed.

Financial concerns at the hospital caused a cut in his hours. Less money could prove a problem soon, but for now, he welcomed the extra free time. He had other work that required no small amount of diligence.

He boarded the bus, its destination of no concern. The chosen were everywhere. They shopped in the stores and strolled the sidewalks. They worked in the tall buildings and groveled in the low alleys. All around him, their pain sought him out. He needed only open his eyes and reach out with his gifts to find them.

The bus wound through the neighborhood of Homewood and into Vestavia. Gabriel gazed out the window watching the city pass, one town giving way to the next, nothing changing except the names on the street signs. Everywhere the same, each place home to identical desires and needs.

As the bus passed over the Cahaba River, he noticed a cross at the roadside with a wreath draped over it—a marker for some poor soul who died there. It was not the tribute that caught Gabriel's eye, however, but the man seated on a park bench near the site. The man stared at the cross, a heartrending sadness in his eyes.

Gabriel exited the bus at its next stop and walked back toward the bridge. The man remained. Like a statue, he did not seem to move. Gabriel sauntered past, never looking directly at him. Once within an arm's reach—his fingers burned, thunder rocked his brain, his stomach constricted like the folds of a feeding python.

Practiced now at masking the blessing's signs, Gabriel concentrated on keeping his pace and ignoring the pain. With a quick glance back, he made certain the man had not taken any special notice of him. He continued up the walk and stopped to watch from a position out of his line of sight.

After an hour or so, the man rose and proceeded along the sidewalk. A potential setback. If he had parked his car near, if he drove away, Gabriel could not follow. Yet, once again, providence watched over him. The man cut across a park area roughly a hundred yards from the bridge. Gabriel followed at a distance until the man entered a house several blocks away.

Gabriel would return tomorrow and watch the house. He now realized the necessity of learning the chosen's movements and habits. Did he live with others? When did he leave and return? Many details he must discover before his visit. Fortune had smiled on his previous endeavors, but his mission now met with greater scrutiny. He did not believe the gods would allow interruption in their work, but they would not reward arrogance.

Gabriel returned to the bus stop and boarded the next one headed toward home. He should arrive in time to meet Wanda at Henry's store. It would be nice to see them. With an odd work schedule and his other ... responsibilities, he had not seen them since last week. He managed not to miss their weekly meetings, at least able to maintain that one bit of routine.

Henry smiled as Gabriel entered the store. Then, his face changed. His mouth turned downward, his eyes misted over. "Gabriel, I … I didn't know how to get in touch with you. You really need to get a phone. I called Paul, he said you guys were working less … he hadn't seen you since Monday. I even went by your apartment, but you weren't in. I'm sorry I couldn't tell you sooner."

"What's wrong, Henry? What has happened? Where is Ms. Felton?"

Henry wiped a hand hard across his mouth. "Wanda … she … some thug attacked her Tuesday night."

"Will she recover? Is she …?"

"No, no. She's not dead, but it's bad. He grabbed for her purse, and you know our Wanda, she was having none of it. Held on like a snapping turtle to a finger, no letting go til the thunder cracked. He shoved her down. The fall broke her leg." Henry slammed his fist onto the counter. "What kind of monster would do such a thing to an old woman?"

"A detestable one," said Gabriel, anger burning in his gut.

"Worse though, a broke leg at her age is serious business. They say a blood clot caused a stroke. She's paralyzed on the left side, and she's … blind. They don't know if it's permanent yet." Henry nodded as if forcing himself to shake his worry. "But she's in good spirits. Tough old bird, our Wanda. She'll pull through this."

"She is eighty, Henry. I'm as fond of Ms. Felton as you, but …"

"No, I hear what you're saying Gabriel. But she'll be all right. She will."

"I would like to visit her."

"She'd love for you to, I know. You mean a lot to her. Her daughter's with her most of the time, but the more folks she has in her corner the better. Wanda's in room 611 over at the hospital. Not sure when she'll get to come home. I'm watering her plants and seeing after her place."

"I can do those tasks if you need assistance. Your hands are full with your duties here."

"I appreciate that, Gabriel. But I want to do it. Makes me feel closer to her, you know?"

Henry had not stopped fidgeting since Gabriel arrived. He needed to keep his mind occupied, it seemed. Rearranging the same shelf for the third time, he appeared unaware of his own actions. The impending loss of a loved one brought his own mortality into alarming focus, Gabriel assumed.

Although several years separated Henry and Wanda in age, Henry had watched others in the neighborhood pass in recent years, and now loneliness crept toward him like an ominous shadow. Gabriel could do nothing to alleviate his fears. For he, more than most, knew death waited for everyone. A week, a year, a decade, none escaped its cold touch forever.

He left Henry to his busy work and his reflections, and headed toward the hospital. He understood Henry's uncertainties. Growing old meant death's shadow drew closer with each passing day. Henry's death paled in comparison to the solitude and grief of being left behind when those he loved parted this world.

Gabriel's view of death had changed dramatically over the years since his father died. It held little fear for him. Instead, it whispered a promise he could not quite make out, but one that stoked curiosity and excitement. Deep down, he knew with certainty that what waited beyond the veil would be wondrous.

He saw the peace on the faces of the dead—those who wished for it and welcomed it. Gabriel still had many miles to go before he slept. The undiscovered country Hamlet contemplated in his musings, yet avoided in his actions, sang to Gabriel in a sweet song. He would not fear its approach.

A middle-aged woman met him at the entrance to Wanda's hospital room. "Excuse me. Do I know you?" she asked.

"My name is Gab—"

"Gabriel," said Wanda in a weakened voice. "Move aside, Charlotte, and let that handsome man in here."

Charlotte smiled and let him pass. "Sorry. Mom, I'm running down to the food court. Need anything?" she said.

"Nope, just some time with my gentleman caller." Charlotte shook her head with a grin and left the room. "Come over here, you."

"How are you, milady?"

"Better now that you're here. Didn't think you would ever show."

"My apologies. I only learned of your condition today."

"My condition …" Wanda rolled the word around in her mouth as if it tasted sour. "Well, get over here and take my hand. It's a stroke, not cooties."

Gabriel stood beside her bed, Wanda's skeletal fingers entwined feebly with his. "Have the doctors informed you of the stroke's severity?"

"They say it was a good one. Seemed surprised I'm still here, but it'll take more than a little stroke to kill me."

"Henry said much the same thing."

"Henry's afraid I'll kick the bucket, and he won't have anyone to fuss with."

"The man who attacked you, did you see him?"

"No, he wore one of those ski masks over his head. But the size of him, I know him. The man selling drugs, the one I always try to run off. You remember?"

"I do," said Gabriel, pure hatred seeping into his voice.

Wanda noticed. "Now, don't go doing anything stupid. That man would kill you. Let the police handle it. They came and took a report. He'll get his."

Gabriel remembered Henry's complaints about the police never catching those who robbed him. "Yes he will."

"Anyway, I'll be fine. Then I might box his big, fat ears myself."

"I do not doubt it at all. I am glad you are facing your situation with such strength."

"Oh, I'm scared. Don't let my tone fool you. But if it's my time, I'm ready. I'd like a few more years. I planned to marry some young stud and have him feed me grapes at a poolside some place. Fan me with one of those palm leaves like I'm Cleopatra. Know where I can find one of those?" she asked, a sly grin trying to find her lips through the discomfort.

"I am quite certain you will have your pick."

Wanda attempted a laugh that morphed into a harsh cough. Her eyes moved in disturbing circles trying to find something, anything in her darkness. "I've lived a long life. Got fewer regrets than most. It's been a good run."

"You are the envy of the world, milady, to face the specter of death with such dignity and grace."

"I don't know about all that. But, no use hiding the checkbook with the taxman at the door."

"Is there anything you need? Anything I can do for you?" asked Gabriel.

"No, Dear. Look after Henry for me until I get outta here. The man will fall apart without me taking care of him."

"I promise I will."

She reached over with her other hand and placed it atop his. "There's one more thing. I've saved some money over the last several years. Not a lot, but some. Charlotte doesn't need it. She and her husband do well enough. I want you to have it."

"I couldn't take your money. There are others in greater need."

"There are, but it's my money, and this is what I want to do with it. I want you to have it. I want you to take it and get out of Westside, like we talked about before. Go to college, do something with your life. You're meant for big things, you hear me? You're like a son to me, Gabriel, I'll rest easier knowing you are on your way to a better life. Let me do what little I can. Make an old woman happy, won't you?"

"If it is truly your wish, I will not refuse."

"Thank you," she said with a tired smile. "Now off with you. I need my beauty sleep."

"I will come again soon."

She did not reply, already asleep. Gabriel positioned her arms beside her and stood watching slow breaths lift her frail body. He waited for Charlotte to return and then left the hospital.

He could not help but believe his visit with Wanda revealed yet another proof of his calling. The contrast between her and the chosen stood so stark as to be blinding. At peace with life and the gods, death held no terror for Wanda. She did not lament a longer future among the living, but neither did she fear an end. The chosen existed in a state of perpetual anguish where the hope of death offered their only solace. He alone could guide them to the other side, allowing them to pass through the veil clean, their souls pure ... and grateful.

FOR TWO DAYS, GABRIEL WATCHED THE HOUSE. THE MAN ONLY LEFT FOR his daily sojourn to the park bench, to sit staring at the wreath. No one else departed the house, and no one visited.

While the man kept his vigil, Gabriel snuck into the house. A living room, kitchen, dining room, and master bedroom with bathroom made up the layout of the lower floor. The upper contained two more bedrooms with adjoining bathrooms and a half-bath along the hallway.

The upper level appeared seldom trafficked, everything neatly in place, a fine film of dust covering the furniture. Gabriel decided to wait in the basement. He could hide amongst the clutter of shelves and stored boxes if the man happened that way.

He did not. Gabriel heard him enter the house and go into the kitchen, soon followed by the television in the master bedroom switching on. He would wait for the man to fall asleep.

Gabriel enjoyed this time. The long moment of anticipation—a time to reflect on the glorious endeavor. So many wandered through life like insects in the miasma of existence, going to work, watching TV programs, the yearly vacation, all the while giving only a passing notice to the greater significance of being. Only when death visited them or someone close to them did they consider meaning. Mortal instruments all, yet dulled and unused, covered in thickening rust, their utility faded, becoming obsolete.

He cracked the basement door, listening. All quiet. Gabriel lifted his bag and eased toward the bedroom. The man slept; boisterous snoring issued from his prone form. Bolt gun in hand, Gabriel stepped alongside and placed the mushroom-shaped tip against the man's skull. The cartridge fired, a crack followed by a thud as the tip indented bone.

Gabriel dragged him to the bathroom. Stepping into the tub, he tapped along the ceiling until he found a stud. After screwing in a thick eyebolt, he attached the hoist and retrieved the gambrel—a metal rod shaped much like a clothes hanger. He clamped it to the hoist, and lifted the man, draping a leg over each arm of the gambrel at the knee and strapping them tight with duct tape.

He cut two garbage bags apart and wrapped them around the man's hanging inverted body. Flicking open his knife, he sliced the arteries and veins in the chosen's neck, those he knew allowed the greatest blood flow. Once the spray slowed to mere drops, Gabriel washed the man's hair and face clean, removed the plastic, and laid him on the tub floor facing upward.

A strip of duct tape, half on the chosen's shirt, half on his breastbone, allowed him to retain dignity while Gabriel worked. He drew the tip of his blade downward from nape of the neck to inches below the navel. Using the tip of the knife, he made a series of holes in the loosened skin. Inserting the hooked ends of the bungee cords, he pulled the flesh open, and attached the opposite ends to the tub's sides.

The hand-sized bolt cutters were not optimal, requiring a great deal of pressure to break the sternum. Fragments of bone shot outward with each snip. Gabriel would gather them once done, and cleanse the tub of any remaining blood.

He moved into the bedroom and opened the window wide. A beautiful night, the stars bright, a quarter moon hung in the sky. Beneath the window, Gabriel laid out the white sheet. He returned to the tub and cut free the organs he would use for the totem. The other unclean materials, bowels and lesser organs, he would discard.

The lungs, he carefully arranged furthest from the window. Beneath them—the liver, kidneys, and stomach. Last, he cut the heart in two, allowing a thin strand to remain, holding the halves together, and set it onto the sheet. He dipped a small brush in the moist muscle, and painted the words:

ζωή

σκοπός

θάνατος

Gabriel admired the symbols. Well-practiced now, their crimson shapes stood out like fine calligraphy. Severing the arms took some patience and effort, yet once done, flaying the skin and drawing it downward proved simple. Magnificent wings to give the chosen the power of flight.

He envied the man's freedom to separate from the calamity of life and fly on the folds of the gods' love and favor into a wondrous new world. Gabriel gazed down on his totem. His monument of worship. Beautiful. Perfect.

The flowers, his mother's favorites, grew wild in the woods near the farm. He remembered picking them for her, how she always laughed and called him her little angel. Gabriel smiled at the memory.

He placed the flowers inside the body cavity and stitched it closed. The coins he laid on the eyes, the small cross on the neck. It was finished. The chosen, sanctified, could now soar for the heavens into the loving bosom of the gods.

Elation filled him as he cleaned his tools and replaced them in his bag. With each chosen he ushered toward the heavens, he felt his own closeness to the gods' presence increase. He was becoming one with them.

Might he transform into a god himself? Might the great ones of Olympus and the heavens grant him a place among them? Forever faithful to their will, what wonders were possible.

Gabriel pressed his finger into the heart. Upon the wall, he wrote a name.

CHAPTER TWENTY

"Judas? Didn't he betray Jesus?" Spence learned forward, his face inches from the wall. He scratched his neck and eyed the name scrawled in blood.

Marlowe stooped to examine the organs on the floor. "Yes ... I think the killer's more interested in the reason Judas hanged himself."

Spence pulled away from the wall and gave him an expectant look.

"Guilt," said Marlowe. "The victim is Terrence Cooley. A few weeks ago, he hit a kid with his car. They declared it an accident; the boy ran right out in front of him. Several witnesses confirmed there was no time to stop or swerve. Mr. Cooley couldn't live with it. According to neighbors, he went to the spot where it happened every day. Withdrew, closed himself up in the house, never left but for that daily trip."

"Sad," said Spence.

"Very." Marlowe stood and moved to the window, glancing up at the clouds. *Another show for God.* "Have the team do the usual. I'm not holding my breath for anything new, but you never know. Koop, let me know if you find anything."

Dr. Koopman moved around the bed, surveying the team checking the scene for prints and bagging items deemed as evidence. He seemed preoccupied.

"Koop, you need anything?" asked Marlowe.

"A new assistant if you have one on you. I'm too old for this heavy lifting." Koop made a show of rubbing his lower back.

"What happened to the vet kid?" asked Spence.

"My question precisely. He said something came up out of town demanding his immediate attention and could not be certain when he might return. Peculiar." Koop wiped a handkerchief across his forehead and let out a sigh.

"Yeah, that is strange," said Marlowe with a sly expression that went unnoticed.

"So, where are we?" asked Spence.

"Same river, one less paddle. We know what the killer's doing and why. We know how he chooses his victims. Still, we're no closer to finding him." Marlowe paced the floor, hands clasped behind him.

"If you're right, and our dude's got some keen sense of empathy allowing him to recognize these people, and no connection between victims, our only hope is he gives us some help." Spence grumbled. "Bastard's clean as a whistle. We couldn't get a hit on his prints anywhere. It's like he doesn't exist. A fucking ghost."

Marlowe pointed to the corpse on the bed. "This poor guy suggests he's real enough. I need to get some distance, clear my head."

Spence edged away from the body to give the forensics team room. "Yeah, you do that. S'pose I'll head back downtown and comb through traffic surveillance tapes, see if anything stands out. I know we haven't had any reports of a common vehicle at the scenes yet, but I can't come up with anything else to do. Even a hook without a worm gets a bite once in a while."

"Yeah …" Marlowe stuffed his notebook in his pocket and trudged outside to his car.

Ten minutes he sat there, not bothering to start the engine, unsure of where to go or what to do. This case was consuming him. He never slept and rarely ate. *I could go spend time with Paige.* He sighed. What good would that do? She'd still refuse to acknowledge him, her glassy-eyed stare again casting a silent reminder of how he'd failed.

Day and night, his mind turned to the gruesome sights and facts associated with this madman's work. The only other thing that gained any purchase in his thoughts, a woman. He spent a moment thinking of Becca, but wound up gazing into space, vaguely aware of the blurry shapes of the crime scene team milling around the door of the house.

His phone went off, startling him.

"Gentry," said Marlowe, answering his cell.

"Marlowe? Hi, it's Becca. I hope I'm not bothering you."

"No, not at all. I'm taking a break. Actually, I could use a distraction."

She drew a breath, remaining silent for ten seconds. "C-could you come by my office? I, uh … need to talk to someone."

Her exhale told him it hadn't been an easy question to ask. "Sure. Be there in thirty."

"Thank you."

Marlowe placed his phone on the dashboard. His heart sped up a few dozen beats per minute. A bad idea most likely, but she probably wanted to discuss something about the case. No use reading too much into it, even though part of him wanted to.

Keep it professional. She's a witness, idiot. Don't do anything stupid.

Becca stood by her office window with her back to the door as he entered. When she turned toward him, dark circles beneath her eyes gave away the fact that she had not slept much more than he had. Attacks by both a serial killer and her husband in the course of a couple of days seemed not to encourage sound sleeping habits. Marlowe admired her strength. How many people would still be standing, much less working, after going through that?

"Thank you for coming." She covered her face with her hands for a moment "It's Michael. I'm at my wits' end. I don't know what to do."

He rushed over to her. "Tell me what's going on."

She paced in circles, shaking her hands in the air as if drying them. "I told you how bad things are, but recently they've gotten worse. He's like a caged animal with the reporters always outside the house. He was furious when he showed up that day. All the media and the cops. He said something about he couldn't have them in his business. I thought he was going to explode, but I guess … all the cameras scared him off."

"His business?"

"Yesterday, he got a call. I heard him yelling about someone getting arrested. I've been able to stay out of his way, but I'm afraid it's just a matter of time until …"

"He's a cop, why would someone's arrest matter so much? A friend? Relative?"

"No, I don't think so. I'm pretty certain he is up to something. Drugs, maybe. He gets these calls, always secretive, at all hours. I don't recognize the voices, and they won't talk to me if I answer."

"Hmm, does sound strange. I'll do some checking. In the meantime, I can call over to county. I know some people there, lodge a domestic abuse complaint."

"No, please don't." Her eyes grew wide. "They won't do anything, and even if they do … he'll blame me and I'll just get it worse."

"Okay, let me see what I can dig up. In the meantime, stay away from him. Is there somewhere you can go that's safe?"

She shook her head. "I have to stay at home. I've tried leaving, not a good idea."

Marlowe moved close and grasped her shoulders, "Listen, I'm going to take care of this, okay?"

"I believe you." Her smile made his knees weak. He stepped back before surrendering to his desire to pull her close and hold on tight.

BECCA PLACED HER HANDS ON HER SHOULDERS WHERE MARLOWE HAD touched her, his eyes gazing into hers. She could still feel the warmth and strength of those hands. A bad idea on every level, she knew. Anything that might develop between them was bound to end badly. The things they possessed in common did not constitute the best foundation for building a relationship. Chief among them … need.

They both struggled with a deep longing she doubted companionship, or even love, could satisfy.

"Tall, dark, and dreamy back again?" asked Rachel with a sly grin. "Three visits here, a couple more to your house. Must have *a lot* of questions. I think you're becoming a person of interest."

"Just questions about the case." Becca attempted to hide her reddening cheeks.

"Yeah, okay. He is handsome though. But another cop? Maybe not. I'm sure Michael seemed the same at first. Not saying he'd be as bad as Michael, but being a cop takes a certain mindset. Hard to turn it on and off."

Dammit, how does she do that? Always say what I'm thinking?

Even so, right now, any port in a storm. She needed something to hope for, some light in the proverbial darkness. Anything seemed better than the dead end her life had become. Becca needed something pleasant to think about. A fantasy, even if it never became more than a fantasy. A place of sanctuary, a place to hide. A safe place.

"You need a vacation. Get out of town for a while. We can stop scheduling appointments for a week. Clear this week and maybe the next, and then find a sunny beach somewhere."

"Sounds nice, but Michael can't take any leave right now with a promotion pending, not that I would go anywhere with him. No way in hell would he allow me to go alone. Plus, I need to work, keep my mind focused. Too much time sitting around thinking … not a good idea."

"I guess I understand. Figuring out how to get rid of that lowlife husband of yours—that's goal number one."

"Miracles happen," Becca said with a forced smile.

"Honey," Rachel raised her eyebrows, "if anyone is due one, it's you."

MARLOWE LOATHED THE COURTHOUSE. TOO MANY VOICES, TOO MANY complaints. Disgruntled people jostled in long lines for one license or another. Reporters shoved microphones into faces, some smiling, eager for the acclaim, while others pushed through the press of bodies, hands covering their faces to block the camera's eye.

He made his way to a fourth-floor office labeled District Attorney Horace Bennett. Marlowe marched past the clerk and knocked on the door belonging to Assistant DA Avery Humphries.

"Yeah, come in." A heavyset man with a bad comb-over popped up and rushed forward when he saw Marlowe enter the office. "Marlowe, you old son of a bitch. Here to pay up on that dinner you owe me for the last Auburn-Alabama game? Been avoiding me, haven't you?"

Avery and Marlowe went back several years. Avery had started as a prosecutor in the DA's office about the same time Marlowe made detective. They had worked many cases together, and became good friends in the process.

"I figured if I avoided you until this season Bama would win and square us even."

"Doesn't work that way. And the Tigers will make it two in a row anyway. Have a seat." Avery plopped down in his chair behind a desk layered in files and papers.

Marlowe surveyed the desk as he sat. "Looks like you're staying busy."

"No rest for the wicked. I haven't seen the wood on this desktop since they rang the Liberty Bell. What brings you to my little corner of hell?"

"Need a favor. You have anything on a Michael Drenning? Patrolman with County."

"Hmm, sounds familiar, actually." Avery went to his file cabinet and rifled through dozens of manila folders. He plucked one out and flipped it open. "Ah, here we go. IA forwarded a few complaints for excessive force."

"Yeah, I found those. Anything else?"

"Appears we're looking at him for drug trafficking. We just nabbed one of his suspected accomplices. Seems Drenning's more of a lookout and drop guy—transports the stash for sale. A lot of cops take on that role. They keep things running smoothly, without interference or surprises. Nothing hard on him. Sorry. Why do you ask?"

Marlowe rubbed a finger over his lips. "Came across him while investigating another case. Something seemed off."

"Drenning … ah. The doctor attacked by Seraphim, right? Her husband?"

"Yeah, abusive prick. Hoped I might find something on him, get him out of circulation."

"That's tough. Why hasn't the doctor lodged a domestic abuse complaint? We take those very seriously now days."

"It's complicated," said Marlowe with a *don't ask* expression.

"Always is," said Avery. "Listen, if you want to bait this guy, see what you catch, we have a man in deep undercover with one of the main suppliers. He can't help directly, you'll need to find your own seller. Still, if Drenning is in the business at all, he should recognize the name and take it as legit. Name he's under with is Carlos Montego."

"Sounds good." Marlowe stood and shook Avery's hand. "Thanks for everything. I promise you'll get that dinner. And Avery, keep this between us, okay?"

"Keep what between who?" Avery smiled mischievously.

Now, with something to work with, Marlowe knew just who to recruit. He drove to Westside and parked in the alley behind Brightbrook Apartments. With any luck, Raze would be holed up in his underwear eating potato chips.

Marlowe pounded on the door. If the asshole was sleeping that should wake him and let him know someone at the door meant business. He waited a few seconds. Not hearing movement from within, he prepared to give the door another thumping.

"Wait a fuckin' second. I'm coming. Jesus Christ."

Raze didn't sound in good spirits, but Marlowe couldn't care less. The little weasel's mood was about to change for the worse, regardless.

"Open up, Raze," Marlowe said as the rat-faced man peeked through four inches of open door.

"Aww shit. Listen, I told you everything. I swear. Your people ripped my place apart. Can't you leave a dude alone?" Raze backpedaled, wide-eyed, into the apartment.

"Time to pay back that favor, Raze." Marlowe strolled into the dank room like he owned the place.

"You've got to be kidding me. Why the hell would I help you? You almost tossed my ass four stories."

"That's one reason," Marlowe said, smiling and nodding to the window.

"Man, why are you fucking with my life?"

"If I wanted to 'fuck with your life,' you'd be looking at charges for tampering with a corpse, disturbing a crime scene—"

"All right, all right." Raze pinched the bridge of his nose and shook his head. "What the hell do you want?"

Marlowe smiled. "That's more like it. I need you to do something for me, and you're going to do it."

"What is *it?*" Raze lowered his arm, staring at Marlowe with a pained expression, his left eye half closed.

"Arrange a drop. I need some cheese on a mousetrap."

"Oh, fuck man. You have any idea what'll happen to me if word gets out about somethin' like that? You can't. Shit … shit…." Raze collapsed into a rickety chair. He looked up at Marlowe like a beaten puppy.

Marlowe wandered closer, appraising the junk strewn about. "You'd be perfectly safe in a holding cell."

Raze wiped a hand down his face, drooping his eyes. "What do I have to do?"

"Call this number. Make sure you talk to Michael Drenning … and *only* Michael Drenning." Marlowe offered him a Post-It. "Tell him you are the new liaison for Carlos Montego, and you've got some product ready for shipment. Say it. Only Michael Drenning."

"You ain't going to get me killed, are you?" asked Raze, almost childlike.

"Say it."

Anger hardened the man's eyes. "Only Michael fucking Drenning. Now, this little escapade ain't gonna get my ass killed, is it?"

"Not if you do what I tell you. All the info for the meet is written here." Marlowe handed Raze a folded piece of paper. "All you have to do is drive up, get out, and wait for Vice to roll in. Think you can handle that?"

Raze looked the paper over, smirked, and let it fall in his lap. "Do I have a choice?"

"We all have choices, Raze. What matters is the effect of those choices."

"Yeah, okay Mr. Fortune Cookie. You some Confucius-ass motherfucker all right."

Marlowe headed for the door. "Confucius? Raze, maybe you aren't as dumb as you look after all. Make the call. I'll check in later."

"Gentry ..."

"What?" Marlowe turned, eyeing Raze with a stare that brooked no arguments.

"After this, we good, right?"

"We'll see, Raze," said Marlowe, with a subtle grin.

CHAPTER TWENTY-ONE

Max could no longer hold down more than small bites of food. The pain in his head and belly grew daily, threatening to rip his body and psyche apart. He could taste colors and see sounds. Sometimes, scenes burst into a million shards of light before his red swollen eyes—walls, furniture, entire rooms exploded like a universe of stars. Reality blurred and became less certain. He saw things ... horrible things.

The worst of it had begun a few days earlier. Max woke near noon feeling lethargic, his mind unable to grasp even simple tasks such as feeding or dressing himself. The house felt confining, too hot; he needed fresh air. The crisp, cool winter breeze might clear his head.

Still in pajamas, he walked outside. A narrow path ran through the woods behind his house leading to Gooseneck Creek. Max had explored these woods a thousand times over the years, following the rabbit trails darting in and out of the trees.

He and the boys often made their way to the creek. Max wanted to teach them about nature and share his love for the forest with them. Cody enjoyed wading into the water and catching crawdads. Unfortunately, he also delighted in chasing his brother with the creatures, trying to pinch him with their claws. Austin, of course, liked that part of the excursion far less.

Max labored into the forest on shaky legs. He should get a cane; two legs no longer seemed to do the trick. He might pick one up the next time he went into town. One with a wolf's head on the pommel like the old German guy in that movie—Max Von something or other. He played chess with Death. No, same guy different movie.

Yeah, that would be fitting. A silver wolf's head on a black cane. Even though I suck at chess.

Once upon a time, Max knew every tree, leaf, and stone in these woods. He found it a peaceful place and came here to think and find solitude when life grew too confusing or hectic. He had always loved these woods. He knew them, and they knew him. One of the few constants in his life—a place that always welcomed him.

Within minutes of entering the forest, Max was hopelessly lost.

He scanned his surroundings, trying to fix his location. The woods. Yes, the woods behind the house. But how far had he come? Was the house further back this way or in the other direction? Fear tightened his throat and rolled in his gut. Sobbing like an infant, he fell to the ground.

The trees swayed, bowing toward him, yet only a mild breeze wafted through the forest. Dry leaves, brown and orange, swirled and coalesced into disturbing shapes. On his knees, Max tore at his hair. He closed his eyes tightly and refused to see what ghosts rose to haunt him.

He heard a rustling in the trees. Steeling himself, he mustered the courage to search out the sound. A small dog came trotting out of the undergrowth. An ugly mutt, wiry fur patched in black and gray, it sniffed Max's extended hand and tasted it with its tongue. The dog growled deep in its throat and retreated several steps.

"It's okay, boy. I won't hurt you."

Pawing at the ground, the dog bared its teeth and shook its head back and forth as if playing a game of tug-o-war. Its head split in two, eyes rolling on thin, spindly stalks. The beady orbs ogled Max from skull halves flapping to each side. A muscular protrusion shot out from the center of the gory mass and latched onto his arm. He screamed, struggling to disengage the hideous tentacle.

Wisps of white, wormy strands erupted from the dog's body, whipping violently like streamers in a gale wind. Blood welled and ran from the wound the tentacle inflicted. A thick, syrupy venom dripped from the translucent protrusion into Max's arm and coursed upward toward his shoulder. His veins rose to the surface of his skin and turned the same scarlet as the venom. His chest quaked as the poison plunged into his heart.

Rain came—lightly at first, turning to a downpour in under a minute. The droplets hit his skin, fizzling and hissing with wisps of acidic smoke issuing from the contact. Half-dollar-sized blisters rose on his arms, face, and legs. The boils cracked under the deluge, breaking open, seeping a vile-smelling pus.

The downpour intensified. The ground soaked into a mire, bogging his legs until he could not move. The mud pulled at him, sucking him downward. Further and further into the earth Max descended, until he could no longer see the surface. The trees extended their roots from the pit's walls, finding his every orifice, seeking to drain him of life.

Such unbelievable agony washed over him; his body shook with vicious tremors. Max clawed at the slick walls of the pit, but could find no purchase. Deeper and deeper he sank, mud congealing with the venom and roots, filling him, ripping him apart.

He crossed his arms over his face in a feeble effort to protect it, and screamed his lungs empty.

All sound ceased, the world went stone still—no pit, no dog's growl, no breeze, no rustle of leaves. Max looked around, all seemed returned to normal. No, not returned, the same as it had always been. Max fell on his chest, panting, delirious with terror.

How long he lay there, he did not know. When he finally pushed himself upright, the sun was setting; an eerie orange-purple glow bled from the horizon. Max fought for balance, unsteady, trying to hold himself upright. His clothes and the ground around him were bone dry. He did not see a dog, or any sign one had been there. The leaves lay motionless on the ground, undisturbed.

Max stepped through a slow turn, looking around at the woods. His gaze found a trail; he looked along the length, spotting his home no more than a hundred yards away. He examined his arm and found no wounds or discolored veins. His chest felt smooth and warm with no signs of injury, and no blisters scarred him.

He stumbled home, wanting only the safety of locked doors between himself and the world. His desire to ever step outside again remained in serious doubt. Once inside, he checked the locks on all the doors and windows. Winded after his adventure, Max changed into a shirt and jeans and staggered into the living room, and stopped dead in his tracks at the sight of Maggie waiting. She stood in the center of the room, her back to him, perusing old photos propped on the mantle. After a moment, she turned toward him, an unreadable expression on her face.

"I've been waiting for you."

"M-Maggie? I didn't know you were coming," said a surprised Max, his voice apprehensive, but hopeful.

"I never loved you, Max." She said it as though reading a soup can label. Max blanched, not certain he heard correctly. Why would she come here now to tell him such a hateful thing? "The boys don't love you either. You embarrass them. They don't want their friends to know you're their father. I don't want anyone knowing I married you. I mean really. What the hell was I thinking? You've always been a loser."

Maggie stopped in front of the fireplace, a cradle full of cold, dead embers. "You couldn't please your father—a poor athlete and a worse student. Dear Mommy hated the sight of you. A disappointment, that's all you ever were to them."

Max stared at her, his mouth gaping open.

"You're nothing but a failure," Maggie said. "You failed as a husband. You failed as a father. Look at you. You can't even die without making a big to-do of it. What ... pills? How hard could that be? Just swallow and die, even you should be able to do something that easy."

"Why are you saying this? Why are you doing this to me? I tried, Maggie. You know I always tried." Max placed his palms over his ears. He did not want to hear any more … no more.

"Oh, poor Max. It's all about you isn't it? I've got cancer. Feel sorry for me. Well, guess what? No one feels sorry for you. We all want you gone. The sooner the better."

"But I didn't tell you. You can't know. I was protecting you … you and the boys. I didn't want you to see me waste away. I didn't want you to have to take care of me."

"Aren't you mister thoughtful?" Maggie scoffed. "Some of that thoughtfulness would've been nice when I worked double shifts just to buy food. Where was it when you were out drinking while your family sat home? Huh? Don't fool yourself. You're only thinking about Max, like always. You didn't want to suffer the feelings that came with us being here—seeing our disgust and pity. Your ego's what this is really all about. So don't sit there and try to say you're doing anything for us."

"That's not true. I love you. I love my sons. I don't want you to go through this." He felt the humiliation of his begging, but could not stop.

"So, we walk in and find you dead one day, or some stranger calls to tell us. Yeah, brilliant plan. Your sons wouldn't have any problem with discovering dear ol' Dad blue and stiff as a board."

"No, that's not how I meant it. You don't understand."

"It doesn't matter. We've moved on. I've found a great man already. Without you around it wasn't hard to find a decent guy. He takes care of us and the boys worship him." Maggie sighed, a look of contentment washing over her face. "And the way he fucks me. You could never make me feel so good. I didn't know what I was missing."

"Shut up. Please, shut up. Leave. I want you to leave." Max shut his eyes tight, but could still feel her there before him, staring with pure hatred.

"How can I leave, Max?" Her voice took on an ephemeral, echoing quality. "I'm not even here."

When he opened his eyes, she was gone. Gone? No, she was never here. Part of him felt relief—relief that she did not say those terrible things, not really. But part of him still hurt. Her words stung too deep, touching him where he would never heal. He knew he imagined it all. So why did it hurt so badly? The accusations, the spite and hatred, felt real and did not dissipate in the hours that followed.

He could not sleep. In light or dark, visions came—a monstrous dog, acid rain, a sinking pit … and Maggie. Max did not sleep for the next two days. Afraid to go outside, afraid to go downstairs, he lay in bed with the covers tight around him. Receding into a second childhood where terrors hid under the bed and in the closets, he prayed for death over and over.

On the third day, Max slept twenty hours straight. He wanted to believe the visions were no more than nightmares suffered during that long sleep. Time, day and night, meant little anymore. Now only the waiting remained. He waited for the next symptom, the next horrible episode of nausea, headaches, or seizures, waited until he could take more pills and ease the edge off the pain, waited for it all to finally end.

A rushing sound emanated from downstairs. Fear pushed bile into his mouth.

Nothing. Just the house shifting.

A moment later, the noise came again. A swooshing rise and fall like waves against the shore.

My imagination. My mind playing tricks like always. Another hallucination. It'll stop, wait it out.

It did not stop, but grew incrementally louder from faint to insistent. Not a particularly threatening sound in and of itself, but the strangeness of it, and his inability to discern its source or cause, unnerved him. Still, even in his fear, a soothing quality accompanied the sound. Like turning on a fan to help him sleep, it dispelled the haunting quiet. The dichotomy made him laugh and question his sanity for the millionth time.

Curiosity joined with fear. The sound would drive him yet madder. Its unrelenting pulse bored into his skull. He pushed himself from the bed, slung on his robe, and inched toward the bedroom door. Once into the hall above the stairs, the sound took on a ringing note, like a bird's call or a flute.

Max eased down the stairs, placing each foot deliberately on the step as though it might decide to fly out from under him. The photos of his family along the hallway seemed to glower hatefully as he passed. His eyes darted about, trying to see around corners and through walls.

What is that sound? In my mind ... or ...

The closer he drew to the source, the more recognizable it became. Somewhere in his jarred and fractured mind, he knew that noise. Tiny bees buzzing? The amplified din of a million ants scurrying across the hardwood floor?

He edged around the corner and into the living room. Relief flooded through him ... the television. Max must have left it on. The station had gone offline and now static white noise hissed from the speakers. He allowed himself a narrow, haggard smile.

Max fell back into his recliner, grabbed for the remote control and changed the channel. A two-level house with dozens of reporters and police roaming about came on the screen, an attractive female reporter in the center of the frame.

WRZK has learned an intended victim of the Seraphim escaped an attack last evening. Dr. Rebecca Drenning is now the only known person to survive this killer....

Dr. Drenning? His Dr. Drenning? The station showed a photo of the doctor dressed in her white coat, posed in her office.

I just saw her on Thursday.

He could only imagine how terrified she must feel, narrowly escaping a brutal killer. Dr. Drenning understood his situation better than most. He liked her. She seemed genuinely to care about him, about all her patients, he assumed.

Max pushed himself from the chair and went into the kitchen. He poured a glass of tea and turned as the female voice changed. The white noise returned, only much louder than before. He moved toward the living room, more puzzled than afraid.

The television showed the photo of Dr. Drenning, but the audio had resumed the static buzz. Max retrieved the remote. Pressing button after button, he tried to switch the channels, but all displayed the same image of Dr. Drenning, accompanied by the same noise.

The dead logs lying cold in the fireplace sprang to life. Flames blazed, casting off an incredible heat. Max tripped over the coffee table, toppling onto the floor. Propped on his elbows, he sought to retreat further, backpedaling like a crab. His legs went stiff. He couldn't move.

Billowing flames leapt from the fireplace, stretching upward to the ceiling and taking on vague shape. Max whined, raising an arm to shield his eyes. Orange became yellow; the brightest patches of fire exuded liquid gold, which defined a human figure, molded of bronze. Angelic wings unfurled, their span reaching from wall to wall across the room.

Do not fear me.

"This isn't happening. Only in my mind. It's all in my mind."

Do not fear me.

"Who … who are you? *What* are you? What do you what with me?"

You know me. I am your salvation. I am the end to your suffering.

Max felt the creature's warmth. A comforting sensation spread out from its extended hands. Palms up, it beckoned, promising deliverance. All Max's fear fled into that warmth. No longer afraid, he desired only to please the angel … to do its will.

"What do I have to do?"

The woman. Will you stand for her?

"Dr. Drenning? Stand for her?"

Will you offer your life for hers?

"Yes."

She is your test. Are you worthy?

Max wept. "I am. I know I am."

Succeed and all of your pain and fear will end. You will find your place in the heavens. No more suffering—only perfect peace and joy.

"Yes ... please. I want that ... please"

I will return for her. Stand for her.

The room went cold. No fire burned; no angel hovered before him, yet, Max felt a sense of euphoria. He laughed until he could not catch his breath. Gasping on hands and knees, he offered up prayers of thanks through hacking coughs.

He understood. The angel touched his mind and showed him ... truth. Dr. Drenning did not *escape* Seraphim. Seraphim released her to allow Max this one chance at redemption—an opportunity to erase so many mistakes and failures. Soon, Seraphim would return for the doctor, and Max would be there.

To stand for her.

CHAPTER TWENTY-TWO

"Knew I'd find you down here. You've got to quit doing this to yourself," said Spence.

Marlowe sat in the basement of Birmingham Metro, the *Churchill Murders* files laid out on the table before him. His red-tinged eyes struggled to adjust when he looked up, making Spence appear blurred. Marlowe thought it a slight improvement.

"Bateman said you're down here every night."

"Need to get a bead on Seraphim," said Marlowe, none too happy with Spence's interruption.

"Bullshit. You aren't going to find anything about Seraphim in those files. This is self-flagellation, plain and simple. I don't need to be a shrink to know you're punishing yourself. Do you enjoy the hell you put yourself through? Get some kind of masochistic pleasure from it? When are you going to give yourself a break?"

"Flagellation? Masochistic? Did you run face first into a dictionary?"

"I'm not joking here."

Spence would not take the bait. Fine. No need for Marlowe to play nice.

"Back off, Spence."

"You've been doing it for years, but now … Jesus, Marlowe, enough's enough. You're losing it, bro. This case has dug up a big, black pile of shit in you. I'm worried, the lieutenant's worried."

"Well don't be. And the lot of you, mind your own goddamned business. I'm doing my job."

"That what you call it? Seraphim's out there, genius. The only thing you'll find down here in the dark is misery and bad vision. You've got more than you need of one, come back up to the land of the living before you have a case of the other."

Marlowe doubted Spence meant that remark the way he took it. The land of the living did not seem to have a place for him anymore. He walked, and talked, and breathed, but as for living—a concept he no longer understood.

Spence's attempt at an intervention did little to improve his mood, or his fixation with these files. He found a sick kind of comfort in them. A closeness to Katy he attained nowhere else. He did not expect Spence to understand. Marlowe questioned whether he understood himself. He didn't much want to go home either. Seeing Paige in her emotionless trance tormented and mocked him, reminded him he failed. Why couldn't she talk? Did she hate him so much? The gun under his arm felt heavier. How close had he come? How often? If not for having a daughter who needed him … but did she? Might she be better off without seeing the reason Katy was dead every day?

No matter how many times he pored over these pages, they offered little catharsis for the vileness worming constantly into his thoughts. Akin to picking at a scab, the wound might heal if he could stop worrying at it, but he could not. All he knew was that he needed this. He needed to stoke the rage … and remember. Remember what his mistakes had cost him.

It seemed Spence might stand there staring for the rest of the night.

"Okay, okay. I promise I'll knock off in a minute. Now get out of here so I can finish up," said Marlowe.

"Finish up driving yourself bonkers? Be my guest." Spence waved him off in frustration and headed up the stairs.

Marlowe closed the files and placed them with care, like holy relics, into the cardboard box. With a few deep breaths, he reined in his emotion, and pushed Katy's terrified eyes out of his mind. In truth, Marlowe had other matters on his agenda this evening—other reasons for staying late, other reasons for this vigil in the basement. The siren call of those old case files had been hard to resist; he hadn't planned on staring at them *that* long.

Although police work demanded around-the-clock personnel, most of the support staff left at six p.m. The department utilized a skeleton crew this late at night. The dispatcher and a few uniforms milled around the lower floor. Detectives from the various units— Homicide, Vice, and Criminal Investigations, would be home, but on call. Custodians worked throughout the complex. Luckily for Marlowe, they took care of the basement first and had completed their duties some time ago.

The basement floor of Birmingham Metro housed two main areas —file storage and the evidence locker. Active case evidence remained in one area under lock and key. Gaining access to the active cases required signing in with the clerk. Evidence for older inactive cases got shifted to storage off site.

Vice employed a different protocol. The evidence locker held drugs associated with active cases. Caches from older, finalized cases, however, were transferred to an adjacent storage unit to await destruction. Normally, seized drugs found their way to the incinerator or were used in sting operations. Marlowe intended to employ them for the latter … more or less.

Someone had busted the lock on the drug cage a while ago. Several requisitions were sent to maintenance, but still not repaired—more important fish to fry, as it were. Marlowe knew a simple credit card inserted between door and frame would pry it open. He placed his card into the crack, and wiggled it up and down.

"Detective? Detective Gentry?" came a voice from behind.

Marlowe felt like an electric shock passed through his spinal cord. He pictured the cartoon scene where the frightened cat launched itself onto the ceiling, claws dug in. How was he going to talk his way out of this one? He slowly turned.

"Jesus, TJ, you scared the shit out of me," said Marlowe.

TJ, a sixty-something custodian, stared at him for a moment. "Sorry bout that. Didn't know no one was down here. I didn't see you during my clean up earlier."

"I think I came in right after you finished. Floor was still wet, almost slipped and broke my neck." Marlowe put on his best disarming smile.

"What you doing there? You need some help? I got a master key if you need it."

"No, no thanks. Case coming up next week, an appeal. I thought we were done with it. I'm just making sure the evidence is still present and accounted for. Drug bust went bad—couple of guys killed," said Marlowe.

TJ, a long-termer with the department, longer than Marlowe, knew everyone's jobs, and that included Marlowe working in Homicide and not Vice. He must have been wondering why Marlowe was presently getting into the drug locker. Marlowe hoped he bought the lame explanation.

"I got ya," said TJ. "Well, I left my key card down here somewhere. Ah, here's the little devil. Hung it on the cage. Mind's the first to go, ya know."

"You're telling me," said Marlowe with a forced grin.

"Okay, see ya later, Detective."

"Later, TJ." Marlowe watched TJ until he disappeared up the stairs. He listened for the basement door to open and then shut.

Christ. I should have brought a second pair of underwear.

He waited several minutes to make certain TJ did not return. Marlowe sighed and regained control of his frazzled nerves. He jimmied the lock and entered the storage locker. It was packed with row after row of rickety steel shelving, and Marlowe needed to turn sideways to navigate between the narrow aisles. Finally, he made it to the rear of the storeroom.

Drugs, here as in most cities, were a popular recreation. So much so, Birmingham Metro was usually backlogged with a stash awaiting destruction. Earlier, Marlowe had prepared several bricks of baking soda wrapped in the same brown paper as used in evidence. He would take the drugs and replace them with the baking soda. No longer needed as evidence, and merely destined for the ovens, Marlowe doubted anyone would sift through individual bricks checking authenticity.

He made the switch, tucked the cocaine into a duffle bag, and left the station. A quick call to dispatch gave him the present location of Officer Michael Drenning. To his relief, Drenning had gotten off duty a few hours earlier; his patrol car was likely sitting in the driveway at home.

Marlowe drove to Emerald Lane and parked two blocks away from the Drenning house. In his suit, albeit a wrinkled one, he would pass for a resident, at least in the dark. Well past midnight, no lights were on in the house, but a single floodlight blazed over the driveway.

Shit. Do I take my chances no one sees, or knock out the light? Decisions, decisions.

He decided busting the light seemed riskier. Marlowe strolled up the behind Michael's patrol car like it belonged to him. Lucky again, Michael was stupid—or arrogant—enough to leave the car unlocked. Marlowe hit the trunk release to the left of the steering wheel and eased the door closed. He hurried to the back of the car, lifting the trunk to expose the Mossberg mounted to the underside. He shuffled through the usual stuff, blankets for victims, spare ammo, first aid kit, and a spare uniform, and pulled up the floor mat to expose a hollow by the wheel well. He packed the duffel into the space and put everything back as it had been. With some luck, Michael would not find it. With a larger dose of luck, he would not have cause to open the trunk at all. At least not for the next forty-eight hours. Now to get Vice involved.

THE NEXT DAY, AFTER CHECKING IN WITH RAZE, MARLOWE MET WITH

Detective Ricky King in Vice. A small man with piercing blue eyes, Ricky had come up with Marlowe in the department. They patrolled together for a year shortly after joining the force.

"Gentry, long time no see." Ricky rushed over to clasp hands with Marlowe.

"Too long. We work in the same building, yet I never seem to run into you."

"Vice is night work. The cockroaches only crawl out after dark."

"How's the family?"

"Gregory is bigger than me now. So is my wife, but don't dare tell her I said so," said Ricky, laughing.

"Not a chance."

"Oh, you'll never guess who I ran into last week. Willie 'Jets' Johnson."

"Really? He finally got out, huh?"

"Yep, only now he's Reverend William Johnson. Pastor down at Trinity Church of God, you know, over on 6th Avenue. Ha, we must have busted him a dozen times. Guy boosted more stereos than Joan Rivers had face lifts."

"Amazing how ex-cons always seem to find religion. Tend to lose it again pretty quick though. Once they're out again."

"Too true. God doesn't pay as well as a good fence," said Ricky. "So, what brings you to our fair corner of crime and mayhem?"

"Dirty cop and drugs. Interested?"

"Singing my song, dude."

"I've got a snitch ready, but I need you guys to orchestrate the bust. Location and time are set."

"Done all my work for me, I likey." Ricky rubbed his palms together in mock excitement.

"Tomorrow night, eleven p.m. Westside Industrial Park. Warehouse 15."

"Good choice. Open, only two ways in and out by car. Two doors on each wall—front and back. Used it once or twice myself. How many perps?"

"Just the one. Name's Michael Drenning. He's a patrolman with

County. Our snitch will be in a white Camaro—'85 model. Black t-shirt and jeans. Safe word is 'Protect and Serve.'"

"Nice touch," said Ricky, grinning. "We'll set up at both exits and cover all the doors once the perp pulls in. Take him down after he makes contact with your snitch."

"Sounds good."

"Want to tag along?" asked Ricky. "It'll be just like old times."

"Love to, but I better sit this one out. I have some history with Drenning. Might taint the bust if I'm present."

"Gotcha. No worries, we'll handle it."

"Thanks Ricky. I knew I could count on you."

Marlowe left Vice and made his way to Homicide Division. Nothing more to do now but wait.

MARLOWE DID NOT TAG ALONG WITH RICKY AND HIS TEAM, HE ARRIVED an hour before them. Most of the old industrial park warehouses were equipped with access ladders. Marlowe made use of the one attached to Warehouse 15 and climbed onto the metal roof. He sat next to a window offering a full view of the warehouse floor.

This particular warehouse had been empty for a while. Formerly part of Odell Steel, it was abandoned when the company moved north a few years back, and no new business had bought it. An aluminum structure with steel framing, beams positioned every twenty yards or so crisscrossed below a bare metal ceiling

At ten minutes until eleven p.m. Raze pulled through the north gate in his Camaro. Five minutes later, Drenning drove in the south end. The cars came to a halt ten yards from each other. Raze stepped from his car, nervous as a rabbit with a crack habit. He couldn't stand still. Thrusting his hands into his pockets, he rocked back and forth on his heels. Marlowe could see the whites of Raze's eyes from his post.

Settle down, Raze. Don't give the game away.

Michael seemed more in his element. Shoulders back, confident, he strolled to the front of his cruiser. He eyed Raze up and down and peered around the darkened warehouse. Not his first rodeo, Michael knew enough to remain wary.

"I don't like this, shithead," said Michael, seeming satisfied the warehouse was empty, and no surprises would spring from a dark corner. "Carlos said you're good, so I'm here, but you make one wrong move and I'll drop you. Understand?"

"Yeah, I got it, tough guy." Raze puffed up and attempted to sound the part.

"So you're the new middleman. A bit scrawny for the job. Alright, let's get this done. Where's the stuff?"

"I'm buying," said Raze.

"What the fuck? I've done this a hundred times. I pick up and drop off, shitlick. Where the hell did Carlos find your dumb ass?"

Raze's eyes bulged as fear and bravado clashed. "You got the shit or don't you?"

Michael's face turned red. "You trying to fleece me, bitch?" For a moment, he simply stood there glaring at Raze. As suspicion deepened, he pulled his gun. His eyes darted around as he backpedaled behind his driver's side door. "Something ain't right here."

Raze ran past the side of his Camaro and ducked down behind the rear, hands over his head. Marlowe particularly enjoyed the expression on Michael's face as the truth sank in.

"You little fucker. You set me up." Michael leaned up over his door, trying to get a clean angle with his gun on Raze. He moved toward the Camaro, but held up at the sight of lights outside the building. He ran back and dove in behind the wheel of his black-and-white.

On cue, police vans rolled up to block the north and south entries, floodlights blazing. Ricky and his team stormed in through each end of the warehouse, with more cops swarming through the side doors. The interior of the warehouse lit up with flashlight beams like a Pink Floyd laser show.

"Down, get down now," yelled Ricky.

Michael refused to give up without a fight. Smoke billowed from the rear tires as the patrol car lurched into reverse. The vehicle smashed into one of the steel support beams, rocking the warehouse with a thunderous *boom*. Michael spun the car to face the direction he had entered the building. He revved the engine, appearing intent on ramming the vans blocking the exit.

The car bolted forward, tires squealing, cops leaping out of its path, and smashed into the pair of vans in the door, aiming for the gap where their front fenders touched. The heavy utility trucks tilted from the violent collision, and slid back a couple of feet with a resounding *bang*, but did not part enough for Michael's vehicle to pass through. The back end of his cruiser pitched into the air and came down hard, bursting both rear tires.

Michael's airbag exploded on impact, knocking him senseless. He sat behind the wheel, head lolling around on his neck. One of Ricky's team grabbed him and yanked him from the car. With a dozen officers surrounding him, guns aimed, and Michael helpless on his stomach, they had him cuffed in seconds.

"Search the car," said Ricky.

Two officers went through the cruiser's interior while a third searched the trunk. It took about five seconds to locate the duffel bag.

"Got a bag here," said one officer.

"Unwrap it, see what our friend brought us for Christmas," said Ricky.

The officer opened the bag and removed several rectangular blocks wrapped in manila paper. Ricky retrieved one, pulled a small knife from his pocket, and sliced into the brick. Touching a finger inside, he withdrew it and placed the tip to his tongue.

"Ah, Merry Christmas," he said.

"That shit ain't mine. You framed me. Somebody's setting me up," screamed Michael. "I'll kill whoever did this. I'll kill 'em...." His voice cut out as the officers unceremoniously tossed him into the back of one of the vans.

Could not have gone better. From his perch on high, Marlowe smiled.

CHAPTER TWENTY-THREE

"**M**arlowe? Can you come by this evening?" asked Becca.

"Sure. You working late?"

"No. Come to my house."

"Your house? What about Michael?"

"I don't think he will be coming home tonight ... or for a lot of nights."

"Hmm, well in that case."

Becca hung up the phone, grinning ear to ear. Dancing across the living room to Alanis Morissette and The Cranberries for hours, she laughed and cried at regular intervals. Not tears of sadness, but of pure joy. She would have swollen ankles tomorrow, and she did not care.

Sweet freedom. She tasted it in the air, felt it swirling around her as she swayed to the beat. No more Michael.

She still couldn't believe it. Ten years of hell ended in one night. It was not something Becca could have done herself. No, all her options and schemes never amounted to more than a fool's hope of being rid of Michael or escaping him. God, fate, something needed to intervene. Yet neither of those rescued her. Her savior was a man, a mere mortal.

For reasons she did not understand, he stepped in and solved a problem that would have killed her in time.

When the doorbell rang, Becca rushed to the entrance. Like a silly teen, she giggled as she opened the door to Marlowe. She wanted to leap into his arms.

Gathering herself, a giddiness coloring her words, she said, "Glad you could make it. Come on in."

"No problem. Everything okay?"

"I think you know it is. I wanted to thank you in person."

"For what?" Marlowe maintained a stoic expression, but Becca could see the roguish hint flitting behind his eyes.

"Michael made me feel weak a lot of the time, but I've never been good at asking for help. I thought no one *could* help. Suffer in silence, my mantra. I don't know how you did it. I don't want to know. I'm just so glad you did."

"Sorry, but you've lost me." Marlowe's facetious tone gave him away.

"Fine, we'll play it your way if you want. Still, you're going to stay and have a glass of champagne with me. I, for one, am celebrating. Do the honors?"

Becca handed Marlowe the bottle and a corkscrew. He popped the cork, quickly turning the spewing froth toward the sink, but not before dousing Becca and soaking her shirt.

"Shit. Sorry," he said, embarrassed.

"No harm done." Becca threw back the glass of bubbly liquid in a few large gulps. She reached down, took her shirt at the waist, and tugged it over her head.

MARLOWE'S EYES WENT WIDE. SHE LOOKED SO BEAUTIFUL STARING UP AT him. Her jet-black hair cascaded down her shoulders and onto her chest, lustrous, glistening in the light, strands raking against the nipples of perfect, ample breasts. She moved to him, pressing her body against him.

"Becca, I … I can't do this. I want to. God, how I want to. But you are a key witness in a colossal case. I could lose my job."

"I'm no help to your investigation. I didn't see anything. I don't know anything. I can't help with the case. But I can help with this.…" She pulled his belt loose and thrust her hand into his pants.

"You don't owe me anything. I'm just glad you're safe now." Marlowe managed only a meager protest against her advance.

"It's not about that. Not all of it. I need this, and I know you do too." She nuzzled against his chest, one hand squeezing his swollen member.

"What the hell." Marlowe grasped her beneath the arms and lifted her onto the countertop.

They tore at each other's clothes, both hungry with need. Marlowe bit her neck, lifting her onto him. She screamed with pleasure as he entered her. Rocking back and forth, aggression and passion, hostility and tenderness, alternated in a struggle to vanquish old wounds.

He did not remember how they made it to her bed. Looking up at her from his back, her fingers digging into his chest, Marlowe grasped at the moment. He gazed at Becca, the silver light streaming through an open window framing her form in an angelic pose. He wanted to hold onto the image—to this feeling—and never let it escape. He wanted to fix it in place forever, to spend the rest of his life in this moment.

They erupted together, a release of everything horrible and feared. Years of self-loathing, shame, and sadness exploded outward, replaced by ecstasy. For one sweet instant, the world hovered between past and future. Nothing outside this one moment held relevance. The world disappeared—only two bodies locked in fulfilled desire remained.

"Wow," Becca said, falling back onto the bed. "You just get out of prison or something?"

"Ha. No, but it has been a long time."

"For me too. We both needed that … badly."

"I agree. I didn't realize how much." Marlowe traced the back of his hand along the outline of her hip.

"You're alright with it? Really?" Becca rolled toward him, her head resting on his shoulder. He could feel his heartbeat against the palm of her hand.

"Yes, really."

"I know why you have reservations. I have them too. How we met, what we have in common. Not the best ingredients for a relationship. But I'm not asking for anything. My mind can't even think long term. Right now, we need each other. We both have demons to exorcise. What happens next ... we'll figure out as we go. Deal?"

"Deal."

Marlowe turned onto his side to face her. "A shrink should know better, don't you think?"

"Should know what?"

"Not to get involved with damaged goods."

"Everyone's damaged, it's merely a question of degree. Even Michael's damaged in his own way. But he manifests it through anger, lashing out at everyone and everything around him. You and I turn it inward. We pour ourselves into our work, as if controlling one part of our lives will help us to control the rest. It never works. We both help others because we can't seem to help ourselves. And I'm not a shrink, I'm a clinical psychologist. Thank you very much." She playfully shoved him, that infectious smile beaming.

"Sounds like you're a pretty good one too. How did you get into that field?"

"A neurotic mother," she said, laughing. "I'm only half joking. I love my mother, but she goes through husbands like a rock star goes through rehab clinics. Listening to all her moaning and bitching over the years gave me tons of theories on emotional distress ... hers and mine. Still, having a high-powered attorney for a mother always comes in handy."

"An attorney, huh?"

"Yeah, Mary Tolbert."

"Mary Tolbert is your mother?" Marlowe shook his head.

"You know her?"

"Of her. Doesn't everyone? I remember when she sued Jonathan

Craft—richest, most powerful man in the state. She had him crying on the stand."

"That's dear ol' mom. Making men cry is her specialty. That, and enticing them to marry her."

Marlowe couldn't remember feeling so at ease in a very long time. Becca had a way of disarming him. She saw him the pain and guilt, but also the goodness.

"What about your father?" asked Marlowe.

"He died when I was young. Heart attack. I don't remember him very well. Only a few memories of his big, rough hands … and his laughter. I think the main reason mom has married so many times is she's trying to find my dad again. Each time she remarried, I can't count the number of times she said, 'your father would never do that,' after they did something to irritate her."

"Sounds like you see people pretty clearly. Must be what makes you good at your job."

"I suppose. I do enjoy helping people. Most of my patients are suffering unimaginably, both physically and emotionally. I deal with patients who have terminal illnesses, progressive dementia, and a lot of the most debilitating conditions you could imagine."

"Must be tough hearing those stories all day, and coming home to your own set of problems." Marlowe reached over and brushed a lock of hair from her brow. He could not seem to stop touching her.

"Sometimes, but it also puts things in perspective. No matter how bad Michael treated me, it paled in comparison to what those people were going through."

"I can see that."

"What about you? How did you become a cop?"

"Stumbled into it. I started college with no idea of what I wanted to do with my life. I got a degree in psychology—don't worry, I'm no match for you. Then I went to law school, which I hated. Found I was pretty good at reading people too. I could figure out why they did the things they did. I trained at the FBI, thought I would be one of those profilers like in the movies. I met Katy and things changed."

"You really miss her a great deal, don't you?"

"Every day," he said, his eyes going dark.

"I can't even begin to imagine what you've been through. Even with the patients I treat, I can't think of anything as horrific as losing someone you love in such a violent way."

"I hope you never have to." He averted his face, trying to hide the pain and weakness.

"I'm sorry. Let's talk about something else."

"I've got a better idea." Marlowe rolled Becca onto her back.

"Now you're talking," she giggled.

This time, they made love slowly and tenderly. Marlowe felt the weight of his world lift off his broad shoulders for little while. For a blissful instant, Seraphim did not exist and the Churchill Murders were only horrible make believe.

When at last they collapsed, spent, into each other's arms, Becca sighed with contentment, lay her head on his chest, and fell right to sleep. Marlowe gazed up at the ceiling, holding Becca close, smelling Becca's hair, touching Becca's skin; yet, when he drifted off, it was Katy who waited in his dreams.

MARLOWE PULLED INTO THE STATION A FULL HOUR LATE. Disentangling himself from Becca had been more difficult than he thought, and not just from the bed. Their encounter was more than a meaningless one night tryst. No, something sparked between them, something beyond lust or a convergence of circumstances. They had both existed alone for so long, hiding somewhere within themselves. Their connection seemed inevitable in retrospect. Still, theirs remained a relationship rife with dangers—for both of them. He wanted to protect her, not hurt her, but the idea of losing what now grew between them terrified him more.

"Where the hell have you been?" Spence rounded the front of Marlowe's car. He seemed irritated, angry even.

"I'm here now."

Spence rubbed his face and tramped across the lot. Obviously, something bothered him. Marlowe wished he would spill it already.

"Something on your mind, Spence?"

"Yeah, yeah there is. Tell me you didn't have anything to do with it. Make me believe it." Spence stopped and turned on him, his eyes locked onto Marlowe's.

"What are you talking about?"

"Michael Drenning. Officer Michael Drenning. Husband of our key witness. The witness you have been getting all chummy with lately."

"I have no idea what you're talking about."

"No? Seems Officer Drenning got nabbed in a sting. Found enough coke in the trunk of his car to put him away for a very long time, possibly for life."

"That's too bad."

"You think so? Well, you'll love this then. Raze supposedly sold him the coke."

Marlowe flashed an appraising frown. "That is a strange coincidence."

"Bullshit. The husband of our witness *and* the two-bit junkie we questioned? Raze couldn't get his hands on that much coke if his life depended on it. You set Drenning up; you framed a cop."

"Listen Spence, if you have some evidence of a crime, you should probably talk to the lieutenant." Marlowe tried to push past toward the building, but Spence moved into his path, placing a palm against his chest.

"Don't do that, Marlowe. This is me. Talk to me goddammit."

"Fine, Spence. You want it?" Marlowe shoved Spence back a step, his anger rising. "The guy beat the shit out of his wife on a regular basis, and he was a dirty cop. He *did* have a side business moving drugs around, and he got what he deserved. I only helped set up the sting."

"Really, that's all? Raze didn't make any sale, he just got Drenning to the site. The drugs were already in his trunk because you put them there."

"I don't know where you're getting your information."

"Wasn't hard to figure out, and if I figured it out, how long before someone else does? Someone not on your side?"

"Nothing to figure out, and even if there was, who's going to question it? A dirty cop with a history of complaints against him, and a DA's office investigation pointed at him … *prior* to this?"

Spence did not have a good answer for that. Clearly, he did not know about the DA investigation. "Why the interest? Why was it so important you stick your neck out, put your career on the line to take this guy down?"

"The right thing to do? Remember the concept?"

"No, it's more. It's the doctor."

Marlowe shifted his eyes and reddened.

"Shit, I don't believe this. You're fucking her, aren't you? Jesus Christ, Marlowe. I was kidding about you two. I knew, or thought I knew, you would never get involved with a witness. You could lose your badge over this. How will you take care of Paige if that happens?"

"Won't happen. No one but you knows. No one else is going to know. Besides, she's no good at trial. She saw jack shit." Marlowe stared hard at Spence, the warning evident in his eyes.

"You're my partner, my brother. I would never rat you out, but shit Marlowe. Why? Tell me why."

"I didn't plan it. The shit he did to her … pissed me off. Attacked by two psychos, she needed my help. I had to protect her. I have to."

"There it is. You've been going downhill for a while now. I blame myself for not jerking your ass out of it sooner. I hinted at it when you tore our vic's house up. I put it more bluntly when you nearly tossed a witness out a window, but now, I'm going to give it to you straight." Spence stepped close, concern and annoyance written in his every feature. "You're obsessed, Marlowe. I understood it and gave you some space. After the Churchill Murders, you changed, and who the hell wouldn't? But you've changed again, and not for the better. This isn't who you are. I can tell you aren't sleeping. I can't remember the last time I saw you eat. You work this case day and night."

Again, Marlowe tried to walk away. Spence grabbed his arm and spun him around.

"Listen to me, please. You're becoming someone you don't want to be. Dr. Drenning is not Katy. Seraphim is not Frank Brumbeloe. Protecting her won't bring Katy back. Catching Seraphim won't change the past. All you can do is be the man Katy loved. Honor her memory with your actions. Be the father Paige needs. Right now, she and Katy would be ashamed of you."

The next thing Marlowe knew, Spence lay on the ground, blood trickling from his mouth. He looked down at his hand, still clenched in a fist. "You don't know what you're talking about. You don't know a fucking thing."

Spence sat there looking up at Marlowe, not with anger, but with sympathy and hurt. "This isn't you. You're better than this."

Marlowe stormed off, leaving Spence on the asphalt, wiping blood from his face, and checking to be certain all his teeth were still in place.

CHAPTER TWENTY-FOUR

T he monitor squawked out its beeps; the intervals between growing inexorably longer as Wanda's heartbeat crept toward ceasing.

"It won't be long now," said Charlotte, offering Gabriel a sad smile. "I'm glad you're here. You mean a lot to her."

"She is very dear to me as well. I can sit with her for a time if you need to rest."

"No. I want to be here ... in case."

Charlotte looked down. "I understand."

"Who?" said Wanda in a barely audible voice, the simple syllable weighted with effort.

"Gabriel, milady."

She extended her hand, begging him to come close. "I'm scared, Gabriel."

He nodded a greeting to Henry, who stood near, looking on through bleary eyes, and moved to Wanda's side. Peering down with aching compassion, Gabriel took her hand. "There is no need to be frightened,"

"I am. I know I shouldn't be. It's the unknown, what's going to happen to me? I believe, I do. Always have. But now, I don't know. I'm just scared."

"Look. Can you see it?" Gabriel said in a soft voice.

Her blind eyes moved side to side, trying to focus, to find something in the black. Death stood close, he knew Wanda could feel its icy touch hovering above her skin. The dark tunnel claimed her, and she had yet to find the light at its end.

"Wait, it is there, not so far," said Gabriel. "A city—white marble buildings shine in the sun. So grand, they eclipse any you have seen. A cool breeze blows off a sea so blue and clear. Beautiful people stroll streets of gold, each and every one young and strong. They know no hardships or suffering. They live perpetually in a state of perfect contentment. Look now, see? They bid you welcome. Eager for you to join them, their faces glow with love." Gabriel leaned to her ear and whispered, "It is time, milady. No need to struggle any longer. Take your place among them. Live anew, free of fear, in peace."

Wanda stared up toward the sound of his voice, and for a brief instant, he felt certain she saw him. "Thank you, Gabriel. My angel."

She squeezed his hand, an almost imperceptible pressure, tilted her head onto the pillow, and lay still. Charlotte stepped over and wrapped an arm around him.

"That was beautiful. Thank you, Gabriel. No one could have found better words to ease her fear," said Charlotte. Though the pain of loss weighted her voice, Gabriel knew she relished knowing her mother no longer suffered.

Gabriel turned toward Henry. He stood near the foot of the bed, blubbering like an infant. Feeling Gabriel's gaze, he moved to the window, ashamed to show his grief.

Gabriel moved to his side and placed a hand on his back. "Do not be embarrassed, my friend. Never be ashamed to love someone."

"I'm gonna miss the old bag. I know she's in a better place, and I envy her that, but this world just went a little colder ... a little darker. Ya know?"

"I do. I feel it too."

"She was always one to light up a place. You shoulda seen her.

What a looker—hair like gold and legs for days. She and her husband moved into the neighborhood in '58, I believe it was." Henry scratched his head, his eyes fixed out the window on something far away. "I spent more time with Wanda and Harold than with my own folks. I worked with Harold at his store downtown. How I learned to manage my own. After he died, Wanda took his place. She knew more than he did about the business. But not just business. Wanda taught me things about life, stuff no one else would." Gabriel knew Henry needed to reminisce, to etch the memories into his mind and guard them from fading. "Sucks hind-tit getting old. Too many gone, too many good ones. With every good one that goes, another scumbag moves in to take their place. Yep, the world's growing darker." Henry rotated away again; this time he let the tears flow.

Gabriel left his friend to his sorrow. He intended to deal with his own grief in another way.

GABRIEL PROWLED THE STREETS OF WESTSIDE SCANNING EVERY ALLEY, store, and bar. Nothing. His prey waited somewhere, unaware a hunter stalked him. Gabriel felt no burden of frustration; he walked with the placidity of purpose, his patience knew no bounds. He would walk and search until he found the one he sought.

He spotted Red Cap in front of an adult bookstore, his back to the wall, one foot braced behind him. The thug appeared so smug and self-assured. Something dark and cold twisted in Gabriel's gut.

No blessing this time, this would be a kill of a different kind. Not mercy, but justice … punishment. A tragedy Wanda died as she did, but a greater tragedy this one still lived. The scales required balancing. Gabriel lurked across the street, watching and waiting.

Red Cap sold his product for another hour until traffic waned. Done for the night, he proceeded down 14th Avenue, turning the corner at 35th Street. Strolling as if he owned the city, not a care in the world, he entered an alley behind one of the government housing projects.

Gabriel followed at a distance, maintaining sight of his mark. Once Red Cap entered the alley, Gabriel increased his pace, pulling up a few yards behind. He remained in the shadows, his glare piercing through the other man. Red Cap sensed a presence and spun around.

"Who's that?" called Red Cap into the gloom.

Gabriel stepped into the dim streetlamp's light, his darkened outline striking an ominous presence. Red Cap squinted, trying to make him out. Once he recognized Gabriel, he smiled.

"You? I'll be damned if it ain't R2D2. Where's grandma?" He laughed. "Thought she fought all your battles for you."

Gabriel said nothing, only stared.

"What the fuck you want?"

"Your life," said Gabriel.

The menace in his voice seemed to give Red Cap a moment of pause, a flicker of apprehension flitted across his eyes. He shook his head and flexed his muscular frame, appearing to remember he outweighed Gabriel by fifty pounds and towered over him by half a foot. Red Cap puffed out his chest and reclaimed his macho bluster.

"Grew some balls, did ya? Best get out of here before I fuck you up."

Gabriel advanced another step. Red Cap picked up a four-foot length of rebar someone had left lying the alley. He waved the bar at Gabriel, taunting him, daring him. Surprise washed over his face when Gabriel dashed from the shadows without another word.

The charge caught him off guard; Gabriel lowered his shoulder and rammed into Red Cap's stomach, knocking the air from his lungs. Stunned, Red Cap stumbled. Noticing a pile of concrete blocks behind the man, Gabriel slid to the side and shoved. Red Cap tottered on the debris. His leg twisted when a cinderblock collapsed out from under him, sending him toppling over hard on his back.

Gabriel leapt onto the big man, attempting to strangle the life from his floundering body. Red Cap proved too strong hand to hand. He worked one forearm between them and heaved, sending Gabriel flying. Gabriel rolled upright, ignoring the burn of a scuffed elbow.

Red Cap tried to regain his feet, but his knee buckled, dumping him on his rear.

Red Cap eyed Gabriel while rubbing his damaged knee. "You're dead, motherfucker." He worked his good leg underneath him.

Gabriel knew only seconds remained before the oaf could stand and his advantage disappeared. He ran at Red Cap with a wild overhead feint. The big man dragged himself backward, raising his arms to defend against a punch that didn't come. Gabriel hauled an intact cinderblock from the pile, and hefted it over his head. Red Cap threw his weight to the side in an effort to get his head out from under the strike. Much to his surprise—and pain—his huge skull was not the target. Gabriel brought it down with all his strength on Red Cap's injured knee. The big man howled. Again, and again, Gabriel smashed concrete into denim; the third time, it shattered into pieces. The crack of bones filled the alley. Red Cap screamed in agony.

Gabriel brushed dust and crumbled stone from his hands, and picked up the length of rebar. He stepped over him, adopting the posture of a knight with a rebar sword. His anger faded to a sense of purpose and resolve. He pictured Wanda lying in the hospital bed, blind and scared. He heard Mother's voice telling tales of valor.

His grip tightened on the rod.

Red Cap stared at the rebar with an expression that comprehended he was about to die. With quivering lips and fear dominating his eyes, he brought his hands up, both guarding himself and waving Gabriel away. Neither would work. Gabriel stood fast, confident nothing Rep Cap did would stop the length of steel from finding his skull.

"God no, please don't. I'm sorry about the old lady. I didn't mean to hurt her. I just wanted her money. I was desperate, man, you gotta understand. I got three kids to feed. Please don't kill me, please...." Red Cap cried. He lay there bawling like a toddler after a vaccine injection.

His pleas did not stay Gabriel's hand. The whisper of the Gods breezed through his mind. *Vengeance is mine, sayeth the Lord.*

Gabriel lowered his arm. Vengeance was not his calling, not his purpose.

Their will be done.

Gabriel numbed. His fingers loosened until the rebar slipped free and hit the pavement with an echoing *clang* that carried through the narrow alley. He reached into this pocket, withdrew the silver ring with a small opal stone, and tossed it to Red Cap.

"You need this more than I."

Gabriel walked away. Red Cap clutched his shattered leg, repeating *thank you* over and over.

As he returned home, he thought of Wanda. Gabriel viewed death differently than most. He did not look upon it with the same fear. Nevertheless, Wanda's passing left a hollow place inside him. His attachment to her and Henry surprised him in some ways. Their acceptance of *him* surprised him more. Perhaps they were surrogates for all he had lost and the family he needed.

Wanda's words echoed through his thoughts, but it was another's voice he heard.

"I'm scared, Gabriel."

Elisabeth weakened with each passing year. Her soliloquies turned from the cheerful to the tragic. No longer did she recite Hermia or Rosalind, but instead, verses uttered by the likes of Ophelia and Desdemona in their most angst-ridden moments.

"They bore him barefac'd on the bier. And in this grave rain'd many a tear. Fare you well my dove!" she said, her voice filled with despair.

Gabriel assumed she mourned his father. When she began to exhibit a new persona, he understood how much she missed Mason, and how lost she felt without him. He soon longed for this Elisabeth to recede back into his mother's subconscious.

"Where is your father? I never wanted it to be like this. After the accident, after things grew so hard … I didn't like this place. Never did. I didn't know anything about the country, how to live. Mason showed me, best he could, but I missed teaching. I had so many dreams. This was not the life I wanted, only your father's love sustained me."

Gabriel had never heard his mother speak this way. Gone the actress and the poet, leaving this frightened woman. She sounded no different from anyone else living in this area. She sounded … normal. The girl, the young woman from years past, before madness claimed her mind, pushed to the surface. The characters she played, mere deceptions designed to hide from herself.

In ways Gabriel could not describe, these rare moments of lucidity frightened him more than her alter-selves. He knew the actress, the poet, and all the rest. He grew up with them, watched them dance and recite for hours on end. This person wore no mask. Visceral, honest pain lay etched in her every feature from the haunted eyes to the sorrow-filled smile. The others he might humor or comfort, this one … nothing eased her pain.

Twenty-four years old now, Gabriel had spent the last decade trying to keep the farm running. He struggled daily to keep food on the table and clothes on their backs. But the heat of recent summers had scorched the land. Little rain and no money for fertilizer or insecticide meant no crops. He had slaughtered the last of the animals weeks ago. The freezer was filled and would last through one more winter.

The bank had claimed all their equipment for back mortgage payments. So little remained, and now Elisabeth's health gradually worsened by the day. Her body followed her mind toward disintegration.

One day, while helping her dress, Gabriel felt a rock-hard knot in her belly, larger than his fist. He knew she would not live long. On occasion, he had witnessed cancer in his animals, and held no illusions about what would come.

"When down her weedy trophies and herself fell in the weeping brook. Pull'd the poor wretch from her melodious lay to muddy death," Elisabeth said, her voice lifeless, monotone.

"No, you will recover. I will take care of you." Yet, in truth, he did not know how. Ill-prepared to care for her, Gabriel could only attempt to keep her comfortable, provide what needs he could, and hope the end came swiftly.

It did not. More than a year passed and Elisabeth hung on. Maybe a hospital would treat her, insurance or no, but she would not hear of it, becoming wild and violent at the mere mention.

"No. No, I will not be cut and prodded by strangers. Unhand me." She screamed and lashed out, striking Gabriel across his chest.

"Mother, calm down. You will hurt yourself. Mother, please." He attempted to restrain her, but she lunged away, falling hard to the floor. "Oh mother. You must not do such things. I am only trying to help you." Gabriel assisted her to her feet.

"Doth the lady protest too much?" She said and began to laugh uncontrollably.

Gabriel, near tears, felt lost. He could overpower her and take her to the hospital against her will. The process would cause her such pain, and in the end, he doubted any treatment could reverse her condition.

So they lived with Elisabeth in constant pain and Gabriel helpless. Day after day, always the same, until the day she asked him to kill her.

CHAPTER TWENTY-FIVE

"How did Michael get bail? They promised me he wouldn't." Becca, livid, stomped across the floor. Near tears, she could not believe her luck. Just when things seemed to be looking up, the bottom fell out again.

"I don't know. Some judge granted it, nothing we can do," said Marlowe. "You have the restraining order. Any violation will revoke his bail."

"If he believes he's facing life in prison already, what's to stop him from tacking on a count of assault? Or murder? You don't know him. He knows someone framed him. He'll blame me. I knew he was into something. The phone calls, the odd hours, and *he* knows I knew. After I called the police the night he … well, it won't be a leap to believe I took more drastic measures."

"Try to calm down. I've got a patrol car in front of the house, and a uniform set up out back. He won't get within a hundred yards without being spotted."

Becca blinked. "You can do that over a restraining order?"

"No, but I can on suspicion Seraphim may return to finish what he started."

Becca sighed. "My guardian angel. I keep getting you in deeper and deeper, don't I?" She embraced him.

"It's okay. I took it on, no one forced me." Marlowe lifted her head with a finger under her chin. "I won't let anything happen to you."

"I believe you. I do. It's just that my nerves are fried. I've been peeking outside and jumping at every sound for hours. I don't know how much more of this I can take."

"You've taken worse. I understand the not knowing can be worse than facing actual harm. The fact is, Michael is an asshole with a nasty temper, but he's also a cop. He knows how this works. He's not stupid. If he has any chance of beating the drug rap, he can't afford to compound things by violating his bail. And besides, it'll take some time to process him out of the tank."

"You're right. Of course, you're right. I'll try to hold it together."

"Good. Now I've got some things to take care of. I still have a job to do, you know. I'll check in on you later, okay?"

"Okay ... and Marlowe."

"Yeah?"

"Thank you, for everything."

"You've done that already." He grinned.

"I have, but then you do more stuff for me. I have to keep thanking you."

"Well, I like the way you thank me, so I'll have to keep doing stuff."

Becca escorted Marlowe to the door and watched him leave, comforted by the sight of the police cruiser parked on the street. Michael would never come here now. She repeated it over and over, hoping eventually she might believe it.

The house's every creak and groan startled her. A shifting shadow sent her rechecking locks on doors and windows. She needed to get her mind off it. Becca turned on the television, finally found a station not broadcasting news on Seraphim, and sat back with a glass of wine.

Only a single glass—need to keep my wits. Just one ... to take the edge off.

MAX WATCHED THE MAN LEAVE DR. DRENNING'S HOME. FORMIDABLE looking fellow—muscular, like a boxer. If the man returned with Max inside, it would be a problem. He could not take on a man that size, not in his condition, not even if he were perfectly healthy. Even so, it did not matter. Nothing could interfere with his mission.

Dr. Drenning stood at the door until the man drove away. Max watched her wave and then disappear inside. Not something he did every day, this endeavor taxed both his courage and his ingenuity. Staring at the house, all the things that could go wrong made his head thump and his pulse quicken.

He might as well try breaking into Fort Knox, out of his element by miles. Max needed a plan. Seraphim might return for the doctor at any moment. He had to get inside; yet, how could he gain entrance to the house with that police car parked so close? The front was obviously too risky. Maybe the back door.

One of the two policemen got out of the patrol car and walked around to the rear of the home. Perhaps, he would simply check around and come back. After several minutes, the cop did not return.

Dammit. What now?

Max was not a thief. Breaking into a locked home seemed hard enough, but while avoiding the notice of two cops ... impossible. Still, there must be a way. Seraphim would not have sent him if it were unachievable. A test? Surely, a test of his dedication—his desire to save her.

Lacking any expertise for breaking and entering, Max felt his stress level climb. The only bit of good luck, his pain had lessened to tolerable. The doctor said his cancer now encroached on the pain centers in his brain, blocking some reception from the nerves. He called it fortunate for someone in Max's condition. Max called it an answered prayer. On the down side, the condition might reverse at any time, amplifying the pain rather than dampening it. Still, for now, it felt like a blessing from heaven, and he owed repayment for the gift.

Max stared at the house and thought of Dr. Drenning. A hero for once in his life, he could be the champion rather than the villain, the savior instead of the destroyer. He would stand for her, take her place and die in her stead. A grand sacrifice.

I will stand for you.

Marlowe did not need another complication. Michael could pose a problem, and Marlowe did not have the time to worry with him. He wanted Michael out of circulation—permanently. Michael needed to violate his bail agreement, and Marlowe intended to give him a little help.

He walked across the street from Birmingham Metro to County lock-up. Michael would be back on the streets soon. Processing bail could take a while, however, especially when Marlowe *suggested* to the guard there might be some problems with the paperwork. Pesky red tape … poor Michael.

Now to make certain he stayed put. Marlowe always prepared a contingency plan, but working it now could prove tricky. Only one play left … and Raze was not going to like it.

A battered white sports car pulled up to the curb in front of the house. Max ducked low in the bushes as a man got out and headed toward the front door. Scrawny, more a kid really, dressed in torn jeans and a shirt that had seen better days. His sandy colored hair, cropped short, sported a long rat-tail dangling down his back. The cop in the patrol car stepped out, his hand resting on his sidearm. He moved cautiously up behind Rattail, and slid the gun free.

"Down. On the ground right now," shouted the policeman, gun trained on the man.

Rattail raised his hands high above his head and said something Max could not quite make out.

"I said down. On your knees, hands behind your head. Do it now asshole," said the cop. The commotion brought the second policeman rushing around the corner of the house. He took a position opposite his partner, leaving Rattail nowhere to go.

As commanded, Rattail fell to his knees and clasped his hands behind his head. The cop jerked them down and snapped handcuffs tight onto the wrists. Seated across the street, Max could just make out the exchange.

"Who are you? What are you doing here?" asked the cop.

"Raze, man, I'm Raze. Shit, these cuffs are too tight. Freaking hurt. I ain't going nowhere, can't you loosen 'em a little."

The cop tapped Raze on the head with the butt of his gun. "I asked you a question. What are you doing here?"

"Ouch. Officer Drenning sent me to pick up a package for him, okay. I got business here."

"Well, Raaaze," said the cop in a mocking tone. "Let's get this package, and then we can go down to the station and have a long talk. What do ya say?"

BECCA ANSWERED THE DOOR. "WHAT'S GOING ON?"

"This guy says your husband told him to pick up a package. I'm thinking he's trying to get rid of his stash. He didn't know we'd be watching the house. Dumbass," said the policeman, a satisfied smile on his face. His partner held their captive by the link between the steel handcuffs. "I'm Bateman, this is Kirkpatrick."

"Come on in," she said, nodding to each in turn. "Please be careful. Don't break anything,"

"Where to, Raze?" asked Bateman.

"Basement, behind the washer."

"Criminals, so predictable." Kirkpatrick shoved Raze toward the stairs.

Becca remained in the doorway above the basement. She prayed they actually found drugs down there. She prayed Michael could have been so stupid. Surely more drugs would keep him in jail, unless they considered it all part of the previous crime. If so, it might not affect his bail.

Stay positive. They'll find the drugs. Michael will remain in jail. Positive.

She could hear clanging and objects shifting below. Becca hoped they didn't damage her new washer and dryer.

"Got it. Nice," Bateman said.

They came up the stairs, Bateman bouncing a sack in his palm, Kirkpatrick still pushing Raze from behind. Oddly, Raze did not appear particularly worried.

Marlowe arrived a half hour after Bateman and Kirkpatrick took off with Raze in tow. Out of habit, he scanned the street: not a soul in sight. Becca waited for him in the doorway, hands on hips, her lips pursed with playful accusation.

"Any idea what that was all about?" she asked.

"I have no idea what you're referring to my dear," Marlowe said with a grin.

"No? Seems Michael sent one of his friends over to retrieve his hidden drugs. I guess he wanted to get them out of the house before someone found them."

"Fancy that. I did hear something about it, now that you mention it. Seems that Raze guy is on parole. I hear you're not supposed to associate with parolees while incarcerated or on bail. And the drugs … not good for ol' Michael. Pretty clear violation of his bail agreement. Looks like he'll stay locked up until the trial. Pity, some people never learn."

"I can't believe I'm thankful there were drugs in my house."

"Bit of luck there."

Becca eyed him closely, catching the glibness in his tone. "You knew they were there, didn't you?"

"I suspected as much … since I put them there."

"What?" asked Becca, her eyes wide.

"Plan B, in case Michael didn't take to the meeting with Raze.

Figured someone could tip the police off he hid a stash here. Glad now I left them in place. You never know when things will come in handy."

"Remind me never to cross you, Detective Gentry. Now, I'll race you to the bedroom." Becca darted for the stairs with Marlowe hot on her heels.

MAX WATCHED THE POLICE SHOVE RAZE INTO THE BACKSEAT OF THE cruiser and depart. Soon after, Boxer returned. Busy place. How many people would come and go? It made him nervous. For the millionth time, Max wondered if his sanity had completely fled. Still, he must trust Seraphim to guide him.

With the police gone, Max relocated to the east side of the house. He did not know if they were gone for good, or would soon return. No choice but to proceed under the suspicion they might be back. From his new vantage point, he noticed a small window slightly above ground level and set into a basement wall. He might be able to pry it open without alerting Dr. Drenning. It seemed his only option. Waiting for the cover of night, Max sat with his back to a large oak and listened for the voice to whisper direction into his mind.

He removed a revolver from his pocket and cradled it in his hands. A rifle or shotgun felt right at home in his grip, but he had never been comfortable with handguns. He had bought the .38 on a whim a few years back, but never fired it. Max knew his plans would frighten Dr. Drenning. Brandishing the gun should prove enough to encourage her cooperation ... he hoped.

Anticipation made him jittery. The sun seemed fixed in the sky, never moving an inch toward the western horizon. He thought of the last time he ventured into the woods. The memory unsettled him and caused his eyes to seek out the slightest sound.

All in the past, he told himself. Seraphim changed everything. He longer needed to fear. With this one courageous act, the past would melt away. Maggie and his boys could smile when they thought of him.

The cops did not return. He gazed into the sky again. The sun had dipped behind the trees. Max smiled.

Not much longer now.

CHAPTER TWENTY-SIX

Marlowe left Becca's at sunset and arrived home to the dark and cold. He found Paige in her room, stone-faced as always. She sat on the floor in her pink nightgown with a doll in each hand, making the man stab the woman in the neck. Marlowe rushed in and scooped her up, carrying her to sit on the bed with her in his lap.

"Oh, Paige ... what are you doing?"

She stared at her lap.

"I'm sorry...." Marlowe pulled her close, sniffling. "I should've shot him."

Paige didn't move. She felt lighter. He worried she'd not been eating enough. The red crayon marks on the female doll's shirt tore at his heart.

"Come on, sweetie. Talk to me. Please ... talk to me." He kissed the side of her head. "If I could go back and take Mommy's place, I would."

She leaned toward him, a half-hearted attempt to snuggle.

An hour passed. Paige sat impassive no matter what he said or how he tried to reach her. Not until he set her on her feet and told her to get ready for bed did she do anything more than stare into nothing.

Once she returned from brushing her teeth, Marlowe tucked her in. She gazed up at him from the bed. Those blue eyes could have held fatigue, sadness, anger, loneliness, or nothing at all.

Marlowe saw blame. Blame for letting Mommy die.

He stiffened. "Good night, sweetie. I love you."

Not expecting any sort of reaction, he didn't wait and walked out, headed down to his study. Alone with the quiet, he could no longer avoid the pain eating away at him. He knew his passion to apprehend Seraphim had grown into an obsession having little to do with the actual killer. Why attempt to deny it?

In this house, surrounded by memories, denials were useless. Reality obliterated all imaginings that life existed as anything but dark and horrible. No happy ending waited, only a chance to remove one tiny speck of evil from the world. In a year, no one would remember, new horrors would rise to take Seraphim's place. It did not matter. Seraphim had become Marlowe's white whale—the only thing keeping him going. He clenched his hands into fists atop his knees, thinking about Paige's dolls. She was trapped in that moment too. Frank Brumbeloe hadn't just killed Katy, he had murdered his daughter's innocence.

Becca distracted him, maybe even gave him some measure of contentment, but she was not here now. Here, only ghosts kept him company. The Marlowe Becca saw did not live here. No, in this house only a husband to a dead wife, a father to a near catatonic child, existed.

This isn't you. You're better than this. You're better than this....

Spence's words echoed through Marlowe's brain, growing louder, he could not shut them out. Even ol' faithful Jim Beam, two-thirds gone, seemed unable to quiet the chastisement. The words came to life bearing steely eyes, glaring with disappointment. Their fingers pointed out his failures, his shame.

Your family would be ashamed of you.

Faces floated in the darkness—mouths moving in silence hurled accusations and broke down his defenses. Why couldn't they understand? He acted, did the hard thing. Standing still, frozen with indecision, playing it safe or by the book, what did that gain him?

The faces drifted closer, their words garbled whispers in his mind.

This isn't you. This isn't you. You're better....

"What do you want from me? I did what I had to do!"

He did not do anything bad. The job got done, that's what counted —the ends justified the means, only the ends mattered. So he lost it in a vic's house, big deal. A bad day, everyone had them.

He hung a slimeball tweeker out a window and made sure a dirty cop went to prison. Good deeds. Anyone going to cry over those two? No.

Maybe he played fast and loose with the rules. Rules ... fuck 'em. Rules did nothing but get in the way. They interfered with getting the job done, the hard things, the things that must be done. Didn't people admire Dirty Harry, his type? People wanted protection and safety, if he bent a law here and there in order to provide it, so what.

Michael got what he deserved. A drug-pushing cop. A wife beater. He'd have killed Becca eventually. Marlowe felt no guilt over Michael's incarceration. So why did he feel so goddamn guilty?

This isn't you. You're better than this.

What if he wasn't better? The man Spence spoke of died long ago. He died with Katy. He died each day watching Paige plod through life like a zombie. Spence, and the rest, needed to start accepting the new Marlowe, because no one else existed. The old Marlowe was gone ... and good riddance. Weak—unwilling to do the hard things, the things that must be done—the old Marlowe got his wife killed, his child fucked up beyond healing.

This isn't you. You're better than this.

Your family would be ashamed of you.

"Shut up! Leave me alone!"

Marlowe screamed into the silence of an empty home. No, not a home ... not anymore. Only a house now, a meaningless structure of wood and brick, no life left in it. The ghosts of the past dwelled here now. They claimed all he once held dear, changing him.

A door creaked in the hall. Marlowe scowled. His yelling must have awakened Mable. Hopefully, she wouldn't be dumb enough to complain right now.

He took another swig and sat staring at his distorted reflection in the amber liquor. Nothing appeared the same anymore. The world shifted into a version of itself he no longer recognized. Marlowe closed his eyes, hoping to find the quiet void. Somewhere distant came the soft *thud* of a shot glass falling to the rug. For an instant, a flash of pink moved in the corner of his eye.

Images flashed. Some sped by too quickly to grasp, leaving only a residue of the emotions they carried—joy and pain, hope and disillusionment, love and loss. Others fell on him like great birds of prey, talons stretched wide, sinking into his flesh. Memory after memory assaulted him, vivid with reality … impossible to deny:

"But I don't want Butters to be dead. I want him back," said Paige. Her bottom lip quivered, tears filming her eyes, as she stared down on the little black dog's still form.

"Sweetie, Butters is in heaven now. He's playing with the angels," said Marlowe. The words sounded silly even in his own ears.

"I want him back. The angels can get their own puppy."

Marlowe had reluctantly allowed Paige the dog—reluctant for this very reason. She was not ready to learn about death. An understanding of death killed a little piece of childhood. Nothing could ever be quite as carefree again.

He would have hid this to protect her from that truth, if he had found Butters first. But every morning, Paige shot out the door to play with her pup. She would run with Butters hot on her heels and roll on the ground as the tiny furball licked at her neck. The sound of her giggling lit up Marlowe's world.

A stray, Butters had wandered into their yard one day. A cute little thing with big, sad eyes and floppy ears, he could not have been more than a year old. Marlowe planned to build a pen, but with his work schedule, he simply never got around to it.

The rural highway running in front of the house doled out pet death on a regular basis. Teenagers racing home before curfew, delivery vans nearing quitting time, a free roaming pet did not stand a chance. Marlowe should have built the pen.

They found Butters's body lying in the ditch. Poor thing must have died on impact to remain so close to the road. Marlowe had heard Paige scream and rushed from the house, fearing she was injured. When he saw the motionless black lump, he knew, and his heart sank.

Marlowe retrieved a box large enough to contain the body and wrapped it in Butters's favorite blanket. They picked a spot high on a hill behind the house beneath a sprawling oak tree. With Paige and Katy looking on, Marlowe dug the grave.

After placing the last shovel of dirt, he hammered a cross made from two by fours into the ground and carved the dog's name into the wood. Paige hung Butters's collar on the cross. Along with Katy, the three stood solemn, holding hands.

"Why did Butters have to die, Daddy?" asked Paige. The pain and loss in her voice broke his heart.

"Listen, Sweetie, death is just a part of life—the last part. It's the period at the end of the sentence. The important thing is to write the very best sentence you can. So, when it's time to put the period on it, you're ready.

"Butters's sentence was too short, and that's sad, but he still wrote one. One you get to read anytime you think of him. Your sentence is what you do in life, all the good stuff... and the bad stuff too. That's why you want to write the best one you can, filled with as much good stuff as possible. Understand?"

"I think so. Daddy ..." said Paige, looking up at Marlowe.

"Yes, Honey?"

"I think you'll have the best sentence."

Marlowe and Spence searched Matthew Young's home looking for anything that might give them a lead on Seraphim. Spence proceeded to the rear of the house, leaving Marlowe with the living room and kitchen. Marlowe walked to a series of shelves near the television set. Several photos lined one level. They depicted Young with his wife and daughter.

A happy family, standing on the beach, wrapped arm in arm ... happy *together. Fury built inside him and exploded outward. He shattered the photos, raked the knick-knacks and trophies to the floor. He tore through the room snatching items from drawers and flinging them into the air.*

A madness seized him. He wanted to obliterate everything, erase the memories of Matthew Young from this home. Erase the pain Young's absence would bring his family. Marlowe wanted to destroy the illusion of happiness. He broke what could be broken, until every item and fixture reflected the turmoil raging within him.

When Spence returned, Marlowe collapsed, his frenzy exhausted. He stared at the upheaval he created. No photos of Matthew Young, his wife, or daughter remained intact or recognizable. Yet, an image still burned in his mind's eye—a man, his wife, and his daughter ... despair ... alone.

"The police? You're really thinking of joining the police?" asked Katy.

"What else am I going to do? I have no desire to practice law. Nothing much you can do with a BS in psychology," said Marlowe.

Katy laughed. "I'm sorry ... I'm not laughing at you. Well, I am, but ... I just can't see you as a cop."

"And why is that, pray tell?"

"No offense, Honey, but you aren't exactly a manly man. You loathe violence. You'll scoop up a spider rather than kill it. Marlowe, you have a favorite opera for crying out loud. How many policemen do you think have even heard of La Traviata?"

Marlowe feigned hurt. "How dare you. I'm as he-man as the next guy. I simply choose to suppress my primitive nature. It's in here, don't you doubt it missy."

He dashed forward, hoisting Katy over his shoulder. "Me Tarzan, you Jane."

"Put me down, ape-man," said Katy, laughing and pounding at his back.

"You don't think I can cut it?" asked Marlowe, once they both caught their breath.

"That isn't it. You can do anything. Maybe I'm not giving cops enough

credit, but you're so smart. Almost as smart as me," she said with a sly smile. "When I think police, I think former high-school jock or class bully."

"A pretty disparaging generalization."

"It is, isn't it? Okay, remember that frat party our senior year? The one where Kap almost drowned? Drunk as a skunk, someone dared him to jump off the balcony into the pool. Fully clothed, he looked like big jellyfish floating on the bottom. You jumped in and pulled him out. He pushed you away and said he had everything under control."

"I remember," said Marlowe, grinning at the memory.

"Well, do you also remember the other drunk? The not so cute or funny one?"

"Hmm, I don't think so...."

"Really messed up guy. I don't recall now what caused it, but he went off. He took out a knife, started threatening people, and then said he would kill himself."

"Oh yeah. Depressed and drunk, not a good combination. Not a bad guy though, I took a chem class with him."

"See that's what I mean. You see the good in people. If someone does something bad, you always think their circumstances caused it. You think if you can understand their situation, you can help them. No one is really bad or evil in your mind." Katy kissed him on the cheek.

"He was drunk. Who doesn't do stupid stuff when they're drunk?"

"But how many people would have stood there talking to him for an hour until he calmed down and sobered enough to surrender the knife? Not one other person at the party, and I'm doubting very few anywhere else. You did, though."

"See, I'm a natural hero."

"Hmm. What if talking didn't work? What if he attacked you and tried to kill you? Or hurt someone else while you were trying to talk sense to him? I'm not sure you have the heart for doing the hard things. You want to save everyone. Darling, I hate to tell you this, but not everyone can be saved."

"I know. I do. But shouldn't they have a chance to prove it before I decide they're beyond saving?"

"That's why I love you. Well, if it's really what you want," she said with a wink. "I do love a man in uniform."

He held Raze out the window, wanting to drop him. Marlowe wanted it so bad he could taste it. In his mind, he saw the little bastard splatter onto the pavement four stories below. The image felt ... good.

Raze deserved it. He fed the poor girl junk, shooting poison into her veins, and then pushed her to fuck strangers. All to keep her under his thumb. All to feed his ego, and his desire to be a player in the drug world. Nikki's life meant nothing to Raze. Why should his life matter to Marlowe?

One less parasite in the world, who would cry? Marlowe loosened his grip, feeling Raze's weight pull him downward. Gravity. Just let go. So easy. Raze deserved it.

"Jesus Christ, I said I don't know anything."

I don't care.

"Oh god, man. I didn't do it. I wasn't even here."

It doesn't matter.

"I swear, I didn't see nothing."

You deserve to die.

Marlowe lay in bed with Becca nestled against him. It felt nice to have someone to hold again. He liked that she needed him. Marlowe wanted to protect her and keep her safe. He needed to do this one thing right—keep her safe, keep her alive.

Sheer curtains waved gently, stirred by the breeze from an open window. Moonlight cascaded across the floor, casting soft illumination into the room. In the shadows near one wall, he saw a figure take shape, the outline of a woman's form posed in inky tones. As she stepped into the moon's glow, Marlowe's breath caught, tightening in his lungs. His heart beat in a slow, thunderous rhythm.

The figure emerged from the shadows. Marlowe's mind struggled to find substance in the apparition. Features solidified, leaving the ethereal plane, and merging with his reality. He could see her face now. Tears coated his eyes. Katy.

I'm so glad you have found someone, my love. I want you to be happy.

"Katy. I've betrayed you. You are the only one I ever wanted—will ever want."

No, you must live. Live and love.

"I can't. I will never try to replace you."

But you have. See her there, lying in my place. You have forgotten me.

"No, never. I can't forget. You are with me every day."

Liar. Liar.

"Please Katy. You must believe me. I'm so alone without you."

I know you are, darling. I only want you to be happy. I'm glad you have found someone.

Marlowe's mind split in two—the betrayer and the man in need. The man capable of love and the man lost to all emotion but despair. Katy stood before him, her expression blank and inscrutable. In one breath, she intoned love and encouragement, and in the next lashed out, blaming him for not taking the shot. He failed her.

THE MEMORIES AND NIGHTMARE IMAGES CEASED LIKE FLICKING OFF A television. The screen in his mind went black. Marlowe opened his eyes. His palms bled from nails digging into flesh through clenched fists. The tears flowed free, and he let them come.

In truth, the best part of him died that day with Katy. Now, he walked the earth sucking in the air rightly belonging to the living. A thief and a trespasser, violating a realm that had forsaken him ... that he had forsaken. Paige would be better off without him. Every time she saw him, he made her think of watching her mother die. Every time he saw those eyes, he felt the accusation burn into his heart. She would go to live with her grandparents up north—a fresh start. Marlowe should not be here.

His eyes found the photo of Katy and Paige on his desk. Like Young's, it depicted them enjoying the beach. Marlowe had not visited a beach since. So many things brought memories of Katy alive, Paige healthy and happy—hearing a certain song, seeing a particular doll.

Still, nothing carried more feeling than the memory of white sands and ocean breezes, Katy talking about their perfect lives. Perfect lives shattered on one tragic day, in one tragic instant.

Marlowe's gaze shifted back and forth from the photo to the gun lying beside it. The cold beauty of the gun's steel matched the radiant beauty of his wife and daughter. Each item held a promise. Photo and gun, in their own way, whispered to him ... *come with me.*

This isn't you. You're better than this.

The alternating memories reflected his two selves—Better and Worse. Two aspects within one form. The loving husband and father, and the man filled with rage and self-hatred. Both existed inside him. He could deny neither. Experience composed their qualities and need gave them life.

Every person possessed the two faces. One smiled on family and friends, seeking the good in life—loving, caring, hoping. The other looked on life with hate-filled eyes, loathing the evil and hardness of the world—fearing, suffering, seeking to destroy.

A war waged within Marlowe's soul, threatening to rip him apart. Anguish racked his mind. He wanted it to end. An end to this meaningless life.

The photo of Katy and Paige. The gun. Love and hope verses pain and despair. Two aspects of a man, each demanding sovereignty.

The question then ... which would rule?

He stared at the gun, trying to get it to leap into his hand by sheer force of will. His arm refused to move. Jim Beam had other plans for him. Marlowe slumped in his chair and passed out. Katy haunted his dreams with blood. The hundredth time she screamed, he woke, his decision made. His hand went to the desktop, fumbling for his gun. Frenzied fingers darted across the surface; pens, papers, and books fell to the floor.

Where is it?!

When he couldn't find it glancing about, Marlowe struggled to his feet and began tearing drawers open, flinging their contents across the room. The clap of objects ricocheting off walls and shelves echoed the thunder pounding in his brain. With nothing else to smash, he hunched in a Quasimodo stance—the sound of his heavy breathing the only mar in the silence.

"I hid it."

Marlowe spun at the sound of a tiny voice in the doorway. Paige stood there in her little, pink nightgown, clutching a doll by its tousled, red hair. She appeared angelic, framed by the hallway's light.

His eyes wide, Marlowe fell to his knees. "Baby ..." Tears streamed down his face, arms extended to his daughter.

"I don't want you to die like Mommy." Paige ambled into his arms. He held her as though she might evaporate into his dreams. "You tried to save Mommy from the bad man." She placed her tiny palms against his cheeks. "It wasn't your fault, Daddy. Please don't go away."

Marlowe collapsed to the floor. Seated with Paige in his lap, he stroked her hair and pressed her body to his chest. Racking sobs tore through him.

CHAPTER TWENTY-SEVEN

B ecca stepped out of the shower and leaned forward to gather her hair into a towel wrap. After shrugging on her bathrobe, she strolled into the bedroom, humming some tune she could not seem to get out of her head. She could not remember feeling this good in years. Maybe life was finally breaking her way.

Gone for only a few days, Michael seemed a distant memory. Becca felt as if she had spent the last ten years asleep, and today awoke to find it had all been a nightmare. It was not true of course. She would never recover all she lost, or completely rid herself of the scars. Even so, a new day dawned full of promise, full of anticipation and hope. The monsters had fled, and, though they were always waiting to crawl forth, for now, she locked them away in a dark corner of her mind.

Maybe she could have a future with Marlowe. She loved being with him, loved his strength and bullish dedication. Becca felt safe with him. Safe. A concept she had almost forgotten existed. Not afraid —when did she last feel this way? So long ago, she could not even recall it now. Safe and unafraid, she could get used to this.

Becca plucked her cell phone off the nightstand and opened to the contacts. She hovered over Marlowe's entry, debating calling him. To hear the sound of his voice would be like a warm blanket around her shoulders. She glanced at the time display. Too late. His daughter would be asleep now. She slipped the phone into the huge pocket on the side of her robe and wandered to the window. The police hadn't returned. No chance Michael would make bail now. Perhaps they decided to take their time with that "associate" of his.

She smiled, closed her eyes, and took in a deep breath of freedom.

A sweaty palm clamped over her mouth as someone grabbed her from behind. So preoccupied with meandering thoughts, she hadn't felt the lurking presence. She struggled, kicking, flailing, and trying to scream. He lifted her off her feet. Becca kicked a lamp over as they went stumbling back and fell on the bed. The arms around her crushed the air from her lungs.

Oh god, Michael. He's here. He's going to kill me.

The hand covering her mouth slid down to her throat and squeezed. She could not scream, could not breathe.

I'm going to die. Please don't let me die.

"Stop. Stop fighting. I'm not here to hurt you."

The voice sounded muffled and distant. Her heart pounded in her skull, threatening to explode. Becca's vision blurred as the room around her faded to black.

When consciousness returned, she found herself in the dining room. Her instinctual attempt to clutch her throat made her aware of tight cords around her wrists, binding them to the armrests of the chair, ankles strapped to the legs. Wet hair hung over her face. Her towel was gone, her bathrobe askew. Panic came on with a squirming fit that got her nowhere. A sound emanated from behind her, a click and shuffling steps. She tried to turn her head, to find him.

What is he going to do to me?

Frantic, Becca felt her fear escalate, becoming uncontrollable. The chair legs click-clapped against the hardwood as she rocked back and forth, trying to free herself. She tilted and started to tip over sideways, but stalled in midair with the clap of a hand on wood. He pulled her upright, setting the chair back in place.

"Don't do that. You'll hurt yourself," said a man's voice. A man's …
but not Michael's.

As he stepped into view, fear merged with puzzlement. She did not
understand. So certain Michael had returned, her mind fought to
accept a quite different reality. Becca knew this man, but the
recognition did little to clear her confusion.

"Max? Max Bannon? I don't … I don't understand. Why are you in
my house? What are you doing?"

He leaned close, staring *through* her. "I'm not going to hurt you. I
promise. I'm here to save you."

"Save me? Save me from what? You're not making sense, Max.
Untie me, we'll sit down and figure this out together."

"I want to, Dr. Drenning. Really, I do. He says you need to stay like
this. So you don't get hurt." Max checked her restraints to make
certain they remained secure.

"What? Who says? Is someone here with you?" Becca wriggled
around, trying to locate anyone else in the house.

"Yes, but you can't see him." His eyes glazed over. "Only I can.
Because he picked me."

"Who picked you? Picked you for what?"

"To stand for you."

A GENTLE HAND NUDGED MARLOWE FROM A SHALLOW SLEEP. HE
rolled over to see Paige standing at his bedside.

"Can I have pancakes?" she asked in a shy tone.

Marlowe blinked, afraid to believe he was awake. In a second, he
smiled. "Of course you can."

She swayed back and forth, biting her lower lip. His head still rang,
but he had not felt so alive in a long time. He forced himself to sit up,
waited for the room to stop spinning, and stood. Paige took his hand
and they made their way down to the kitchen where Mable stood by
the sink with her back turned.

"Good morning, Mable," said Marlowe.

The plump nanny jumped at the sound and whirled about with a suspicious squint—he never said good morning, or much of anything to her. Mable spotted Paige and tilted her head.

"Hi," said Paige with a narrow smile.

Mable stumbled into the counter with one hand pressed to her chest. After a few gasping breaths she burst into tears and shouted at the ceiling. "Thank the Good Lord!" She threw her hands into the air, and rushed over to envelop Paige in a hug. She put the girl down a moment later and regained her composure. "Good morning to the both of you. Coffee's in the pot." She knelt down to face level with Paige. "What would you like for breakfast, little angel?"

"I got this," said Marlowe.

Mable grinned and stepped aside.

Marlowe made pancakes, chocolate chip for Paige. As they ate, he asked Paige questions and tried to blow the dust off some of his old jokes. She offered succinct replies and giggled at his humor. A long way from returning to normality, but it was a start—a good start.

Marlowe sucked down two cups coffee and poured a third. Ah, Dunkin Donuts Dark—perfection. Nothing sobered him up or cleared his mind quicker. Marlowe left Paige playing with her dolls in the den and went to his study.

He retrieved the photo from his desk. The feelings remained a dull ache in his chest. The beach, its white sands and the blazing sun in the background, made him squint. He could hear Katy's laughter and the sound of Paige splashing in the waves.

His gun, found under the sofa, offered no more allure than a tool. A necessity of the trade. Marlowe tucked it into its holster.

This isn't you. You're better than this....

The words still haunted him. Along with the memories of that beach, Spence's words stung, but something else lay underneath. Hope.

Maybe somewhere inside hid the man Katy and Paige had loved, the man Spence believed still existed. Paige, with two simple sentences, rekindled his hope and woke him from a dark slumber. He shuddered at the realization of how close he'd come to slipping off the edge. Had Paige sensed it?

Marlowe let the thoughts come, not shying away. He tried to view them objectively, acknowledging the pain, but keeping it at a distance. *She spoke....* Tears gathered at the corners of his eyes. So close, cracks appeared in a wall he had built to remain impenetrable. With Paige, and perhaps Becca, it felt so close....

The phone rang, interrupting his meditation.

"Gentry," said Marlowe.

Dead air on the other end. A half-second before Marlowe thumbed the phone off, Becca's muffled voice said something indistinct.

"Becca?" Marlowe raised his voice.

"What was that?" asked an unfamiliar man in the background.

"Nothing.... Probably Bill next door yelling at his son. Please don't hurt me. Untie me. I can help you."

Marlowe's mouth went dry.

"I'm sorry, I can't do that," the man said.

Feminine grunting and wood creaking accompanied the brushy sound of cloth over a microphone.

Seraphim? Did he come back?

It did not make sense. Still, it was the only possible explanation. Maybe Becca did fight him off. Maybe she hurt him badly enough he fled and now returned to finish the job. If so, why the Judas kill first?

To let the scene cool down, of course. Goddammit. How could I have been so blind?

Why was Seraphim talking to her? *Becca got to him ... bought herself time.*

It was happening again. He could not let it happen again. Not again, no fucking way.

Marlowe snatched Paige into the air, hugging her tight. "Daddy's gotta work, babes. Be back soon." He lowered her to the floor and dashed up to his bedroom.

After dressing hastily, he pounded down to the stairs, two at a time, and headed for the front door.

"Daddy." Paige gazed at him. When she caught sight of the gun under his arm, a trace of worry appeared in her eyes.

Marlowe halted and turned. "Yes, baby?"

"I love you."

Marlowe smiled in spite of his worry; pride and affection swelled his chest. "I love you, too. More than anything." He kissed her on the forehead. "Be back soon."

She smiled.

Marlowe rushed out the door and jumped into his Explorer. He shoved his cop light onto the dashboard and ran over the trashcans on the way to the street. He floored it, trying to hold the cell to his ear.

Silence. He pulled the phone back enough to look. The call had dropped.

"Goddammit. No fucking way. No ..."

BECCA KEPT HER VOICE CALM. "EXPLAIN IT TO ME, MAX. TELL ME WHY you're doing this. What's this all about?"

Max paced back and forth, kneading his hands. "I have to, doctor. It's the only way. I can't go on like this. It gets worse every day. The pain ... I can't take it anymore. I tried to kill myself, you know. But I couldn't do it. I don't know why, I just couldn't."

He scratched his brow with the muzzle of his gun. "Can't even do that right. This is my chance. Don't you understand? I can do something important, something big to make up for ... everything."

Max looked skeletal—thin arms, sunken cheeks. He must have lost fifty pounds since their last session together. His rapid decline shocked her, and she had seen hundreds of patients with similar conditions.

Most frightening, however, was his descent into madness. She could see it in his eyes. The cancer had wormed into his brain and warped his reality. His mind created a new world. Whatever he saw or believed was real for him. Talking Max down would not be easy, perhaps impossible.

"He came to me. The Seraphim. He said he would return for you, and I could take your place. I can stand for you."

"That's crazy, Max. Listen to yourself. Seraphim is a brutal killer. A maniac. It's all in your mind. Your cancer is affecting your thinking, making you hear and see things that aren't real."

He seemed to consider this, and then shook his head. "No, I know the difference. Yeah, I've seen things, things that weren't really there. But this is different. It's real. He's real. *You* know, he came to you. He's come to others. All that isn't just in my head."

"No, it isn't. There's a real killer out there. And yes, he did attack me, but he only kills those who no longer want to live. I wanted to live, that's why he spared me. He let me go, Max, because I am not suicidal. He isn't coming back. He has no reason to."

"I don't want to live. He'll come for me. He *promised* he would. Maybe what you say is true, about why he didn't take you, but this is how he wants it. This is where he can find me."

"If that's the case, Max, how did he come to you and give you these instructions? He found you then without a problem. Why would he need you to be here now in order to find you?"

Max opened his mouth wide, wiggled his jaw, and closed it several times. He stared at the wall. "You're trying to mess with me. You're mixing it all up. Seraphim said he would come for you, and I can take your place. He'll take me with him. Take away all my pain. All my mistakes and failures won't mean anything anymore."

Becca needed to keep him talking. The call had gone through. Max almost heard Marlowe on the other end … a beep told her the phone ran out of battery, and she tried not to lose hope. Marlowe would come, she just needed to keep Max occupied. She was not certain at this point what he intended to do with her, but in his condition, she had no way to know what he might be capable of.

Max turned away, putting the heels of his palms to his temples. "I'm s-sorry for having to tie you to the chair, but you have to be here for him. Be quiet now, okay. He'll come soon and it'll all be over."

MARLOWE TURNED ONTO EMERALD LANE, SLOWING ONLY ENOUGH NOT to screech the tires as he stopped in front of Becca's house. From the foot of her driveway, the silhouette of a man walking around appeared plain as day on the closed blinds. Marlowe thanked whatever lived upstairs that her side windows faced east and let in the morning sun.

He grabbed the radio and called for backup before jumping out and rushing up to the front door. No sense in subterfuge; Seraphim would know what was up soon enough. Still, kicking his way in might startle him enough to hurt Becca. Marlowe edged to the corner of the window. A finger-width slice of glass by the blinds offered only enough of a view to see Becca seated in a chair in a peach-colored bathrobe, wrists bound with black cord. Her attention focused on something out of sight.

Two quick steps brought him to the door. He tried the knob, finding it locked. He glanced at the small flowerpots and decorative stones on either side of the stoop.

Maybe ... it always works in the movies.

He lifted the first flowerpot and peered underneath. Nothing.

Shit. Two more, fingers crossed.

Nothing under the second, but the third ...

Yes. Gotta love predictability.

He retrieved the spare key. With a little luck, he might slip in and get a clean shot before Seraphim realized he was there. As quietly as possible, Marlowe slipped the key in the lock and turned. No shots fired—a good start. He moved through the foyer and backed against the wall between the living room and kitchen. He had a partial view of the dining room, but no sight of Becca or Seraphim.

"You need help," said Becca, calm and steady. "I can help you. I understand you're in a scary place now. There's no need to press charges."

Good girl. She was obviously using her skills to keep him pacified and buy some time. Marlowe, gun in hand, slid along the wall to the edge of the hallway. He still couldn't see into the room without exposing himself to fire. Only one choice: a quick spin into the dining room, acquire the target, and take him down.

Two hands on his Glock, the cold steel pressed to his chest, Marlowe took a deep breath. As he leapt around the corner, time slowed to a crawl. Seraphim was behind Becca, a small revolver pressed to the back of her head.

Shit.

Seraphim stood, she sat. Marlowe had a clear line of sight ... a clear shot. Yet, even if he put one right in the man's eye, a spasmodic muscle contraction could cause Seraphim to fire. With it against her head ...

Marlowe had been here before. He had rounded another corner to see Frank Brumbeloe with his arm around Katy's waist, his knife at her throat. He broke out in a cold sweat as reality fell away.

"Just in time, Detective," said Frank, a smarmy man with greasy black hair and bad teeth. He nodded toward Marlowe's gun. "I wouldn't do that if I were you. My hand's not so steady these days. Even if you get that shot off in time, can't say this knife don't still cut her pretty little neck to the bone."

Katy trembled in his clutches. Her lips quivered, her eyes pleaded in silent terror. Paige cowered against the kitchen cabinets, crying.

"It's okay, baby. I'm here. You're going to be fine." Marlowe trained his gun on Frank and stalked closer.

"Ah, ah. That's about close enough," said Frank.

"Mommy," cried Paige.

"How sweet. Makes me miss my own mom. Oh, wait, never knew the whore," said Frank.

"Let her go, you bastard." Marlowe's heart threatened to pound out of his chest. He fought for calm, and failed.

"Now, now, no need for name calling. We're all friends here, aren't we?"

"I killed your low-life brother. Let them go. I'll put down my gun, and you can do what you want with me."

"Tempting, but I'm gonna have to say no. See, it's like I told you. You took my family, I'm gonna take yours. First, Mrs. Detective here, then maybe I'll have a go at that little one there. No? I know what you're thinking. You'll waste me. Yeah, I'm sure you will, but don't matter. I still win. You get to live

a long time with the memories in your head. Ain't no getting rid of them. Ah, a bonus, you'll probably have one messed up kid to boot." Frank raised his voice. "How bout it, sweetie-pie? You're gonna be dreamin' about me till you're all grown up."

Paige sniveled. "No!"

Marlowe's gun hand shook. "Goddammit, Brumbeloe, don't do this."

"It's been fun, but I'm getting bored."

Marlowe yelled, "Noooo!"

Frank Brumbeloe drew the blade across. As soon as he twitched, Marlowe fired, but it was too late. Blood, so much blood. Katy grabbed her neck and fell to her knees as Frank staggered away with an idiot grin. She never even managed to look up at him. Marlowe's scream echoed through his skull only slightly louder than Frank's laughter. He fired until his magazine clicked empty, reloaded, and fired into Frank Brumbeloe's dead body over and over again, deaf to all but Paige's sobs.

The last time Marlowe was here, he failed. Not again. Maybe if he had taken the shot, Frank's hand would not have pulled the knife across Katy's throat. Maybe, she would still be alive.

Maybes and what ifs had haunted his every waking hour since that day. If he had taken the shot, Frank's knife might still have sliced through her flesh. There was no way of knowing, and the not knowing left Marlowe in his own private hell. What if he had fired, and Frank had still killed her? Would he blame himself for her death anyway?

If he took this shot, a death spasm could blow Becca's brains out. If he did not, Seraphim might kill her at any time.

Marlowe put his finger on the trigger … and squeezed.

CHAPTER TWENTY-EIGHT

T he groundskeeping crew sat at a picnic table outside the hospital eating lunch. Gabriel rarely spoke, but he enjoyed listening to his coworkers' banter. A colorful lot, the five men ranged in age and race, but everyone got along. A band of brothers, fighting and name calling included.

"Mr. Compton told me our hours should get back to normal in the next week or two," said Paul. "I don't know about you guys, but I've tightened my belt so much this last month, thought my innards would come out my nose."

"Patty Jr.'s got his heart set on playing baseball this year. You know how much uniforms, gloves, cleats, all that jazz costs? I need a different job for each member of my family," said Patrick, a small man, but stout as a tree trunk. "Stacy starts dance classes soon, too. The twins always need new clothes or something. Little suckers are growing like weeds, the whole lot eating me out of house and home."

"No one made you have four kids, Pat," said Marty. Marty considered himself the brains of the operation, which meant he liked to stand back and give orders. His commands usually met with a fair share of profanity and threats.

Pat glanced to the clouds. "God keeps blessing us with children."

"God blessed me and my wife with birth control." Clive glanced up from his copy of Reader's Digest.

"Glad He did too, last thing we want is your genes polluting the pool," said Paul, chuckling.

"You should know. You been firing blanks for years," shot back Clive.

Paul crumpled up his empty sandwich wrapper. "Anyhow, things are looking up. Summer gets here, we might even see some overtime."

"One of these days, I'm going to find a real job," said Marty.

"Okay, daylight's burning, let's get to it," said Paul. "Clive, you and Marty finish up the yard around East Wing. Pat, you're with me. Gabriel, what are you working on?"

"I am trimming limbs in the exercise yard in West Wing."

Paul clapped his hand on the table like a judge's gavel. "Sounds good. See you guys at punch out."

Rehabilitation and Physical Therapy occupied the west wing of the hospital. The interior contained patient rooms, a pool, a gymnasium, and separate treatment areas for brain trauma and spinal cord injuries. The facilities were state of the art and the finest in the southeast.

Outside, a spacious yard spanned a horseshoe-shaped area encircled by English boxwoods and azaleas. Therapists brought patients onto the lawn on pleasant days, to give them some exercise. Encouraged to walked certain distances or move against restrictions, patients worked to increase muscle strength and flexibility.

Gabriel had noticed the old woman before, laboring through the workouts designed to give her better mobility. A hip replacement and a mild stroke left her requiring a walker and often a powered wheelchair to get around. She preferred the walker, arguing the wheelchair made her feel lazy.

A talkative sort, the old woman spoke to nurses, other patients, and anyone who listened. Gabriel overheard much of her conversations.

"My Thomas, he died, you know. His heart gave out. Always

thought I'd go first. Always hoped I'd go first," she said to the therapist assisting her.

"You'll be with us a long time yet," said the young man, prematurely balding, with thick arms and legs.

"Hush your mouth. I go home to my empty house. Never had any children. We wanted to, but I couldn't get pregnant. It's only me now. I'm ready to see my Thomas again."

"Don't say that. I'd miss you too much."

She sighed. "You're a sweet dear, but I'm so lonely now."

"You should really consider the home Dr. Mathis recommended. You'd have friends there. You wouldn't be lonely."

"No, I'll die in my own house. No one's going to put me in some old folks' home," said the elderly woman. "I'll join my Thomas soon."

Gabriel listened, hearing the sadness in her voice and feeling *the blessing*. The chosen. He would answer her prayer and bring an end to her loneliness and pain … his gift of mercy.

Two days later, Gabriel watched her from across the street. The old woman moved gingerly behind her stroller, its miniature wheels clicking against the pavement. Fragile hands, covered in paper-thin skin, clutched tight the apparatus's arms. Tiny, hesitant steps followed each push forward. Even this mundane trip to the mailbox required all her effort.

No mail today. He watched her progress as she labored up the walkway, stepped through the door, and disappeared inside her home. His mind drew back to another time when he watched a sickly woman making the slow, arduous trek toward death.

"To bed, to bed. There's knocking at the gate. Come, come, come, come, give me your hand. To bed, to bed, to bed…" raved his mother.

"Mother, please. Let me help you," said Gabriel.

Elisabeth's mind seemed completely lost to her now—her days spent lying in bed moaning or reciting verses in a pain-filled voice.

Gabriel stood over her, a damp cloth in hand, dabbing the perspiration from her forehead. His arms ached from constantly carrying her to the bathroom, to the bed, or outside to sit for a time under the sun. She could not walk or do even simple things for herself.

He grew weary right along with her. Gabriel loved his mother and would do anything for her. It shamed him when her complaints annoyed him. Akin to a ringing in his hears he could not stop.

Still, her incessant raving unnerved him more. She made little sense. Deciphering what she wanted became a trying ordeal all its own.

"And, most dear actors eat no onions or garlic, for we are to utter sweet breath; and I do not doubt but to hear them say, it is a sweet comedy. No more words. Away! Go, away!" Elisabeth said.

"I don't understand, mother. Are you hungry?"

"Some pigeons, Davy, a couple of short-legged hens, a joint of mutton, and any pretty little tiny kickshaws, tell William cook." She yelled.

"I'll bring you some soup," he said, but when he returned it to her, she knocked it from his hands in frustration.

She ruminated on death much of the time. It demoralized him that he could find no way to comfort her. Hearing her plead for death, in so much misery, he could not bear it.

"I wonder if it hurts to live. And if they have to try. And whether, could they choose between. They would not rather die."

"Please stop it. Just stop it," said Gabriel. Emily Dickinson seemed her favored verse when in her poet persona. Surprisingly, she remembered long passages of prose and complete poems, yet seldom recalled his name.

Why must he suffer these dire ravings? He felt his own sanity slipping away with his mother's.

All his life, Gabriel had learned his speech through his mother's stanzas and verses. He came to understand the vernacular of her personas. Gabriel had no one to talk to aside from her, so Elisabeth's poetry and prose colored his language. Her words now morphed into something horrible and nonsensical even he could not understand.

Worse still, worse than her quotes and mad gibberish, were the brief moments of lucidity when she became fully aware of her suffering. When she gazed at him with understanding and complete cognizance of her situation. In those instances, he longed for the madness to return and take her from this prison of flesh.

"Gabriel," she said, reaching out to him. "You are my angel. My gift from heaven. It's why I named you Gabriel. Please, my angel, please don't let me go on like this. You can do it, son. You're strong. Don't feel bad. It's a mercy. Please help me."

"No, mother do not ask this of me. I am here with you. I'll care for you. You will be well again soon."

"You know I will not. I see it in your eyes. A day, a week, soon I will die. Why make me continue this way when there is no hope?"

Each time this Elisabeth spoke, his hands were set on fire. His head pounded, shutting out all sound except the rush of blood into his brain, like a crashing waterfall. His stomach balled tight, squeezing, a vice twisting his insides.

Death shadowed Gabriel. Through the momentous events of his life, Death had held his hand. Thinking back, each occurrence pushing him toward adulthood involved the demise of someone or something he loved. Death guided the chisel, chipping away the excess stone to reveal the statue, already present, yet hidden beneath.

Athena lay in the mud. Her short, fat legs kicked at the air. Eyes, confused, lacked the understanding to puzzle out what was happening to her. Fear and panic in her squeals at a sound from behind—another wild dog come to tear at her flesh. When he stood before her, recognition and yearning filled her eyes. Gabriel answered her pleas. He fulfilled her need and ended her pain.

His father lay in a pool of his own blood, brain matter splattered upon the wall. Serenity and peace written on his face ... what remained of it. Gabriel stood over him, unnamed feelings swirling through him.

And now, his mother.

"I can't. I love you. Do not ask this of me ... please."

"I would do it myself, but I'm not strong enough. You're my only hope."

"Let the gods decide. Is it not what you taught me? They will come for you soon. Try to be patient."

"The gods give us reason. They have granted me the ability to understand my life is no longer worth living. This is not life, Gabriel. I'm already dead. My body simply will not give up. You would not kill me, son ... you would set me free."

Torn, Gabriel walked outside. He prayed to every god whose name he recalled—Jehovah, Zeus, Apollo, Asclepius, Panacea. To hundreds of divine entities he prayed.... He searched the moon and stars for answers and for strength. No burning bush spoke to him, no god disguised as a hermit revealed himself. No one came.

Elisabeth appeared pregnant. The tumor in her belly grown so large it filled her. Pressing outward and inward, it left no room for anything else. Gabriel could not be apart from her, and he could not be with her. Hearing her screams, he rushed to her side, yet once there, his own agony quickly pushed him away.

The day he left, Gabriel heard her moans rise from a delirious sleep. He stood paralyzed, unable to step forward, unable to pace back. Another day, the same day, recurring over and over.

Whether an act of cowardice or acceptance, he retreated from his mother's bedroom. He packed his clothes into one bag. In another, he took what few tools remained—the bolt gun, the gambrel and hoist used for slaughter, a few others. Perhaps he could sell them, though they were old and probably of no value.

She would die soon. His mother would not suffer much longer. Certainly, she could not hold on. Too frail, too weak, it would end soon.

With a last look back at the farm that had been his home, the only world he knew, Gabriel walked away.

His mind slowly returned to the present. He gazed down at the old woman, and remembered … everything. He shook his head and focused on the blessing warming him inside—the still, small whisper of the gods.

The chosen. My purpose.

Gabriel moved to her bedside, bolt gun poised and ready. With the tip pressed to her temple, he set his finger on the trigger. She turned her head and gazed up at him. Her eyes showed no fear or alarm. Gabriel fell back a step.

The old woman smiled faintly. "I knew you'd come. I'm ready."

Surprised, he froze. The blessing blazed through him, yet he could not move.

"I'm ready, my son."

"It's a mercy you do for me. I'll be with my Thomas."

"It's a mercy, my love, my angel. I'll be with your father."

"You're an angel. I know it."

Gabriel retreated another step, then another, soon backpedaling out of the room. He stumbled on the stairs, falling and crashing down the last several steps. His tools scattered, clanging across the floor. Fumbling, groping in the darkness, he shoved his things into the bag and fled into the night.

CHAPTER TWENTY-NINE

"Marlowe, don't!" shouted Becca, straining at her ties. "He's not the Seraphim. Please don't shoot."

Marlowe released pressure on the trigger a hair's width before the hammer fell. He stared at Becca in disbelief.

Has she lost her mind?

"His name is Max. He's one of my patients. He has brain cancer. He doesn't know what he's doing."

Marlowe's eyes darted from Becca to the gun in the other man's hand. Pretty simple equation for a cop. A shrink might try to talk it out with some nut job. Marlowe himself might have tried it in college with a knife-wielding drunk, but since then he'd learned crazies were like a mean dog, wagging their tails while biting a hand off. A similar dog bit him once, to the bone ... not this time.

His arm shook. His focus shifted between the gun sight and the man's face.

"He thinks Seraphim sent him to die in my place. He thinks Seraphim's coming back here." Becca's voice held no trace of the panic her eyes conveyed.

Marlowe trembled. *Not again.* The room swirled into a morass of sound.

"Marlowe!" yelled Becca.

He flinched as if slapped, blinked, and made eye contact with her.

She raised her hands as much as the restraints allowed, waving him off. "He doesn't want to kill me. Please don't shoot him."

Shit. This is a bad idea.

"I made that mistake once, Becca." He aimed at the man's forehead.

"Marlowe..." Her voice seemed strangled halfway between whispering and yelling.

His shoulders slumped as he lowered the gun to a nonthreatening posture.

Max stared in Marlowe's direction, but did not seem to see him. Glazed eyes flitted about, fixing on nothing.

Marlowe slowly waved a hand in the air. "Max. It's Max, right? Hey, it's okay, we're all fine. I'm going to put my gun down. Right here on this table. See? We're fine."

Taking a step away from his gun, Marlowe kept his attention locked on the other man. Max seemed to notice him now, puzzlement spread across his face. He squinted at Marlowe as if trying to make out some far away object.

"You're not him," he said.

"I'm Marlowe. I'm a friend of Dr. Drenning's. I'm going to wait here with you, if you don't mind."

Max tilted his head, listening for something. After a moment, Marlowe's words finally registered. "Okay, but stay over there," Max said, his voice distant. "He'll be here soon. Very soon."

Max waited. Seraphim would come. He promised. Keeping Dr. Drenning tied up made him feel guilty, but she would run if given the chance. Now this man, this Marlowe. Yes, the boxer, he might try to interfere. Max wished Seraphim would hurry.

Something moved inside his head. Max not only felt it, he saw it ... somehow. There behind his eyes—a small stone, like a marble. It floated amongst the fleshy folds of his brain, turning as if on an invisible axis. Spiked protrusions slid from the surface, fanning out into triangle shaped blades. The sphere began to rotate, expanding to the size of a golf ball, now a baseball—spinning faster, the blades sliced through his brain. Excruciating pain laced through his head and pulsated down his body.

Max slumped forward, clutching the back of the chair to keep from collapsing to the ground. He screamed in agony, his free hand clamped to his temple, pressing hard, trying to crush the ball, to still it. It only spun faster and grew larger. His world faded, black coloring his surroundings.

A bright light rose above his head. With the little strength remaining in him, Max gazed upward, and in that hovering orb saw a shape. Seraphim had come at last.

Tears poured down his face, part joy, part pain. Such awesome beauty. The Seraphim leaned down, seeming to embrace him. Arms held wide, his majestic wings spread out behind. Glorious. On his knees, prostrate before the angelic form, Max begged for his reward.

"I did all you asked. I stand for her. Take me. Wipe away my failures."

The doctor needs your help. She must be set free from this life. Kill her.

"What? That wasn't the deal. You promised me. You can't change it now. I won't do it. I won't kill her."

Your pain can last. The wasting of your body can take a great deal of time before death releases you.

"No. You wouldn't. Please. Take me ... like you promised."

The radiant seraphim dimmed. Inky black streaks exuded from seams in the bronze armor, running like thickening veins over his body and wings until the figure had become pure black. *Take her life and all you were promised will be given. Not only will your pain cease, and your loved ones look on you without contempt or pity, and you will join with us. You will find a place at our side.*

Max could not think. He tore at his hair. He rocked back and forth, making the chair creak. What he wanted lay inches away. Maggie stood before him, smiling, hands reaching out to him. His boys ran to him from across a field of the greenest grass, joyous laughter filling the air.

The Seraphim only came for those ready to die. That's what the news said. He came for Dr. Drenning, so she must be ready. Max could be an instrument of mercy—ending her pain, and his own, with one gentle squeeze of the trigger. A simple thing. A righteous thing.

BECCA TRIED TO HIDE HER TERROR. SHE SHUDDERED EVERY TIME THE chair moved, afraid to turn her head to look. Max muttered under his breath, shaking his head side to side. Still on one knee, he shuffled around to her side, sweat pouring down his face. Crisscrossing blood vessels webbed his eyes. His screams tore at her heart, but her fear of him did not diminish. In his condition, he might do anything. As if summoned to life, Becca's unspoken fears manifested before her.

Marlowe stared at the revolver. Even in his agony, Max could fire at any moment. The anguish in Marlowe's eyes tore at her heart. He ached to act, but seemed trapped in his past trauma, and his fear she would be killed.

Max tilted his head upward, staring at something she could not see —something only he could see. He began speaking, not to her or Marlowe, but to some apparition conjured from his delusions.

"I did all you asked. I stand for her. Take me. Wipe away my failures."

"What? That wasn't the deal. You promised me. You can't change it now. I won't do it. I won't kill her."

"No. You wouldn't. Please. Take me ... like you promised."

I won't kill her? Yes Max, fight it.

Marlowe crept closer.

When Max went still and silent, she held her breath and waited. When he stood and turned his gaze toward her, she knew he had lost the fight. His gun rose, the barrel—a gaping black hole she could walk down with both arms held wide—inches from her face.

"Max, listen to me. Seraphim is *not* here. It's all in your mind. You know that. It's the cancer. It's making you see and hear things that aren't real. This isn't you, Max. You're not a killer. You're a good man. Please, don't do this," said Becca.

Her words were getting through. She could see his confusion, the battle still raging within him. She needed him to lower his gun. With it fixed on her, Marlowe could not act. If she could get Max to relax, just for a second, and point that thing somewhere else....

Keep his attention. I've got to give Marlowe an opening.

MARLOWE HAD SEEN JUNKIES LOSE IT, BUT NEVER ANYTHING LIKE THIS. He watched Max, and in some way, sympathized with his pain. He recognized the confusion, the self-hatred, his need to find hope in anything, even something fashioned within his own imagination.

Marlowe, too, knew such a place. He had spent most of the last five years locked inside it. But, the big difference—Marlowe knew it. This guy could not tell up from down. So lost in his nightmare, the darkness engulfing him encompassed his entire world.

Becca spoke in a soothing voice, attempting to coax Max back to reality. Marlowe thought, for a moment, maybe she could talk him down. Once his gun swung toward her, Marlowe knew this would not end well, not on its own. He had to follow Becca's lead. He needed an opening.

"Max," he said in a sharp voice. Max turned at the sound, but kept his gun on Becca. "I know what you're going through."

"You can't know. No one can," said Max, defeated.

"I do. No, I'm not dying from cancer like you. I hate that for you. It sucks, it really does. But life can suck in a lot of ways. I lost my wife. She was murdered, brutally. I saw it, Max. I saw it happen, and I couldn't stop it. I live with my failure every day. You have kids, Max?"

"Two boys. Austin and Cody." He seemed to picture his sons in his mind. The image brought a sad, thin smile to his lips.

Marlowe nodded. "My daughter Paige watched it happen too. Eight years old. This Seraphim got into my head too. I thought taking him down would bring some peace. Instead, I became obsessed with catching him. I've become someone I don't want to be. Done things I regret. I've become someone my family wouldn't know and wouldn't be proud of."

Marlowe inched closer as he spoke. "You want your boys to be proud of you, don't you?"

Max trembled. "Yes, yes I want that."

"If you hurt Dr. Drenning, they won't be. They'll be ashamed of you. And worse, you'll be a killer. Austin and Cody's dad—a killer. They will never outlive the stain. It will follow them for the rest of their lives."

Tears trickled from Max's eyes. A broken man, struggling within two worlds, unsure which was real. "But ... but, I don't know. I'm confused. I don't know what to do. *It's right behind me.* It wants me to set her free from her pain. B-black wings ..."

"It's okay. We all get confused sometimes. Put the gun down and we'll help you. Dr. Drenning and I will get you the help you need."

"I don't want to live like this. I can't face what my life is becoming. I'm afraid." Even for a tough, hardened cop like Marlowe, Max's expression, his utter despair, hit him in the heart. Marlowe had rushed here to save Becca, but now he needed to help this man as well. To know he could come back from this. Redemption took many forms, and Marlowe had focused on the wrong one.

Marlowe reached out, palm up. "I know. I promise you, we'll get you the care you need. Medications to make sure you don't suffer. You can die with dignity. Your boys will know you were a good man with the courage to do the right thing," said Marlowe.

Max lowered his gun.

While Max spoke with the man, the Seraphim's blackness dripped onto the rug, seeping to a puddle of midnight ichor that slithered around his feet. Now, Seraphim roared and blazed anew with crimson flame. The heat radiating from the angel charred the walls, ignited the curtains, and scorched all it touched—and it touched Max, burning away all remaining resolve. Its words flowed into his mind in a language he did not consciously understand.

As if something, some force, seized control of his body, Max watched in horror as his gun rose in the air. He saw his hand on the grip, his finger against the trigger, his gun pointed at Dr. Drenning.

The ball fixed with razors resumed its rapid spin. The pain came not in waves, but constant—no pause, no cessation.

The room teetered like a seesaw. The rise and fall accented a perception of the house constricting and expanding. Nausea roiled in his gut. His vision blurred. A dozen versions of the doctor danced before him like a mirage in a desert heat shimmer.

To Seraphim, he said, "Guide my aim."

To Dr. Drenning, he said, "I'm sorry."

A KNOT TWISTED IN MARLOWE'S GUT AS MAX'S FINGER TIGHTENED ON the trigger. Becca's scream snapped him out of his fog. Dread took his spine in a cold embrace. He lunged for his Glock, swiping it from the table as he fell on his side. He took a split second to aim … and fired.

Thunder exploded in the close confines.

BECCA HELD HER BREATH AS MARLOWE LEAPT. MAX STOOD NO MORE than a foot away from her. No possibility he could miss at that range. She strained with all her might to break free, but couldn't move. Deafening blasts erupted around her amid flashes of muzzle fire. The wall behind her, the chair beneath her, erupted in a spray of splinters and plaster.

A BULLET STRUCK MAX'S LEFT ARM AND SPUN HIM TO ONE SIDE. A

second hit him in the chest. He fell into a sideways stagger and collided with the dining room table. The force of his impact shattered the legs. The crack of breaking wood echoed the gunshots, bringing the entire table crashing to the floor.

He lay there, blood saturating his shirt and pooling at his sides. The Seraphim dissolved into tiny pinpoints of light, flickering out one by one. He reached for them, his hand shaking weakly in the air. He felt cold, but there was no more pain. No more pain. Max let go of the tablecloth and slipped onto the floor.

He smiled.

MARLOWE'S FIRST SHOT STRUCK MAX HIGH ON HIS LEFT ARM. THE .45 caliber bullet spun him on impact, twisting his body to face Marlowe. His second shot found Max's chest; bone fragments and blood misted the air. In the tumult, a third and fourth shot fired, and not from Marlowe's gun. Becca crumbled to the floor in a cloud of smoke and shards.

No, oh God. Please, no. Not again.

BECCA LAY ON THE FLOOR, GULPING THE AIR, THE ODOR OF GUNPOWDER filling her nostrils. She pawed at her body in a panic, the shattered armrests still tied to her wrists. She was certain the bullet must have gone cleanly through her and into the wall. But no, she appeared unharmed. Somehow, miraculously, Max had aimed wide and low, the bullets striking the seat an inch behind her and the wall beside her. Dumbstruck, she pulled her arms loose from the bits of destroyed chair.

Marlowe rushed to Becca's side and untied the bindings from her legs. His expression of unrelenting terror and relief broke her heart. She embraced him as if she might never let go, trying to pull herself *into* him.

"Oh god, I was so scared," she said.

"I know. Me too."

"Is he...?"

"I think so," he said.

Max gurgled. Marlowe pushed Becca behind him and aimed his Glock at Max, who raised a bloodied hand into the air.

Marlowe edged over and kicked the .38 well out of reach. He knelt and peeled Max's shirt back. After examining the wound, he glanced back to Becca and shook his head.

Her hands went to her face. Why did it have to end this way? Why couldn't Max have just put the goddamned gun down? He didn't need to die like this.

It surprised her how attached she felt to him after meeting him for only a few sessions. Becca knew him far less than many of her patients. Nevertheless, he had made an impression. He'd been the one to make her see the truth of her situation.

Becca didn't know what she'd expected. Max would have died from his cancer. He was not going to have a long life either way. Maybe she'd hoped he would find some measure of peace before he ran out of time. Selfish, but she'd wanted to believe, no matter the circumstances, things could work out. Not a happily-ever-after maybe ... but something better than this.

Outside, approaching sirens grew louder. She heard Marlowe mutter something.

Max jerked to life and seized Marlowe's wrist. How he managed it defied logic. He should not be alive, much less able to muster such strength. Marlowe's hand darted to his gun. Max mouthed something and tugged Marlowe toward him. Marlowe seemed to relax and leaned down, listening.

Marlowe gently touched Max's face and stood, staring down on him. Max coughed once more, blood spitting onto his lips. His body sagged, and he let out his last breath.

Becca wanted to turn away, but could not take her eyes off the poor man lying dead in her living room. Marlowe turned and embraced her, a tear trailing down his cheek. For a long moment, they said nothing. They held each other, both struggling with a myriad of conflicting thoughts. Noise from the foyer announced the police storming into the house.

"Clear," yelled Marlowe. "Suspect down."

Becca pulled back and gazed into his eyes. She saw pain there, but also compassion. He wore the countenance of a child who had mended a bird's broken wing and set it free to fly.

"What did he say?" she asked.

Marlowe stared at the dead man. "He said thank you."

CHAPTER THIRTY

Arriving home after fleeing the old woman, Gabriel had searched his books for answers, for any consolation. None came. He tore the pages from his beloved books, flinging them until they filled the air like confetti.

He needed no answers. Gabriel understood all too well. He had failed.

He failed with his mother all those years ago. The young prostitute was not the first time he experienced the blessing with a person. He had felt it every time he came close to his mother, but denied it. Gabriel placed his revulsion toward killing his mother above her wishes, above the command of the gods.

The doctor ... she was not the test. She was a lesson. No ... a warning. The Gods in their omnipotence knew what would come. They knew the old woman would be the true test. They offered a foreshadowing to remind him of his failure, his disobedience. A warning—the price of placing his own will above theirs.

The memories of the boy at the market, Red Cap, and all the people who had ever taunted him merged into one form. Their harsh voices cut through the façade. Their eyes saw the frightened boy and dismantled the man Gabriel had thought to become. They knew him, all he was, all he would ever be.

Isolation and insecurity rose to the surface of his skin, peeling it back, every nerve exposed. Yet, beneath, a boiling rage screamed at his weakness, his fear. His mother had begged him to spare her the pain, yet he had abandoned her. For all the love she had shown him over the years, when she needed him the most—he ran like a scared little boy. The *blessing* had come to him. Gabriel had known what he must do, but could not bear the thought of killing his mother. With each moment he ignored the blessing, his own pain grew more intense. He could not endure. Unable to kill her—he had to flee.

Gabriel sobbed.

He did not even know if she was still alive. Likely not. The woman could not walk on her own. He left her to a cruel, lonely death.

Coward.

There could be no consolation for him. The gods had gone quiet. He could not feel them or hear them.

Alone. I am alone.

He fell to his hands and knees and clawed frenziedly at the floor, as if salvation hid beneath the floorboards. He tore at the wood until his fingers bled, his nails ripped from their beds. He collapsed onto his back and yanked at his hair, pulling bloody locks free. With his chest convulsing in spasms, Gabriel fought to breathe. He lay there, staring at the ceiling, but saw so much more.

A deafening silence overtook him. The buzz of the sign outside the window, the roar of cars on the streets, the voices of people talking, arguing, and laughing, all ceased. He heard nothing except the pounding of his own heart; its frantic pulse thundered against the inside of his skull.

Images crawled across his mind. Bodies sliced open, organs displayed to the night sky. A river of blood flowed into his eyes, coloring his world crimson. Drowning beneath the flood, he clawed at the torrent, screaming as the sweet, sickly liquid filled him.

Gabriel floated amidst the congealing waves—a pig cut to pieces, brain matter splattered upon a barn wall, a woman impregnated with a black, rotten mass. Memories, too many memories.

Stone faces turned toward him. The disappointment in those divine visages ripped through him. All he did, he did for them. He only desired to please the gods, to worship them. Now, with this one failure, this one sin, they exiled him. They reached down and plucked his purpose from him.

Without it, without his calling, what was he? No one.

Life. Purpose. Death.

There could be no life without purpose. Without purpose, only death remained.

He stumbled into the bathroom. Standing at the sink, he ran water into the basin and dunked his head beneath the frigid stream—once, twice. With arms taut, gripping the cool porcelain, Gabriel raised his head and stared into the mirror....

His hands felt pierced by a thousand needles, sudden violent pressure in his head caused blood to trickle from his nose. His stomach churned and contracted, he vomited into the sink.

The blessing.

CHAPTER THIRTY-ONE

"I was out of line," said Spence. "I need to learn to keep my big mouth shut."

"No, you were right ... about everything," said Marlowe.

Spence blinked. "Uh, could you repeat that? The part about me being right."

"Don't push it, unless you want another pop in the mouth."

"No thanks. You've got a decent right hook for an old timer."

Marlowe's eyebrows came together. "I'm only two years older than you."

"Yeah, but I've aged better." Spence puffed out his chest.

"Wanting to punch you rarely needs a reason, but I might have gotten a tad carried away."

"A tad," said Spence. "No one can blame you, though. I'd be modeling a straightjacket in the funny farm after seeing all you have. I'm impressed you didn't go in guns blazing on that Max guy."

"I wanted to kill him. I wanted it so badly I could taste it. When I entered the house, my mind was set. He was Seraphim, and he deserved to die." Marlowe shook his head. "Becca wound up talking us both away from that cliff. I saw the guy standing there—the pain and confusion written all over his face ... I couldn't do it. Maybe there's a little humanity still in here someplace." Marlowe tapped his chest.

"Never left. What could be more human than suffering? Than grief?"

Marlowe chuckled. "Never figured you for a philosopher."

"I'm smart as Einstein, bro. Just don't show it. Show it, and people start expecting stuff from you." Spence grinned and ran a hand over his top of his head.

"Hmm. Still, it was touch and go the whole time. I admit I was rooting for Max. Everyone should be able to come back, you know? No matter what's happened, or how far you've fallen, you should have a chance to come back."

"Well, I'm rooting for *you*. I see a change in you ... another one. Something in your eyes. Hell, you're like that chick with all the personalities. Sylvia?"

"Sybil," said Marlowe with a grin. "And that was a hoax."

"Whatever. Listen to what I mean, not what I say. Anyway, you seem less distant now. More ... optimistic? I don't know. Different. In a good way."

"A work in progress. For the first time in a very long time, I feel like I might get there. I might make it back to something near my old self. Paige pulled me out of deep, dark hole ... and maybe ... maybe, you had a tiny bit to do with it, too."

Marlowe expected another off-handed quip from Spence; instead, he turned with a serious expression. "I care about you. You're my partner and my brother. There's nothing I wouldn't do for you, I hope you know that."

"I do. You're a great cop Spence, but a better friend than you? There isn't one."

"What to hug or something?" said Spence.

"Not a chance."

BECCA VOLUNTEERED TO GIVE MAGGIE AND HER SONS THE NEWS. NOT

normal police protocol, of course—the victim informing the assailant's family of his death—but her experience with Max, and her dogged insistence, swayed the argument.

She did not relish facing them. Though Max tried to kill her, she felt nothing but pity for him. On some level, she even understood. His mind, turned to mush, incorporated all his fears and delusions into a horrible reality.

He could not live, and he could not die. Trapped in a hellish netherworld between the two, his mind created a savior. One who could do for him what he could not do for himself. He envisioned a way his pain might end, and his family might see him as a hero. Insanity delivered gaping holes in logic, but Max could not see the discrepancies, the rips in the design.

On the drive toward Maggie's sister's house, Becca rehearsed what she would say a thousand times. She dealt with the suffering and the grieving every day, and now, her words lacked the significance of the moment. Where were the grand axioms to comfort? The psychological brilliance to dispel the anguish of loss?

The tactics she employed daily seemed paltry things. She felt certain she would be a better therapist as a byproduct of Max's death. No more simply going through the motions, saying the words some book prescribed. The wall her training taught her to erect between herself and her patients must come down. For only through the prism of her own experiences could she understand theirs. They needed to know this person counseling them was not some sterile, static machine, but a living person with their same fears. These were the lessons Max taught her. Lessons she would put to good use from here on out.

She parked by a white mailbox and walked to the porch. It took a moment and three breaths to summon the nerve to push the bell.

"Yes? Can I help you," said the woman who answered the door.

"My name is Dr. Rebecca Drenning. We spoke on the phone earlier."

"Oh, yes. I … pictured someone older. Come on in. Please have a seat in the living room, I'll get Maggie."

"Thank you."

The woman left, and Becca sat on the sofa, appraising the house. Quiant. Nothing fancy, but nice. She noticed a family photo on the mantle. A dozen people stood in front of a Christmas tree, Max among them. He appeared so healthy and alive, a wide smiled stretched across his face, eyes bright, seeming to see a future full of promise.

Becca felt a weight settle in the pit of her stomach. She felt cheated that she never had the opportunity to know *that* Max. Becca remembered a line from Hamlet, something about the fear of death making cowards of us all. It could also drive a person to desperation and even madness.

Children's laughter accompanied the sound of feet stomping on hardwood. Becca shook the morose thoughts from her mind as two boys came dashing around the corner.

"Hello," said Becca, smiling.

"Who are you?" asked the smaller of the two, rather bluntly.

"I'm Dr. Drenning. Who might you be?"

The boy blanched and took a step back, "Doctor? You going to give us a shot?

Becca laughed. "I'm not that kind of doctor, and no, I'm not going to give you a shot."

"Oh, good. I'm Austin."

"I'm Cody," said the older boy.

"Handsome men," said Becca. The boys blushed, shoved one another, and darted out of the room.

"No running in the house, you two," said a pretty brunette, entering the room behind the boys. "And close the door if you're going outside."

She turned to Becca, an embarrassed smile on her face, "Sorry about them. Wild animals."

"It's okay, they're adorable." Becca stood and shook Maggie's hand.

"My sister said you wanted to see me?"

"Yes. I wanted to talk to you about Max."

"Max?" The woman stiffened. "Is something wrong?"

"I'm afraid so. Sit with me, won't you?"

Maggie, hesitant, sat beside Becca. "Laura said you're a doctor. Is Max sick?"

"There's no easy way to say this." She placed a hand on Maggie's knee. "Max died yesterday."

"What? No, no, I don't believe you." Maggie shook her head, tears welling in her eyes.

"Max was very sick. Brain cancer. There wasn't anything the doctors could do. He was too sick by the time they found it. I'm so sorry."

"Why didn't he tell me? Cody and Austin, oh my God, how do I tell them?" Through her tears, anger flared. "This is so like him. So selfish. His sons didn't even get to say goodbye … I didn't …"

Maggie collapsed into Becca's arms. Becca decided then, they did not need to know *how* Max died. He died of cancer. That was enough.

"Listen to me, Maggie. I counseled Max during his treatment. Let me tell you, he did not do this out of selfishness. He loved you and his sons. Max knew if he told you, you would try to care for him out of obligation. He couldn't bear you and the boys seeing him waste away."

"I couldn't be with him any longer, but it didn't mean I stopped caring about him. Families … they're there for each other." Maggie dug her fingers into her thighs.

"That's hindsight speaking. You're here with your sister. If Max left you, if the situations were reversed, would you want your estranged husband taking care of you as you withered away to skin and bone?"

"No, no I wouldn't." Maggie's hands stilled and she gave a slight nod. A thousand thoughts raced past Maggie's eyes.

"The cancer attacked his mind. Max wasn't himself anymore. You and the boys didn't need to see that. Let them, and you, remember Max healthy and strong. Most of all, I want you to know that in the end, he died heroic. His death was self-sacrifice. Nothing would have pleased him more than to have his family around him, but out of love, he chose to die alone."

Becca understood the doubt and regret. Maggie could not stem the flow of her tears. She would hate herself for a time, question every decision, and find no solace. Eventually, Becca hoped Maggie could come to grips with Max's death. Perhaps, someday, Maggie would realize no one was at fault.

MARLOWE LEANED BACK IN HIS CHAIR, SMILING AT AN EIGHT-BY-TEN OF Paige, a speck of pancake on her chin. Wonderful things, these new color laser printers. He'd taken the picture that morning. Let McCann say a word about "misuse of department resources."

"Detectives," said Officer English, "Seraphim hit again."

"Where?" Marlowe looked up.

"Westside."

"Hmm, no shortage of down-on-your-luck types out there. Who's on scene?"

"Everyone. Well, pretty much. The lieutenant wants Dr. Koopman and you two out there ASAP. S.W.A.T. and a dozen patrols already present."

"S.W.A.T.?" said Spence. "And a dozen patrols for a dead body? Seems overkill to me. How do we know it was a Seraphim attack?"

"Apartment building's super found the vic. Scared the shit out of him. He didn't stick around, but said he saw some creepy symbols on the floor. Said the guy was cut open, blood everywhere. Lieutenant was apprised of the call and told the EMTs to hold back until we check it out."

"The victim was on the floor? Not the bed? And blood everywhere?" Marlowe stood. "Sounds like the super interrupted the ritual." His eyes went wide. "Jesus, let's go, Spence. Seraphim's still in the vicinity!"

POLICE HAD SURROUNDED THE BUILDING BY THE TIME MARLOWE AND Spence arrived. A couple of S.W.A.T. snipers observed from the roof across the street. A horde of onlookers, including a few dozen reporters, pushed against a barricade.

Lieutenant McCann had pulled out all the stops. Along with S.W.A.T. and the regular patrol cruisers, he'd brought in armored vehicles and officers in body armor carrying assault weapons. If Seraphim got away, it would not be on his feet.

The lieutenant waved them over as soon as he spotted them. "We have the place locked down. S.W.A.T.'s cleared the premises. Teams are coming out. Finished up door-to-door searches and all apartments are clean. No sign of Seraphim. I want you two in there. Marquez, Kirkpatrick, and Bateman will back you up, just in case. Koop and his team are with you. Doc, you and your people stay to the rear."

"No need to tell me," said Koop. "I abhor violence."

"No one but you three go into that room." McCann pointed to Marlowe, Spence and Koop. "Once they have a handle on things, Koop, your team can go in. This is the closest we've been. The bastard is going down this time."

"He's out of the building? What time did the super make the call? What's the perimeter?" asked Marlowe, a thousand questions whirling through his head. He knew the lieutenant would have every contingency covered, but Marlowe's anxiety soared. He did not want this maniac slipping through.

"I've set a six-block perimeter. All our resources are in, and County sent everything they have. Seraphim isn't getting out of the net."

Marlowe and Spence strapped on their vests and waited for S.W.A.T. to restore power. With the team on their heels, they proceeded into the building. The flicker of the florescent lights overhead set nerves further on edge, blinking out for an instant every few seconds.

McCann said all the apartments had been cleared, but that did not keep the team from staring at every door and hallway they passed. Nor did it ease Marlowe's white-knuckle grip on his Glock. Kirkpatrick and Bateman carried AR-15 rifles. Marquez, a Mossberg

590 assault shotgun. Spence followed as few steps in front of Koop, his own Sig Sauer 9mm at the ready. Overkill with the weaponry seemed preferable to getting killed.

Once onto the third floor, the team slowed their progress, tension growing with each step closer to the target apartment. A sudden *bang* and a door flew open. Weapons raised in unison, all trained on the entrance. A boy of no more than ten came barreling out and ran headlong into Kirkpatrick's leg.

"Shit," said Bateman. "I almost ..."

"We all did," whispered Marlowe. "But we didn't. So, hold it together. The kid must have hid somewhere during the search. Marquez, get him outside."

Marquez escorted the child down the hall as the others steadied themselves. At the door to apartment 311, Marlowe directed Kirkpatrick and Bateman into positions on the opposite side. Spence moved in on Marlowe's back while Koop remained several feet further down the hall, out of harm's way.

Marlowe raised a hand and counted one ... two ... three. He shoved the door open, took a quick peek inside, and pivoted into the room, followed by Spence. Kirkpatrick and Bates held guns ready in the doorway.

The victim lay on the floor, a bloody mess. His torso and abdomen slit open, entrails overflowed his belly like grotesque cords of rope. Kirkpatrick doubled over and backed into the hall.

"Jesus Christ," breathed Bateman.

"Get Koop in here, but you two stay out there. Spence, take a look around." Marlowe circled his finger in the air.

The small apartment looked as if a tornado had torn through. Pages from a half dozen books lay strewn across the room. The bed leaned against one wall, toppled onto its side. Moonlight peeked through sheer curtains, setting a gloss to the congealing blood pooled around the corpse. Arterial spray splattered the floor and walls.

Marlowe moved to a small desk near the solitary window, sifting through the paltry stash of objects. Spence crept to the bathroom, behind his gun. After an inspection revealed nothing threatening, he examined the rear area of the room.

Koop knelt beside the corpse, looking over the victim's wounds. A few minutes later, he took a handkerchief from his jacket and wiped it across his forehead. His head rose, confusion written in his eyes. "I don't think they will be catching the killer out there."

"No, we'll get him. Have a little faith, Doc," said Spence.

"You misunderstand me. I believe ... well, I'm reasonably certain ... this *is* the killer."

Marlowe and Spence stopped in their tracks, both wearing expressions of disbelief.

"What?" asked Spence. "I don't think I heard you right."

"You did. This man killed himself."

"You're telling me this guy cut himself open and pulled his own insides out?" asked Marlowe, his eyes wide.

"And more. It appears he tried to cut his sternum with the cutters there—same as with Seraphim's other victims. When that failed, he attempted to pull his own ribcage apart with his hands. Look at these marks here on the bones, and the blood saturation on his hands."

"Probably from trying to stanch the blood flow," said Marlowe, still unable to accept Koop's explanation.

"No, look at the breaks on the ribs. Pulled apart, not snipped with the tool. Also, the trail of blood droplets from his hand to the symbols. This is the killer."

"How ..." Marlowe cringed. "Nobody could've stayed conscious long enough to do that."

"Marlowe, I think he's right," said Spence. "Got a bag here, full of tools. We've got a bolt gun."

Marlowe's mind refused to process what he heard. It seemed impossible. He searched for answers written on the wall. A scrap of yellow drew his eyes to a vase of flowers—the same flowers found in the victims' body cavities. On a small desk sat a mason jar filled with familiar halfpennies. Dozens of small metal bars and copper wire such as Seraphim used to fashion his crosses filled a desk drawer.

There could be no doubt. Seraphim did not bring all his supplies, far more than one crime scene would have required, and leave them in a rush when the super surprised him. No, the Seraphim lay right there with his body torn open.

"This fellow did not possess the full complement of mental faculties." Koop's bewildered tone did not match his humor.

"What the hell? This makes no fucking sense," said Spence. "Any idea what's going on here?"

Marlowe paced, rubbing at his brow. The wheels inside his head turned, trying to lock into place. He stared around the small apartment. Each item flew into his mind and took position in a mental jigsaw puzzle. Every nuance filled in the space that formed like pixels in a digital mosaic. He thought back to Paige trying to force the piece in where it didn't belong.

Finally, Marlowe shook his head and stared down at the crimson-coated body. "A guess, though with this guy, who knows. We'll probably never know ... not for certain."

"And your guess?" asked Koop, kneeling beside the corpse.

"He tried to duplicate his ritual on himself. Seraphim thought he brought peace to people who could no longer endure their suffering. He intervened on behalf of those ready to die. I think ... maybe he discovered he was one of them."

"Or simply very, very insane," said Koop.

"Then there's that," said Marlowe.

"Un-freaking-believable," said Spence. "So what now?"

"Get the teams in here. Process everything, clean it up," said Marlowe, making for the door.

"Where are you going?" asked Spence.

"The beach."

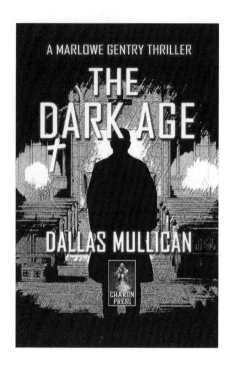

Marlowe's story continues in book 2
The Dark Age

The Heretic knows they lied. Now, he will make them confess.

The first murder, a small town pastor burned at the stake, seems personal; an act of rage committed on impulse. But when a second victim is found brutally tortured to death, Detective Marlowe Gentry realizes he's dealing with a serial killer who is drawing inspiration from the Inquisition.

The killer's methods grow more gruesome with each victim. He's escalating, racing toward an endgame. How far will The Heretic go to punish those who betrayed him? And can Marlowe stop him before the ultimate trial?

ACKNOWLEDGMENTS

Melea Mullican, daughter, inspiration, best friend.
Margie and Alan England for their unwavering support.
Melissa Grinder, Tonya Loveless, and Natalie Wright for their valuable insights.
Elizabeth Rubio, Rick Pieters, and Matthew Cox for their expertise and guidance.

ABOUT THE AUTHOR

After spending twenty years as the lead singer of a progressive metal band, Dallas Mullican turned his creative impulses toward writing. Raised on King, Barker, and McCammon, he moved on to Poe and Lovecraft, enamored with the macabre. During his time at the University of Alabama at Birmingham, where he received degrees in English and Philosophy, Dallas developed a love for the Existentialists, Shakespeare, Faulkner, and many more great authors and thinkers. Incorporating this wide array of influences, he entices the reader to fear the bump in the night, think about the nature of reality, and question the motives of their fellow humans.

A pariah of the Deep South, Dallas doesn't understand NASCAR, hates Southern rock and country music, and believes the great outdoors consists of walking to the mailbox and back. He remains a metalhead at heart, and can be easily recognized by his bald head and Iron Maiden t-shirt.

Facebook Page: https://www. facebook.com/authordallasmullican/

Website – http://www.dallasmullican.wixsite.com

ALSO BY DALLAS MULLICAN

Detective Marlowe Gentry Thriller series
The Dark Age
October's Children

The Horde and the Host Trilogy (Fantasy)
Blood for the Dancer (Book I)
The Sun at Night (Book II) (Forthcoming)
Cry of the Unspoken (Book III) (Forthcoming)

Stand Alone Novels (Dark Fiction)
The Music of Midnight

Made in the
USA
Columbia, SC